SHADOWS *of* SWANFORD *A*BBEY

Books by Julie Klassen

FROM BETHANY HOUSE PUBLISHERS

Lady of Milkweed Manor

The Apothecary's Daughter

The Silent Governess

The Girl in the Gatehouse

The Maid of Fairbourne Hall

The Tutor's Daughter

The Dancing Master

The Secret of Pembrooke Park

The Painter's Daughter

The Bridge to Belle Island

A Castaway in Cornwall

Shadows of Swanford Abbey

TALES FROM IVY HILL

The Innkeeper of Ivy Hill

The Ladies of Ivy Cottage

The Bride of Ivy Green

An Ivy Hill Christmas: A TALES FROM IVY HILL *Novella*

SHADOWS *of* SWANFORD ABBEY

❧

JULIE KLASSEN

BETHANYHOUSE
a division of Baker Publishing Group
Minneapolis, Minnesota

Published by Bethany House Publishers
11400 Hampshire Avenue South
Minneapolis, Minnesota 55438
www.bethanyhouse.com

Bethany House Publishers is a division of
Baker Publishing Group, Grand Rapids, Michigan

Printed in the United States of America

Library of Congress Cataloging-in-Publication Data
Names: Klassen, Julie, author.
Title: Shadows of Swanford Abbey / Julie Klassen.
Description: Minneapolis, Minnesota : Bethany House Publishers, a division of
    Baker Publishing Group, [2021]
Identifiers: LCCN 2021031568 | ISBN 9780764234255 (cloth) | ISBN 9780764234248
    (trade paperback) | ISBN 9780764236211 (large print)
Subjects: GSAFD: Christian fiction. | Mystery fiction.
Classification: LCC PS3611.L37 S48 2021 | DDC 813/.6—dc23
LC record available at https://lccn.loc.gov/2021031568

Unless otherwise indicated, Scripture quotations are from the King James Version
of the Bible.

Scripture quotations labeled NKJV are from the New King James Version®. Copyright
© 1982 by Thomas Nelson. Used by permission. All rights reserved.

Cover design by Jennifer Parker
Cover photography by Todd Hafermann Photography, Inc.
Front cover background photograph is of the interior of the Cloister of Lacock Abbey,
Wiltshire, UK © Alamy Images.

Author is represented by Books and Such Literary Agency.

Baker Publishing Group publications use paper produced from sustainable forestry
practices and post-consumer waste whenever possible.

21   22   23   24   25   26   27   7   6   5   4   3   2   1

In Memory of Katy Banton,
whose smiles, prayers, and friendship
brightened the world

1986–2020

The part of the abbey you inhabit
is undoubtedly haunted.

—Jane Austen, *Northanger Abbey*

The GENTLEMEN'S HOTEL in King-Street, Saint
James's Square
TAKES this opportunity of acquainting all
Noblemen, Gentlemen, Foreigners,
and others, that they may be accommodated with
genteel Lodgings for one night,
or as long as they think proper.

—Eighteenth-century London advertisement

A large party in an hotel ensured
a quick-changing, unsettled scene.

—Jane Austen, *Persuasion*

For God has not given us a spirit of fear, but of power and of
love and of a sound mind.

—2 Timothy 1:7 NKJV

1

March 1820
Worcestershire, England

Miss Rebecca Lane quaked at the thought of returning to Swanford after more than a year's absence, even though her heart had never really left.

Inside the jostling post chaise, she prayed, *Please don't let him do anything foolish before I get there.*

Lines from their housekeeper's recent letter echoed through her mind.

> *Your brother's behavior has grown more alarming. I fear what he might do.*
> *I could not in good conscience wait any longer to write. I pray I have not waited too long as it is.*

Dread filled Rebecca again, as it had when she'd first read the words. Was John threatening to harm himself, or someone else, or what . . . ?

Rebecca sighed and leaned her throbbing temple against the

vehicle's smooth, cool window. Outside, the rolling countryside lay draped in March mist, its fields dotted with white sheep and new lambs.

Soon the tower of All Saints Church appeared above the treetops, and there, the tall chimney stacks of the Wickworth mansion.

Rebecca gestured out the window toward the village. "There it is. Swanford."

Beside her, the French maid slept on, but Lady Fitzhoward, their employer, gazed out as directed. "Ah yes." The older woman looked at her. "Are you glad to be home?"

Rebecca summoned the expected smile and nodded, though it was a weak effort. Inwardly, she thought, *Where is home?*

With her parents passed on, the vicarage, which was never actually theirs anyway, was occupied by the new vicar and his family. The underkeeper's lodge where her brother lived belonged to the Wilford family estate. And except for a brief visit the Christmas before last, she had spent the previous two years living out of trunks and bandboxes in one inn or hotel after another as a lady's companion. Perhaps in time, she could learn to be like Lady Fitzhoward and enjoy endless travel rather than longing for home. But she had not managed it yet.

The chaise turned off the main road and made its way past farmyards, cottages, and the village itself. Beyond it, imposing Swanford Abbey rose from the misty ground like an ancient headstone.

Before the sight of the old abbey-turned-hotel could rouse its customary trepidation, the chaise rumbled under an archway and into the adjacent stable courtyard.

A porter appeared to help them alight. Miss Joly, the lady's maid, awoke and climbed out first to direct the care of their employer's belongings. Lady Fitzhoward stepped down after her, leaning heavily on the porter's hand until her cane reached the ground.

Following her out, Rebecca asked, "May I leave my trunk with you?"

The maid looked annoyed at the request, but Lady Fitzhoward agreed.

"Yes, of course. Joly shall have it stowed for you."

An old man in coarse work clothes hobbled into the stable yard, spade in hand. He paused, faded blue eyes fixing on Lady Fitzhoward.

"Purty flower . . ." he murmured.

The porter shooed him away.

When he'd ambled off, Lady Fitzhoward turned to Rebecca. "If a week with your brother is not sufficient, let me know. If I am not here at the hotel, leave a message at the desk. As I mentioned, I hope to visit friends while I'm in the area."

Rebecca nodded. "I shall, thank you. And thank you again for changing your plans to accompany me."

Seeing her preparing to depart, the porter offered to summon a fly to take Rebecca the rest of the way.

She politely declined. The distance across the village and through the wood to the lodge was more than a mile. But the day was fine and her purse light, so she decided to go on foot.

She retrieved her valise and bandbox from among the pile of baggage, bid the two women farewell, and turned to go. After a few steps, her valise felt heavy, but it was nothing to the guilt she carried.

Rebecca walked up Abbey Lane, past the busy High Street, and along the village green framed by thatched cottages on two sides. Reaching All Saints Street, she turned right and walked by half-timbered houses hugging the cobbled street, and the Swan & Goose, the tang of sour ale emanating from the public house.

She crossed the river bridge and walked out of town. It would have been faster to continue past the church and vicarage, but she was not ready to face those poignant memories just yet.

As she followed the river toward the wood, a child's wail pierced the air, followed by heartbroken sobs. She glanced around, trying to locate the wee sufferer, and there, under a sprawling English oak, stood a boy of four or five in long pantaloons with high waist buttoned to a jacket above. A wide, frilly shirt collar rested on little, heaving shoulders.

Rebecca set down her things and hurried over to him.

"What is it? What's wrong?"

Eyes wet and nose running, the boy pointed up into the tree.

There, high above, a kite lay snared in the branches, its tail and string entangled in the gnarly limbs.

"Oh dear. That is a pity." Rebecca looked around for help. "Where do you live?"

He wiped his sleeve under his glistening nose and pointed over the river, narrow here, to the back of the vicarage.

"And are you out here alone?"

He shook his head and began sobbing again.

A girl a few years older appeared, carrying a long stick.

"Do hush, Colin. You are not a baby anymore. I will try to get it down for you."

Seeing her, the girl hesitated, then explained, "He was given that kite for his birthday and breeching. I was supposed to help him fly it, but the wind grabbed hold and would not let go."

"I see." Rebecca surveyed the tree and considered the situation. "I shall go up for it," she offered. "You stay here and watch over your brother, will you?"

The girl's eyes widened, then swept over Rebecca's neat carriage dress and hat. "You, miss?"

Rebecca nodded and unpinned the ornate hat—Lady Fitzhoward's choice, not her own. The feather would only get caught in the branches. Then she tied her petticoat between her knees to keep from showing more than she wished.

She looked around again, glad there was no one but these two children to witness her unladylike act.

Seeing a cracked wagon wheel abandoned beside a nearby tree, she rolled it over and propped it against the trunk to form a sort of step stool. The lowest branch grew almost horizontally before curving upward. It had always reminded her of an elephant with its trumpeting trunk, like the one she'd seen at Astley's Amphitheatre. The branch was too high for the children to reach, but with the help of the wheel, she managed to lift one foot to the Y between it and the trunk, grasp the branch with gloved hands, and half swing, half lift herself up, the bark rough against her delicate stockings, which would no doubt be ruined.

From there, she righted herself and began the relatively easy feat of climbing the remaining branches as one would a ladder.

Below her, the children clapped, and she felt rather like a performer at Astley's herself.

Rebecca had never been afraid of heights and had happily scrambled up trees, including this one, as a girl, heedless of scraped hands and knees. But she was a woman now, out of practice and condition, and was soon breathing hard as she scaled the great oak.

Nearing the kite, she sat on one accommodating branch and propped her half boot on another for support. Then she began the tedious task of untangling the kite tail and string.

She looked down at the waiting children. The canopy of branches hid the girl from view, but the teary boy was in plain, vivid sight.

"Can you get it?" he asked. "Can you?"

Unexpectedly, her vision tunneled, and she felt strangely dizzy.

The scene and plea were all-too familiar, and upon its echoes she hurtled back through the years, looking down from a similar perch to a tearful John below, although several years older than this boy.

"May I?" he'd pleaded. "Please? Just this once?"

He'd wanted to climb up the tree with her. Begged to. Her parents had charged her with keeping an eye on her little brother—keeping him safe. She knew John was too young. Too unsteady. But he kept begging and whining and finally she'd relented, thinking if she kept him close, all would be well. She'd helped him up to the lowest branch and he'd climbed up from there, ignoring her warnings and entreaties to wait for her and not climb too high.

Heart pounding, she'd hurried after him but before she could reach him, he slipped and fell, landing on the hard-packed earth below, where he lay deadly still. . . .

"Are you all right, miss?" the girl called up, scattering her dark cloud of reverie.

"Em, yes. Just taking time to untangle."

Rebecca lowered the kite, freed at last, to the outstretched hands awaiting it, then dropped the string as well.

She climbed carefully down, finally sitting on the lowest branch and preparing to jump. It seemed higher now for some reason.

Rebecca took a steadying breath and pushed off, stumbling to the ground. Getting to her feet, she saw the grass stain on her gown and inwardly groaned. Lady Fitzhoward had an exacting eye. She reached down and swatted ineffectually at the stain. Hopefully, Rose could help her remove it.

The little boy threw his arms around her knees, adding snot to the brownish-green stain.

The girl bobbed a curtsy. "Thank you, Miss . . . ? May I ask your name?"

"I am Miss Lane, and you are most welcome." Rebecca gathered her things and straightened. "May I suggest the village green for your next kite-flying adventure?"

Grinning sheepishly, the children nodded in agreement and waved her on her way.

Reaching the narrow footbridge, Rebecca crossed back over the river and continued through Fowler's Wood, approaching the lodge from behind. The thatched cottage had once been the underkeeper's lodge, but the Wilfords employed only one gamekeeper these days and had let the lodge to John and Rebecca on very easy terms. She had lived there with her brother for a few years until financial and relational strain had spurred her to seek a position as a lady's companion.

At her knock, the elderly cook-housekeeper, Rose Watts, met her at the door, the dear, sagging features lifting into a smile at the sight of her.

"Miss Rebecca! What a happy surprise. Thank the Lord."

Uncertainty flickered. "Is it a surprise, Rose? I did write and asked John to let you know when I would be arriving. Perhaps he has not yet received my letter."

The woman's gaze shifted to a basket on the sideboard, overflowing with newspapers and correspondence. "Or perhaps it is still in that pile." Rose looked back at her. "You did receive my letter?"

"Yes, that is why I am here. Is John home?"

"'Course he is. He's always home."

Rebecca glanced from the dining parlour into the sitting room and saw that both were empty.

Rose sighed. "He's in his room. Still asleep, most likely."

"Asleep? It's after three in the afternoon!"

The housekeeper's lined face creased into an odd expression, half apology, half long-suffering frown. "It's as I told you. He stays up all hours, pacing back and forth and muttering to himself, then sleeps the day away. And when I try to talk to him about it, he becomes devilish angry."

Rebecca went to knock on her brother's bedchamber door.

"John? It's Rebecca. I am back."

No answer. She removed her hat and gloves and tried again. Still no response.

To distract herself from mounting alarm, Rebecca walked down the passage to the spare room where she usually slept, planning to stow her valise. She opened the door and froze. The room was an utter disaster. Between the door and bed, a small table haphazardly sat, piled high with sheaves of paper, as was the bed itself. Twine hung with pages stretched across the room. The side table and dressing chest were strewn with reference books, ink pots, spent candles, coffee cups, plates, piles of old clothes, and even John's viola, which, as far as she knew, he had not played in years.

Rose stopped in the doorway behind her. "I am sorry, Miss Rebecca. He's taken to using this room as an office and store-room of sorts. I would have asked him to clean it—or done it myself—had I known when you were coming. What you must think of me! In my defense, John has kept me busy writing a clean copy of his new manuscript."

"I understand."

Rebecca gestured toward the pages hanging on the line. "Why are those there?"

"I believe he spilled something and is drying them out."

"I see. I shall . . . em, sleep on the sofa tonight, and we'll sort it tomorrow."

"Very well. Come with me to the kitchen. I have something else to tell you."

She joined Rose for tea at the scarred wooden table. The

older woman said, "Since I wrote to you, I have learned that a certain author, and you will guess who I mean, wrote to reserve a room at the Swanford Abbey Hotel. I heard it from Cassie Somerton herself—she's head housekeeper there. He arrived last night, and word is spreading fast round the village. I worry what John might do."

Rebecca nodded, a new wave of dread washing over her. Why was that man in Swanford?

As they were finishing their tea, the Wilfords' steward arrived, and again Rebecca tried to rouse her brother. "John?" she hissed through the door. "Mr. Jones is here for the rent. John?"

In the entryway, the stoic man shifted from foot to foot. "That's all right, miss. Don't want to spoil your homecoming. I'll return another time."

Face hot with embarrassment, Rebecca replied, "Thank you, Mr. Jones. I apologize for the inconvenience."

And later, when Rose began setting platters of food on the dining table, Rebecca tried again. "John? Dinner is almost ready. Please join us."

No reply. She pressed her forehead to the solid wood and added on a plaintive note, "John? Do answer. You begin to worry me."

Finally, she returned to the kitchen and said, "You have a key to his room, do you not?"

Rose nodded as she poured gravy into a sauceboat. "Used it once when he didn't respond, but he flew into a rage and warned me never to use it again."

Rebecca raised her chin. "Well, he has not warned *me*."

Rose handed over the key from her chatelaine, worry lines on her brow. Rebecca didn't blame her. She was worried too. Worried her brother might have done himself a harm.

Rebecca strode down the passage, took a deep breath, and

inserted the key into the lock. Then she pushed the door open, the hinges creaking in protest.

There he lay, eyes closed, half-dressed, disheveled, lying amid jumbled bedclothes, wadded papers, teacups, empty whiskey bottles, smaller suspicious-looking brown bottles, and plates of half-eaten food. The air was foul with the cloying odor of sweat and spoiled meat.

She wrinkled her nose. "John?"

No reaction. Her heart banged hard.

"John!" she repeated sharply, slogging through the debris to the bed and shaking his shoulder.

His eyelids fluttered open. "What!" Displeasure and confusion puckered his face. "Becky? Why are you here? Leave me alone."

What's wrong with you? She wanted to shout, but the lump in her throat stopped her. She knew what was wrong—to some degree at least. He had never been quite right since that fall from the tree. The resulting head injury had left him confused, lethargic, and moody. A condition that had grown worse over recent years, exacerbated by a deep depression of spirits and too much drink.

And the cause?

She knew it all too well.

Frederick Wilford glanced around the Wickworth drawing room into the hall beyond. Everywhere he looked, the furniture, mirrors, and silent clocks lay shrouded under protective white Holland cloths—and had been for two years.

Will I never be able to put the past behind me? he asked himself. *Forgive her . . . and myself?*

The sound of hammering from upstairs seemed to pound

right into his brain. He rubbed ineffectually at his throbbing temples.

The front door burst open, the caller not bothering to knock. "Freddy? I'm here!"

Frederick stepped into the hall to greet his younger brother, who lived in London but visited every year at Christmas and Frederick's birthday.

Dapper, fair-haired Thomas set down his valise and handed his greatcoat to the suddenly appearing footman.

Frederick looked past him, expecting to see his valet. "Your man not with you?"

"No. Went off and got himself married, poor fool." Then his brother glanced around, eyes wide. "You still have everything covered? Really, Freddy, this place is like a mausoleum."

"Good day to you too, Tom. Welcome home."

Thomas shook his head. "Wickworth has not been my home in ages, thankfully. Who would want to live here? Ghosts? Certainly not living, breathing people."

"You know why everything is covered. We are renovating."

"Are you? I thought you stopped all that after Marina died. The refurbishments were her idea, after all."

"I have put off the plans for this floor. The men are working upstairs for the present, finishing the guest rooms." He gestured behind himself. "But I can't leave that gaping hole open between the library and drawing room forever."

His brother's eyes glinted. "Like a wound refusing to heal?"

Frederick frowned.

"Look, I can't stay here again," Thomas announced. "Not with these paint fumes and all this dust flying about. I left here with a rattling cough after Christmas. Let's stay at the abbey— a birthday treat for you and a little holiday for us both. What do you say?"

Hammering started up again from above, making Frederick's headache all the worse.

"Come on," Thomas wheedled. "You are holding the canal meeting there anyway. Besides, when is the last time you've spent a few nights away from this place?"

And from all the memories it holds . . . Frederick silently added. "Very well. Assuming they have rooms."

Thomas beamed. "Excellent. You won't regret it. We shall have a merry time."

Frederick highly doubted it.

In the morning, while Rebecca was still asleep on the sitting-room sofa, her brother burst from his room with a stack of pages in hand.

"It's fate you're here now, Becky."

Startled awake, Rebecca surveyed her brother's unkempt appearance and fevered gaze. "Have you even slept?"

He shook his head, greasy dark hair flopping over his forehead. "Up working and thinking all night, and I've decided. You are the perfect person to place my new manuscript into his hands."

Confusion pinched. "What?"

"I've tried sending it to other publishers directly, and they all rejected it. Most without reading it. 'Declined by Return of Post'! My only chance is if Oliver will recommend it to *his* publisher."

Rebecca struggled up into a sitting position. "But would he? Considering your history with him?"

"Rose made a clean copy for me. He doesn't have to know it's my work until he passes it on to his publisher. We'll use a pen name."

Rebecca considered the plan and felt her brow furrow. "Will Mr. Edgecombe be at the hotel too? I met him that day, we—" She broke off, not wanting to remind John of that unhappy scene, and instead said, "Perhaps I might give the manuscript to him directly?"

John shook his head. "William Edgecombe died over a year ago. His brother, Thaddeus, has taken over, and he doesn't accept unsolicited manuscripts either."

"Then, might we not work on Mr. Oliver's sympathies— remind him what he owes you?"

John sat on the sofa near her feet. "No, Becky. Do not mention me. You know it will put him on his guard. He'd probably burn it out of spite."

"Or steal it," Rebecca muttered.

"Maybe. But if I want to risk my own work, that's my decision." John's eyes gleamed. "And if he does steal it again, we'll be prepared this time. We have a copy and Rose has read it. Perhaps you might read a few chapters as well, as you failed to do before. Then it would not be my word against his."

Remorse stabbed her. His fall from the tree was not the only injury she felt responsible for.

"There are no other options," John went on, voice rising. "This is the only way."

Rebecca didn't trust Ambrose Oliver and couldn't believe her brother would either. Moderating her tone, she said, "I don't think it would be wise to—"

"Stop!" he interjected. "Don't talk about things you don't understand. I know far more about publishing than you do."

Rebecca bit back a retort, realizing he was working himself into one of his fits of pique.

Oh, John. He could not be thinking rationally. Would his mind ever be right again? At peace?

She laid a hand on his rumpled sleeve. "You must forgive him, John, for your own sake. You are eaten up with bitterness."

He scowled. "Forgive him? He stole from me. Ruined my chances and my name. Called me a liar. I should be threatening *him* with a defamation suit instead of the other way around. And would—if I had more evidence. Or the money for a more powerful lawyer."

Rebecca sighed. She had heard it all so many times before. She said, "I don't want to leave. I just got here. And I want to help—"

"You can help me far more at the abbey," he insisted. "I already have Rose here. I don't need two women scolding me. And take your things. Might be a few days until you have an opportunity to speak with him."

"John, an unmarried woman cannot stay in a hotel alone."

"Is not your Lady F staying there?"

"I am not certain. She said she might visit friends."

He shrugged. "Either way, no need to be fastidious. It is not some gentlemen's club in London. This is Swanford Abbey—perfectly respectable."

She regarded her brother, another rebuke on her lips, but before she could reply he looked her in the eye and implored, "Please, please help me, Becky."

In that moment, she saw John as a little boy, climbing onto her bed, his hair untidy and book in hand. *Read me a story, Becky. Please?*

Taking a deep breath, she said, "I will think about it." She reached for the pages, but he held them away from her.

"Not these. You'll smudge them. Read from my copy, if you care to. Not that you've ever cared about my work before. . . ."

Her stomach churned with that old familiar guilt along with unease. What should she do?

She just wanted her brother back as he had once been, but she feared that John was gone forever.

Donning her spectacles, Rebecca read a few chapters of John's draft—actually quite good, she thought—then set it aside to dress. She went into the kitchen and found Rose bent over a book of household accounts.

The cook-housekeeper looked up with a rueful shake of her head. "I am behind on my bookwork as well as the housework."

Rebecca sat down across from her. "John asked me to take your copy of his manuscript to Mr. Oliver."

Rose nodded. "I overheard."

"It seems a fool's errand to me, not to mention improper. I don't know that I should even try."

Rose lifted a veined, work-worn hand and framed Rebecca's chin with it.

"If that's all he wants, give it to him. Besides, better you than John himself. Best thing we can do is keep him away from the abbey until Ambrose Oliver leaves."

Rose was right. But the last thing Rebecca wanted to do was to go inside Swanford Abbey, a place she had avoided since childhood.

With a sigh of resignation, Rebecca made quick work of repacking her valise, then looked around the sitting room to see if she had forgotten anything.

She noticed that the Lane family portrait was no longer hanging above the fireplace. Had Rose or John moved it for some reason?

She stepped closer to the mantelpiece and saw that someone had propped three sketches there—awful, amateur, adored. Her mother had drawn them in the vicarage garden. The first showed the vicarage's paneled front door and listing porch, woodbine climbing its columns. The second showed two children at play with a ball, meant to be her and John, she knew, although the simple drawing resembled neither. And the third was of a man in black—her father—standing beside the old rosebush, which reminded Rebecca of the hothouse flowers she had laid upon their grave when last she was home.

Rebecca looked above them, at the empty place on the wall. The sketches were dear, because her mother had done them, but they were a poor substitute for the professionally painted portrait of her parents and herself, with John as a toddler.

Rose shuffled past with a broom.

"Rose, where is our family portrait?"

The housekeeper hesitated, the lines on her face deepened by a wince. "Gone. John sold it."

Rebecca's heart sank. "Sold it? Why?"

"Needed the money. Or at least, wanted the money."

"But who would even want our family portrait?"

"Don't know. Was it done by someone famous?"

Rebecca shrugged. "Samuel Lines, I believe. Or one of his pupils. I was rather young at the time." Betrayal heated her veins. "He had no right to sell it!"

"I understand your anger, my dear. But trust me, it's not worth losing your only sibling over. Your living, breathing family is more important than any portrait."

Rebecca squeezed her eyes closed and drew a shaky inhale. "I suppose you are right. I will wait to raise the issue with John. We have a more pressing matter to deal with first."

2

Portfolio in one trembling hand, valise in the other, Rebecca walked back to the medieval stone abbey—the setting of many childhood nightmares. Her heart beat painfully hard. It had been one thing to alight in the stable yard, but to enter the abbey itself?

As a girl, she had taken pains to avoid the place, walking around Mr. Dodge's field rather than using the more direct path past the abbey. Every All Hallows' Eve, the children of Swanford told tales of the evil abbess who roamed the ruined church that slumped beside the abbey like the bones of an ancient mastodon, which Rebecca had once seen at an exhibition.

Local children still considered Swanford Abbey haunted, inhabited by the spirits of long-dead nuns who'd lost their home and some their lives during the dissolution centuries before, when icons had been smashed and church property claimed by the monarch. Afterward, the abbey had been given to a nobleman loyal to the crown who built a large private residence over and around the old cloisters. Sharington Court had been a two-and-a-half-story house with a slate roof, twisted chimney stacks, and mullioned windows. Many generations of the

Sharington family had lived there until the last of them died without heir or offspring more than thirty years ago. The house had been locked up, while the adjacent church, with its collapsed roof, continued to crumble. Since then, children of the parish had dared one another to climb the fallen walls, and the bravest among them had played among its ruins.

Rebecca still remembered the one and only time she climbed atop a partially crumbled wall of the ruined abbey church. A childhood companion had told ghost stories until fear froze her in place.

And then Rebecca had looked down and seen Frederick Wilford standing below her, an amused smile on his handsome face.

"May I help you down, young lady?"

Relief and a secret thrill had washed over her. She nodded and trustingly leaned into him as he lowered her to the ground. . . .

Rebecca blinked away the memory, wishing she could leave behind her girlish infatuation as easily.

Several years ago, Sharington Court had been purchased and, after a few financial setbacks, had eventually been renovated into a grand hotel. Rebecca was still not keen to enter the place in any state. With thoughts of dispossessed spirits in mind, the hairs at the back of her neck stood on end as she walked up the graveled drive.

Taking a deep breath, she ascended the double-sided stairway, where an officious-looking commissionaire opened the door for her.

With a start, she recognized him as Sir Roger Wilford's former valet, now attired in fine livery.

"Mr. Moseley, good day."

"Ah, if it isn't Rebecca Lane, all grown up. Goodness, how ancient you make me feel. I remember you running around the village green in a grass-stained pinafore."

She dipped her head, neck warm. "That was a long time ago. Well, a pleasure to see you again."

"And you, miss. It's been an age."

"I have been traveling."

"Have you? I would say, 'How pleasant,' but the truth is, I am a homebody who likes his own bed."

He offered to carry her valise, but she shook her head and held it close. She wasn't yet sure she would be staying as a guest. She rather hoped not.

He looked about to insist, but at that moment a stately traveling chariot arrived, and he quickly turned his attention to its occupants, calling for two porters to come and carry their baggage.

Rebecca entered Swanford Abbey alone.

Inside, she found herself in what had once been a Gothic great hall of impressive height, now a spacious reception hall. A magnificent log fire burned in a hearth with crossed sabers carved into the chimney piece above. On either side of the fire, decorative andirons shone, polished to a high sheen. A plush Turkish carpet served to soften the echoing sound of the open space. Atop it were arranged a cluster of small tea tables, red velvet armchairs, and sofas.

All around her was opulence to a grand scale. Rebecca supposed she should be used to such finery after traveling as companion to a wealthy dowager, but today she was on her own—former vicar's daughter and now humble lady's companion—and felt out of place.

She wondered if Lady Fitzhoward was still there or if she had already left to visit friends. But it was not Lady Fitzhoward she had come to see.

As she tentatively approached the gleaming oak reception desk, the clerk looked up, his gaze sweeping over her in practiced study. Perhaps she should have worn one of the fashionable gowns Lady Fitzhoward had purchased for her instead of a simple day dress and unadorned spencer.

"May I . . . help you?" the young man asked.

He did not appear eager to do so, nor familiar. He must be new to the village.

"Good day. I was hoping to speak with Mr. Ambrose Oliver. I understand he is staying here?"

Again his gaze swept over her and his lips thinned. "May I ask your connection to Mr. Oliver? Are you a . . . friend?" His tone dripped with lurid suspicion.

"Not at all. I wish to speak with him on a matter of business. Publishing business." She lifted the leather portfolio to substantiate her claim, then added, "My brother was an . . . associate of his."

The clerk shook his head. "Mr. Oliver sees no one. He has left strict instructions not to be disturbed."

Dismay and relief swirled within her. "Then, perhaps I might speak with his publisher, Mr. Edgecombe?"

Another shake of the head. "We have no one by that name staying here."

Disappointment pinched her stomach. Rebecca hoped she didn't appear as crestfallen as she felt.

Mr. Moseley, escorting the new arrivals inside, said, "Now, Raymond, this is Miss Lane, our former vicar's daughter. Do be polite."

The clerk lifted a pugnacious nose and said in a lower voice, "I can tell you that a Mr. Edgecombe was here yesterday to meet with a certain famous guest, and that we expect him back for dinner sometime in the next few days. Beyond that I cannot help you."

"I see. Well, thank you." Rebecca turned and stepped aside to make way for the others awaiting their turn at the desk.

She walked blindly across the reception hall to one of the cushioned armchairs and sat down to think, settling her valise beside her. Rebecca would have preferred to avoid the expense of an overnight stay, even though her brother had made it clear he didn't want her in the lodge criticizing his habits or untidiness. But a young, unmarried lady, staying in a hotel on her own?

Perhaps if she were quiet and kept to herself, her presence would go unremarked.

Movement at the far end of the room drew her attention. She glanced past a grand pianoforte to an impressive, curved staircase that led to a gallery above. From there, a tall, dark-haired man started down the steps. Recognition jolted her. *Not him. Not here. Not now.* She swiftly turned her face away, praying he had not seen her.

Too late.

"Miss Lane, is that you?"

She pressed her eyes tight. Was there any chance of slipping away? No. So much for keeping to herself.

She looked over with feigned nonchalance, hoping he would not notice her lip tremble. He'd reached the landing and walked toward her like an image from those old romantic dreams she'd tried to root out of her mind.

"Yes?" It was the only syllable she managed over her tight throat and racing thoughts.

As he neared, she noticed Sir Frederick looked a little older. He must be five and thirty now, but still meltingly handsome, and more intimidating than she recalled.

At her unenthusiastic response, he stopped where he was, smile fading. "Forgive me." He bowed. "I hope I am not intruding."

27

She rose and curtsied. "Not at all. I am only surprised to see you here."

"And I you. It has been far too long."

"I have been away traveling."

"Here in Swanford to visit your brother, I imagine?"

"Y-yes."

"Are you staying here, or in the lodge with him?" Sir Frederick raised his hand. "Don't worry, we would not raise the rent!" He chuckled, and she managed a small grin in return.

She did not, however, answer his question.

When she said no more, he asked, "Did you travel somewhere pleasant?"

"Oh yes, we did. Bath, Brighton, Paris . . ."

"We . . . ?" His dark brows rose in expectation.

She swallowed. She shouldn't be embarrassed to admit she had taken a position as lady's companion, but she was. Did he already know? Rose or one of the Fenchurches might have mentioned it. Before she could reply, a second man swept across the hall to join them, a younger, fairer version of the first in immaculate gentlemen's attire.

"Paris? *J'adore* Paris. So beautiful." His gaze seemed to linger on her face as he said the words, but she was likely imagining it. He elbowed his brother. "Do introduce us, Freddy."

Sir Frederick hesitated, then complied. "Miss Lane, I am not sure if you will remember my brother, Thomas Wil—"

"Tommy Wilford," the younger man interrupted with a bow. "How do you do?"

Thomas was good-looking and closer to her age, but she had always preferred his older brother.

Frederick added, "Miss Lane's father was our vicar and my boyhood tutor."

The golden eyebrows lifted. "Ah yes! I am afraid I did not

recognize you, Miss Lane. You have grown up—and very well, I might add!"

Sir Frederick's mouth tightened at Thomas's flattery. He said, "You were at school for much of Miss Lane's childhood and away in London a great deal in recent years."

"That must explain it. And I did not know the legendary Mr. Lane as well as my brother did, as he had given up tutoring by the time I was old enough, but Freddy speaks of him often and fondly."

Frederick nodded, then said, "Her brother, John, lives in the underkeeper's lodge. Perhaps you have met him."

The light of interest in Thomas's eyes dimmed somewhat. "No, I have not had that pleasure."

Sir Frederick turned back to her and explained, "We are staying here as guests this week. The house is undergoing renovations."

"Ah. I see. I wondered why you would stay here when Wickworth is so close."

"And you, Miss Lane?"

Two similar pairs of eyes regarded her curiously.

She dampened dry lips. "I may be staying a night or two as well. My brother is . . . um . . . busy writing, you see. I rather surprised him, coming to visit just now."

"Well, whatever the reason, we are delighted to find you here. Are we not, Freddy?" Again, Thomas elbowed his brother's side.

"Indeed we are. I hope we shall have an opportunity to talk of old times while you are here."

"I would enjoy that."

She nodded to each brother in turn, then made her way back to the desk. The same clerk stood there and did not look especially pleased to see her return.

"Yes, miss. How may I help you now?"

"I would like a room, please."

"For one?"

"Yes." Self-consciousness burned her ears.

"Have you a reservation?"

"No. Is that a problem?"

"Well, we are quite busy." He opened the register and made a pretense of running a finger down an inked page. "And I am not sure we have any rooms available."

Even though a part of her would be glad for an excuse to return to the lodge, she would be mortified to be turned away in front of the Wilfords. She added in a lower voice, "I am meeting Lady Fitzhoward here."

They were not planning to meet for a week's time, but Rebecca kept that bit to herself.

"Lady Fitzhoward?" The clerk's disapproving expression relaxed somewhat. "Ah. I do have one room available, although not our finest."

"That is all right. I don't need anything grand."

Even if a better room were available, she would rather not pay any more than she had to for this unplanned stay.

"For how many nights?"

"I am not yet certain. May I let you know?"

"Very well, miss." He swiveled the registration book toward her.

While she filled in her information, the clerk extracted a key from a drawer and gestured for a porter.

"Neville, please take Miss Lane to number thirteen."

"Thirteen?" the young porter repeated in surprise, then with a shrug picked up her valise. "Very well. Right this way, miss."

Neville nodded to the curving staircase. "There are two ways to reach your room. We can take the main stairs there to the first floor. Or, if you don't mind a bit of fresh air, we can go through the cloisters. I think it's quicker."

The haunted cloisters? Rebecca thought. She swallowed a foolish lump. "I don't mind."

He led her from the hall, across a passage, and out into the four-sided cloister walkway, which framed a grassy inner court-yard. The cloisters had a solid wall on one side and a colonnade on the other, which supported a series of stone arches with ornamental openwork above. From a distance, the arches looked like windows, but they held no glass. Through them, sunshine cast bars of light onto the flagstone floor, the "windows" appearing like tapered candles with flames above.

Gazing up, Rebecca admired the fan vaulting of the cloister ceiling. So much beauty for women who had taken vows of poverty. Or was the beauty for God? Either way, Rebecca was glad the nuns had been surrounded by loveliness in this place where they'd spent many hours praying.

"The cloisters were the very heart of the abbey," the porter explained. "The oldest part too. Pretty when it's sunny and mild like today, but cold in January."

"I can imagine. Is it . . . haunted, as people say?"

With his free hand, he scratched his ear and sent her a sideways glance. "I am not really supposed to talk about that. You don't want to get me into trouble, do you?"

"Of course not."

He reached the far corner and gestured up a dim stairway. "Your room is at the top of the night stair."

"Night stair?"

He nodded. "The nuns came down from their dormitory to services while it was still dark. The church is just through that door." Neville pointed to the right. "What's left of it, anyway."

Rebecca looked up the shadowy stairway. Dips had been

worn into the center of each stone step, as if a stream had flowed over them for centuries. In this case, she realized, a stream of dutiful feet, making their way to and from worship.

He led the way up. "Watch your step."

Turning on the half landing, he continued upstairs. At the top, a door stood on one side, and on the other, an open archway into the main corridor. He turned to the door, which bore a brass plate engraved with the number 13. Unlocking the door with effort, the porter then gestured her inside. He set down her valise and stepped to the room's small window to open the shutters.

"Don't use this room very often. Once part of the nuns' dormitory."

The spartan room held a single bed, armchair, washstand, dressing table, and a small closet. Probably usually reserved for a lady's maid or valet, Rebecca guessed. An unadorned crucifix hung over the bed, a vivid reminder of the devout women who once slept there.

"It may be small, but it has a balcony." He pointed to the narrow door that led out to it.

Then he frowned at the basin—empty save a dried spider— and the single towel beside it. "I'll ask one of the chambermaids to bring up water and fresh towels."

"Thank you." She extracted a coin from her reticule and handed it to him.

"Appreciate it, miss. Enjoy your stay."

Rebecca summoned a feeble smile in return. "I hope to."

After he left, she removed her bonnet, laid out her dinner dress to smooth its wrinkles, and set her toiletries on the dressing table. Even though she bemoaned the cost of the room, she found herself nervously excited about being in the hotel, especially with Sir Frederick Wilford staying there as well.

Frederick went to look in on the young thoroughbred he was boarding at the abbey stables. He wanted the convenience of being able to ride—and to leave the abbey—whenever he wished. After so much solitude over the last few years he was unaccustomed to being surrounded by people, and quickly wearied of having to make polite conversation. Moreover, he was not a man made for sitting about, chatting aimlessly or playing cards—pastimes his brother seemed to relish. Give him a blood horse, clear skies, and miles of good road any day.

Reaching the stall, he saw his chestnut stallion munching contentedly from a feed bucket. The horse looked up, nickering in recognition.

The scene took Frederick back to the many hours he'd spent in the Wickworth stable over the years, often with a young Rebecca Lane for company.

He'd always had an affinity for the spirited girl with the big hazel eyes, the firstborn of his beloved tutor, Mr. Arthur Lane.

When she had shown every interest, and her parents had not objected, Frederick had taught her to ride and care for horses. Rebecca had taken to it quickly and was a natural-born rider. She also possessed a keen mind and had borne his lessons—first in riding, later in chess and other games—with patient interest, far more so than Thomas ever had.

But later, when Frederick met and fell in love with the beautiful Miss Seward, he had drifted apart from the Lane family. Compared to spending time with an alluring woman, games and rides with an adolescent girl held little appeal.

Rebecca had clearly been hurt by his dismissal and inattention, but what could he do? The time had come to take a wife, and thoughts of Rebecca Lane had faded. She was just a girl, he'd told himself. She would get over her disappointment, grow up, and someday meet a love of her own.

But now . . . ?

Rebecca Lane was a little girl no longer. As Thomas had said, she had grown up very well, and grown remarkably pretty. He had seen her in passing over the years since his marriage and across the church two Christmases ago. But meeting her again now, close up, and after a long absence, he could find little trace of the precocious girl he had known. Instead he saw an elegant, well-spoken, and well-traveled woman.

For the first time in years, the rusty hinges of his shuttered heart gave an experimental creak.

No. He pressed his eyes shut and his heart with it.

Rebecca was still young and innocent. She deserved better, far better, than a disillusioned widower nearly ten years her senior with bitter experience and a sullied soul.

⁂

With sunlight spilling through the window into her tidy, simple room, Rebecca's earlier visions of the abbey—dark and dangerous—began to fade.

Pushing aside her uneasiness about what John had asked her to do, she decided that as soon as she was settled, she would explore the hotel. Having seen the beautifully renovated great hall, she wanted to see more of this place that had once seemed forbidden and frightening.

While awaiting the maid, Rebecca tried the balcony door, which opened with a cranky whine of disuse. The narrow, wrought-iron balcony overlooked the abbey gardens and held one small, ornate chair of the same material. Perhaps she might sit out there at some point, or even explore the gardens below, but first she wanted to see more of the abbey itself.

The chambermaid arrived with a pitcher of warm water, towels, and a friendly smile.

Rebecca recognized her with surprise. "Mary?"

The young woman looked up, eyes widening. "Miss Lane! Whatever are you doing here?"

"I am . . ." She faltered. What was she doing there, when her brother lived in a perfectly adequate house less than two miles away?

"I am *so* glad to see you, Mary," she said in a rush, sidestepping the question. "We miss you at the lodge."

Mary Hinton had been employed by them as a housemaid, assisting Rose, until they could no longer afford to keep two servants.

"I did not know you had a place here," Rebecca added. "I thought you had taken one with the Griffiths?"

The girl nodded. "I had. But this one pays better, so I gave my notice and came here. Must be nearly a year ago now."

"Are you enjoying the position?"

Mary shrugged. "It's all right. I get tips sometimes. I like that. Otherwise, the work is much the same as anywhere else."

"I imagine you meet some . . . interesting people here."

"A few. Though I don't really 'meet' the guests, do I? Just tote and clean for them. Some are kind and some are a right bother." The girl seemed to realize whom she was talking to and bit her lip. "Pray, don't be offended, miss. I don't mean you, now you're a guest. I'm happy to do my job—'specially for you."

"Thank you, Mary. While I am here, I shall endeavor not to be too much bother."

The girl's worried gaze flew to hers, but seeing Rebecca's

grin, she returned it with relief and then finished the tasks she had come for.

Stepping to the door, Mary said, "Indoor water closet just down the passage. Breakfast served in the refectory, or I can bring it to your room. You need anything else while you're here, you just let me know."

"I will. Thank you, Mary."

After the maid left, Rebecca washed her face and hands and tidied her hair in the small mirror. Then she stepped from her room, locked the door, and slipped the key into her reticule.

Instead of going back down the night stair, she passed by it and went through the archway into the main corridor. She walked past numbered doors at intervals, while the inner walls held windows that overlooked the cloister courtyard below.

She strolled along first one side and then the next of the quadrangle that composed the upper floor. Turning down the third side, she passed a few more doors and then reached the gallery balustrade, open to the reception hall below.

Ahead of her, just beyond the main stairway, a man sat on a chair outside the final door along this corridor. She wondered what he was doing there. Even while seated, he displayed the excellent posture of a military man, although he wore ordinary civilian attire. If not an officer, perhaps a coachman, she guessed.

He glanced her way, eyes narrowing. Disconcerted to be caught staring, she lowered her head and started down the stairs, holding on to the railing to avoid slipping from such a height.

Reaching the ground floor, Rebecca avoided the gaze of the rude clerk as she crossed the hall. Stepping into the corridor behind, she passed the refectory dining room and the coffee room around the corner. The savory smells of roasted coffee beans and fresh bread wafted out, and in reply, Rebecca's stomach growled a vacant protest. She wondered if it would be inappropriate to venture into the dining room on her own. She supposed she could ask Mary to bring a tray to her room to avoid the awkwardness of dining alone.

Continuing on, Rebecca noticed that while many of the hotel furnishings were clearly new, some ancient scent lingered in the air. She breathed it in, trying to place it. A slight mustiness paired with . . . what . . . chalk dust and incense?

The tall ceilings and doors with high transoms lent the place an institutional atmosphere, like a university or a church. And, she supposed, it had once been a bit of both.

Turning another corner, she went by a closed door marked *Grand Suite* and a passage that led to a rear exit.

Just past it, an open doorway and the pleasanter smell of leather and old books beckoned her. The library and writing room, she realized, where guests might borrow books or keep up with correspondence. Rebecca decided she would first complete her circuit with a peek into the chapel, then return to peruse the hotel's books.

Passing the night stair, she reached the final door, which, the porter had said, led to what remained of the church.

Inching open the heavy door, Rebecca hoped she would not disturb a service of some sort. Perhaps she would pray for John while she was there.

Inside, she saw a woman kneeling at the altar rail, head bowed. The chapel was dim, but a shaft of colored light from the stained-glass windows shone on her, and Rebecca glimpsed a brimmed hat and the outline of her profile.

At the sound of soft weeping, Rebecca retreated, quietly closing the door behind her.

Retracing her steps to the library and writing room, Rebecca entered to find two walls filled floor-to-ceiling with books, high-back armchairs facing a fireplace, a game table laid with chess pieces, and several writing desks.

She paused. A woman sat at one of the desks, her back to the door, putting pen to paper. She crumpled the page, tossed it into a nearby rubbish basket, and then rested her head in her hands in a hunched posture of defeat.

Rebecca walked closer. As she did, her slipper scuffed the floor and the woman turned to look over her shoulder.

Surprised, Rebecca said, "Good day, Lady Fitzhoward."

Her employer was dressed in her striped rust-and-gold open-robe, which fastened under the bosom of a muslin day dress, the style old, but the garments new and the fabric of finest quality. A filmy fichu around her shoulders covered her decolletage.

She wore a lace-trimmed cap over hair that appeared flat and in need of a washing rather than her usual lofty, elegant coiffure. Nor was she wearing powder and rouge. She looked careworn and older, more like the woman of nearly sixty that she was.

"I am surprised to find you here," Rebecca added, feeling suddenly awkward in her presence.

The woman straightened, and her confident demeanor slid back into place. Her lower lip buttoned over a thin upper lip in an expression of disapproval. "I could say the same of you. I thought you were visiting your brother."

"I was. I stayed at the lodge last night, but he . . . he is not prepared for a house guest. He suggested I come here and deliver something to an acquaintance staying in the hotel."

The woman's hooded eyes narrowed with doubt.

Before Lady Fitzhoward could press her, Rebecca asked, "And I thought you planned to visit friends?"

The woman lifted a haughty chin. "I changed my mind. Apparently both of us have had a change in plans. I hope you are not disappointed to find me here. You were no doubt hoping for a respite from my company."

"Not at all, my lady. And I hope you are not sorry to see me again so soon."

The woman hesitated, then coolly replied, "It makes no difference to me."

Rebecca's stomach growled again. Perhaps she could sit with Lady Fitzhoward at dinner. Would it be presumptuous to ask? She was not there in her role as companion now.

Pressing a subtle hand to her midriff, Rebecca said, "Are you planning to dine here tonight, my lady?"

"Why? Do you wish to join me?"

"Only if you don't mind. I am not certain it would be seemly for me to dine alone. Not in the coffee room, of course, but in the main dining room."

"I don't see why not. I dined there alone last night. But then, I am old and don't draw any attention, whereas you are young and pretty." Her disapproving gaze swept over her once more. "That frock, however . . . Yes, assuming you change for dinner, you may share my table as usual."

Relief overcame offense. "Thank you."

One sparse eyebrow rose. "Will you be sharing the bill as well? Or do you wish to cancel your week's holiday and resume your onerous duties?"

"Oh, I did not presume you would pay for my meals. I will pay my own way, to be fair."

Lady Fitzhoward waved an impatient hand. "No matter. I have more money than companions. And you don't eat much. That is . . . unless you have suddenly acquired a taste for French wines and choice game?"

"No, my lady," Rebecca hurried to assure her, and then saw

the humor glimmering in the woman's eyes. Rebecca grinned tentatively, almost holding her breath, relieved when her employer smirked in return.

Something in her expression reminded Rebecca of something, but the fleeting impression flickered away before she could identify it.

The gleam faded from Lady Fitzhoward's eyes as quickly as it had appeared. "I dine at seven. Don't be late."

Rebecca dipped a quick curtsy and turned to go, postponing her plan to search the library shelves.

"Which room have they put you in?" her employer called after her.

Rebecca turned back. "Thirteen."

Lady Fitzhoward nodded. "I am in the Grand Suite. I shall send Joly to help you dress at half past six."

"Thank you, my lady."

Rebecca walked back upstairs to her room, reaching into her reticule for her key as she went. The metal edge caught in a small tear in the lining. As she stood outside her door, carefully extracting it, she noticed movement down the corridor.

A woman in a broad-brimmed hat stood at a door beyond the night stair, struggling with her lock and key. She gave a small cry of frustration. A man emerging from the water closet seemed to hear and turned in her direction.

"Having trouble, miss? Mine sticks too. Happy to help, if you like."

"Oh, that is kind of you. Thank you." She stepped aside.

"The trick is to lift up while you turn the key," he explained, his tone friendly. "Like this." He demonstrated and the lock gave.

"There you are." He handed back the key, and the young woman thanked him again.

"No trouble." He bowed respectfully and turned, walking in Rebecca's direction.

She recognized him as the man she'd seen sitting outside one of the rooms a short while before. As he strode smartly toward her now, she dismissed the notion that he might be a coachman. Definitely an officer, she decided, though in civilian dress. Middle forties, perhaps, brown hair receding slightly at the forehead, long side-whiskers a shade lighter than his hair.

She turned her attention to her own door, unlocking it as he'd advised. He nodded politely in her direction as he marched away down the passage.

His demeanor and offer of help had struck her as honorable and almost paternal. For a moment, it made Rebecca miss her own dear papa.

Shaking off the bittersweet thought, Rebecca entered her room with a resolute smile, determined to make the best of her unplanned stay.

3

Dressed in a gown of willow green, her hair freshly arranged by the dexterous Nicole Joly, Rebecca made her way to the hotel's cavernous dining room a few minutes before seven.

Lady Fitzhoward was there before her and dressed to the nines. Her hair was now curled and fashioned in its usual fluffy coiffure. Pearl earrings dangled, a necklace graced her neck, and a jeweled ring shone on her finger. Expertly applied rouge added vibrancy to thin lips and lined cheeks.

Miss Joly had been busy.

Lady Fitzhoward's gimlet gaze swept over Rebecca, and her only sign of approval was a curt nod. She turned to the maître d'hôtel standing just inside the door with a large leather-bound book, greeting guests.

"Two tonight, Pierre."

"Very good, your ladyship."

He led them to a table, where a waiter pulled back chairs for them and laid linen serviettes across their laps.

Rebecca looked around the long rectangular room. White

cloth–covered tables filled the space, dark beams striped the ceiling, and a wooden dais with a cross above reminded guests of the room's origins as the abbey's refectory.

Only a handful of the many tables were occupied. At one sat four older gentlemen, at another, a middle-aged couple who barely spoke to one another, and at a third, Sir Frederick and his brother.

Both Wilfords glanced in her direction. Sir Frederick nodded to her, and Thomas smiled.

"Who are they?" Lady Fitzhoward asked.

"Sir Frederick Wilford and his brother, Thomas."

"Ah. Frederick is the older one, with dark hair?"

Rebecca was not surprised the woman had noticed him. Sir Frederick was striking with broad shoulders and finely chiseled features. He was perhaps not quite as good-looking as his fair-haired brother, but his air of self-possession garnered respect above and beyond simple admiration for his appearance.

"Yes. How did you know?"

"I have . . . heard of him."

Surprise darted through her. "Have you?"

She nodded. "Though a long time ago now."

Rebecca was about to ask in what context, but the waiter returned to explain the evening's bill of fare: spring soup, followed by sirloins of beef and saddles of mutton accompanied by salads and sauces.

They had just been served the soup course when a general stir caused Rebecca to look up from her bowl.

The commotion was followed by a rolling pause in conversation. From table to table, people stopped talking, some in midsentence, until the entire room seemed to still. Even the silent middle-aged couple looked over, spoons suspended, to stare at the newcomer.

Rebecca looked over as well, steeling herself, expecting to see Ambrose Oliver.

Instead, a strikingly beautiful woman strode into the room, a shimmering white evening gown revealing delicate collarbones and a slim feminine figure. She wore her coppery-gold hair in a simple style and held herself with grace and poise, as if aware all eyes were upon her but unaffected by the attention.

In their hurry to seat her, two waiters collided, and only the quick hands of the maître d'hôtel averted disaster, catching a wine bottle slipping from one young man's grasp before it could fall splashing to the floor.

Rebecca could not resist glancing over at Sir Frederick, expecting to see admiration in his eyes even as she dreaded it. Surprisingly, he looked from the woman to his brother, dark brows drawn low, expression thunderous. Thomas Wilford, meanwhile, smiled and sipped his wine, eyes glimmering over his glass.

"Who is she?" Rebecca whispered across the table.

"She looks familiar, but I don't know," Lady Fitzhoward replied, then studied the reactions of the Wilford brothers with interest. "But those two seem to know something."

Lady Fitzhoward leaned closer, her focus remaining on the gentlemen. "Frederick does not seem happy to see her, while his brother looks altogether too pleased with himself."

The maître d'hôtel proceeded to seat the beautiful woman by herself at a table for two. She did not appear at all self-conscious to be dining alone.

Now that Rebecca could see a profile, a tingle of recognition prickled through her. Was this the woman she had seen crying? The chapel had been dim, and the woman had worn a hat, but the upturned nose and high cheekbones seemed familiar.

The long-case clock showed a quarter past seven. A minute later, male footsteps advanced toward the refectory entrance.

First to appear was the man Rebecca had seen in the upstairs passage, now marching like an infantry officer, his posture erect, arms at his sides, eyes sweeping the room as though expecting an enemy attack. Apparently satisfied, he pivoted and stood just inside the threshold, his back to the wall.

After him came Ambrose Oliver. She had seen the author once from a distance and recognized him instantly. He appeared older, heavier, and more dissipated than she recalled. Dark hair hung in untidy waves around his face. He was perhaps five and forty, and a big man, several inches over six feet tall. His rounded belly and full cheeks attested to his love of food and drink.

Apparently aware he was being watched, he gave a general nod to the room before taking his chair. His gaze landed on the beautiful woman. Something flashed in his eyes, but Rebecca wasn't certain if the spark was recognition or attraction. He paused in the act of sitting, hovering there in a strange half-bent posture.

The waiter began fluttering around him, settling him into the chair and spreading a serviette over his lap.

The awkward moment passed.

"Our illustrious guest has arrived," Lady Fitzhoward observed. "Same time as last night."

"Are you acquainted with him?" Rebecca asked.

"Only through his books."

"Why is that man standing guard by the door, do you think?" Rebecca whispered.

The older woman considered. "Perhaps Mr. Oliver feels he is in danger."

"Danger? Why should he be? From whom—avid readers?" Rebecca inwardly scoffed. Ambrose Oliver was not *that* famous.

Lady Fitzhoward shrugged. "Never mind. That Gothic novel

you lent me has me seeing danger everywhere. Come, our meal is growing cold."

Frederick leaned across the table and speared his brother with a look. "You know that woman, don't you. You arranged to meet her here."

Thomas touched smooth fingertips to his cravat. "Upon my soul, I did not."

"Then, you knew she would be here."

His brother dipped his head and looked up with a coy grin. "I may have had a hint."

Frederick rolled his eyes. "And here I believed you when you said the paint fumes and dust made you ill last time. A birthday treat for *me*, indeed."

"Come, Freddy. Let us not quarrel. I truly believe a change of scenery will do you a world of good. You have been stuck inside that house of mourning long enough. How you glower!" Thomas leaned his elbows on the table and lowered his voice. "Consider. If I simply wanted to meet a woman in a hotel, would I have brought my brother along?"

"I suppose not," Frederick grudgingly allowed. He glanced over at the tall man who'd entered late and scowled anew. "What is Ambrose Oliver doing here?"

"The author? Where?"

Thomas swiveled to gawk, then looked back at him warily, gaze shifting from Frederick's face to clenched fist.

"Now, Freddy. Calm down. I never really thought his book was about Marina, for all your embarrassment."

One of the man's novels had described the love affairs of a baronet's unfaithful wife. Frederick hissed, "'Sir Roderick and his roving Lady Willing?' How much more obvious could he be?"

"See? He did not use real names. If it did describe her, it was a veiled reference. Beyond a few local people, perhaps, no one would guess—"

"Many people *did* guess. If it was veiled, it was thinly veiled. One might say, gossamer. That man made me a laughingstock."

"If anyone made you a laughingstock, it was Marina herself, and she is gone. I do wish you would move past this already."

"You have never been married, Tom. You don't understand."

His brother shuddered theatrically. "You're right, I don't. It is the bachelor's life for me."

The hotel proprietor, making his nightly round through the dining room, approached their table. "Pardon me. Is everything all right, gentlemen?"

Frederick sat back, glad for the interruption. "Ah yes, the meal is excellent. Thank you."

The well-dressed, ginger-haired man looked down at Frederick's barely touched plate. "Your full plate disagrees with you."

"My fault," Thomas interjected. "Kept his maw too busy gabbing."

Frederick, who knew the owner slightly, said, "How are you, Mr. Mayhew?"

"I am well, thank you. A pleasure to have you both staying with us."

Thomas lifted an index finger. "My idea."

"How are things going here?" Frederick asked. "Business brisk?"

Was it his imagination, or did the man's smile dim?

"Good, good," Mayhew said, avoiding their eyes and looking around the room, his focus lingering on Ambrose Oliver.

Following his line of sight, Thomas said, "Having a celebrated author here ought to be good for business."

The owner said, "That remains to be seen." He bowed and then walked toward the neighboring table.

After they'd eaten, Thomas wiped his mouth, folded his napkin, and set it aside. "Please excuse me while I pay my compliments to that enchanting woman in white."

He rose and walked over to her table.

At the same moment, Mr. Oliver stood, sights fixed on the woman like a target.

Seeing the younger man stop to talk with her, Oliver sat back down, thick lips curled into a frown.

Frederick rather liked seeing the author disappointed. Heaven help the man who tried to compete with Thomas where women were concerned. For a moment, Frederick watched his brother bow and chat, and the woman smile in return, her countenance nearly glowing in the face of Thomas's good looks and impeccable address.

Frederick turned away. His brother had always had a way with women, a confidence and easy charm that made him a favorite wherever he went. Far more so than Frederick.

Of its own accord, his gaze traveled over to Miss Lane. She was one female who had admired him. Granted, that had been years ago, when she was barely out of the schoolroom. Now she was an attractive woman in an evening gown that flattered her feminine figure. Rich honey-brown curls framed a lovely face with smooth skin, delicate nose, and fine, full mouth.

She looked over and caught him staring. Politeness dictated he acknowledge her, so he rose, tugged down his waistcoat, and slowly crossed the room. Noticing his approach, Miss Lane sat up even straighter and dabbed a nervous table napkin to her mouth.

"Good evening, Miss Lane. I hope you don't mind my coming over to greet you."

"Of course not."

He glanced at her dining companion. "Would you introduce me to your friend?"

"Oh, forgive me. Lady Fitzhoward, may I present Sir Frederick Wilford."

The woman looked up at him with interest. "*Sir* Frederick now, is it?"

An odd thing for a stranger to say, Frederick thought. Or was she? Something about the older woman struck him as familiar. "Yes. My dear father, Sir Roger, passed on several years ago."

"Ah. I see. My condolences."

"Were you . . . acquainted with my father?"

After a slight hesitation, she replied, "No. We were never . . . introduced."

Another odd response.

He said, "And I don't believe I am familiar with the name Fitzhoward. You are not from this county, I take it."

No shake of the head. Only her eyes moved. "My husband's name. From Manchester. We spent his last few years in Cheltenham. Spa town, you know, hoping to restore his health. The effort did not succeed."

"Then you have lost a spouse as well."

"Have you?"

"Yes, almost two years ago now."

"I am sorry." The woman's gaze slid to Rebecca and away again.

"Well. I won't keep you. Good night, ladies."

"Good night," Lady Fitzhoward replied.

Miss Lane said nothing, but her large hazel eyes held his, making him reluctant to turn away. With effort, he bowed and took his leave.

Throughout the meal, Rebecca had tried to rouse her courage to walk over and speak to Mr. Oliver, but doing so seemed like such a presumptuous intrusion. He, not to mention Lady Fitzhoward, would likely think her incredibly forward. That thought kept her rooted to her chair.

Sir Frederick's coming to their table had given her a welcome excuse to put off the uncomfortable task.

After he left the dining room, Lady Fitzhoward turned speculative eyes her way.

"That honor was due to you. You two are apparently well acquainted?"

For some illogical reason, Rebecca's face heated. She lowered it, looking down at her serviette again as she folded it with far more precision than the task required.

"Oh, I have known him for years," she said in what she hoped seemed a casual manner. "My father was his tutor when he was a boy. And after Papa married as a mere curate, the Wilfords granted him the living of All Saints Church. My brother and I grew up as neighbors to them."

"I see." Lady Fitzhoward studied her face. "And were you acquainted with his wife as well?"

Rebecca fussed with the cloth. "I met her, once or twice."

"I suppose she was very beautiful and accomplished?"

Rebecca felt the old ache, and said in a hollow voice, "Yes. She was."

Rose had written to let her know Lady Wilford had died, and Rebecca had felt no joy at the news. *Poor Frederick.*

Lady Fitzhoward watched her a moment longer, then gathered up her reticule and stood. "I shall see you tomorrow, I trust?"

"I shall be here."

After her employer left, Rebecca finished her coffee, and then followed her out. Passing by the hall, she noticed Sir Frederick standing within, looking up at something. The walls held carved niches from portrait level to the ceiling. In place of the old religious icons that must once have filled them now stood small statues of Greek gods and other fanciful figures.

"What has caught your attention?" she asked, walking over to join him.

He pointed to one of the niches. "That statue. It's meant to be the first abbess, the one who built the abbey. How young and carefree she looks."

The female figurine had curled locks, and a bird had landed on her outstretched arm.

"And here's another of the same woman." He pointed to a marble bust. The woman, now older, wore a veil, her shoulders were lifted, and although there were no arms, one could imagine them reaching out. "That's from later in life. After she lost her husband and built the abbey in his memory."

Rebecca licked dry lips. "Speaking of . . . loss, I was sorry to hear about your wife."

He dipped his head in acknowledgment. "Thank you."

When he said no more, she felt compelled to fill the awkward silence. "I . . . only met her in passing, but I remember her being very beautiful. At least you will always have your memories."

He winced and replied, "Sadly, yes."

She blinked, uncertain what he meant, and embarrassed about her clumsy attempt to comfort him.

"Well." She swallowed a gristly lump of regret. "Good night."

He nodded but said nothing more, his gaze returning to the first statue in all her youthful beauty, before loss and time had stolen her charms.

Frederick looked over his shoulder and watched Miss Lane walk away, cursing his dull, awkward tongue. Why had he not engaged her in more pleasant conversation? Talking of long-dead abbesses and lost spouses was not exactly the way to put a young lady at her ease. Thomas would certainly chide him had he heard.

How strange to find himself speaking to a grown-up Rebecca Lane here in Swanford Abbey of all places.

Frederick was still unaccustomed to being in the abbey now that it was a hotel. He well remembered the years it had stood deserted, left to ruin, and supposedly haunted.

He recalled coming upon a few children clambering about the ruins of the abbey church long after the last Sharington had died and before it had been acquired by investors.

Walking past the abbey, Frederick heard a young lad, Robb Tarvin, teasing two girls. One he didn't recognize, but the other was Rebecca Lane, perched atop a half-crumbled wall.

The lad was telling them a story about the soldiers who came and smashed the altar and chased out the nuns and abbess, scaring them to death, one quite literally.

Walking closer, he saw Rebecca's big eyes fill with tears.

"No one would be so cruel, Robb Tarvin. You are a brute to tell such lies."

"It's no lie, and you are as ninny-headed as Kitty there if you don't believe me. They say the ghost of the abbess roams these ruins even now, crying out for justice."

"That's enough, young man," Frederick interrupted, stepping over the fallen coping to reach them. "I think you've frightened these girls more than enough for one day."

The boy scowled. "Bah. It's all true and you know it. I read the history in one of your father's books!"

"I don't think that bit about a ghost was in any book he

might have lent you. Nor do I think it kind of you to take quite so much pleasure in scaring these girls."

The boy scowled again, mumbled something unflattering under his breath, and slinked away.

Frederick approached the vicar's daughter sitting high on the partial wall. "May I help you down, young lady?"

"Yes, thank you."

He reached up his hands and lowered the trusting Rebecca easily to the ground.

"Are you all right?"

"Perfectly well. I was not scared."

"No?" he asked, barely restraining a smile.

"Well. Maybe a little."

"May I walk you back to the vicarage?"

"Yes, if you please," she said in a rush of relief. "May we drop Kitty on the way?"

"Of course."

"Thank you, Frederick."

"My pleasure, Miss Rebecca."

The memory faded.

He wondered if Miss Lane still trusted him as she once had. He hoped so. Although if she had heard the rumors about his wife's death, her opinion of him may very well have changed, and if so, he could not blame her.

That night, Rebecca settled into bed with her reading spectacles and an old novel she'd brought with her. She struggled to concentrate on the print, guilt still chafing her over that awkward attempt to console Sir Frederick. Recalling her words, she winced again. *"You will always have your memories"*? What were memories to a flesh-and-blood woman? A lover? A wife? Did the fact that Rebecca had her memories alleviate the pain she still felt over her parents' deaths? No. It had been a stupid and thoughtless thing to say. She had been nervous, yes, but that did not excuse her.

Determined to put it from her mind, she turned a page in *The Italian, or the Confessional of the Black Penitents*, a Gothic novel by Ann Radcliffe. The story was about a young man kept from the woman he loved by a ghostly monk.

Rebecca read a few more lines, then looked up midsentence. What had she heard? Footsteps outside her room? Porters and page boys going about their duties, she supposed. It was not her first time in a hotel, she reminded herself. She should be used to such sounds by now. She continued reading.

When the young man refused to stay away, abductors carried off his love and hid her. He eventually found her imprisoned in a remote convent at the mercy of a cruel lady abbess. . . .

Rebecca shivered and shut the book. It was definitely not helping allay her nerves, nor would it help her sleep.

Setting the book on the nearby table, she leaned over to blow out her candle but changed her mind and let it burn. She settled under the bedclothes, the flickering light casting disconcerting shadows on the walls. Finding her pillow too flat, she bunched it up and lay back down. Wind whistled through the abbey in a low moan.

She closed her eyes, but when a door whined open somewhere nearby, she abruptly reopened them. Merely a guest returning to his room, she decided, and turned over.

Footsteps sounded outside her door, followed by a cry, quickly stifled.

Rebecca sat upright in bed. Was someone hurt?

She folded back the counterpane and climbed from bed, wrapping a shawl around herself and wriggling her feet into shoes. Picking up her guttering candle, she inched open the door and listened.

Silence.

She tiptoed into the main corridor, lifting her candle high to survey the closed doors. All was quiet.

She stepped to the nearest window overlooking the inner courtyard. A flutter of movement drew her eye to the right. Across the quadrangle, a figure in black hood and gown floated past window after window, head covering fluttering behind, then disappeared from view.

Rebecca's heart thudded. Real person, or apparition?

She told herself the Gothic novel she'd been reading had invaded her imagination. Or perhaps it was all those terrifying stories she'd heard as a girl about the ghost of the abbess who haunted Swanford Abbey. Whatever the cause, Rebecca chastised herself for a fool.

She turned back, not sure if she had remembered to shut her door. A chill slithered up her spine at the thought of someone entering while she'd been creeping about. She returned to her room and searched beneath the bed and in the closet before locking her door, and with a sigh of relief, climbed back into bed.

But it was a long time before she fell asleep.

4

The next morning, Rebecca awoke feeling muddled and queasy. She had not slept well, tormented by the late-night scare, her worries for John, and the question of how to meet with Mr. Oliver.

As Rebecca climbed from bed, Mary Hinton arrived with warm water and asked what she wanted for breakfast, offering eggs, bacon, kippers, kidneys, ham, toasted muffins, and orange marmalade.

"Goodness," Rebecca breathed, stomach roiling at the thought of so much rich food. She selected tea and toasted muffins, hoping the comforting combination would settle her stomach . . . and her nerves.

"Shall I help you dress, miss? I'll have to hurry, though. It's almost time to deliver a certain guest's breakfast. He is most particular that it's delivered at nine sharp."

Rebecca guessed, "Mr. Oliver, do you mean?"

"Yes, miss." Mary winked. "Though you didn't hear it from me."

Rebecca washed quickly and pulled on a fresh shift. "What is he like?"

"Oh, he's an odd one, he is," Mary explained as she tightened Rebecca's stays. "Talks to himself while he writes. Ink on his fingers and on his lips! Crumpled up paper everywhere! I'll have a time cleaning that room once he's out of it."

Rebecca stepped into her gown and turned again so Mary could lace the waist while Rebecca fastened the front. "And how does he treat you?"

"Like I'm beneath his notice. Just mumbles to set the tray down and pick up his dirty dishes. If I dally, he urges me to finish and be gone without looking up from his page, which suits me perfectly well. His man outside warned me to take care around him, but Mr. Oliver has never paid me any attention *that* way. Some guests do, you know, but not him. Even so, I'm happy to leave his room without vexing him. If he complained to Mr. Mayhew, I'd be out on my ear in two shakes." Finishing up, Mary hurried to the door. "I'll be back as soon as I can with your breakfast."

"Thank you."

While she awaited Mary's return, Rebecca put on her stockings herself and brushed and pinned her hair.

When traveling, the lady's maid assisted Rebecca. Lady Fitzhoward had generously sent Joly up last night before dinner but had said nothing about sending her back in the morning. And since Rebecca was not at the hotel in her official capacity as companion, she was reluctant to ask.

Over the years, Rebecca had learned to dress herself when needed, having acquired wraparound stays and frocks that laced, pinned, or buttoned at the front. She could have donned the same simple frock she'd worn yesterday, but anticipating a meeting with Mr. Oliver or Mr. Edgecombe, she'd deemed it wisest to dress well to make a positive impression.

She regarded her reflection in the mirror. The promenade

dress hugged her figure with military-style frog lacings and a velvet collar, its lines giving it the look of a riding habit or frock coat, which made her feel less vulnerable than she would have felt in a thin muslin day dress.

Returning with her breakfast a short while later, Mary announced, "Mr. Mayhew is offering a tour of the abbey at eleven, if you are interested."

Rebecca thanked her and sat down at the dressing table to sip her tea, but her jittery stomach would tolerate only a few bites of food.

Before leaving her room, she put on a modest hat ornamented with a ribbon. Then, having time to spare, she took a walk around the hotel's garden, admiring its central fountain.

Might Mr. Oliver join the tour? If so, perhaps she could talk to him then. She decided it was worth a try.

At eleven, interested guests gathered in the blue parlour, a room off the reception hall, just beyond the stairs. Paneled in dark wood, the parlour was filled with comfortable furniture upholstered in rich blue fabrics.

Rebecca saw no sign of Mr. Oliver but was pleased to see Lady Fitzhoward, Thomas Wilford, and the lovely woman who'd caused a stir at dinner, whom Thomas introduced to her as Miss Selina Newport.

Mr. Mayhew, tall and lanky with dark ginger hair, rubbed his hands together in boyish enthusiasm. "Welcome, everyone, and thank you for your interest in the Swanford Abbey Hotel. I am Carl Mayhew, proprietor, and it will be my distinct pleasure to show you . . . or rather, show off"—here he chuckled—"the features, architecture, and history of this grand place.

"As you may know, it began its life as a monastic community. A devout woman named Elena de Wyke built the abbey in her husband's honor after his death in the Crusades. Now, that's devotion, gents. Would you not say?" Another chuckle. "She became abbess and lived here with a clutch of sisters for many years until her death, followed by a succession of other abbesses and nuns until the 1500s.

"After the dissolution, the Sharingtons became the new owners and renovated the old abbey into a commodious family home. And such it remained for many generations, until the last of the family died and the place was abandoned.

"Several years ago, a group of investors bought the property and hired architects and builders to convert it into a grand hotel. Sadly, the investors went bankrupt and the project was disbanded before completion." Here he touched his lapels. "That is where yours truly comes in. I bought the place at a very good price and undertook to finish the work started by my predecessors. I have been successful, as you see." He gestured around himself.

Then he continued, "The refectory and gentlemen's coffee room you will see as a matter of course during your stay, so we won't venture to those now. But do come with me upstairs, if you will." He backed through the open parlour doorway into the hall. "The builders had already installed this staircase, but I personally chose the Turkish carpet, which is, I believe you'll agree, exceptionally fine."

He led the way upstairs, a middle-aged couple at his heels. Thomas Wilford and Miss Newport went next, heads near and whispering flirtatiously, while Rebecca lagged behind to accompany Lady Fitzhoward, who was gripping the railing tightly and breathing heavily before they were halfway up.

She panted, "Now you see why I requested a suite on the ground level!"

Sir Frederick appeared in the hall, the picture of a well-dressed sportsman in forest-green frock coat and buff breeches. Rebecca could not help but admire his confident bearing and long, athletic stride.

Glancing up and seeing them, he quickly ascended the stairs. "May I offer an arm, my lady?"

"Indeed you may," the older woman said. She added wryly, "If you like, you may offer me two!"

Sir Frederick grinned and helped her up the remaining stairs, and Rebecca was touched by his kindness.

He said, "What are you ladies doing, if I may ask?"

"We are taking a tour of the abbey."

"Ah."

Rebecca reached the top first and saw the others grouping around Mr. Mayhew. The military man sitting at his post rose and regarded the gathering warily.

She waited for Lady Fitzhoward and Sir Frederick on the landing, and asked him, "Will you join us?"

"I had not planned to, but why not? I see Thomas is taking part as well."

Looking over at them, Mr. Mayhew said, "Good. We are all here. Now, I shan't point out other rooms, but number three is special, as it was formerly the abbess's private apartment. It retains the stained glass and ornamental woodwork of the original chamber. It is occupied at present or I would show you. In fact"—his eyes twinkled—"our illustrious guest is—"

The guard coughed significantly.

Mayhew broke off and then continued, "Eager not to be disturbed, so let us move on."

He led the way down the south side of the quadrangle, which had no guest rooms leading from it.

"This I call the long gallery. The abbey church was originally just beyond this outer wall, and since it collapsed, there was nothing to build over. A waste of space from a business point of view, but I've tried to give it merit historically by displaying paintings left by the Sharingtons. I especially like this landscape of the house as it once stood, before the village grew up around it."

Rebecca's gaze, however, lingered on a family portrait, and she felt a renewed sting of loss.

The proprietor stepped to another. "And this one is by the famous Thomas Gainsborough. I believe the subject is the last mistress of the estate. I forget her name."

"Lady Sybil," Lady Fitzhoward supplied. "Daughter of the Earl of Witney."

"Really? Well. Good to know. Thank you. Something of a historian, are you?"

"Something like that."

The group moved on, but Lady Fitzhoward lingered, studying the portrait of the fine lady. Rebecca walked over to join her.

"What do you think of her hair, Miss Lane?"

"Um . . . there is a lot of it." The subject's dark hair billowed above her head like a brunette cloud, interlaced with pearls, while a long curled tendril hung over one shoulder. She had a widow's peak on her forehead, however, which looked quite natural. "Do you think it was a wig?" Rebecca asked.

"No, I do not." Lady Fitzhoward seemed to suddenly recall her surroundings. "Come. We're missing the man's *thrilling* commentary."

They hurried through the rest of the gallery and followed the sounds of echoing footsteps and voices down the night stair. Slipping into the library and writing room, Rebecca winced as the door banged shut behind them, interrupting Mr. Mayhew's talk.

He sent them a tolerant smile before continuing. "As I was saying, this spacious room originally housed the chapter house, where the nuns discussed abbey business, and the chaplains' room, which accommodated those who ministered to the sisters."

He turned to the wall behind him. "During renovations, several medieval wall paintings were discovered. Here are the largest two. The first depicts St. Andrew the apostle—notice he's shown on the X-shaped cross of his crucifixion. And the second is believed to be Elena de Wyke, who built the abbey for her order and became its first abbess."

The willowy woman in headdress and flowing robes held one hand to her breast, while the other palm extended, holding a bird. It was very like the statue Sir Frederick had pointed out to her the previous night.

"Rather than covering over these ancient paintings, I engaged an artist to restore them. Notice the deep frames? They allowed us to plaster over the rest of the room, while preserving this artwork for generations to come."

He looked at his audience, clearly expecting applause. Rebecca and the middle-aged couple halfheartedly obliged him.

He bowed. "Now. We shall end our tour in the chapel."

They all filed out after him and processed into the nearby sanctuary, lit today by candelabras. Rebecca smelled dusty hymn books and tallow candles, and saw a vase of tulips left to molder, their bent heads weeping yellow pollen onto the polished wood altar.

"This is the only surviving section of the original church— the rest was too severely damaged to save. The Sharingtons walled it off and installed the altar and pews. It was then used as a chapel of ease for the family. Nowadays, it is simply a peaceful sanctuary for prayer or reflection, as well as the final resting place of the first abbess."

Within the dim, reverent place, he pointed to a gravestone in the floor, worn almost unreadable by the hands and feet of time.

Sir Frederick lowered himself to his haunches to peer at the Latin words. Rebecca knew Frederick had studied Latin, as did most upper-class males.

He then translated for those gathered around. "Below lie buried the bones of the venerable Elena, who gave this sacred house as a home for the nuns. She also lived here as abbess, full of good works."

"Clever boy," Lady Fitzhoward said. Then she announced, "I'm done in. I'm going to my room." She turned to take her leave.

"Shall I walk with you, my lady?" Rebecca offered.

"I am not an invalid yet. Oh, very well. Come if you're coming."

Rebecca took her arm and was glad when the older woman did not pull away. "Indeed you do seem tired."

"Revisiting history is a taxing business."

"Shall I send for tea? Summon Joly?"

"Don't fuss, Miss Lane. I shall be my old cantankerous self again after a nap."

Rebecca bit back a grin. "I am excessively glad to hear it."

After walking with Lady Fitzhoward to her room, Rebecca rejoined the others, now lingering in the cloisters.

"It is a lovely day," Thomas Wilford observed. Then, with a glance that encompassed her, his brother, and Miss Newport, he said, "How about a game of lawn bowls?"

The four of them agreed and met outside on the bowling green half an hour later. Sir Frederick and Rebecca had remained as they were, while Miss Newport had donned a pelisse over her day dress and Thomas had changed into casual coat and trousers.

The mid-March air was brisk, but the garden wall and hedges protected them from the wind.

"Let's play in teams of two," Thomas suggested. "Miss Newport and myself against Frederick and Miss Lane. Any objections?"

When heads shook, Thomas smiled slyly. "I, too, thought the arrangement most agreeable."

Frederick produced a coin, and the brothers flipped to see who would go first.

Their team won the toss. "Will you deliver the jack, or shall I?" Frederick asked her.

"I will, if you don't mind."

He had obviously expected her to demur, and Rebecca found she enjoyed surprising him.

She stepped to the marker, placed her left foot forward, bent her knees, and gave the smaller white ball an energetic roll.

Now that their target had been placed, the game began in earnest, with each player trying to roll nearest the jack.

Sir Frederick played with ease and skill. Rebecca watched him, hoping her attention was not obvious. She admired his broad shoulders, masculine build, and prowess.

When Miss Newport's turn came, her bowl rolled weakly less than halfway toward the goal.

Thomas said, "You cannot just toss it, my dear Miss Newport. You must really put some effort into it."

"I am sorry." Selina pouted prettily. "I have not done this in an age."

"That's all right. It will be my pleasure to show you how the game is played."

Thomas clearly relished the role, letting his hands linger at her narrow waist, demonstrating how to position her feet, and advising her how to aim.

The game continued, Miss Newport flirting and teasing and praising the men's skill. When it was again her turn to throw, her bowl missed the others by a wide margin and disappeared under the privet hedge.

"No, no," Thomas chided gently. "Remember, these balls are slightly biased instead of perfectly round. If you aim directly at the jack, it will curve to the side."

He stood behind her and guided her hand to show her how to deliver.

Watching their antics, Frederick shook his head. "At this rate, we shall be here all day."

Thomas grinned. "Then my strategy is working. A pity Miss Lane is so terribly competent."

Rebecca replied, "That is what comes of growing up with a brother."

"Two brothers, if you count Frederick," Thomas quipped. "After all, did he not teach you to play chess and lawn bowls, not to mention how to ride?"

"He did, though we are not really so much brother and sister," Rebecca said, her neck growing warm.

"Brother and sister?" Frederick echoed. "No, indeed. We were friends, and I hope we always shall be." He held her gaze, and her heart gave a foolish little leap.

"If you say so," Thomas replied. "Now quit stalling and take the mat. I believe we are about to win."

Frederick sized up the clustered balls, took aim, bent low, and threw hard. The bowl rolled fast in a narrow arc and knocked into the other team's, scattering them and leaving his and Rebecca's in winning position.

Hands on hips, Thomas shook his head and groaned. Rebecca and Sir Frederick, meanwhile, shared conspirators' smiles of triumph.

At that moment, Mr. Jones, the Wilfords' steward, strode out of the hotel with a handful of correspondence.

The brothers excused themselves and walked over to meet him. While the men's backs were turned and their attention focused on the steward, Selina Newport looked from them to Rebecca with an impish gleam in her eyes.

She crouched low, aimed, and rolled with strength and precision, her bowl curving and slowing and finally nestling right beside the jack.

Then she straightened and dusted off her gloves. With a grin of satisfaction, she winked at Rebecca, turned, and strolled gracefully away.

5

Later that afternoon, Frederick prepared for the canal investors' meeting he had organized, to be held in the library and writing room. At his request, hotel staff had arranged chairs in rows, a lectern at the front, and two long tables on one side.

Mr. Mayhew had also posted a sign on the door, handwritten on heavy card stock:

Room reserved 2–4 pm.
We apologize for any inconvenience.

On one long table were spread drawings of the route of the proposed canal spur. On the other, a buffet meal to reward attendees for their time and also to put them in the mood to open their minds to possibility . . . and their purses as well.

Frederick had personally put a notice in the newspapers and had written to invite various gentlemen of the county whom he deemed might benefit from the project and be willing to invest. Unfortunately, it was not a very long list.

The first arrival was a complete surprise to him and a mostly pleasant one, although painful memories followed in the doctor's wake.

"Charles. What an unexpected pleasure."

"Sir Frederick." Dr. Fox extended his hand.

Frederick shook it, blinking away the recollection of the last time he had seen the man. His wife's funeral.

"I did not expect to see you here."

"Saw the notice in the paper and wanted to come. Thought I'd enjoy a few days' holiday with my wife in the bargain." Dr. Fox winced at his own words. "Forgive me if that is salt in the wound. I hope you know how sorry I am, that I could not do more to help her."

Frederick replied, "I do know. And it's all right—not your fault, Charles."

"Thank you for saying so. I still feel guilty, I admit."

"Then that makes two of us."

Dr. Fox drew back his shoulders. "Well, enough of that. I am here for the canal meeting."

"You are most welcome, though I feel honor-bound to caution you that, as an investment, I can't guarantee it will generate a high rate of return. I see the project as more beneficial for those of us who live here."

"I understand. Regardless, I'd like to help."

"That's good of you. And I am not too proud to admit we need it. Well, help yourself to refreshments and have a seat. We will begin shortly."

The physician nodded with a wisp of a smile and walked away to claim a chair.

Thomas appeared at Frederick's elbow. "Who is that?"

"Dr. Charles Fox."

"Fox? The mad doctor?"

Frederick frowned. "I don't like that term and neither does he. He's here as a potential investor in our canal scheme."

"*Your* canal scheme," Thomas corrected. "Too much dashed bother in my view. But why is *he* here? I thought Marina's doctor was from farther afield. Bristol, was it not?"

"He used to live there. Now he practices near Cheltenham."

Thomas shrugged. "Even so, I am surprised he'd come. Perhaps he likes to stay busy, as you seem to do."

Frederick sent his brother a weighty glance but did not bother denying it. He did like to keep busy. It distracted him from thoughts of the unpleasant past.

Eight other men arrived, two acquaintances traveling together from the Malvern district, Mr. Wigley, Mr. Russell, Esq., the Reverend Mr. Gilby, and three others—merchants and men of industry—who arrived one after another and headed straight for the buffet table. Lord Deerhurst, he realized, was noticeably absent even though Frederick had chosen a meeting date well before Parliament was scheduled to begin its next session.

He repressed a sigh and swallowed his disappointment on a bitter sip of coffee.

Frederick was just about to call the meeting to order when one more person entered the room. Lady Fitzhoward. Had she come to read periodicals or write letters? Had she not seen the sign? He hated to be rude, but he had paid a significant sum for the private use of the library.

He walked over to speak with her quietly. "My lady, I hope you are feeling better. I am sorry, but we are having a meeting in this room. We should be finished by four, if you would like to return then?"

"Yes, I know. Why do you think I am here?"

"Oh. Forgive me, I . . . I am grateful for your interest, truly.

But as I told Dr. Fox a few minutes ago, as an investment, I don't know that this particular canal spur will generate a high rate of return. I see the project as beneficial for those of us who actually live here rather than for someone with no connections to the area."

She held his gaze, hooded eyes steely. "Are you asking me to leave?"

"Heavens, no. Only being honest with you."

"Then I will stay. Unless you object to a female being present?"

"Not at all. Your interest is unexpected but welcome. Do help yourself to refreshments, just there."

Lady Fitzhoward took a slice of cake and, foregoing the chairs in rows, sat in one of the cushioned armchairs at the back.

Frederick walked to the front of the room and addressed the ten prospective subscribers, wishing there were more of them. He went on to explain his vision for the project—a spur connecting their parish to the River Severn and the Worcester and Birmingham Canal beyond.

He described the scheme, referencing the drawn plans, cost estimates, and benefits in terms of reduced prices in coal shipments, lumber, and other imports as well as readier access to markets for local bricks, pottery, and gloves.

At some point during his speech, he glanced back and noticed Lady Fitzhoward pick up a magazine and begin flipping through it. Was he such a boring speaker? He tried not to let her obvious inattention distract him and pressed on.

When he finished, he looked up to ask for questions and noticed that the woman had fallen asleep in her chair. So much for her interest! It did not bode well.

A time of discussion and debate followed. A few gentlemen were undecided while two refused outright to participate, decrying the expense and the vague nature of the return, not to mention the time involved in pursuing such a scheme all the way through Parliament.

The three merchants and men of industry, seeing the benefits to local trade, willingly agreed to take shares. Together they pledged significant backing.

It was a good start. But not enough.

After the men left—Dr. Fox gesturing to the chess set and promising to meet him later for a game—Frederick gathered up his papers. At the back, Lady Fitzhoward slept on, undisturbed.

Finally, a soft snore of her own making roused her awake. She sniffed and looked around.

Thomas walked over and offered her a hand in rising. Frederick thought the woman might rebuff him, but she took his hand and allowed him to help her to her feet. "Thank you, young man."

Thomas grinned. "Sorry my brother put you to sleep. He seems to have that effect on people. Women especially."

Frederick shook his head, lips pursed. "Very funny."

She glanced with mild surprise from her empty plate to the empty chairs. "Sweets, a warm room, and a dull talk does it to me every time. Capacity and tonnage, rises and locks . . ." She yawned for effect. "If some apothecary could bottle the combination, he'd make a fortune selling it as a sleeping draught."

Thomas chuckled. "Now, *that* I would invest in."

"If your tailor did not pocket your every farthing." Frederick could not resist adding a jab of his own.

The woman eyed him and asked, "Did you raise the needed capital?"

"Not by a long chalk," Thomas replied for him. "We're done for."

Frederick sent him a chastising look. "Not as bad as all that.

A few have asked for time to consider the matter further before giving an answer."

"Which means they will turn us down eventually," Thomas said, "but they'd rather not do it in person."

Frederick sighed. "Probably right."

Lady Fitzhoward looked from one brother to the other and observed, "You two have an . . . interesting . . . relationship. Sparring and roasting each other one minute, then supporting each other the next."

Was that disapproval or admiration in her expression? Difficult to tell.

"Can't argue there." Thomas slung an arm around Frederick's shoulder. "But down deep, *very deep*, we really do like each other. At least, I like Freddy. Can't speak for him."

Frederick said acidly, "Yet you try to at every turn."

"True," Thomas allowed. "I hope you don't think us barbarians, my lady."

She studied them for another long moment, something unfathomable glistening in her eyes. "Not at all. It is how siblings ought to be, I think. At least brothers."

"Have you brothers, my lady?"

She stared off into her thoughts, then seemed to recall herself to the present. With a raised chin and tart voice, she said, "Heavens, no. And after seeing you two tease and provoke one another, I am glad I have not!"

Thomas chuckled again, but Frederick watched the woman with curiosity. He guessed that beneath her curt reply and haughty expression lay buried deep, *very deep*, quite an opposite emotion.

Realizing it would be difficult to speak privately with Mr. Oliver when he came down only for dinner, Rebecca decided to go to his room and try to speak to him there.

So after luncheon she slipped the manuscript into a large envelope and walked around the hotel's upper story toward room three. Palms damp and pulse pounding, Rebecca wondered if she looked as self-conscious as she felt.

Turning the corner, she saw the same man sitting on a chair beside the door, sunshine from a nearby window casting his face in half light, half shadow. Had the publisher truly hired a guard to protect the popular author?

The man raised his head at her approach, and she noticed razor stubble darkened his jaw although it was still early afternoon.

When she hesitated near the top of the main stairs, he waved a hand. "Move along, miss. Nothing to see here. Tour's over."

"Ah yes. I saw you here then." Rebecca adopted a friendly, casual manner. "You must be bored sitting out here all hours. Is there really so much danger in Swanford?"

"More'n you know, miss."

She pointed to the door marked 3. "The proprietor mentioned the abbess once slept in that room. Surely you do not believe the tales of her ghost haunting the place?"

Sunlight glinted in the man's knowing eyes. "It is not the ghosts I worry about, miss, but creatures who are very much alive."

He jerked a thumb toward the door. "Do yourself a favor, young lady. Steer clear of this man and spare yourself a great deal of heartache. I would say you're not his sort, but he's not exactly particular."

"I was only hoping to have a word with him."

He shook his head. "No one goes in and no one goes out, except at dinner. I'm here to make sure of it."

"No one?"

"Except his publisher."

She thought of Mary. "Surely a chambermaid must go in and tidy up?"

He lifted one shoulder. "Only to deliver his breakfast and such."

"His publisher's orders, I presume?"

"No, miss. Mr. Oliver's orders."

"Oh. I see. How . . . novel." Her feeble chuckle fell flat. "Well. Thank you for the warning, Mr. . . ."

"George. Jack George."

"Mr. George." She started to go and then turned back. "I do hope you are allowed to sleep?"

Another shrug. "I sleep when he does. But my room's just beyond the stairs and I'm a light sleeper. Comes from years in the army."

"How . . . dedicated. Well. Good-bye."

She continued down the stairs, sour failure sweeping over her. Now what was she to do?

Needing to think, Rebecca crossed the hall and walked outside, with no particular destination in mind. Seeing a familiar man exiting the stable courtyard, she drew up short.

"Robb Tarvin! I am surprised to see you here."

The tall, broad-shouldered man might have intimidated her, had she not known him since childhood.

He stared back and his eyes widened. "Becky Lane, as I live and breathe. A sight for sore eyes."

"Are you working here now?"

"In a manner of speaking. I have my own fly." He gestured through the stable-yard entrance to a horse and two-wheeled gig. "I transport hotel guests hither and yon and make deliveries on the side."

"So . . ." she rephrased in a positive light, "you have your own business. Well done."

"Suppose I do." He seemed to stand up straighter. "Though a lot of my runs are for the hotel."

Rebecca said, "I was sorry to hear about your father."

The young man nodded in acknowledgment. "We have that loss in common."

"Yes." She added, "I thought you would have taken over the family business." His father had owned Swanford's livery and wheelwright's shop.

"So did I. But Mamma and I had to sell it to cover Papa's debts."

"I am sorry. Surely if the new owners knew of your skills and experience, they would have wanted to keep you on?"

He lifted an indifferent shoulder. "So I thought. But Mr. Fornoff made it clear he likes doing things his own way. Said I was a know-all."

She saw the resentment in her old friend's face and tried to tease it away. "Well, you always were the cleverest lad in the village. That's what my father always said."

"I remember." He grimaced. "Much good it's done me."

Robb Tarvin had been something of a prodigy to her learned father. A boy raised by uneducated people who thirsted for knowledge like a scholar. He read Johnson's Dictionary and every book he could lay hands on. Mr. Lane had given him leave to borrow books from his own library, and the boy had been insatiable, reading one scholarly tome after another, without apparent limit to his interests. Later, the Wilfords had allowed him to borrow from their vast collection as well, and when a circulating library had opened in Worcester, her father, the Wilfords, and a few other neighbors had joined forces to pay the lad's subscription fees.

Rebecca had accompanied her father when he went to speak to Mr. Tarvin, Senior, to offer the boy access to education, to a future beyond the limits of his birth.

The man had responded none too kindly. "What use has he for education? He knows all he needs to manage our business here. And when I am gone, all this will be his. Why would I send him off for more useless book learning?"

The man had called Robb over then and there. "Do ya want to go off with a bunch of bookish snobs and learn hoity-toity ways, or do ya want to work here with me?"

For a moment, hope had sparked in the lad's eyes—a flash of eager interest and intelligence. But then he looked at his father and the spark faded. The lad wanted to please his parent, as was only natural. So he'd swallowed and said, "Why would I want to go anywhere? When the good parson lets me read all the books I want while I work here."

The elder Tarvin nodded triumphantly. "There, you see? He has all he wants and needs. Don't go filling his head with a lot of useless nonsense."

Her father, seeing his efforts were in vain, had given it up and taken his leave.

Blinking away the memory, Rebecca asked, "And how is your mother? In good health, I trust?"

"Oh, she is all right. Misses Papa, of course."

He looked toward the hotel and asked, "And what are you doing here? Does not your brother still let the Wilfords' lodge?"

"He does. I saw him there yesterday." She was not keen to spread her brother's troubles nor to admit that the once proud and respected vicar's daughter had been compelled to seek employment. However, considering the young man's recent setback, she deemed it a kindness to tell him the truth. "I am companion to a woman staying here."

"Ah. I see. Well. Nothing to be ashamed of."

Yet she did not miss the gleam of satisfaction in his eyes.

After her uncomfortable reunion with Robb, Rebecca walked back through the hotel and out into the cloister courtyard, tucking the manuscript under her arm as she went.

She strolled along its perimeter, enjoying the smell of freshly clipped grass and a border of cheerful tulips. Then she tilted up her face and closed her eyes, relishing the warm sunshine penetrating her skin and the peace of the secluded place.

After a moment, she opened her eyes again and glanced around. A few wrought iron tables and chairs were placed here and there, lent shade and elegance by potted trees.

At one of these tables several yards away, a man sat silhouetted against the stone wall, a gracefully spouted teapot at his elbow. It looked like Sir Frederick, but was he not at his canal meeting?

Torn between greeting him and slipping back into the cloisters unnoticed, she stood there, vacillating.

A waiter in crisp black and white came out with a plate of something. Looking up at his arrival, Frederick saw her as well and lifted a hand.

"Miss Lane. Will you join me? Another cup, Bernard, if you please."

"Right away, sir."

Frederick stood, and Rebecca walked slowly across the grass, feeling reluctant. Was he just being polite? She glanced around. The courtyard was visible from the cloisters and the windows above. It was a public place, though at the moment, quiet. Would it look like a private tête-à-tête to a passerby?

As if reading her thoughts, he said, "I don't think there is anything untoward about taking tea together out here. After all, we are old friends. At least, I am old." One corner of his mouth quirked in a boyish grin, and he pulled back the chair for her before the waiter, returning with an extra place setting, could do so.

"Thank you," she murmured as he bent to push the chair in again, a feat over the thick turf. Hands on either side of the chair, Frederick's shoulders seemed to envelop her, and she breathed in the smell of his shaving tonic, spicy and slightly sweet, like citrus with a hint of cloves. Or perhaps the aroma of the tea was influencing this impression.

She set the large envelope on the ground, hoping he would not inquire.

"Important papers?" he asked.

"Oh, just something of John's I was reading."

He nodded his understanding and when he didn't probe further, she sat back with relief.

On the large crested tray stood a milk pitcher, sugar bowl, and two fine cups and saucers—which she recognized as Worcester porcelain.

"The waiter assures me this tea is the finest souchong, but if you prefer coffee . . . ?"

"No, tea is perfect."

He eyed the small pitcher. "Do you still take milk?"

Surprise flared. *He remembered.* "Yes. Thank you."

He poured milk into her cup, followed by tea in both. Her gaze lingered on his long, lean fingers. His were not the doughy hands of a man of leisure but were instead strong and callused from holding rein and whip, bat and bowl.

He lifted the newly arrived plate. "I have ordered seed cake. Takes me back to childhood, I own. But Bernard could bring buttered muffins or anything else you wished."

"Seed cake sounds a treat." She reached for a piece and took a delicate bite. "Delicious. Rose used to make it for us after . . ." She swallowed, hard. A seed caught in her throat and she lifted a serviette to cover her cough.

Concern furrowing his brow, he slid her cup closer. "Here, drink this."

She nodded, eyes watering, and sipped the stout brew.

When she recovered, she avoided his eyes, saying, "Sorry. Not very ladylike."

"Not at all, Miss Lane. You strike me as every inch the lady."

Her gaze flew to his. Was she imagining it, or was a flush creeping over the top of his white collar?

He took a bite of his own cake, then asked, "Did you see Rose when you visited your brother?"

She nodded. "Yes, I did."

"How is she? My former nursery maid, remember? I have not seen her in some time."

"She is . . . em . . ." How to be truthful and yet vague enough not to expose her brother? *How was Rose?* She was concerned, fretful, feeling helpless and hopeless as to how to help John. Emotions Rebecca shared.

"She's in good health," Rebecca said. "As spry and hard-working as ever. Thank you again for arranging for her to live and work in the lodge. She has been indispensable."

He watched her closely a moment, then stirred his tea, although he'd added neither milk nor sugar. He glanced up at her from beneath a fall of dark hair. "And . . . how is John?"

Again she hesitated. How to reply? She didn't want to say anything about her brother's mental or financial state that would cause Sir Frederick to evict him. Did he know John had failed to pay the rent the last few months? His steward had likely reported the lapse. Did she want to be the one to mention it if Mr. Jones hadn't?

She took another sip of tea to delay and dampen dry lips.

"He is . . . struggling, truth be told. He hasn't been able to interest a publisher in the book he finished recently and is finding it difficult to write another."

A line tensed between his eyebrows, and Rebecca hurried to add, "Thankfully, he is also correcting proofs for the newspaper. He was . . . distracted by work when I called at the lodge."

"So was it your idea to stay here instead?"

"Actually, John suggested it. He had not read my letter announcing my arrival and was not prepared for company. He has taken over the room I usually use, as his office." She added lightly, "Reference books and stacks of paper everywhere! I spent the night on the sofa, and in the morning, I realized what John really wanted was . . ."

"Solitude?" Frederick suggested.

"Yes, I suppose so. He believes I can help him more by staying here." She hurried to change the subject. "Speaking of solitude, what has you sitting out here all alone?" She managed a small smile. "Your brother abandon you?"

He chuckled. "In this case, I rather abandoned him. We hosted a meeting with potential investors in a proposed canal spur, and afterward, I just wanted a little time alone."

Her smile faded. "Oh. Then forgive me for intruding." She made to rise.

"No. Not at all. Please stay." He reached out and touched her hand, then snatched it away again just as quickly. "You misunderstand. It is only large crowds that tire me. And speaking before such a group—an argumentative group, I might add—with so much depending on the outcome . . ." He shook his head. "But talking with one person, especially you, has quite the opposite effect. You are like fresh air and sunshine after a storm."

She blinked, then ducked her head, pleased but self-conscious under his praise. When she looked up, she saw him reach up and adjust his cravat, again reddening above it.

He cleared his throat. "Forgive me. I sound a very poor poet."

"Not at all."

"Poet? Freddy? This I *must* hear."

Thomas strode into the courtyard, dragged over a chair from a nearby table, and plopped down next to them, helping himself to the remaining piece of seed cake and licking his fingers like a child.

He eyed her expectantly, golden eyebrows high.

A quick glance revealed Frederick's discomfort. When he said nothing and shifted in his seat, Rebecca said, "Sir Frederick was only telling me about the meeting." She added, "Something of a . . . storm . . . apparently."

"Oh, is that all." Thomas sighed. "I had hoped for something more interesting. But yes, the meeting had its stormy bits. Flashes of lightning and drenching rain . . . but also a few bright moments amid the clouds."

Frederick smirked. "Now you sound the poet."

"Miss Lane has inspired me. Although I am sorry to report that Frederick put your poor Lady Fitzhoward straight to sleep."

Now Rebecca raised her eyebrows. "Lady Fitzhoward was there?"

"Indeed. Until she snored and woke herself up."

Rebecca grinned and shook her head. "I must say, I never before heard anyone use the word *poor* to describe her."

Thomas grinned back then looked at his brother. "So what's the final tally? Seems our mad doctor is in as well as Hess and Fernsby."

Frederick nodded. "Not enough, however."

"Mad . . . doctor?" Rebecca echoed, attempting a laugh, which came out as a warble.

"Dr. Fox," Frederick corrected. "A highly reputable physician. His new methods are far more humane than those of others of his ilk."

"Who cares about his methods; how deep are his pockets?" Thomas asked with a sly wink. "It is good of him to involve himself at all, after he—"

Sir Frederick sent his brother a warning glance. "Thomas . . ."

The younger man raised his hands in surrender. "Never mind. Surely Miss Lane knows not to heed anything I say? Or if not, she will soon figure that out."

6

Rebecca tentatively approached the room adjacent to Lady Fitzhoward's suite to ask Nicole Joly to help her dress for dinner an hour earlier than the evening before.

She felt oddly nervous. She knew the lady's maid resented that Rebecca dined with their employer while Miss Joly took her meals in her room or—when at Lady Fitzhoward's home—with the housekeeper. So Rebecca knocked and clasped her hands, bracing herself for a sullen response.

Instead, the Frenchwoman agreed without rancor. Setting aside her sewing, she adjusted her beribboned lace cap and followed Rebecca upstairs. As the maid helped her into the same evening dress, Rebecca glimpsed the woman's reflection in the mirror and was surprised to see a hint of a smile on her thin mouth.

"And what has you looking so happy?" Rebecca dared ask.

Joly shrugged. "I don't know. Perhaps because I am eating well here. The chef is *Français*."

"Ah. And have you met this French chef?"

She nodded. "When I go to the kitchen for my lady's chocolate, I hear someone speaking *en français*. I respond in kind, *et voila*! Monsieur Marhic asked where I come from, and offered to prepare for me the special dishes from home. A welcome change from the bland English food." Nicole Joly sighed wistfully. "He is very kind."

"Apparently." Seeing the dreamy look on the woman's usually dour face, Rebecca bit back a grin.

When she was ready, Rebecca thanked Miss Joly, went downstairs, and positioned herself on one of the comfortable sofas in the hall. She picked up a newspaper from a side table and skimmed over the print, only half-aware of what she read.

The clerk had told her that Mr. Edgecombe would be dining there in the next day or two, and she didn't want to miss his arrival and her chance to talk with him.

Yes, John had told her to get the manuscript into Mr. Oliver's hands and ask him to recommend it to his publisher. But why not bypass the man who had betrayed him and deal with the publisher directly? John had said Edgecombe & Co. did not accept unsolicited manuscripts. But perhaps if they met personally, Thaddeus Edgecombe might make an exception. She hoped.

A notice in the newspaper caught her eye:

Eminent author Ambrose Oliver is currently staying at the Swanford Abbey Hotel, Swanford, Worcestershire. He can be seen nightly at 7:15 in the commodious dining room, where guests partake of excellent French cuisine prepared in the cleanest manner, with the best wines of all sorts. The hotel offers elegant accommodations for Gentlemen and Ladies of the first Quality. . . .

It read like news and an advertisement in one. Mr. Mayhew was certainly making the most of the author's presence.

Rebecca thought of the half-empty dining room last night. She guessed this notice would bring in more customers.

A few minutes later, a well-dressed man with curly dark hair, bushy side-whiskers, and small gold spectacles came through the front doors, parcel under his arm and newspaper in hand. He resembled William Edgecombe, whom she had met a few times. *This must be his brother*, she decided, her pulse quickening.

Setting aside the paper, Rebecca rose. But before she could walk over, the man advanced on the desk where Mr. Mayhew was speaking to the clerk.

The proprietor looked up at his approach. "Ah, Mr. Edgecombe. A bit early for dinner, but if you would like to wait in the parlour or perhaps the coffee room . . . ?"

The man frowned, eyes blazing. "I am not here for dinner. I am here to drop off a dictionary and ink for Mr. Oliver. Apparently I am errand boy now as well as publisher. Man consumes more ink than brandy, and that is saying something."

He set down the parcel, then slapped the broadsheet against the desk. "And I suppose you are responsible for this article in the newspaper? It was bad enough when they announced Mr. Oliver's plan to retreat here, but now to detail his schedule, specifying when he dines so he might be gawked at like an animal in a menagerie? Mr. Oliver is here for solitude, to focus on his next book, not to entertain hordes of curiosity seekers."

Having read the notice, Rebecca could understand Mr. Edgecombe's point.

The owner squinted at the newsprint. "I am as surprised as you are, Mr. Edgecombe."

"I doubt that." The publisher spun on his heel and stalked away, leaving the hotel without giving her a chance to speak to him. Lead filled her stomach. Dare she go after him?

Rebecca gathered every scrap of courage she could muster and followed the man outside. *You can do this. For John.*

From the top of the stairs, she saw the publisher beside the drive, talking to the commissionaire. "Please have my carriage brought back around."

"Yes, sir." Mr. Moseley stepped away to summon the coachman.

Rebecca hurried down the stairs. "Mr. Edgecombe?"

The man turned. "Yes?" His gaze raked over her, his expression inscrutable.

She began, "I wonder if you, as Mr. Oliver's publisher—"

"What of it?" he snapped, eyes narrowed.

"I would like to ask you . . . for advice about my brother. He is an excellent writer and editor. He has worked for . . . another author and corrects galley proofs for the newspaper. He has also written a few novels and—"

Edgecombe's jaw tensed. "My firm does not accept unsolicited manuscripts. Most are not worth the paper they are scribbled on, and we cannot invest the time."

"But my brother was acquainted with yours. Might you not make an exception?"

"Where is this brother?" He looked past her. "Is he not with you?"

"Unfortunately, no. He is . . . ill, so I have come in his stead. I hoped to—"

"I see. Well. Can't talk now. I have a meeting in Birmingham. Hoping to convince Washington Irving to let us publish his next book. So, if you will excuse me . . ." A carriage rumbled up the drive.

Frustrated tears threatened, but Rebecca forced herself to try once more. "I understand. Perhaps . . . another time?"

He seemed about to refuse, then glancing at her and seeing

her tears, desperation, or maybe only a pretty face, his gaze softened infinitesimally.

"Perhaps. I am having dinner with Mr. Oliver tomorrow. Are you staying here at the hotel?"

"I . . . Yes, I am."

"Well. I shall try to make time beforehand. Give you a little advice if nothing else. Good-bye for now, Miss . . . "

Rebecca hesitated. Had his brother told him the whole sordid story? If so, he might refuse to speak to John Lane's sister. And what about the pen name on the manuscript?

She beamed at the man as though she'd not heard the implied question. "Until tomorrow, then. Thank you. Thank you so much!"

Apparently she was staying at least another night.

At dinner that evening, Frederick noticed several more tables were occupied than had been the previous evening. Rebecca Lane, however, sat alone, and he idly wondered where Lady Fitzhoward was.

The ornamental Miss Newport swept in, wearing, he recognized, the same gown as the night before. So was Miss Lane for that matter, but still unease niggled him. Was it a sign of the Newport woman's penury? He could well believe her an impoverished beauty looking to land a wealthy husband at a grand hotel. He frowned at the disparaging thought. His own disastrous marriage had apparently jaded him.

Still, I wonder why she is here.

The likely answer strode in, in the form of his younger brother. How he managed to look rumpled and perfectly groomed at the same time was a mystery to Frederick.

Thomas grinned. "Sorry, brother dear. Only meant to rest my eyes for a few minutes and fell asleep. Late night, em, reading."

Reading? Balderdash, Frederick thought. His brother had no doubt taken advantage of the gentlemen's billiard room and bar tucked away belowstairs. Or worse.

Thomas bowed to Miss Newport before taking his chair at Frederick's table. "May we not invite her to join us? Seems less than chivalrous to let her dine alone again."

"I am not sure that would be wise."

"Why not? What an old codger you are. It won't exactly be a romantic tête-à-tête, now, will it? Not with the three of us."

"So I am to serve as chaperone for appearances' sake?"

"A sour, disapproving chaperone? It is, I believe, the role you were born for." Thomas leaned closer. "Better yet, let's invite that sweet-faced Miss Lane to join us too. Make a proper foursome of it. I don't see the old lady she usually dines with, and she looks deuced uncomfortable over there alone."

She did indeed; Frederick had noticed.

When he hesitated, Thomas took that as consent. "Excellent!" He rose before Frederick could object and first asked Miss Newport to join them. She accepted with a coy smile, as if such invitations were customary and her due. Thomas led her by the elbow to their table and pulled out a chair for her. Frederick rose politely and offered a bow while Thomas crossed the room to Miss Lane. Her thick brows rose as his brother approached. He could not hear what was said, but she replied without smiling, her gaze darting around the room, clearly uncertain.

At that moment, Frederick's view was blocked as the maître d'hôtel led two people across the dining room—a well-dressed mother and a daughter of perhaps eighteen or nineteen.

When they had passed, Frederick was surprised to see Miss Lane rise and allow Thomas to escort her to their table, looking supremely self-conscious. He fleetingly wondered what his brother had said to win her agreement, when she had seemed intent on politely refusing him. But his brother had always been able to charm women and was much more at ease in their company than he had ever been.

Frederick had thought, after he married and had a wife to share his life with, that his days of having to make inane conversation with attractive females was over. He had been mistaken in that, and in so many other things.

Again he rose, bowed, and murmured a greeting.

Miss Lane dipped an awkward curtsy, looking as uncomfortable as he felt, yet pretty too, with dark glossy curls framing her face, her hazel eyes looking almost green by candlelight.

Thomas's warm smile and gallant words smoothed over the uneasy moment as they all settled themselves once more, and the waiters laid more places.

Seated close to him, Miss Newport looked a bit older than Frederick had at first supposed. He noticed she wore powder and rouge, compared with Miss Lane's fresh face with a sprinkling of freckles across her nose.

When the four of them had played lawn bowls together, most of their conversation had centered on the game itself. Now, Thomas explained, "Miss Newport and I met in London last year. She was the toast of Town."

Selina Newport demurely dipped her head. "Mr. Wilford exaggerates."

Thomas turned to Rebecca. "And Miss Lane is, em . . ." He faltered, his smooth tongue for once failing him.

"An old friend," Frederick supplied. "Miss Lane's father was our vicar before his untimely death, and before that my tutor. An excellent man."

Both Thomas and Rebecca sent him appreciative looks.

One of Miss Newport's shapely eyebrows rose. "A vicar's daughter. How . . . respectable." She added in self-deprecating tones, "You may wish to move to another table, Miss Lane, for I am but a lowly actress and singer."

"Not at all. I . . . like music," Miss Lane kindly replied.

An actress! Frederick inwardly groaned. It was worse than he'd thought.

Thomas added, "Miss Newport is very talented. Sings like an angel."

Frederick changed the subject. "Even though Miss Lane was our neighbor for years, we have not seen her in some time. She has been away traveling."

"How exciting!" Miss Newport said. "Where did you go?"

"Bath, Brighton, France . . ."

"I would love to travel," Miss Newport said dreamily.

"But you have traveled here, Miss Newport," Frederick said. "May I ask where you come from?"

Thomas kicked him under the table.

"I have lived in several places, but I grew up in Birmingham. My family are all gone now, except an uncle."

"I am sorry to hear it. Have your parents been gone long?"

"Yes, Mamma ages ago and Papa during the Peninsular War."

Before Frederick could pose another question, Miss Newport asked one of her own. "Are you back to stay, Miss Lane?"

"Oh. I am . . . um, just here visiting my brother."

Miss Newport leaned nearer. "I always longed to have a brother. Does he travel with you?"

Rebecca shook her head. "He prefers to stay at home."

Frederick wished the woman would change the topic, which clearly discomfited Miss Lane.

"A man of leisure, is he?"

"No. A writer and proofreader. Quite talented."

"Would I have read something he's written?"

Miss Lane met her gaze, a parade of emotions flickering behind her eyes, turning them from hazel-green to dull brown.

"I am afraid not," she replied. Then added in an undertone, "Not knowingly."

"Ah! A writer for hire, ey?" Thomas sagely observed. "A 'freelance' so to speak. A publisher I met once boasted of employing a large contingent of writers and illustrators." He turned to Rebecca. "And are you a writer as well?"

"Heavens, no—I leave that to John. Although we have always been avid readers in my family."

Frederick nodded. "Yes, Miss Lane's father often promoted the benefits of reading."

Miss Lane looked at him. "That sounds like Papa."

"And I remember your mother as a gracious and intelligent woman."

"Thank you for saying so. I quite agree." She smiled at last. A truly lovely, toothy smile that carved deep dimples in her cheeks. Frederick's heart warmed at the sight. *Careful, old boy. She's too young for you. Too . . . everything.*

At a quarter past seven, Ambrose Oliver appeared in the dining room doorway.

Miss Newport noticed his entrance and ducked her head, making a show of looking for something in her reticule.

Mr. Oliver swaggered inside, leaving his . . . associate . . . standing guard at the door.

What a pompous prig, Frederick thought. As if any of them would swarm the man, celebrated author or not.

But then Frederick had cause to repent of his acidic thought. The mother-daughter duo left their seats, mincingly approached the writer's table, and began telling him how much they enjoyed his latest novel, lifting their copy as proof.

The man at the door straightened to attention, but Mr. Oliver waved him off.

"Why, thank you, ladies," Mr. Oliver politely replied. Gaze lingering on the charming younger female, he added, "Would you like me to sign my autograph inside?"

His autograph? Frederick rolled his eyes.

"Ohhh! Would you?" Both women cooed and offered up their treasured volume.

Mr. Oliver signaled the waiter and asked for pen and ink, which was quickly appropriated from the desk of the maître d'hôtel.

The author signed his name with a flourish, blowing it dry with thick, pursed lips. He ended up with a smear of ink on his mouth, or perhaps it had been there already and Frederick just now noticed.

Looking back at his table companions, Frederick saw that Miss Newport had returned her attention to Miss Lane, asking for more details about her travels, although she seemed to barely attend the answers.

Rebecca was able to relax when the first course arrived and everyone's focus turned to their meals. The *crème d'asperge* soup was hot and savory with asparagus tips floating in a creamy broth and served with crusty rolls and butter. This was followed by trout amandine and then tender filet mignon adorned with mushrooms, potatoes, tiny kidneys, and crisply fried onions. *Delicious*. If Miss Joly ate half as well, then no wonder she was happy.

After the main course had been served, Mr. Mayhew entered the dining room with a shorter man dressed all in white, from double-breasted jacket and apron to the pleated toque atop his dark head. The two men moved from table to table, accepting compliments.

Mr. Mayhew approached them and said, "If you will pardon the interruption, my friends, I should like to introduce our most talented chef, Monsieur Marhic."

"*Merci, mon vieux*," the man humbly replied. He looked from person to person, wearing a closed-lip smile, then asked, "Everything you want you have?"

Around the table, they all nodded and declared everything delicious.

He touched fingers to the double row of buttons near his heart and bowed. "You gratify me."

Then the chef turned to Rebecca, his dark eyes merry. "And what to follow, mademoiselle? Cheese? A little fruit?"

"Nothing more for me, thank you. I cannot remember the last time I ate so much and so well."

The chef beamed, bowed again, and departed a happy man.

After the meal, Rebecca visited Lady Fitzhoward's room and found Miss Joly offering the older woman a draught and laying a cool cloth on her brow.

Concern washed over her. "Are you unwell, my lady? Shall I fetch some bouillon, perhaps? Or ask Mr. Mayhew to summon a doctor?"

The patient frowned. "A doctor? Why? I am not on my deathbed—however much my husband's son might wish it. A simple case of the megrims. A doctor! Let us have none of that tribe here. I go on very well as it is. Do I not, Joly?"

"Yes, my lady."

"Are you certain?" Rebecca persisted. "It is not like you to miss dinner."

She waved a dismissive hand. "Oh, they sent up a tray, and I even ate a few bites. Don't fuss, Miss Lane."

"But there must be something I can do. A book from the library, perhaps?"

Lady Fitzhoward winced. "My head pounds harder at the mere thought of reading. But you could do one thing." Her eyes brightened. "Tell me what I missed at dinner."

"Very well."

Joly moved away to tidy the dressing table, and Rebecca sat on a chair near the bed. "Tonight we were introduced to the chef, a Monsieur Marhic, who seems as amiable as he is skilled." Here she sent Nicole Joly a telling glance and had the satisfaction of seeing the woman blush.

What else? Rebecca asked herself. She was reticent to divulge that she had sat with the Wilford brothers, sure Lady Fitzhoward would either disapprove or read more into the invitation than it merited. Instead, she described her conversation with the beautiful Miss Newport. And since the woman had offered the information herself, Rebecca hoped it was not wrong to repeat. "She mentioned she is an actress and singer."

"Ah," Lady Fitzhoward mused. "I thought she looked familiar. I wonder if I saw her perform at a theatre in Cheltenham?"

"Perhaps. Beyond that, the only other occurrence worth mentioning was that two women approached Mr. Oliver to praise his book and he offered to write his autograph inside."

Lady Fitzhoward scoffed. "His autograph? Who does the man think he is, Sir Walter Scott?

"That reminds me." Lady Fitzhoward picked up a broadsheet from the side table. "Did you see the notice in today's newspaper about Ambrose Oliver staying here?"

"Yes. And I overheard Mr. Oliver's publisher expressing his displeasure about it to Mr. Mayhew."

"Wonder what he's squawking about," Lady Fitzhoward replied. "Both men ought to be glad for any publicity." She tapped the broadsheet for emphasis. "The dining room shall be busy tomorrow. Mark my words."

Satisfied her employer would not be so tart-tongued if she were seriously ill, Rebecca went upstairs to her own room. From her window, she saw the sky was already dark, but she was not yet sleepy. She wrapped a shawl around herself, opened her balcony door, and stepped out. The night air felt cool and refreshing after the stifling warmth of Lady Fitzhoward's suite.

For a moment she closed her eyes to savor it, then gazed up, admiring the stars and the sliver of new moon.

Hearing a click to her left, she looked over. The balcony closest to hers was empty, but a man stepped out onto one farther down. He stood there in evening clothes, also looking at the night sky. Others might not have recognized him in the darkness, but that posture, that profile, that presence were all too familiar to Rebecca. She would recognize Frederick anywhere.

Years ago, as a smitten adolescent, she had admired him and foolishly believed he admired her too—that he was content to wait for her to come of age. He had always been unfailingly kind and attentive. Ready to listen to her youthful chatter or console her various disappointments with single-minded focus, while her parents were sometimes impatient and quickly wearied of her tales of village injustices. When her mother died, Frederick had climbed up and sat beside her on the garden wall as she sobbed, offering his handkerchief and his presence and his silent comfort.

Later, he'd given her a pony, or at least the use of one, and taught her to ride.

She well remembered the rush of joy and gratitude she had felt, and could still hear the sound of her young voice in all its girlish exultation.

"Thank you for letting me ride Ladybird, Frederick. She's fine!" The beautiful creature was a Connemara pony, a small horse ridden by adults and children alike.

He'd smiled indulgently. "I am glad you like her. She gets far too little exercise now that Tommy has gone to school."

They had ridden together almost once a week after that, when the weather allowed. And how she had looked forward to it.

But then one day when she went to Wickworth at their usual meeting time, Frederick was too busy to ride.

"Sorry, Miss Rebecca, I have other engagements today."

"Tomorrow, then?"

He grimaced. "I am afraid not. We have house guests, you see."

"Oh, who?"

"Miss Seward and her parents. I don't think you know them."

Disappointment deflated her hopeful heart. "I see."

He chucked her under the chin. "Another time?"

"Yes, of course." And she had smiled in anticipation, never guessing that it was the beginning of the end. That she was soon to lose her special place in Frederick's life. . . .

With a resigned sigh, Rebecca slipped back inside her hotel room. Soon after, Mary knocked and helped her undress, and then Rebecca climbed into bed.

She wasn't sure how long she'd been asleep when voices outside the door woke her.

A man and a woman were talking quietly near the top of the night stair.

She couldn't make out their low words at first, but then the man's voice rose.

"No!" he ordered sternly.

And the woman began to cry.

Uneasiness needled Rebecca. Should she get up and see what the matter was? Come to the woman's aid, if aid was needed?

Neither of them might appreciate a stranger's interference, but she could not in good conscience do nothing.

Rebecca got up, put on her dressing gown, and slid her feet into slippers.

Tiptoeing across the small room, she pressed her ear to the door, but heard nothing. She gingerly turned the key and opened the door a few inches, then, seeing no one nearby, opened it farther and stepped into the passage.

Footsteps. She looked straight ahead and saw the figure of a man retreating down the dim gallery passage. A moment later, she heard a door slam somewhere to the right.

A quarrel of some kind, now ended, Rebecca decided. Relieved it was over, and to see no sign of a hooded figure, she thankfully went back to bed.

7

The next morning, Frederick awoke feeling restless. After dressing, he set out on foot along the North Road toward Wickworth, which stood on the opposite side of the village. Turning at Swanford Road, he approached the dower house nestled beside the estate's long drive, lofty hedges lending it a modicum of privacy on the relatively busy street.

He stopped at the dower house to visit his mother and found her busy in her conservatory. She was pleased to see him, and irritated that Thomas had done no more than wave as he went past. Frederick followed her around the glass house she'd had built on since moving there, despite the high glass taxes. He dutifully expressed interest as she showed him her orchid specimens—ghost orchid, lady's slipper, and spotted—and a newly imported staghorn fern.

After their visit, Frederick took his leave, but then hesitated on the drive. He supposed he could go into the house since he was so close, yet the prospect felt oppressive.

Instead he walked through the grounds and along the bridle way—the more peaceful, roundabout way to All Saints Church. It wasn't that he didn't like his neighbors. He did. And they, in turn, treated him with respect and deference. He simply was not in a sociable frame of mind, nor in the mood for idle pleasantries.

His solitary walk was soon disturbed, however, when he saw Rose Watts, his childhood nurse, walking from the wood toward the village, market basket in hand. He had always been fond of the woman, and could not in good conscience pass by without stopping to chat.

"Good day, Rose. How are you? In good health, I trust?"

The older woman smiled. "Ah, Master Frederick, what a pleasure to see you. Yes, I am well. And you?"

"Tolerable. Thomas is visiting. He took it into his head that we should stay at the abbey this time. He blames the ongoing renovations, but frankly, I think he finds the hotel more to his liking after his years in London."

She shrugged. "Why not, if that's what he wants?"

Frederick tucked his chin. "You surprise me. I thought you would decry the expense and call Thomas a wastrel." He grinned, saying it partly in jest, but her lined face remained serious.

"Not worth disappointing your only sibling over such a trifle. Besides, might be just what you need."

"What I need?" He eyed her warily. "What do you mean?"

"I think you know. Time to get out of that house and move on with your life."

Frederick had almost forgotten how outspoken the woman could be. "Ah. Well, you have given me good advice in the past, so I will consider what you say."

One wiry brow arched. "And when did the young ever listen to advice?" Now the twinkle returned to her eyes. "Good-bye, Master Frederick."

He tipped his hat. "Good-bye."

The woman ambled away, and he continued on toward All Saints.

Passing through the rear gate, he entered the walled churchyard—a shady haven of reverence and memories, filled with new and well-tended gravestones as well as age-spotted monuments tilting at all angles, their epitaphs worn unreadable.

Following the uneven path as it wound between tombs and trees, Frederick walked slowly from plot to plot, headstone to headstone, most of the surnames familiar to him, and many faces appearing in his mind's eye to match the names of those now laid to rest.

He walked to his family plot, to a stately headstone unmarred by time or the elements, the carved words and symbol still painfully clear. Its rounded top had been engraved with the emblem of a bluebell, meaning *sorrowful regret*. The inscription read:

In Memory
Marina Seward Wilford
1790–1818

He stared at the headstone, but saw his wife instead. Her disdainful expression falling away at the last moment as fear gripped hard, her face elongated in shock and terror.

"I am sorry. Truly," he whispered, guilt lancing between his ribs like a rusty blade.

Despite everything, he would never have wished such an end on anyone.

❧

Wearing pelisse and bonnet, Rebecca walked across Swanford toward the churchyard. She had mixed feelings about seeing All Saints Church again and the vicarage where she had grown up—and which always stirred bittersweet memories of happier times. Even so, she had not visited her parents' graves since the previous Christmas some fifteen months ago, and felt she had neglected the duty too long.

As she walked up All Saints Street, she passed the Fenchurch residence, one of the larger houses in the village. Her childhood playmate had lived there and probably still did.

As if in answer, a voice greeted her over the stone wall that separated the narrow front garden from the street. "Welcome home, Rebecca. Didn't know you were back."

She looked over the waist-high wall and saw the round, rosy cheeks of her old friend. "Kitty! How good to see you."

"Is it?" She seemed a bit piqued. "You know, I was sure I saw you in Bath a few weeks ago. I called out but you did not answer. Perhaps you did not hear me."

Rebecca hoped her former friend could not see the warmth spreading up her neck. She *had* heard Kitty but pretended not to and kept walking. She'd been helping Joly carry parcels for Lady Fitzhoward at the time, and she had been embarrassed to be seen looking like a servant by someone from home.

"Bath?" Rebecca said. "I trust you enjoyed it."

"I did, yes. My parents and I travel somewhere every year. I adore Bath. Brighton has the sea, but Bath has better shops, don't you find?"

"I . . . suppose so. And your parents are in good health, I trust?"

"Yes. Going along famously. If you'd come by a few minutes earlier you might have greeted them, but they've already left to call on friends."

Kitty cocked her head to one side. "And how is John keeping? Still living in the Wilfords' lodge? I almost never see him. Keeps himself to himself, apparently."

"Yes, yes. Writing away."

Kitty formed a closed-lip smile, which rounded her cheeks into red orbs. "Anything of his in the circulating library yet? I have a subscription, you see."

"Not yet. Hopefully soon."

"He's been at it a long time, has he not? Oh well. He's still young. Unlike the pair of us, ey?" Kitty reached over the wall and gave Rebecca a playful slap on the arm. "We're nearly on the shelf!"

Kitty laughed, but Rebecca thought she saw a sheen of desperation in her eyes.

"Not quite yet," Rebecca reassured her—and herself.

Kitty asked, "Have you seen Sir Frederick since you've been back?"

"Yes," Rebecca replied then added quickly, "though only in passing. At the hotel."

Kitty shivered theatrically. "We dine there now and again, but I would not want to sleep in that old place, would you?"

"I . . . am, actually. It's a long story. The spare room in the lodge was not ready for me. John did not receive my letter and has been doing some work in there, so . . ."

"Does the abbey not give you nightmares?"

"It does, rather. In fact, one night I even thought I saw the ghost of the abbess."

"You're joking!" Kitty burst out laughing, and Rebecca immediately wished she had not told her.

Kitty collected herself, then said, "Thomas Wilford is staying there too, I hear. Apparently he can't abide being in Wickworth nowadays and keeps to London as much as possible. And of course their mother lives in the dower house and won't think of returning, even though Sir Frederick's wife is gone now."

"Yes, I was sorry to hear it."

"Were you indeed?" Speculation glimmered in Kitty's eyes. "I wonder how long it will be until he remarries. I haven't heard of him courting anyone yet. Have you?"

Rebecca shook her head, uneasy at the thought. "No. But I have only just returned and would be the last to hear the latest *en dit*."

"But you two were always friends."

"Family friends, maybe. But that doesn't mean he would confide something so personal."

Kitty shrugged. "Maybe he shan't marry again. Maybe no one will have him."

Rebecca gaped at her. "Why would you say that?"

Kitty leaned closer. "There were lots of rumors about his wife's death. Maybe you didn't hear, being away so much as you were."

Rebecca knew she should insist she didn't want to hear any rumors, but curiosity stifled her rebuttal.

Kitty went on, "Some say her death was not an accident as the official report claimed."

Incredulity flared. "Whatever do you mean?"

"A fall down the stairs? And her as graceful as could be, and using those same stairs every day for years? It does beggar belief."

Kitty lowered her voice. "Others say Sir Frederick discovered she was having an affair—maybe with his brother or maybe with someone else—and pushed her."

"I don't believe it."

Kitty nodded. "She was always going off to Birmingham. None of our shops were good enough for her. Or maybe she had a lover there—some say maybe even Mr. Oliver."

"Ambrose Oliver?" Rebecca felt more incredulous than ever.

"Exactly. You read his last novel, did you not? The couple's names were changed, I grant you, but even so, it seemed pretty obvious he was describing an affair with Lady Wilford, her husband none the wiser. Maybe Sir Frederick took revenge."

Rebecca slowly shook her head. Had John written about a struggling couple, and then Mr. Oliver changed the names to ones resembling Sir Frederick's and his wife's? Why would he? Out of spite? Or personal experience?

Kitty continued, "And I have it on good authority that—"

Rebecca held up an adamant palm. "That's enough. It's all lies; it must be. I was not well acquainted with his wife, but I have known Frederick Wilford all my life. He would never do anything so odious."

Kitty raised her own hands in surrender. "All right, all right. Don't get pettish. I don't say it's fact. I was not there. But that's what people say."

Rebecca frowned. "You really ought not to spread such baseless, mean-spirited rumors."

Kitty's eyes narrowed. "Well, well. Are we not high-and-mighty all of a sudden."

"I don't mean to be." Rebecca felt chastised. "I am only shocked and disappointed to hear what people are saying. I can't believe any of it's true."

"Can't believe or don't want to believe?"

Hoping to lighten the tension, Rebecca grinned. "Both!" She took a deep breath and placated, "Well, enough of that. It truly is good to see you again, Kitty, and looking so well too."

Kitty grinned back, her apple cheeks mounding once more. "Kind of you to notice. And you are still too skinny. Better eat more while you're at the hotel," Kitty teased. "How do you think I keep my *generous* figure?"

She giggled, and Rebecca was relieved to see her pique had faded.

Rebecca drew herself up. "Well, I am on my way to the churchyard."

"To visit your parents' graves, of course. Here, let me give you some flowers. . . ." Kitty disappeared behind the wall, bending to retrieve her basket. "I was cutting them for the parlour, but I can easily cut more."

She handed over an informal bouquet of daffodils and tulips.

"Thank you, Kitty. That is very kind of you. I hope to see you again while I am here."

"I shall make sure of it!"

Rebecca continued up the street past the vicarage, which was—perhaps mercifully—mostly out of sight behind a tall hedge.

Reaching the church where her father had faithfully served as vicar, she pushed open the old gate, which swung wide with rusty reluctance.

Eyes lowered to watch her footing on the cracked path, she walked by listing, lichen-spotted monuments until she came to her parents' gravestone.

Gone to their Redeemer
Elizabeth Stephens Lane
and
Rev. Arthur Lane
Beloved Parents
Forever In Our Hearts

Rebecca bent and pulled the weeds that had cropped up during her absence. One sapling clung tenaciously to life. She tugged hard and almost fell in extracting the stubborn root.

Finally satisfied, she laid the flowers before the shared gravestone.

"These are from Kitty Fenchurch," she whispered. As she straightened, tears heated her eyes. "I think of you both every day, and I miss you." Her voice thickened, and she added hoarsely, "Though in some ways, I am glad you are not here. You would hate to see John like this, struggling so. But then, maybe if you were here, he would not be." The old feelings of inadequacy and guilt sluiced through her, running down the deep gullies carved into her soul.

A voice startled her, and she looked up.

Several yards away, beyond the shady sprawl of an oak tree, a man stood before a headstone that appeared fairly new. He wore a green frock coat and buff trousers, hat in hand, head bowed. Frederick Wilford. She decided she would quietly retreat and leave him to grieve in peace. But as she turned to tiptoe away, his words reached her ears.

"I am sorry. Truly."

She paused, struck by the lament in his voice.

Heart squeezing, she walked slowly toward him. Her half boots scuffed a stone, and he looked up, expression stricken.

She said, "Forgive me for intruding. Are you . . . all right? If you prefer to be alone, I will go. But if there is anything I can do . . ."

"Stay a minute, Miss Lane, if you would."

"Of course." She moved to stand beside him, reading his wife's epitaph. Reserved words, she thought. No *Beloved*, or *Forever in Our Hearts*. She cautioned herself not to infer too much from the simple, though dignified, inscription.

Rebecca twisted gloved fingers, searching for something to say. "I . . . suppose you . . . visit her grave often?"

He shook his head. "Not in some time. But I felt drawn here today. To try to come to terms with what happened. I have . . . regrets."

Rebecca's chest tightened. "I am sorry."

He nodded. "Thank you, but please don't pity me. I neither want nor deserve it."

The rumors Kitty had whispered snaked through her mind. Surely, he'd had nothing to do with his wife's death. Had he?

Hands clasped, he shifted and looked over her head in the direction she had come.

"Visiting your parents' graves?"

"Yes."

"No regrets there, I imagine. They were the best of people, and they clearly loved you. You are more blessed than you know."

"It does not feel like it some days, but you are right. John and I never wanted for anything." Then why, she silently wondered, was John so unhappy? And bent on making everyone around him as miserable as he was?

Rebecca briefly laid her hand on Frederick's arm, then turned and left him to mourn alone.

With a final look at her parents' resting place, she departed the churchyard with little solace from the visit.

On the way back, Rebecca again strolled along All Saints Street, past the Swan & Goose, and then turned at Elderberry Lane.

A woman stood there, deep bonnet tilted up as if studying the modest, half-timbered house on the corner.

Rebecca almost went on past, but the woman's walking stick and embroidered mantle struck her as familiar. She angled her head to see past the woman's bonnet brim.

"My lady," Rebecca exclaimed. "I am surprised to find you here."

Lady Fitzhoward turned to her. "I simply went out for a walk to see something of this village you are forever talking about. Is that a crime?"

"Of course not."

The woman favored jaunty hats. Rebecca wasn't sure she had ever seen her in a poke bonnet before. Noticing Rebecca's gaze linger on it, the woman frowned. "What's wrong with it?"

"Nothing."

"I did not wish to fuss with a parasol, which can be such a bother when windy."

"True," Rebecca allowed, although the day was quite mild.

If Lady Fitzhoward wanted to see something of Swanford, Rebecca would have thought she'd have chosen to visit Wickworth—a great house known for its striking architecture and beautiful gardens—rather than the ragtag shops and houses crowded cheek by jowl in this narrow lane.

Lady Fitzhoward thrust her stick toward the neatly painted sign on the door that read *Henwick Cottage* and asked, "Who lives here?"

"Mr. and Mrs. Brown and their five children. They have the linen drapers shop on the High Street but outgrew the rooms above it."

"Ah." The woman's eyes lingered on the place, vaguely focused.

"Do you know them?" Rebecca asked.

"That is unlikely, is it not? Just curious. To hear you talk, you must be acquainted with almost everyone in the village."

"At one time, perhaps." When her father was vicar Rebecca had often gone with him to visit the sick and elderly.

Lady Fitzhoward glanced at a rope swing hanging from a sturdy oak beside the house, swaying slowly back and forth on a gentle breeze. She stared and seemed to sway with it.

Rebecca watched the woman with curiosity bordering on concern. Such a faraway look in her eyes. Such . . . sadness.

"Have you been to Swanford before, my lady?"

"A lifetime ago." The woman blinked. "Anyone named Westergreen hereabouts?"

"Not that I know of, no."

She nodded absently.

"Growing weary, my lady?"

Rebecca expected to hear the woman's oft-repeated rebuke, *"I am not an invalid."*

But instead she said, "I believe that is far enough for today." She straightened her shoulders and started determinedly down the lane, stick clacking with each step.

Rebecca noticed how heavily she leaned upon it and hurried to catch her. "Shall we walk back together?"

"If you are going back now anyway."

"I am." Rebecca took her arm, lending her strength, and the two made their way steadily to the hotel.

8

That evening, Miss Joly again helped Rebecca change for dinner earlier than usual.

Hearing the lady's maid hum a tune as she arranged her hair, mischief tickled Rebecca's stomach. She said, "Apparently you saw your chef today."

The woman flashed a frown in the mirror. "He is not mine."

"But you did see him?"

The maid's thin lips twitched. "Curiosity does not become you, Miss Lane."

"I cannot help myself. I have only experienced romance vicariously."

"Vi-care-ious? I do not know this word."

"It means, since I don't have my own romance, I enjoy hearing about yours."

Nicole Joly shook her head. "It is not 'romance.' He is very busy, cooking all the day." She paused, then allowed, "But I like talking with him when he has the moment. We speak of our families and all we miss of France. We have much in common, he and I. Both *catholique*. Both have sisters. And of course we both detest the English food."

"Sounds a perfect match, then," Rebecca agreed.

Miss Joly looked up and caught Rebecca's grin in the mirror. "Enough now. You like too much teasing me."

"I confess I do," Rebecca replied. "It is a new experience." She was gratified when the maid did not scowl in reply but grinned back instead.

A short while later, Rebecca was once again dressed and waiting in the hall an hour before their scheduled dinner time.

Mr. Edgecombe entered, and hope rose even as nerves quivered through her limbs.

She stood on shaky legs. "Mr. Edgecombe."

"Ah, yes. Miss . . . ?"

She couldn't avoid giving her name forever. If he agreed to read the manuscript, she would simply leave off the title page with its pen name. "Miss Lane . . . John Lane's sister."

She glanced at him timidly. Did he recognize the name? His expression revealed little.

He gestured for her to sit at one of the tea tables in the reception hall. She did so, setting the portfolio on the floor beside her chair. With trembling fingers, she handed him the first, thin envelope, which held two neatly written pages and a few typeset pages marked with handwritten changes.

His gaze dropped to the envelope and his expression flattened.

She said, "I thought it might be helpful to see a summary of my brother's experience and qualifications. As you can see, he worked as secretary to Ambrose Oliver, taking dictation, writing clean copies, et cetera. And now he corrects galley proofs for our newspaper. The second page is a letter of recommendation from that publisher. And after that are examples of his skill as a proofreader."

"I see." He opened the envelope and idly flipped through

the pages. "Unfortunately, we are not hiring anyone at this time."

She swallowed and reached for the second, much thicker envelope.

Edgecombe sat back with a sigh. "I admit I am relieved. When you handed me pages, I feared you were going to ask me to read a manuscript. You cannot imagine how wearying it is to be a publisher. Everyone wants me to read their prosy twaddle, sure they'll be the next Defoe or Burney. People hand me their manuscripts so often, I don't even read them anymore. I use them for kindling. These days I only consider work recommended to me by one of our own authors."

Rebecca snatched back her hand, leaving the larger envelope where it was. She straightened, cheeks heating at the thought of how humiliated she'd have been if she had handed it to him. The thought of him burning all those hard-written, handwritten pages!

Rebecca licked dry lips. "Your brother published Mr. Oliver's last few novels, is that right?"

Sadness lit his eyes. "That's right. I inherited the firm upon his death. Before that, I worked as a solicitor."

She made herself hold his gaze. "I was sorry to hear of your loss."

His nostrils flared as he drew a long inhale. "Thank you."

She hesitated, realizing she needed to tread carefully. How much did he know? His brother, William, had threatened John with a defamation suit, and promised to make sure he never worked in publishing again if he continued to slander Ambrose Oliver. John could not afford to pay any amount of damages, let alone to have access to all respectable publishers closed to him.

She slowly asked, "Were you aware of the . . . details of Mr. Oliver's last book?"

His eyes narrowed. "What details?"

Was it a trap? Would repeating the accusations trigger the long-threatened action for libel?

She hedged, "Your brother engaged John as Mr. Oliver's secretary, to help with dictation and the like, as I mentioned. Do you know why your brother gave John a small settlement even after Mr. Oliver insisted he be dismissed?"

Thaddeus Edgecombe gave an unconcerned shrug. "I imagine it was because he believed he'd earned it. Working for Ambrose Oliver cannot have been easy, as my brother learned to his detriment."

"No, it was not, as *my* brother learned to the detriment of his own writing career. Mr. Oliver took advantage of John's trust and talent. You could say Mr. Oliver's last book would not have been written without John, and I am talking about far more than dictation and clean copies."

He gave her a hard stare, then slowly slid the first envelope back across the table to her. "I regret I cannot be of more help."

Say it, Rebecca told herself. Push for John's rights. Ask, no, demand that he publish John's new book. Or, at a minimum, read it. Certainly Edgecombe & Co. owed him that much.

As she sat there vacillating, he stood and curtly bowed his farewell. He started to walk away, then turned back. "If you are referring to John Lane's claim that he wrote Mr. Oliver's last book, I hope we can agree that *if* there had been anything owed to him, it has been paid in full by the settlement your brother accepted. And I trust you will not raise the topic with me or anyone else again. For doing so would be violating the injunction against him."

So he does know. A nervous lump rose in Rebecca's throat. Had she said too much? Done more harm than good? Would he warn Mr. Oliver against her?

Edgecombe went on, "Furthermore, I insist that you not . . . disturb . . . Mr. Oliver with a repetition of old grievances which would be disgusting to him, not to mention an unwelcome distraction and waste of time. I will not have his concentration broken by a reminder of past unpleasantness."

Past unpleasantness? Was that all it was to them? A man's life ruined? His work stolen? His dreams dashed? At least, she hoped this meant he would not mention her to the author to avoid breaking his precious concentration.

"Have I made myself clear?" Edgecombe asked.

Rebecca choked down bile and a furious rebuttal. Shouting would not help their cause, although that was exactly what she wanted to do. She rose, nodded, and turned away, biting the inside of her cheek to stem the exasperated words and tears.

She strode into the passage, longing to retreat to her room. Instead she ran smack into the chest of Frederick Wilford.

"Oh!"

He caught her by the elbows. "Steady on, Miss Lane. Are you all right?"

"Forgive me. I was not looking where I was going."

He studied her face in concern. "What has happened? What's wrong?"

"I . . . had an unpleasant encounter—that is all. I am well. Or will be."

He looked past her into the hall. "Did that man say something to upset you? Or insult you?"

She shook her head and stepped back, although a part of her longed to throw her arms around him and cry out her woes. "Not directly, no. Never mind."

His long-lashed eyes narrowed. "Are you sure?"

She nodded.

"Here, let's sit down a moment." He led her to a bench in the cloisters.

When they were seated, she explained, "I am merely disappointed. I hoped Mr. Edgecombe might consider publishing John's book or at least give him some work, but no."

"I am sorry to hear it. Did John send you here to speak on his behalf?"

She nodded.

"You know, we used to see him often, rambling about the estate, but I have not seen him in weeks, if not months."

"He is . . . not well, I'm afraid."

"Has he seen a physician?"

"Not recently. I appreciate your concern, but he will be all right. In time." She prayed the words were true. In the meanwhile, Rebecca would do anything—or almost anything—to help him.

He tilted his head and regarded her pensively. "I don't like seeing you unhappy." He paused, then gave her a crooked grin. "Shall I bring you rout cakes?"

For a moment she blinked up at him, not comprehending.

"Do you not remember?" he asked, with a touch of disappointment.

Then it came to her. "Oh yes! New Year's Eve at the vicarage." Rebecca had been sent to bed early and had sat sadly at the top of the stairs to watch the party from there. Frederick had sneaked upstairs with rout cakes and together they'd sung, "Auld Lang Syne." A promise not to forget old friends.

His dark eyes held hers. "If only I could make you smile as easily now."

She managed a weak grin in reply. "Thank you for trying."

At dinner, even more tables were occupied than had been the previous evening. Lady Fitzhoward looked around and clucked like a self-satisfied hen.

"That newspaper notice was quite effective. Did I not tell you it would be?"

"You did indeed."

Lady Fitzhoward's gaze swept over her—wearing the same dinner dress—and her lips compressed. "If you intend to stay the whole week, we should have your trunk brought out of storage."

"Good idea, my lady."

The stunning Miss Newport came in, wearing the same gown as the night before as well. Empathy and surprise rippled through Rebecca. Was she simply traveling with minimal baggage, or was the evening gown her only one?

Lady Fitzhoward's keen eyes noticed her interest. "What?"

"Oh. Just curious. She wore the same gown last night too, when you were not feeling well."

Lady Fitzhoward humphed. "One would think an actress would have an extensive wardrobe."

A waiter approached. While he described the bill of fare for the evening, Rebecca noticed Lady Fitzhoward's eyes stray several times toward a man about her own age dining alone across the room.

When the waiter had taken down their selections and departed, Lady Fitzhoward beckoned the maître d'hôtel to their table.

"Yes, my lady, how may I be of service?"

She lifted her chin toward the table in question. "That man seated alone. I have seen him before somewhere but cannot place him. Who is he?"

Rebecca surreptitiously glanced over. The man was well dressed and distinguished-looking, with dark brows, silver side-whiskers, and an aquiline nose.

"That is Mr. Isaac King."

"Ah . . ." Lady Fitzhoward nodded. "Yes, now I remember. The moneylender."

She said it in a matter-of-fact tone without rancor, but the maître d'hôtel shifted uneasily.

"I . . . hope this will not inconvenience or distress your ladyship?"

"Heavens, no. I don't owe the man a farthing. Nor does his presence surprise me unduly. From what I hear, Ike King is acquainted with the highest ranks of society, called upon by many aristocrats who find themselves in pecuniary difficulties. I would be the last to raise any objection."

"Very good, your ladyship. You are most gracious."

The man bowed and backed away, returning to his duties with an expression of obvious relief.

Rebecca waited until he was out of earshot, then leaned near and asked in teasing tones, "And how, pray, are you acquainted with such a man?" She made little effort to quell her curiosity, nor the grin quivering on her lips.

"Cheeky girl!" her employer chastised mildly, but her rebuke held no bite. "My husband considered doing business with him once when he needed capital to expand. But Mr. King's business practices were too mercenary for his tastes, as were his interest rates. I saw the man briefly as he left Donald's office. He bowed and wished me a good evening, as polite as could be."

Rebecca asked, "Was he not disappointed to be rejected by your husband?"

The older woman shrugged. "Did not appear to be. He has

no shortage of clients, from what I understand. The *ton* is riddled with unbridled gamblers."

"I see."

Lady Fitzhoward dipped her chin, regarding Rebecca with a sardonic gleam in her eye. "Disappointed I had no seamier tale to tell?" She leaned back and spread her hands. "Feel free to make up your own."

"Not disappointed. Impressed, actually. You were quite affable about the man."

She waved off Rebecca's praise. "I have no interest in ostracizing anyone."

Rebecca nodded her agreement. "You remind me of my father. He believed there were good and bad eggs in every basket, and was kind to all."

Lady Fitzhoward eyed her thoughtfully. "I think I would have liked your father."

"I think so too."

"And your mother?" she asked.

"Oh. I loved her dearly. But I am fairly certain you would have thought her a 'silly creature,' as Rose would say."

"Rose . . ." Lady Fitzhoward echoed. "Your brother's housekeeper—is that right?"

"Right. And our friend. We have known her most of our lives."

Frederick sat alone, waiting for Thomas to join him. Late, again.

His gaze kept sliding over to Miss Lane, who sat with Lady Fitzhoward at their usual table.

Catching his eye, the older woman nodded to him. He still wondered why she seemed familiar.

Miss Newport, seated alone once more, smiled in his direction. He smiled back but did not ask her to join him.

Again at a quarter past seven, Mr. Oliver entered, this time with two companions. The man with military bearing remained near the door, while a second man with curly hair and spectacles joined him at the table. This was the man he had seen Miss Lane talking with earlier—the publisher who had disappointed her.

While Frederick awaited his brother's arrival, he could not help but overhear the publisher's conversation with Mr. Oliver.

"Any progress?" the bespectacled man asked.

"Not yet. Rome was not built in a day."

"Or even in a year, apparently. At this rate, I shall go bankrupt waiting for you to earn back the money William advanced in good faith."

Their soup arrived, and for a time, the tense conversation ceased.

The maître d'hôtel stopped at Miss Newport's table to ask if everything was to her liking. She beamed up at the man and answered in the affirmative, her voice melodic, her smile white, her face lovely.

The author's words from the next table caught his ear.

"I say, Edgecombe. Well done arranging for Selina to be here. I almost didn't recognize her, out of context and without stage paint. I applaud you."

The publisher scowled. "Me? I had nothing to do with it. What do you take me for? The last thing I would do is arrange a meeting with one of your paramours. The only reason I agreed to pay for this charade was because you promised seclusion would help you come up with a winning book idea. *Not* to facilitate love affairs or the adoration of your public." He gestured emphatically around the crowded dining room.

Mr. Oliver glanced over as well, and several heads swiftly turned away, feigning interest in their meals. "You're the one drawing attention now, old boy. Lower your voice. If it wasn't your doing, I wonder why she is here."

Thomas finally arrived. On his way to the table, he bowed to Miss Newport, Miss Lane, and Lady Fitzhoward, and exchanged greetings with Mr. and Mrs. Okeham seated nearby, neighbors who were no doubt dining in the hotel in the hope of seeing the acclaimed author. Then he sat across from Frederick, his cheerful excuses drowning out the conversations around them.

Only half listening, Frederick watched as waiters served another course to Mr. Oliver and his publisher. Suddenly Mr. Oliver tossed down his table napkin, his meal only half-eaten. "I'll not write another word tonight, thanks to you. Keep hounding me, and I never shall again!"

He rose and started across the room. As he passed the table of a dark-haired, sharp-nosed older man, the two locked gazes. Oliver's steps faltered. But a second later, he continued on and stalked from the room, his guard on his heels.

A moment of stunned silence followed his exit, and then a whispered buzz rose among the diners.

The publisher sat stone-faced. Then he rose slowly and followed Mr. Oliver from the room.

⸎

After dinner, Rebecca returned to her bedchamber but felt too restless to sleep. Knowing she had a little time before Mary stopped by to help her undress, she left her room and went down to the library and writing room, glad to find its lamp still lit. She put on her spectacles to peruse a set of novels she had heard of but not yet read, *Northanger Abbey* and *Persuasion* in four volumes. She wrote her name in the log book by lamplight, the flame dancing in a sudden draft. Had someone opened the door to the cloisters? Perhaps she ought to have closed the library door, but she would have felt a little uncomfortable shut inside the dim room alone.

Was she alone?

At the thought, she glanced up at the wall painting above her and met the doleful gaze of the abbess. Her eyes glowed red by candlelight, and Rebecca shivered.

Suddenly a rush of wind blew out the candle lamp, plunging the room into darkness.

For a moment Rebecca froze where she stood. Then, leaving the book, she stepped into the passage and saw the door to the cloisters slowly closing. She opened it and looked out. Diagonally across the courtyard, a figure in flowing black robes sailed through the covered walkway.

Alarm jolted her.

Suppressing the urge to retreat, Rebecca stepped forward to peer through one of the ornamental stone grilles. The figure turned the corner, a sliver of moon-white profile visible for just a moment before it slipped from view. Rebecca's stomach tightened. She had only caught a glimpse, but whoever it was definitely wore a hooded black robe . . . or habit. Had an actual nun come to stay at Swanford Abbey, or who . . . or what . . . had Rebecca seen?

The image brought back all those terrifying stories she'd heard growing up about the ghost of the abbess who haunted the church ruins, bemoaning her fate and the fate of all demolished monasteries, and taking revenge on anyone who dared to enter her domain.

Even as fear pulsed through Rebecca's veins, her feet moved as if of their own accord. She hurried along one side of the cloisters, and then turned the corner down the other side where the figure had disappeared. Had she gone into the hotel? It certainly seemed that way, unless the figure truly was a phantom who could disappear into thin air. *No, that is childish foolishness*, Rebecca reminded herself. She was a grown woman now and no longer believed in such things.

It had been a flesh-and-blood person. It must have been. But why would anyone wear a monk-like hood indoors, unless he or she meant to conceal his or her identity for some clandestine purpose?

A shiver passed over her. *Why indeed.*

Rebecca reached the next corner, saw no one lurking there, but heard faint footfalls. She continued through one of the doors into the hotel and then along the interior passage, past the hall with a bored-looking clerk at the desk, past the dining room, dark and deserted at this hour, past the coffee room, also dark, and then to a narrow stairway leading belowstairs.

There she paused. Was this where the person or specter had gone? Dare she follow?

Perhaps whoever she'd seen had been merely a staff member going down to the cellars for some reason.

Another possibility entered her mind. She had heard whispers that tucked away belowstairs was a club of sorts where gentlemen could drink and play cards away from the exacting eyes of gently bred females. That destination seemed far more likely at this hour.

Rebecca didn't belong in either cellar or club. She ought to return to her own room and try to sleep. Mary might be knocking on her door even now, wondering what had become of her.

Instead, by the light of a candle sconce high on the wall, she carefully made her way down the narrow stairs, the smells of tobacco and sour oak barrels growing stronger as she descended.

Reaching the bottom, she looked one way, then the other, surveying the dim passage and its shadowy corners.

She found herself in a basement far less polished than the levels above, with tiled floors and brick walls lit by lanterns hung at distant intervals. To the left was a door marked *Kitchen Staff Only*, which she guessed might be a cold cellar or larder. She turned right, passing padlocked rooms marked *Baggage Storage* and *Wine Cellar*.

She turned another corner and followed the sound of muffled voices to the end of the passage. There she saw an open doorway to an anteroom. This room held leather armchairs and a few small tables, with paintings of horses and hunts on the walls.

Beyond this lay an inner chamber from which wafted men's voices and cigar smoke. Through its open door, she glimpsed green felt and heard the telltale click of billiard balls striking one other.

So the rumors were true.

Had the hooded figure fled into this male bastion? Certainly not if it had been the ghost of a righteous abbess. But something told her the figure she'd seen was far less upright.

Rebecca was not brazen enough to enter this male sanctuary. Woe to her reputation if she ventured into such a place!

She slowly backed away, stepped on the edge of her hem, and stumbled, colliding with a firm object—a man's chest?

She gasped.

Masculine hands gripped her elbows to steady her. "Careful."

Whoever it was turned her to face him.

Thomas Wilford.

His handsome features creased in surprise, followed by a roguish grin. "Miss Lane. What an . . . unexpected pleasure."

Rebecca guessed most women would be charmed by the blond man's smile, but she had always been more attracted to Frederick's dark good looks and serious demeanor.

"Mr. Wilford. Pardon me, but I thought I saw . . . someone . . . come down here."

"Oh, who?"

"Never mind. You will think me silly."

"Never! Try me."

"Someone in a hooded robe. I could not see a face."

"Ah. A mystery!" His eyes glimmered. "Shall I look inside for you?"

Before she could decline, he stepped to the threshold and looked around the inner sanctum. A moment later he turned back. "No one wearing a cloak of any sort, hooded or otherwise." He teased, "Perhaps you saw the ghost of the abbess in her habit?"

"And here I have been trying to convince myself otherwise. You are not very reassuring, Mr. Wilford."

His expression sobered. "I must say, you do look like you've had a fright. Shall I walk you to your room?"

"That won't be necessary."

"Come, you are trembling. Allow me to walk with you back upstairs at least."

"Very well. Thank you."

He laced her arm through his, and she did not pull away, glad for his supportive presence. Together they walked through the passage and up the narrow stairs.

They met someone at the top. Someone Rebecca would rather not have seen when she was coming from somewhere she had no business being and on the arm of his flirtatious brother.

Sir Frederick.

He stopped abruptly, staring down at them, lips parting and then pressing tight. Self-conscious, Rebecca tugged her hand from Thomas's arm.

Sir Frederick asked, "What are you two doing down there at this hour? Or do I not want to know?"

She hated the disapproving, suspicious look on his face—hated that she'd put it there.

"We were ghost hunting," Thomas said with a wink. "No luck."

Frederick's dark brows rose and his eyes shifted to her.

Warmth infused her cheeks. "It was my fault," she said. "I saw someone in a hooded robe go belowstairs, and I wanted to find out who it was."

Fredrick frowned. "And you thought it might be . . . the abbess?"

Rebecca ducked her head. "I know how foolish that must sound. Especially when there are no nuns in England anymore."

He said, "Actually, several orders from France have taken refuge in our country, or so I have read. Though I have never seen one in this area."

"Nor I," Thomas agreed.

Even so, another shiver passed over her.

Thomas said, "In any case, Miss Lane has had a fright. Why don't you escort her to her room, Freddy? I am eager for a game of billiards."

"If she would like," Frederick solemnly replied.

"Excellent. Join me later."

When Thomas had gone back downstairs, Rebecca said, "There is no need to walk with me . . . at least, not all the way to my room. Perhaps just across the cloisters?"

He studied her face. "Were you really afraid?"

"Again, you will think me foolish, but yes."

"And yet you followed whoever it was down there anyway?"

Reading censure in his question, she ducked her head once more.

He added, "That is the Miss Lane I remember. Climbing the wall. Riding the horse. Standing up to her brother's tormentors. Confident, brave Becky."

She blinked. Not only were his words utterly unexpected but she barely recognized herself in them. Yes, she had climbed things, but confident? Brave? She only vaguely remembered that girl.

"That was all a long time ago now."

"Not so long," he said. "Our vicar, Mr. Gilby, attended the canal meeting. He mentioned you climbed a tree to rescue a kite for his children only a few days ago."

Her face heated anew, but glancing up and seeing his grin, she returned it.

He walked her to the bottom of the night stair. "I shall wait here until you are safe in your room."

"Thank you."

Reaching out, he squeezed her hand and said warmly, "Good night, brave Miss Rebecca."

"Good night," she replied, still grinning foolishly in the dark.

But as she climbed the stairs, Rebecca's grin slowly faded. What was she doing? She was not there to flirt with Sir Frederick or to make a fool of herself. She was there to help John. And here she was, about to spend another night in the Swanford Abbey Hotel.

She hated to think how much her bill amounted to already, and she still had not given John's manuscript to either Mr. Edgecombe or Mr. Oliver. Rebecca wanted to finish what she'd come for and leave, before she made things worse for John or jeopardized her position with Lady Fitzhoward—or, worse yet, before she broke her heart again over Sir Frederick Wilford.

She decided she'd had more than enough of Swanford Abbey, haunted or not.

When she reached her door, she saw Mary knocking. "Oh, there you are, miss! I wondered what became of you."

"I hope you have not been waiting long."

"No, miss."

Rebecca asked, "You have not seen a nun or someone dressed as one, have you?"

"No, miss. Don't tell me you've seen the ghost of the abbess!" Mirth twinkled in the girl's eyes.

Rebecca sighed. "Never mind."

The two entered the room, and Mary began helping her undress. Rebecca found her gaze lingering on the maid's reflection in the mirror, head lowered, mobcap half covering her face, apron over a dark, nondescript dress. An idea struck.

"Mary, I wonder if you might help me with something?"

"'Course, if I can."

"I need to speak to Mr. Oliver. Privately. But no one gets into his room except you. Except a . . . chambermaid."

"What are you saying?"

"May *I* deliver his breakfast tomorrow morning?"

"Mr. George won't let you in."

"Not as me, perhaps. But as a chambermaid, he might."

Mary's eyebrows rose. "You want to work as a maid?"

"Just for a few minutes. Unofficially."

"Un-oh-fishal . . . ?"

"In secret. Just between you and me." Rebecca gestured toward her attire. "Perhaps I could borrow your apron and cap?"

"I couldn't let you wear these," Mary said. "I have to attend to my duties properly dressed."

"I understand," Rebecca replied, feeling defeated. She did not want to get the girl into trouble.

"But I do have an extra set," Mary said, brightening. "You could wear those, as long as you return them no worse for wear."

Relief and terror warred within Rebecca. What was she doing? "It would only be for a short time," she assured the girl. Hopefully not too short, for that would mean he'd refused to talk with her. Refused her request.

Mary nodded. "I'll bring them to you when I finish for the night."

"Thank you. And keep this between us, please."

"If I may be so bold, I'd say the same to you, miss. I don't want anyone to find out either. I'd lose my place."

Half an hour later—time Rebecca had spent in doubts and second thoughts—Mary delivered the promised articles of clothing, carried over her arm, covered by a towel. She delivered instructions as well.

"I've given it some thought. Monsieur Marhic has a keen eye. Instead of you going down to the kitchen, I'll prepare a tray myself and meet you outside your room at five till nine. You can carry the tray from here."

Rebecca expelled a jagged sigh. "Thank you, that does sound less risky." Especially as the chef might remember speaking with her in the dining room.

"Keep your head down," Mary went on. "No one looks at maids anyway, except Mr. George. Usually when he sees me coming with the tray, he rises and knocks on the door for me. If he asks, say you're new. Later, I can deny everything if need be."

"Very well. Sounds a simple plan." Rebecca inhaled a long breath, solidifying her resolve. "And truly, it's not as though we are doing anything illegal."

"I should hope not!"

Now if only it would work . . . and get neither of them into trouble.

9

The next morning, Rebecca dressed herself in the shapeless grey dress, which fastened in the front, and tied on the long white apron with trembling hands. Stepping to the mirror, she pulled her hair back tightly and pinned it away from her face, then covered it all with the floppy, frilly cap.

Her reflection revealed pale skin and crescent shadows beneath her eyes. She had not slept well, worrying about the morning's mission and imagining all that might go wrong. Then she reminded herself of John's desperate state, and the quickly amassing sum she owed the hotel. She hated to imagine the total if Lady Fitzhoward had not offered to pay for her meals!

Studying her face in the mirror, Rebecca decided she still looked too much like herself. Retrieving the tortoiseshell case, she put on the spectacles she usually reserved for reading or mending. Then she ran a finger through the oily soot collected on her lamp and used it to darken her brows. She applied it with too heavy a hand and recoiled from her own startling image. She wiped most of it away until it looked more natural.

She glanced at the small mantel clock. A few minutes to spare. She clasped damp hands, gazed at the cross above her bed, and in the quiet of her solitary chamber, prayed, "Dear God, I know you don't approve of deception but . . ."

Unbidden, thoughts of women from Scripture who had deceived scrolled through her mind. Sarah, Tamar, Rebekah . . . Most of their stories had not ended well.

"I hope you will forgive me," she murmured rather lamely. "I mean no harm." She only wanted to get in to speak to Mr. Oliver, to urge him to recommend her brother's manuscript to his publisher. To help John. To save him.

"Please, let Mr. Oliver listen. Soften his heart and grant me favor in his eyes." She also prayed that Mr. Edgecombe—to avoid distracting the author—had not warned him about John Lane's sister.

Rebecca then inched open her door and peeked out. Seeing no one, she waited until she heard quick footsteps on the nearby night stair and saw a white mobcap emerging from below. Rebecca picked up the large envelope containing the manuscript and tucked it under her arm, hoping it would look like a folded newspaper to any casual passerby. Then she stepped out, quietly closing the door behind herself.

Mary appeared, looking only half as nervous as Rebecca felt.

"Here you are, miss," she whispered. "Careful not to spill. Bring back yesterday's dishes and any dirty laundry he gives you. I'll take care of them from here."

Rebecca nodded her understanding and held out her hands.

The tray felt heavier than her father's thousand-page Bible. Rebecca walked slowly, keeping a wary eye on the piled-high plate of food and pitcher of cream, glad the coffee had not yet been poured into the empty, rattling cup.

Nearing room three, she saw Mr. George glance up. She

quickly ducked her head and kept walking, pulse pounding hard with each step.

Open the door . . . open the door, she silently begged.

He rose to do so, by habit as Mary had said, or by God's favor, or both? He knocked on the door and stood there, waiting.

"Morning," the man said to her as she approached.

She mumbled the same in reply, keeping her head down, trying not to draw the guard's watchful eye.

Come on, come on . . . she inwardly pleaded.

A few seconds later the lock clicked open from within, and the guard pushed the door wide for her.

She stepped through, and the door shut behind her. So far so good.

Inside the room, Mr. Oliver had already reclaimed his seat on a chaise longue, rosewood writing slant on his lap, head bent and dark hair flopping over his forehead. He murmured a barely audible grunt of acknowledgment without looking up. He scribbled with quill and ink to the end of the line, licked his finger to turn a page, and began scratching away again.

When she hesitated, he gestured toward the low end table. "Just set it down there."

She bobbed a curtsy and moved to comply, setting the tray down with a clank of china and cutlery.

"Dirty laundry there." He jerked an ink-stained thumb toward the corner. "I am out of stockings."

She stammered, "I-I have brought you something."

"Coffee, I hope. Eggs, kippers, kidneys, and bacon as usual?" He glanced over at his breakfast.

"That too."

He looked up at her at last, then squinted—a deep crease

connecting his brows. "You're new," he murmured, clearly not pleased about this interruption in routine.

"Yes." She took a deep breath, pulled the manuscript from under her arm, and held it out to him. "And I entreat you most earnestly to ask your publisher to read this manuscript. He won't accept any submissions unless one of his authors recommends it."

Ambrose Oliver growled and threw up his inky hands. "Now even the chambermaids are penning novels and begging me to get them published! Is there no peace for me? No place a man can avoid desperate quill-drivers?" He sat back hard and ran a jaded gaze over her. "In truth, I am surprised you can read, let alone think you've written a work of literature worthy of Edgecombe's attention, let alone mine."

"I believe it is."

"Bah! I don't know whether to be impressed or offended. 'Cheeky' doesn't begin to describe you. Good thing you are pretty or I would call for Sergeant George and send you packing—have you sacked as well."

She bit her lip to keep from retorting that she didn't work there, knowing she should conceal her identity to have any chance of securing his help.

"Please, sir. Simply ask Mr. Edgecombe to read it."

"Is it a novel or poetry or what?"

"A novel. And if he doesn't think it worthy of publication, so be it. You will never see me again."

He narrowed his eyes in searing scrutiny. "You look familiar to me. Have we met?"

"No."

"Yet you do seem familiar. . . ."

Rebecca swallowed. Had he seen her from a distance as she had seen him? Or was he observing a family resemblance? She and John did resemble one another slightly, she knew. But surely with spectacles and her hair hidden under the mobcap he would not guess.

She lifted her chin. "Will you help?"

"Why should I? What's in it for me?"

Forgiveness and redemption, Rebecca thought. *The chance to right a wrong.* But she could say none of those things without revealing or at least hinting at the author's true identity.

Instead she said, "Because it might very well save a life."

"Mine? Is that a threat?"

She sucked in a shocked breath. "Heavens, no! That is not what I meant."

He set down his quill and eyed her. "You could make it worth my while. . . ." His gaze moved from her face down her neck to her bodice, clearly trying to make out the figure beneath the shapeless frock and apron.

Mr. George had been right. Mr. Oliver didn't have a sort. Any female would do.

But not her. That was a line she would not cross. Not even for John.

"What is your name?" he asked, setting aside the lap desk and rising. He stood to his full, impressive, intimidating height.

Rebecca took a step back. "I had better go."

A rap of knuckles shook the door. "Mr. Oliver? Everything all right in there?"

Mr. George.

Would the author detain her? Make good on his threat to send her packing? He could not have her sacked, but he could definitely have her thrown out of the hotel and disgraced in Sir Frederick's eyes as well as Lady Fitzhoward's.

"Please," she whispered, forcing herself to keep her head high and hold his piercing gaze.

His dark eyes gleamed with speculation. "You have certainly aroused my attention."

"I'm all right," he called through the door, then turned back to her, impudent humor quirking his mouth. "May I at least have a cup of coffee before you go?"

"Oh. Of course." She poured a cup with trembling fingers and handed it to him.

She forced herself to ask again. To push. "So . . . will you?"

His focus lingered on her face. "I will think about it. In the meanwhile, you can do something for me."

She was instantly on her guard.

He stepped closer and lowered his voice. "Do you know who Selina Newport is?"

Rebecca weighed the question for a trap. Finding none, she said, "I know who she is, yes."

"Ask her to come and see me. Apparently, Sergeant George will let in any attractive female."

She shook her head. "He won't allow it."

"You leave the sergeant to me. He is in my employ, after all, and not the other way around."

Not wanting to refuse and harm their chances, she said, "I will give her your message. How she responds is up to her."

Those thick lips puckered into a smug smile. "Oh, she'll come to me all right. Of that I have no doubt."

Would she? Why would a beautiful woman like Miss Newport, who had clearly caught Thomas Wilford's eye, be interested in an older, unpleasant man like Ambrose Oliver? Did he hold some power over her?

Mr. Oliver sat back down. "Leave your *opus* on the table and close the door on your way out."

"Yes, sir." Unsettled, Rebecca set down the prized manuscript and opened the door, darting back to pick up an armful of dirty laundry. She didn't see any used dishes except a coffee cup, but swiped that up too. Then she let herself from the room, head low. She swept past Mr. George without looking at him and hurried away, intending to go the long way around, so he would not see which room she was heading for.

"Are you all right?" he called after her. "Did he . . . bother you?"

Without pausing, she shook her head and continued past the main stairs and railing that overlooked the hall below.

From the corner of her eye, she glimpsed a tall man standing near the hotel entrance and glanced down, only to immediately wish she had not. Robb Tarvin stood there, no doubt awaiting the arrival of a guest who'd reserved his fly.

He looked up at that very moment.

She turned her head toward the opposite wall and hurried around the corner and out of view, hoping against hope that he had not seen her.

Mary was waiting for her beside her door. Together they stepped inside.

"How did it go?" Mary whispered eagerly. "Everything all right?"

"I think so." To herself, Rebecca added, *I pray so*. Hands still trembling, she handed over the dirty laundry and coffee cup. "I did not see another tray."

"Oh, that's right. He rang for a second pot of coffee yesterday, and I picked it up then."

Rebecca pulled the cap from her head and untied the apron.

"I'll pick those up later," Mary said. "I've got to get on now."

Rebecca nodded and laid a hand on the girl's arm. "Thank you, Mary. I am indebted to you."

"How could I not help? You're the one who gave me a chance

when I needed a place—me with no experience and my family being what it was. And you who wrote that fine character that got me another place at the Griffiths' and eventually here."

How glad Rebecca was that she had done so. "I did that because I believed you capable, not to get anything in return."

"I know. Even so, I couldn't say no to you now, could I?"

Rebecca stilled, fear curdling inside her. She hoped neither of them would live to regret what she had just done.

Worried that Robb might have recognized her, or even *wonder* if he had seen her in the garb of a maid, Rebecca decided to try to dispel that image as quickly as possible. Thankfully, her trunk had been delivered to her room, and with it, several additional clothing options.

From within the folds of tissue, she carefully extracted one of her more elegant garments, which Lady Fitzhoward had recently purchased for her, saying, *"We are in fashionable Bath, Miss Lane. You must dress the part."*

It was a beautiful spencer of patterned pink satin with a gathered waist, short, ruffled peplum, and bow at the back with long ends trimmed in pleating. The spencer was topped by a matching cape-like collar with a high ruffled neck.

This she put on over a spotted muslin gown of the same hue, and also selected a bonnet with a pert, upturned brim.

Then she went downstairs and knocked on Miss Joly's door to ask her to do something with her hair.

The woman set about the task, although she sighed heavily to have to lay aside a purloined copy of *La Belle Assemblée* to do so.

She curled and arranged Rebecca's hair to show to advantage beneath her high bonnet brim, leaving tendrils on either side of her face.

Suddenly Joly peered closely at her. "You have something . . . just there." She lifted a cloth and wiped at Rebecca's left eyebrow.

Inspecting the smear, Joly frowned. "Lamp-black, Miss Lane?"

She must have missed some. Abashed, Rebecca replied, "Just thought I'd try it."

"It does not suit you."

Perhaps hearing their voices, Lady Fitzhoward knocked once and opened the adjoining door. "Ah. Miss Lane, you look very well, I must say."

"Thank you, my lady. I should. . . ." Rebecca tugged on the short spencer. "You selected both the pattern and the color yourself!"

"Ah yes. Are you seeing Sir Frederick, perchance?"

"No. That is, I don't believe so."

"Pity." She waggled her brows and returned to her own room.

Rebecca took a final look at her reflection and saw no resemblance to the "maid" she had seen in her mirror earlier that morning.

She thanked Joly and went out, walking through the corridor and into the main hall, shoulders back, head held high. Two gentlemen in conversation paused to glance her way, and their expressions shone with admiration.

As she continued across the room, the commissionaire opened the front door for her and tipped his hat. "Miss Lane."

"Good day, Mr. Moseley."

She stepped outside and made her way down the stairs, intending to stroll past the entrance to the stable yard and hopefully encounter Robb if he was back from delivering his last customer.

Not seeing him, she sat on one of the benches nearby to

surreptitiously await his return. As the minutes ticked by, she realized that perhaps she ought to have brought a book.

While she sat there, a man rode out of the stable yard—Sir Frederick Wilford on a chestnut horse. He did not notice her as he directed his mount down the lane and out of the village. She wondered where he was going. For a moment, she imagined herself riding beside him in a fashionable new habit and jaunty hat.

Rebecca was abruptly transported back to her youth, and recalled a mortifying scene as though it had happened weeks ago rather than years ago. Her neck heated as the memory revisited her.

Eager to see Frederick again, Rebecca walked over to Wickworth. One of the stable hands told her he had just ridden off, bound for Ravel Lake, so Rebecca had asked the young man to help her saddle Ladybird. She wasn't supposed to ride on her own, but Ravel Lake, she had justified, was not at all far.

Emerging through the trees a short while later, she saw Frederick on his horse, Warrior, and two other riders near the lakeshore. She decided she would just let him notice her and then wave, sure he would invite her to join them.

Drawing closer, she noticed one of the riders was a striking woman in a formfitting blue habit that accentuated her developed figure. The other was one of the Wilfords' grooms, who rode a respectful distance behind. Frederick did not notice Rebecca, focused instead on his lovely companion as they directed their horses to the picnic grounds. Well-dressed and graceful, the two were a living portrait of fashionable English country life.

Frederick and the groom dismounted first. While the groom held the horses' reins, Frederick reached up and grasped the woman around her tiny waist and helped her down, his hands lingering even after her polished boots touched the ground, his expression besotted.

Rebecca's stomach knotted at the sight, and jealousy slithered through her. She turned Ladybird's head, hoping to ride away before anyone saw her there.

Suddenly an all-too-familiar voice shouted, "Becky!"

John. He stood at the edge of the clearing. Through the trees, she saw their father waiting in the gig on the road beyond.

"Papa says come here—now! You are not allowed to ride alone!"

Mortification flooded her. To be chastised like a little girl, and a naughty one at that, in front of these two elegant adults . . .

She urged Ladybird on, kicking the horse's sides as she almost never did, wishing she could disappear.

From the corner of her eye, she saw Frederick turn in her direction, but she kept her head down and urged the horse to go faster, even as the stubborn creature stretched its neck to steal a lusty bite of grass.

Rebecca vaguely heard low feminine laughter and Frederick's voice call after her, but she rode on, face flaming.

Later, Frederick had come to the vicarage, but Rebecca, too embarrassed to face him, hid in a niche in the garden wall, where a flowering elderberry shrub sheltered her from view.

She heard her father talking to him on the porch. Frederick's low words were indecipherable, but her father's voice—projecting loudly after years of sermon-making—was perfectly clear and painful to hear.

"Don't take it to heart," he said. "Becky has a case of calf-love—that's all. And that was before you offered her the use of that horse! No, no. I don't blame you. You have been very kind to her but have done nothing improper. Just a young girl's romantic fancies . . ."

Frederick said something else that Rebecca did not hear.

"Congratulations!" her father replied. "Who is the fortunate woman? Miss Seward? Ah yes. Lovely lady."

The men talked for a few minutes longer while Rebecca remained in her hidden bower and silently wept.

Sitting there now, Rebecca felt like that awkward, eager adolescent all over again.

She heard the approach of jingling tack and glanced over. Robb Tarvin had returned in his fly. Reining in his horse there on the drive, he looked from her to the retreating rider. "Still pining after Frederick Wilford, I see."

She raised her chin and said coolly, "Good day to you too, Mr. Tarvin."

He narrowed his eyes. "I saw you, you know."

Her heart thudded hard and her mouth went dry. "Saw me?" Rebecca rose and turned to face him.

He tied off the reins, alighted, and walked closer. "I could hardly believe it. You—masquerading like that."

Perspiration heated then chilled her. She wet her lips and said, "Robb, I . . . I can't explain, but I had good reasons."

"Oh sure. And I can just guess at your reasons. Sir Frederick and Thomas Wilford. That's fine company for the daughter of their former tutor."

"Wait. What?" Confusion addled her mind. Had she misunderstood?

"I saw you through the refectory window. Having dinner with them the other night, all cozy like."

Relief flooded her. "Oh! Yes. They invited me to join them.

No doubt out of respect for my father's memory. Sir Frederick was always fond of him."

"But your father was fond of *me*—said *I* was the cleverest lad in the village."

She had never told Robb that, even though her parents admired his thirst for learning, they had discouraged her from pursuing a relationship with the young man.

When Robb had tried to court her when she was seventeen, she had ignored his overtures as long as she could, purposely misinterpreting his flirtation as a continuation of their friendship. Eventually, he had grown frustrated and tried to kiss her, and she'd had to push him away and tell him she had no romantic interest in him, that while she appreciated his friendship, there could be nothing more between them.

He had been angry and resentful, and she'd felt terrible for hurting him. At his disapproving expression now, all those uncomfortable feelings came rushing back.

She tried to assuage his pride. "Yes, my father admired your intelligence. Your capable mind—"

"Nothing's changed. I am still that same lad."

Many things had changed, Rebecca knew. He was no longer a promising lad of fifteen, but an embittered man of five and twenty.

Robb crossed his arms. "Too bad your father liked me more than you did." He slowly shook his head, lips curled in disgust. "You're wasting your time with Sir Frederick, you know. He's not going to remarry. The first go was bad enough, from all accounts, to turn him off the institution."

Rebecca shrugged. "What is that to me?"

"I know you consider yourself his . . . special . . . friend."

"That was years ago. And he was a friend to my entire family, especially to my father."

"He didn't give your father a horse."

Offense flared but she bit her tongue. She could not dispute it. Instead she asked, "Why do you dislike him so much?"

"Because he has everything I want, or could have, without lifting a finger. It isn't fair."

"Life isn't fair," Rebecca said. "God never promised it would be."

"If you say so." Robb climbed back into the fly and drove it into the stable yard.

Rebecca remained where she was a moment longer, turning to watch Sir Frederick and his horse grow smaller and smaller and finally disappear over the hill.

She could not deny that she had long dreamed of being Frederick Wilford's wife. But those were the foolish dreams of a foolish young girl. She took a deep breath. Robb might be resentful and jealous, but he could be right about one thing. Perhaps it was time to lay aside those old dreams and get on with her life.

Returning inside, Rebecca saw Miss Newport in the hall. The lithe, beautiful performer sat at the hotel's grand pianoforte, running her fingers experimentally over the keys.

Finding the hall otherwise unoccupied, Rebecca decided to accomplish one more unpleasant task. "Miss Newport?"

The woman looked up but kept playing softly. "Yes, Miss Lane?"

"I am sorry to disturb you. But I have been asked to pass along a message."

"Oh?"

Rebecca stepped nearer and lowered her voice. "From Mr. Oliver."

The woman's arched brows rose. "Mr. Oliver? Is he not sequestered in his room?"

"Yes, well, he . . . em, asked a chambermaid who knew I had

met you, and I agreed to deliver the message. Pray forgive the interference. He asks that you go and see him."

Miss Newport pursed her rouged lips. "Why would I?"

"I wondered that myself. He is in room three. But don't go on my account. I agreed to pass along the message—how you respond is completely up to you."

Miss Newport struck a jarring chord, then squared her shoulders. "You have delivered the message, Miss Lane, and may consider your duty dispatched." She rose. "Now, please do take tea with me."

Rebecca was taken aback by the abrupt invitation but saw no reason to decline.

Selina Newport spoke to the clerk, and then the two young women sat in armchairs near the fire. While they waited for their tea, Lady Fitzhoward walked into the hall, and Miss Newport asked the older woman to join them as well.

Rebecca worried her wealthy employer might not wish to associate with an actress, but she displayed no such reluctance. She thanked Miss Newport and selected a chair. In short order, a waiter delivered a tea tray and, seeing the newcomer, quickly procured a third cup.

As she poured for them, Miss Newport began, "You mentioned having a brother, Miss Lane. I envy you. Are the two of you close?"

Rebecca hesitated. It seemed odd that she should ask about John again. "In childhood, yes. But we . . ." She looked down at her teacup and murmured, "We are grown now."

Miss Newport picked up her own cup. "It must have been grand to have someone to protect you and tease you in equal measure. Was growing up with a brother as delightful as I imagine?"

"Actually, I was the older sibling. So I tried to protect him, but sadly I failed. He was hurt because of me."

Miss Newport stilled, cup halfway to her lips. Her sparkling eyes dulled. "I am sorry. I sympathize with you. I failed to protect someone I loved too."

"Oh?" Rebecca asked expectantly.

Miss Newport looked down, her stillness transformed into a sudden flurry of little agitated movements—lowering her teacup, adding another lump of sugar, followed by a rapid stir.

"I should not have mentioned it," she said. "You will think me maudlin."

"May I ask who?"

"My sister. My little sister."

"Oh . . ." Rebecca breathed. "I am sorry." She impulsively reached over and squeezed the woman's hand.

They sat in silence, but Miss Newport did not expand on her reply.

Instead, Selina diverted the attention to Lady Fitzhoward. "And have you any siblings, my lady?"

Lady Fitzhoward sipped her tea, then answered somberly, "A sister."

To lighten the conversation, Rebecca said brightly, "Sisters, the both of you. Now I envy you! It must be wonderful to have someone so close to you, sharing dresses and confidences and all your secret hopes and romantic dreams."

"I wouldn't know," Lady Fitzhoward replied. "I haven't spoken to mine in years."

Meanwhile, Miss Newport wiped damp eyes with a serviette. "You make me quite miss my Edie. Do let's talk of something else. What a gloomy trio we are!"

"Then tell us something of your career," Lady Fitzhoward suggested. "Might I have seen you in something in Cheltenham?"

"You very well may have. I performed several roles at Watson's Theatre and even once played opposite the great John Kemble."

"Ah! I thought you seemed familiar. That explains it."

They spoke about music and theatre for several more minutes, then Miss Newport rose and excused herself, thanking them both warmly for their company and friendly conversation.

When she had gone, Rebecca said quietly, "It was kind of you to join us, my lady."

"What? You are shocked I should show polite interest in the woman because she is an actress? I have not such a high-and-mighty opinion of myself, whatever you must think of me."

"Not at all. I was simply . . . pleasantly surprised."

Lady Fitzhoward took another sip of tea, then set it down with a frown. "What is this? What's wrong with a traditional, strong black tea?"

"I could ask for some."

"Never mind. Thing is, Miss Newport reminds me of someone."

"Who?"

"I know you will think I am deluding myself, but she reminds me of myself, as a much younger woman, of course." She sent Rebecca a shrewd look. "Wait and see. You too may be unhappily surprised by the changes age and loss bring. You will not believe it, but I was once reckoned a handsome woman. And like many handsome women, I relied too heavily on my looks. Used them to get my way, sometimes to my regret. I see a bit of that in her. A hollow, costly pursuit, in the end."

Rebecca glanced over and saw Miss Newport speaking to Thomas Wilford on the stairway landing. "Mr. Wilford seems to admire her."

"Yes, although his brother clearly does not approve."

"Will that stop him, do you think?"

Lady Fitzhoward shrugged. "Family disapproval didn't stop my Donald, thankfully."

Rebecca teased, "Were you an actress too?"

The older woman arched a sly brow. "Who among us is not?"

10

Later that afternoon, Rebecca sat with Lady Fitzhoward on a bench in the abbey garden, chatting companionably and enjoying the peaceful burble of the fountain, surrounded by daffodils, tulips, and primroses.

An ancient-looking man in a flat cap worked amid the flower beds. He laboriously got to his feet, trowel in one hand, daffodil stem in the other. Rebecca recognized him as the same old man they'd encountered upon arrival. He slowly approached their bench and extended the bloom to Lady Fitzhoward, head humbly bowed. "A flower fer a flower."

Lady Fitzhoward frowned up at him, wincing against the sunshine and the unexpected compliment. When she made no move to accept the sweet offering, Rebecca gently nudged her.

She belatedly took the stem. "Thank you." As the man ambled away, she added under her breath, "Old fool."

Rebecca teased, "It appears you have an admirer here."

"Yes," the lady dryly replied. "How soon can we leave?"

Rebecca grinned.

Then Lady Fitzhoward rose with the help of her stick and

excused herself, going inside for her daily "restorative," or customary afternoon nap.

A few minutes later, Sir Frederick appeared from around the corner of the abbey. Anticipation thrummed through her. She reached up to touch her hair, reassuring herself it was no longer pulled back severely nor covered by a mobcap.

"Good afternoon, Miss Lane."

She smiled back. "Sir Frederick. Did you enjoy your ride earlier? I saw you leaving."

"Thank you, I did. My horse and I both needed the exercise. I wonder—might you have any interest in visiting Wickworth with me? I have been putting off a decision about the refurbishments and would appreciate your opinion."

"Of course. Happily."

His lower lip protruded. Her acceptance had apparently surprised him. "Excellent. Shall we ride or walk? Or I could hire the fly?"

"No need for that," she quickly replied, preferring not to involve Robb Tarvin. "A ride would be enjoyable, but I haven't a riding habit here. Nor a horse! I don't mind the walk, if you don't."

"Not at all. It is not far."

He offered his hand and helped her to her feet. Standing before him, her hand still in his, their faces close, his eyes seemed to grow large, kindled with warmth and—dare she hope—attraction?

"Miss Lane," he breathed, "you are . . ." He broke off, then faltered, "Are you ready as you are? That is, you look very well as you are, but do you need anything from your room first?"

She shook her head. "I am ready."

Together they walked from Abbey Lane to the North Road outside of Swanford. Arms at their sides, they strolled past fields and pastures, talking companionably about villagers they both knew and the changes the passing years had brought.

Rebecca inhaled a deep breath of fresh air and gazed out at the misty fields. She noticed sheep huddled beneath the outstretched arms of a flowering blackthorn, new lambs frolicking nearby, and father and son farmers preparing the ground for planting.

They raised hands in greeting and walked on. Soon Rebecca felt her recent tensions melting away beneath the invigorating spring sunshine.

She wondered why Sir Frederick wanted her to see Wickworth again. How long had it been since she'd stepped foot in the place—four, five years ago? Then she remembered the last occasion. It was a few months after her father died. The Wilfords had invited her and John for dinner to gently let them know that a new clergyman and his family would be moving into the vicarage soon. And to soften the blow of losing the house, they had offered them the use of their underkeeper's lodge as well as the services of Rose Watts, whom they already knew and liked.

How Rebecca had lamented the loss of their home. If John had aspired to make the church his profession, Sir Roger might have given the living to him rather than to a stranger. But John had no interest in being ordained. Nor in the military. He'd always wanted to be a "great writer" and nothing else.

As they turned into Swanford Road and neared the dower house, Rebecca asked, "And how is your mother? In good health, I hope?"

"Yes. According to Dr. Pope she is in excellent health, though to hear her itemize her aches and pains, you would think she was very ill indeed."

"Will we see her?"

"Unlikely. She keeps to the dower house and has done since shortly after my marriage."

The aloof woman had always intimidated her. Rebecca said, "I heard she relocated there, but I thought, perhaps after . . . ?" Recalling what Kitty had told her about his wife's death, Rebecca trailed off.

"No. She has made the dower house her own, with new furniture and carpets. Even had a glass conservatory built to one side." He pointed it out. "She likes living in her own home— queen of her own snug castle. Says she has no desire to uproot herself again when I might decide to . . ."

He let the sentence dangle, unfinished, and she stole a glance at him, noticing the red flush above his collar. She guessed at what he'd started to say—"*I might decide to marry again.*"

They turned up the long gravel drive flanked by topiaries that led to the main house. "I can understand her sentiments," Rebecca said. "A home of one's own sounds appealing to me as well."

Head tilted, he turned to appraise her. "Have you been unhappy?"

"Oh no. Do not mistake me. I am not complaining. The lodge is a comfortable place. We are grateful for it."

"But it's nothing to the vicarage, I realize."

"The vicarage was not ours either. Simply part of Papa's living while he served the parish." She shrugged with resignation. "It is part and parcel of a clergyman's life to depend on the generosity of others. And of a woman's too, if she does not have independent means of her own."

"Or marry."

Heat toasted her cheeks. She opened her mouth to respond, then closed it again, every possible response that rose to her tongue too mortifying to utter. *I have never had that chance.*

No one has asked. At this point, that seems unlikely. . . . Worse, he might think she was hinting that she still yearned for such an offer.

Filling the awkward gap, he said, "You have barely lived in the lodge the last few years. Where did you reside?"

Relieved for the change of topic, Rebecca replied, "My first situation was with a Mrs. Brocklehurst. She had a commodious home and rarely ventured from it, until ill health prompted her to seek a cure in Cheltenham. That is where I first met Lady Fitzhoward. I remember she seemed interested in where I was from and asked me about Swanford. She even hinted that if I was ever in want of a new place, I should let her know. So when Mrs. Brocklehurst died, I did."

"If it's not too impertinent, may I ask if you sought those positions for the financial benefit, or for the opportunity to live elsewhere?"

She looked up at him, taken aback by his astute question. "Both, if I am honest. I hoped living elsewhere would put less strain on John's limited finances."

Memories of John's erratic behavior, his shouting and re-criminations, flickered through her mind. "And yes, many were the days I longed to be anywhere else but here."

She wished the last sentence back as soon as she had said it, fearing he would ask why. Instead he asked, "And I imagine Lady Fitzhoward has a commodious home as well?"

"I suppose so. Though we rarely stay there. She prefers to travel—spa towns, seaside resorts, and the Continent. She spends more time in fine inns than in her own home. At least for the last year or so."

"I wonder why?"

"She is recently widowed. I take it the house holds more sad memories than present comfort."

"That I do understand."

She looked over at him, but he kept his face forward, his profile grim.

They walked in silence for a few moments, then he asked, "What is Lady Fitzhoward's Christian name, by the way? I have been trying to place her."

"Marguerite."

He frowned and slowly shook his head, the name clearly not familiar.

Soon they arrived at Wickworth, a three-story Palladian house with a pedimented portico supported by four columns. He led her up the stairs and into the entry hall, which was much as she remembered, then through the ground-floor rooms, where the furniture sat covered by white Holland cloths to protect it from construction dust.

She noticed a gaping hole between the library and drawing room.

Following her gaze, he explained, "Marina thought the drawing room too small, so we were going to enlarge it by annexing the library."

"Where were all the books to go?"

"Into my much smaller study. But I had resigned myself to storing some of them in the attic."

"And now?"

"The workmen had already knocked through the wall when she died, and it has remained that way since. For a time, I vacillated between removing the entire wall as planned or patching the hole. Now I am considering having an archway built between the rooms, but to otherwise leave the library as is."

"That sounds a good compromise."

"Do you think so?"

"Yes. I like it. A clever solution."

"Good. Thank you. That eases my mind."

Eventually, he led her up to the first floor.

As they ascended the long flight, Rebecca wondered if these were the very stairs his wife had fallen down. Kitty's words whispered through her mind, *"A fall . . . ? And her as graceful as could be, and using those same stairs every day for years? Others say Sir Frederick . . . pushed her."*

A chill crept up her neck at the thought.

To dispel it, she said brightly, "I recall a remarkably pretty sitting room up here. Your mother's favorite, I believe."

"Yes, it is much as it ever was."

He led her to it. The corner room was a snug, cozy size for family use, with windows on two sides.

She walked to one, then the other. One three-light window overlooked the bowling green where she had learned to play, and beyond it, a patchwork of pastures and fields backed by rolling hills—a lovely, bucolic view she had often admired. The other looked toward the church and graveyard, with Fowler's Wood beyond.

"My wife did not like this room," he said. "The view of the churchyard was distasteful to her, and she judged the furnishings too old-fashioned. She had plans to alter it as well, but that never happened."

"Again, I am sorry for your loss. I hope it is not disrespectful to disagree with her. I think this room delightful as it is, but then, I always have."

She didn't say it to contradict his departed wife, nor to place herself in a more favorable light. It was simply the truth.

She looked up to find him watching her—his expression curiously intent. He crossed the room, stopping just in front of her and taking her hand. She inhaled sharply and held her breath.

Voice low, he said haltingly, "Miss Lane, I wish . . . That is,

I . . . don't want to make you uncomfortable, but I would like to say that being with you again—"

A loud bang shattered the air and the tension between them.

"What the deuce." Frowning, he dropped her hand and turned, striding from the room.

She followed to search for the source of the unwelcome and untimely noise, her hand still tingling from his touch.

They found a workman crouched in the passage, picking up a large brass wall plate. "Sorry, sir." He inspected the engraved surface. "No harm done."

"Good, good." Frederick glanced at her. "Well, as we are here . . ."

He showed her an opulent guest room and his wife's bed-chamber and adjoining boudoir, all fitted up in a lavish, oriental style popular with the recently ascended King George IV.

Rebecca did not like it at all, but refrained from saying so. Then again, she doubted she would like anything that changed the Wickworth of her youth.

He gazed dully at his deceased wife's toiletry items on the dressing table: hairbrush and combs, scent bottles, and rouge pot.

"I suppose it is time to discard these things."

Rebecca thought it wisest not to reply.

Before leaving the estate, Frederick took her out to the stable so she could see his old horse, Warrior, beginning to show his age in the greying of his muzzle.

He whickered at her over the stall and snuffled her hand. She scratched his wiry chin and stroked his ears.

"How are you, old boy?"

Frederick observed, "He remembers you."

She grinned and asked, "Whatever happened to Ladybird?"

"When you lost interest, we sold her to a family in Kempsey."

She nodded, not explaining why she had stopped riding. "Did you and your wife ride together often? I saw you once or twice before you married, but not after."

"No. She gave up riding after we wed."

Rebecca looked over, saw his pained expression, and compassion filled her. She did not ask why, afraid to pry further. Nor did she ask what he had started to say in the sitting room, *"Being with you again . . ."* Was he referencing their long friendship, as he had during the lawn bowls match, or something else?

Thinking back to their rides together and his many kindnesses to her as a child, Rebecca felt renewed gratitude. Yes, Frederick had later disappointed her, but now she decided to be thankful he cared at all. To appreciate his friendship, even if that was all it ever was.

As they left the stable together, she smiled over at him. "This has been lovely. Thank you for inviting me."

"My pleasure." Holding her gaze, he returned her smile.

Her heart gave an odd little somersault. That sparkle in his eyes, that dimple, that flash of white teeth made her breath hitch.

He added, "I have missed our times together."

Has he? Rebecca blinked in surprise and admitted, "So have I."

Upon their return to the abbey, Rebecca thanked Sir Frederick again and went up to her room. She wanted to reflect in private upon the moments they had shared and, eventually, to dress for dinner.

But she had no more than taken off her bonnet when a knock sounded at her door. She opened it, expecting Mary, but instead a surprise stood there, and not a happy one.

"John! What are you doing here?"

Her brother looked rather wild—hair hanging over his collar, in need of a wash and a cut. He hadn't shaved recently either. At least he was fully dressed, although his cravat was stained and untidy.

"Did you see him?" he blurted. "Ambrose Oliver?"

"Yes."

"Did you give it to him?"

"Yes, I—"

"Did he realize who you were?"

"I don't believe so. I went in as a chambermaid. Mr. Edge-combe knows I am staying here and may have said something. But if Mr. Oliver guessed, he hid it well."

"Then I'll wager he hadn't a clue. Never one to hide his feelings. Man's face is an open book."

"I hope you are right."

John's eyes gleamed with satisfaction. "You've done it, Becky. Well done. Now all we have to do is wait."

"Do you mean, for him to give it to Edgecombe?"

He scoffed. "Pfft. We'll see. I'm not holding my breath."

Then why did John seem so pleased?

She asked, "How did you know which room I was in? Did you ask at the desk?"

"No, I found Mary. She told me."

"Oh. Well. I had planned to stay one more night, but since you are here, perhaps we could walk back to the lodge together. Or hire Robb Tarvin's fly."

John paced across the room, looked out the window, and paced back again. "No. Let's stay the night."

"Why stay?" she challenged. "I have done what you asked."

He raked fingers through his hair, causing the fringe to stand up like a cockscomb. "Who knows, perhaps ol' Oliver will surprise me and ask his publisher to read the manuscript. If we see Edgecombe with it, I could reveal the author's true identity."

He looked around the small room. "In the meantime, I can sleep in the chair here, so we won't have to pay for another room."

He did not ask if she would mind, she noticed. But he was right, they were spending too much money as it was. He snored terribly, so she doubted she would get much sleep. Even at the lodge, she had heard him through the wall. At least it would be for only one night.

She told herself she ought to be glad John was out of the lodge. Out of his bed. Perhaps it was the beginning of better times. However, his fiery, almost feverish gaze vaporized her hope like a drop of water on a hot stove.

She took a steadying breath. "I have been taking my meals with Lady Fitzhoward in the dining room. Will you accompany me?" She quailed at the thought of Lady Fitzhoward's reaction to John's disheveled appearance.

"No, go on as usual and report back any developments. I had better stay out of Oliver's sight."

"Then I shall have something sent up for you."

"No, thank you. I am not hungry."

"Very well."

Someone knocked, and they both jumped.

Rebecca opened the door to Mary.

"Just making sure your brother found you all right."

"He did, thank you."

"Shall I help you change for dinner while I'm here?" Mary sent John a telling glance.

"I'll step out," he said, pausing in the doorway to look right and left before exiting. Was he so afraid to be seen by Mr. Oliver?

Mary lingered in the passage, and she and John stood for a few moments, heads near in whispered conversation.

Rose had suspected their attachment years ago, and that had been one reason, along with financial constraints, to dismiss the girl.

Mary came in and helped her dress. Rebecca had neglected to ask Joly, so she was grateful for the assistance.

She said nothing to Mary about John for the time being, and Mary avoided the topic as well. The secrets between them were piling up, and that, Rebecca realized, made them both vulnerable.

Thanks to the returned trunk, she decided to wear something she had not worn since arriving at the abbey—a dinner gown of ivory net over green satin. Mary curled and pinned her hair high atop her head and added a headband of green ribbon. The girl might not have been as skilled as Joly, but she was a deal more pleasant.

When Rebecca was ready, she thanked Mary and made her way downstairs.

In the hall, she saw Kitty Fenchurch fashionably turned out in an evening dress of white gauze trimmed with ruffles. Her parents stood a short way off, talking with Mr. Mayhew.

"Kitty! I did not expect to see you again so soon, but I am glad of it."

The young woman replied, "We are having dinner here. My parents in hopes of seeing Mr. Oliver, and I"—she lowered her voice—"in hopes of seeing Robb Tarvin."

"Oh?"

Kitty nodded. "We saw him briefly in the stable yard when we arrived, but he was on his way somewhere and sadly had little time to talk."

"Ah." She noticed Kitty's attention had been captured by

something behind her and turned to follow her gaze. Thomas was coming down the stairs with Miss Newport.

Kitty said quietly, "Mr. Wilford is handsome, one must admit. A shame he has to marry for money. Of course, that does not stop him from flirting with pretty females."

No, it does not, Rebecca silently agreed.

Then she looked back at her old friend and said, "By the way, I hope I do see you again, whether here or in Bath or Brighton. And if I do, I shall definitely stop to talk."

Kitty grinned. "I shall hold you to it!"

After greeting Mr. and Mrs. Fenchurch, Rebecca went to join Lady Fitzhoward, who stood at the desk of the maître d'hôtel. The older woman gave Rebecca's appearance a pursed-lip look of approval.

The dining room was soon crowded with hotel guests, including Mr. King, the mother-daughter pair, and the middle-aged couple, along with several visitors, like the Fenchurch family.

Sir Frederick and Thomas Wilford nodded from their usual table, and Miss Newport fluttered a girlish finger-wave.

At a quarter past seven, Rebecca looked over, but Mr. Oliver did not appear. Several others watched as well, likely having come to Swanford Abbey to see the famous author.

There was no sign of Mr. George—or was it Sergeant George?—either.

A few minutes later, Mr. Edgecombe entered alone, smiling around the room at the other diners with uncharacteristic cheerfulness before sitting down and ordering, Rebecca noticed, a bottle of champagne.

"Someone's pleased with himself," Lady Fitzhoward observed.

"Yes," Rebecca murmured in agreement. But for some reason, the sight of the cheerful publisher filled Rebecca with misgivings.

When Mr. Mayhew made his nightly round, making sure all his guests were well satisfied, Lady Fitzhoward asked, "And where is our illustrious author tonight?"

"Ah." Mr. Mayhew stepped closer and said in conspiratorial tones, "I have it on good authority that Mr. Oliver has hit upon a new book idea at last. According to his publisher over there, he is in his room working away feverishly. He asked for a tray to be sent up instead of coming down for dinner. Mr. Edgecombe, as you see, is a happy man. He even decided to take a room here."

Rebecca looked over as Mr. Edgecombe took a long sip of champagne, and her stomach soured at the sight.

"Jolly good for him," Lady Fitzhoward observed, "but some of your other guests do not look as pleased, no doubt hoping for a glimpse of the celebrated scribe."

The three of them glanced around and saw a few disgruntled-looking diners.

He said, "True. Alas, I cannot control the great man any more than his publisher can. Enjoy your dinner, ladies."

Later that night, after Mary helped her undress for bed, the young maid again lingered in the passage with John, giving Rebecca time to wash her face and clean her teeth before climbing into bed.

After a few minutes, John knocked softly and let himself in, closing the door quietly behind him.

"It's all right," Rebecca whispered. "I am awake."

"Don't stay up on my account. Get some sleep, Becky."

"Are you sure you will be all right on the chair?"

"Yes, as I assured you earlier."

"Will you not take off your coat at least? If you are cold, you may have my counterpane."

"Don't fuss so, big sister," he said lightly. He slouched in the armchair and spread the blanket Mary had given him over himself. "Good night."

"Good night . . . R. J.," she said, using his pen name.

She heard his low chuckle and closed her eyes, expecting him to begin snoring any minute.

The room remained quiet, and soon drowsiness lured her gently away.

Rebecca was already dreaming when someone knocked on the door, startling her awake. Her room was dark except for the faint glow of embers from her fire. Who would be coming to her door so late? She looked across the room, trying to see John. Had he gone out to use the water closet? As her eyes adjusted, the chair across the room became more visible—empty, except for a heaped blanket.

She was about to whisper, *"Who is it?"* when a deep male voice breathed, "Halloo . . . ? Anyone home?"

The voice sent uneasiness washing over her. Faintly familiar, but not John's. Nor Sir Frederick's either.

Confusion puckered her brow. An unknown man at her room at night? Should she answer? She was not dressed for a caller, especially a male one. Quietly climbing from bed, Rebecca reached for her dressing gown, just in case.

It might be a page with a message, she reasoned, but if so, would he not identify himself?

Whoever it was rapped again. "Are you in there?" he hissed. "Look, it's Ambrose Oliver. The author? I just want to speak with you a moment. Actually, just *see* you a moment and satisfy my curiosity."

161

Rebecca froze, heart pounding. *Please, God, don't let John return while that man is at the door!*

Oliver continued, "Mr. Edgecombe came to my room tonight and told me a young lady had sought him out. Wanted to talk to him about her brother—John Lane?"

The author's voice, Rebecca noticed, was a bit sloppy, as though he'd been drinking.

"It made me wonder if you and I had met quite . . . recently. You see, a certain young woman—perhaps a chambermaid, perhaps only dressed like one—came to my room earlier, asked me to read a manuscript or at least to pass it on to my publisher. You wouldn't know anything about that, would you?"

Rebecca cowered there near the closet, glad now she had not answered his knock. Surely he would give up soon and go away. He wouldn't try to force his way in, would he? Just in case, she tiptoed over and quietly turned the key in the lock.

As if in response, the door latch shook. Rebecca pressed a hand to her mouth to stifle a gasp. The nerve of the man!

Could Mr. Oliver somehow see her? Sense her presence? At the thought, her pulse pounded all the faster and she backed toward the balcony door and into the folds of its velvety draperies to hide.

Another rap, louder this time. "I know you are in there!" he goaded. Then he added, "At least, I think you must be."

A second male voice joined the first. "May I ask what you are doing?"

Sir Frederick. Relief flooded her.

"Oh, good evening. I simply want to speak to the guest in this room, if that is any of your business."

"I think it is. The occupant of that room is a friend of the family. A lady."

"I just need to see her. See if she is who I think she is."

"And I think you had better return to your own room."

Oliver challenged testily, "Don't you know who I am?"

Sir Frederick's voice grew closer and chillier. "Yes, I know who you are and what you are. And I repeat, go back to your own room."

"Ah . . . now I recognize that stern face of yours," the author slurred. "Sir Frederick Wilford. And is your . . . friendly wife with you? Oh wait. That's right. I heard she died. Do forgive me."

Frederick's voice dropped to a dangerous, grating tone. "I realize you have been drinking, so I will endeavor not to lose my temper. But I warn you, another word and I shall—"

"Now, now. No need for pistols at dawn. I'm going."

Rebecca could almost hear, and could certainly imagine, the large man stumbling and grumbling back through the long gallery to his room.

After a quiet moment, a soft knock sounded.

"Miss Lane? It's Frederick. Are you all right?"

Rebecca stepped to the door, laying her palm on the cool wood as though to touch him through it. His room was at the opposite end of the corridor, but she was thankful that he had been the one to hear and respond.

She turned the lock and opened the door, surprised to find him standing there hastily dressed in only trousers and shirt-sleeves—open at the neck. At the sight, her mouth went dry and the fear of moments before transformed into an emotion of a far different kind.

———

Frederick had been lying awake in bed, unable to sleep, when he'd heard a voice in the corridor. How glad he was now that he'd come out to see what the matter was. He stood there, aware of his partial state of dress but at the moment not caring. He would not rest until he assured himself Miss Lane was well.

Relief washed over him as Rebecca appeared in the doorway. Light from a nearby wall sconce illuminated her pale face, and her eyes shone large and luminous.

"Are you all right?" he asked again, not sure if she had heard his question.

"I am now, thanks to you," she softly replied, pulling her dressing gown more closely around her slender frame.

In the warm apricot glow of the candle, she looked sweet and beautiful and vulnerable, and he wanted very much to protect her. She glanced down shyly and something tugged in his chest, drawing him closer. The urge to touch her overpowered his self-control. A strand of hair fell across her face, and he slowly reached out and tucked it behind her ear. Then he cradled the side of her face with one hand and gently lifted until her eyes met his.

"Did he frighten you?" he asked.

"Yes," she whispered.

"You are safe." His thumb caressed her chin. What he wouldn't give to lean down and kiss her. At the notion, his heart banged against his ribs.

As if reading his thoughts, she breathed, "Frederick . . ."

His name said in that husky whisper quickened his desire to take her into his arms. His gaze dropped to her lips and the space between them dwindled.

Footsteps sounded in the corridor. Thomas appeared from around the corner, humming a tune as he came.

Dash it. Frederick blinked and stepped reluctantly away. "If you need me, send for me directly."

"I shall," she said. "Thank you again for . . . dispatching him. Good night."

He nodded. "Sleep well, Miss Lane." And with a slight bow, he turned and retreated to his own cold and lonely room.

There, he closed and latched the door with a sigh. Sleep would be difficult to achieve, he guessed, if his racing heart had anything to say about it.

11

Rebecca had planned to wait up until John returned and tell him about Mr. Oliver, but the chill of the room had forced her back under the blankets. As she lay there, the sweet tension of her encounter with Sir Frederick slowly dissipated and her eyelids grew heavy, but John still had not returned. Eventually, she fell back to sleep.

At some point in the night, Rebecca awoke to the sound of snoring. She glanced over and, by the faint glow of the moon, saw John slouched in the chair, leg over its arm, blanket under his chin, fast asleep. He looked like a sweet little boy . . . although the manly rattling snore ruined that image. Either way, she had not the heart to wake him and decided she would wait until morning to tell him about Ambrose Oliver's visit.

When she next awoke, dawn was just beginning to seep through the window. By its dim light, she looked over at the chair but found it empty, save a tossed-aside blanket.

Had John gone out to the water closet again? Or perhaps he'd simply wanted to give her privacy to dress. At the thought, she rose and washed her face in cold water from the pitcher, wishing Mary or one of the other maids would deliver warm water.

Eventually, she rang the bell pull to summon a chambermaid to help her dress.

No one came.

Odd.

It was early, but not unreasonably so.

Rebecca dressed herself as best she could and wrapped a shawl around her shoulders to cover a few unfastened buttons at the back of her frock.

She let herself from her room, hoping to find Mary or another maid coming up from the kitchen. Miss Joly, she knew, would be busy dressing Lady Fitzhoward.

She tiptoed down the night stair and through the cloisters, where the chill March air nipped at her. She shivered and pulled the shawl more tightly around herself.

Ahead of her, she saw a man slip through the door into the main hall. John? She wasn't sure but hurried her pace and followed, eager for the warmth of the hall's large fire.

Entering the reception hall, quiet at this time of day, she saw no one, but heard the front door close. Striding to one of the tall windows, she glimpsed the top of a man's head as he trotted down the stairs and out of view.

Curious, she hurried into the adjacent blue parlour and to its window, pushing aside the heavy drapery.

A man rapidly crossed the hotel lawn and climbed the stile into Mr. Dodge's field—bypassing the village instead of taking the lane into Swanford. Was it John? Whoever it was walked through the cold morning dew with neither hat nor greatcoat. Very much something her brother would do.

"Foolish creature," she muttered.

"Miss Lane. Is something the matter?"

She turned in surprise and clutched the edges of her shawl, hoping Sir Frederick would notice nothing untoward in her attire—or in finding her watching a man from the window.

"Oh! You startled me. G-good morning."

He stepped to the window beside her. "What are we looking at? See something interesting?"

"Oh, em, nothing. I thought I saw . . . someone I knew, but I can't be certain."

He squinted out into the grey fog. "I don't see anyone."

A scream and a crash rang out from above.

Rebecca jumped.

"What the devil?" Sir Frederick bolted out of the parlour and loped up the stairs by twos.

Rebecca followed more slowly, palms sweating, fearful of what they might find.

At the top of the stairs, Sir Frederick turned toward room three. As she reached the landing after him, movement to the left caught her eye—a black-gowned figure disappearing around the corner. Turning to the right, she saw something worse.

In the corridor outside room three, two bodies lay on the floor.

Clutching her heart, Rebecca gasped.

Sir Frederick put out his hand. "Stay back."

Jack George lay on his belly on the floor, legs sprawled, bloody wound on the back of his head, eyes closed.

A few yards away lay Mary, surrounded by shattered dishes and strewn food.

Bile climbed Rebecca's throat and her pulse beat a drum inside her skull. *No!*

Concern overrode her fear. Disregarding Frederick's command, Rebecca rushed forward and knelt at Mary's side. As a vicar's daughter, she had seen death before. Closer now, she was relieved not to see it in the girl's pale countenance.

"Mary?" She patted her cheek, still warm, though ghostly white. "Mary . . . ?"

Sir Frederick knelt at Mr. George's side, felt the side of his neck, and reported, "He's alive."

"Mary too. Thank God."

Mr. George groaned and his eyelids fluttered.

Frederick asked him, "What happened here?"

The injured man tried to push himself up.

"Lie still. You are injured."

Ignoring him, the man struggled into a sitting position with another groan.

"Don't know." He reached a hand to the back of his head and brought back fingers stained with blood. "Someone must have struck me." He peered at the prostrate maid through narrowed eyes, wincing against the pain. "She all right?"

Mary's eyelids fluttered open, much as Mr. George's had done.

"Mary, it's me, Miss Lane. I believe you fainted, poor dear. Lie still awhile." Rebecca balled up her shawl and gently placed it under Mary's head, heedless of her exposed shoulders.

A more pressing thought struck her. Why would anyone attack Mr. George unless it was to get at Ambrose Oliver?

Oh, John, tell me you did not . . . Oh, God, please no.

She rose, went to the door, and knocked. No answer. She tried the latch but found it locked. Returning to Mary's side, she fished the keys from the maid's apron pocket.

Then she straightened and hesitated, looking inquiringly at Sir Frederick.

He grimly met her gaze. "I will go in." He accepted the keys from her and inserted the one marked 3 into the lock.

Rebecca stepped near, afraid to go in, afraid not to.

Gently guiding her behind his back, he inched the door open. She followed him across the threshold. To steel her nerves, she drew a fortifying breath, and the faint smell of garlic met her nose.

Inside the room, the fire had burned to embers, but morning light shone through a stained-glass window high on the wall—a reminder that the room had once been part of a religious house.

Its muted green-and-gold light revealed a tableau more horrid than the one they'd come upon in the corridor.

For there on the chaise longue lay Ambrose Oliver, eyes open and unseeing, his ink-stained mouth ajar.

Sir Frederick walked over and pressed fingers to the man's neck. "Nothing."

Ambrose Oliver was dead.

Frederick and Miss Lane stepped back into the corridor. Mr. Mayhew and the head housekeeper appeared, roused by the commotion.

"What is it? What's happened?" the proprietor asked, expression harried.

Frederick replied, "Mr. Oliver is dead, I'm afraid."

"What?" The man's face elongated in horror. "How? It can't be."

"And yet it is so," Frederick said. "We shall have to summon the constable."

Mayhew nodded vaguely. "I can send a groom for Mr. Brixton."

Frederick pointed to the man now seated in the chair, bloody handkerchief pressed to his head, and to the pale young woman on the floor. "First, please send someone to fetch Dr. Fox, who is a guest here. Room six, I believe. These two have been injured."

The doctor and his wife had stayed on after the investors' meeting, enjoying some time away together.

Miss Lane spoke up. "Mary just fainted, I think."

"I must have," the maid said, struggling to sit up. Rebecca hurried to assist her.

"I saw Mr. George lying there dead, or so I thought! And then I felt sick and everything went black."

The housekeeper, Mrs. Somerton, shook her head in understanding. "And no wonder. What a shock!"

What a shock indeed.

A few minutes later, his old friend Dr. Fox arrived, Mr. Mayhew trotting behind.

"Hope you don't mind, Charles. I know this is not your specialty, but—"

"Not at all. Happy to help." He started toward the man with the head wound, but Mr. George gestured toward the chambermaid. "See to Mary first."

Frederick approved of the injured man's gallantry, even as he worried he might swoon from blood loss.

The physician examined Mary's eyes and limbs and listened to her heart, and he soon confirmed Miss Lane's assumption that the girl had merely fainted and was otherwise unhurt.

Together, he and Frederick gently helped the maid to her feet.

In motherly tones, Mrs. Somerton said, "A rest for you, my girl." She took one of Mary's arms and Rebecca the other, and the two women led her away.

Dr. Fox tended to Mr. George next, cleaning and bandaging his wound.

When he'd finished, Frederick asked Dr. Fox to confirm that Mr. Oliver was dead, and to give a preliminary opinion on the cause of death.

Dr. Fox agreed and gave Ambrose Oliver a cursory examination, careful not to disrupt the scene. "There's a head wound here. Looks like he was struck from behind, much as befell Mr. George, but with enough force to kill him."

Dr. Fox stepped around to look at Mr. Oliver's face, and then pointed to one of his hands. "Black smudges on his lips and fingers."

"I saw that too. Assumed it was ink."

"Probably right. Arsenic poisoning can cause blackening of the tongue and lips in some cases. But with all the ink on his hands and shirt cuffs, I agree ink stains seem far more likely." He grimaced. "Either way, I'm afraid there will need to be a coroner's inquest and perhaps an autopsy as well."

Frederick nodded his agreement. He was thankful for the older man's presence and experience, as he had never dealt with such a crime before. When his father died a few years ago, Frederick had assumed his title as baronet along with his duties as magistrate. During his brief tenure, he'd handled a few property squabbles, a poaching charge, and a drunken brawl. Nothing of this magnitude. Even in his father's time, Frederick did not recall anything as dire as murder in their sleepy little parish. He hoped he would not make a muddle of it.

Frederick asked his brother to notify Mr. Smith—the nearest of the county's elected coroners—and ask him to come as soon as possible. Thomas begrudgingly agreed and set off on horseback for the county town of Worcester, five or six miles away.

Frederick returned to room three, again surveying the scene. He noticed Oliver's room key on the side table and no sign of forced entry, nor any sign of a struggle.

Mr. Mayhew tentatively followed him into the room, wringing his hands. His eyes flickered toward the still form on the chaise and quickly away again. "I still can't believe it."

Frederick said, "I must ask you to leave everything as it is until the coroner arrives. Please see to it that this room is locked and not disturbed, even by staff. May take a few hours."

Mr. Mayhew nodded. "I understand." He turned away, then sent a regretful look back. "That chaise dated to Queen Anne's reign." He sighed heavily as he departed.

A wait of a few hours would be of no consequence to Ambrose Oliver. He was not going anywhere and was beyond help.

On the heels of Thomas's departure, the local constable, Noah Brixton, arrived. Mr. Mayhew led him upstairs.

The baker and father of two stood outside Oliver's room in Sunday best, hat in hands, hair slicked back. The young man had even less experience as constable than Frederick had as magistrate.

Mr. Brixton stepped close, lowered his voice, and asked, "What do you suggest, sir?"

"Perhaps we should search the hotel and grounds first, and then the local area? If this was done by an intruder, he might still be nearby. Or a villager might have seen someone leaving the abbey in a hurry."

"Good idea."

With Mr. Mayhew's help, several staff members were mustered to search the hotel for anyone lurking about who shouldn't be there. Meanwhile, Frederick, a groom, and Robb Tarvin each took a horse and followed the roads leading away from the abbey and out of the village to see if they could spy anyone fleeing the scene.

Neither search turned up anything—or anyone—suspicious.

An hour later, aided by the hotel's page and porters, the guests and staff were all summoned into the library and writing room, where Frederick had held the canal investors' meeting.

Rebecca Lane and a shaken but plucky Mary Hinton entered first. Miss Lane gave Frederick a small smile of encouragement. The trust and approval radiating from her eyes boosted his confidence.

Next Mr. George arrived, looking stoic but weary, a bandage around his head.

Other guests entered. Lady Fitzhoward, Miss Newport, Dr. and Mrs. Fox, and several others Frederick did not know by name. They settled into seats and whispered among themselves.

Mr. Mayhew came in and sat in one of the chairs. His staff gathered behind him but remained standing, backs against the walls.

Finally, Mr. Edgecombe appeared. Now all the people who seemed most likely to have a vested interest in Mr. Oliver's fate or to know something about it were present.

Frederick addressed Mr. Mayhew first. "Is everyone here?"

The proprietor surveyed the room. "I believe so."

"No one else has arrived or departed the hotel today?"

Mayhew turned to his commissionaire. Mr. Moseley replied, "We received our customary deliveries, but otherwise, no, not as far as I am aware."

Frederick looked at Miss Lane, thinking of the person she thought she'd seen from the window that morning, but she said nothing.

He decided not to single her out in front of all these people and instead began with introductions. "If we have not met, I am Sir Frederick Wilford, local magistrate. And this is our constable, Mr. Brixton."

Mr. Edgecombe spoke up. "I heard the others talking. Is it true? Is Ambrose Oliver dead?"

Frederick nodded. "I am afraid so."

"Dash it!" Mr. Edgecombe's voice shook, the tightened cords in his neck protruding. He removed his spectacles, pressed thumb and fingers to the bridge of his nose, and groaned.

Frederick was taken aback by the vehemence of the man's reaction. "I am sorry for your loss."

"Condolences won't help. He was the firm's highest-selling author. Thunder and turf! How did he die?"

Sir Frederick glanced at Dr. Fox, then said, "The coroner has been sent for, but it will be some time until we have an official verdict."

Edgecombe persisted. "An apoplexy, do you think? He was overweight and drank a great deal."

"Unlikely. Especially as Mr. George there was knocked sense-less while on watch outside his door. It appears Mr. Oliver was bludgeoned, but again, that is not yet official."

Murmurs and tense whispers rose, and Frederick made a downward gesture with his hands. "Please remain calm. As I said, the coroner has been summoned. In the meantime, did any of you see or hear anything that might help us apprehend whoever did this?"

Around him, people shifted and exchanged uneasy looks.

He urged, "Please speak up so we can take action directly." Again he paused, but still, no one spoke. "Well. If you think of something later, don't hesitate to let me know. Otherwise, I must ask everyone to remain in the hotel until further notice. Some of you may be asked to testify at the coroner's inquest."

Grumbles arose at this, and one man said he was sailing for Naples in three days' time and could not delay. Frederick promised to do all he could to speed the process.

Then Frederick allowed Mr. Mayhew and his staff to return to work. Keeping them all idle would have been a significant inconvenience, as the hotel served both staying guests in the dining room as well as villagers and wealthy travelers passing through in private chaises.

Frederick next excused the guests. They slowly rose and filed out of the room, looking uncertain and concerned.

At the door, Miss Newport turned back. "Are the rest of us in any danger here?"

"I think that unlikely," Frederick replied. "Especially now that Mr. Brixton is here."

The constable forced a smile and nodded reassuringly, no doubt wishing he were back in his bakery and had never agreed to serve a term as village official. Frederick did not blame him.

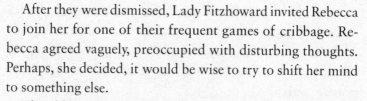

After they were dismissed, Lady Fitzhoward invited Rebecca to join her for one of their frequent games of cribbage. Rebecca agreed vaguely, preoccupied with disturbing thoughts. Perhaps, she decided, it would be wise to try to shift her mind to something else.

The older woman sat at the small table in her suite, setting out cards and cribbage board while Rebecca slowly paced back and forth, clutching trembling fingers.

Ambrose Oliver discovered dead. The very morning after John came to the hotel and then sneaked out again. His manuscript—the one she had delivered herself—in the author's room. What questions that might raise! She was glad now John had used a pen name.

Her employer frowned up at her. "Do sit down, Miss Lane. Watching you is giving me a neck ache."

Rebecca paused. "Sorry." Yet she remained standing, going to look out the window, only to turn back again.

Lady Fitzhoward studied her through narrowed eyes. "What has ruffled your petticoats?"

"Hm? Oh, well, you can imagine."

"Are you so upset over Mr. Oliver's death?"

"Of course."

Lady Fitzhoward positioned the pegs on the board. "I thought you were not acquainted with him, nor even read his books."

"Even so . . . Are you not upset?"

"Not in the least. But . . . I haven't a guilty conscience. Have you?"

"What?" Rebecca stared at her in alarm. Had the woman somehow divined her thoughts?

Lady Fitzhoward shrugged and began to shuffle the cards. "I know I had nothing to do with the man's death."

"Nor did I!"

"Certainly not. Just putting things into perspective for you. Now, do sit down and let's play." The older woman smirked. "In your distracted state, I might finally win."

While awaiting the coroner's arrival, Frederick stood in the hall talking quietly to Mr. Mayhew.

He recognized Ludlow Smith as soon as he entered—a thin, balding man, short on patience and in stature.

"Mr. Smith, thank you for coming."

"Sir Frederick," he acknowledged with a slight nod of deference.

Mr. Smith then turned to the proprietor and said brusquely, "Take me directly to the body, if you please."

"Right this way," Mr. Mayhew obliged, pulling keys from his pocket and leading the way.

Following them, Frederick said, "Dr. Fox happens to be staying here. Would you like him to go in with you? Lend his professional expertise?"

"Fox?" Mr. Smith said sourly. "The mad doctor?"

Frederick bristled. "He may run such an asylum now, but he is a fully qualified physician."

"Maybe later. First, I will go in alone."

Arrogant fool, Frederick thought.

While he and Mayhew waited out in the passage, Frederick asked the proprietor, "Who has keys to the guest rooms?"

"The maids, Mrs. Somerton, and myself. I also keep spares locked in my desk, which I lend as needed to a repairman, but no one has borrowed any for some time."

"Can you look to make sure no keys are missing?"

"Certainly. And of course each guest is given a key upon arrival. Oh, and I should clarify. Our policy is for the maids to knock and wait for the guest to invite them inside. They are only to use their key if they need to clean a room while a guest is absent."

"I see. And do the maids rotate or keep with the same rooms?"

"In general, they remain with the guests throughout their stay. That way, they learn their preferences."

"And the only maid who attended Mr. Oliver's room was Mary Hinton?"

"That's right."

"I believe the coroner will wish to speak with her. And with Mr. George."

If Smith does his duty, Frederick thought, but kept his doubts to himself.

He wished he had more confidence in Mr. Smith's competence as coroner. His father never had much faith in the man. Smith had spent a great deal of time and money getting himself elected, but his qualifications were in short supply. He was neither lawyer nor doctor nor officer of any kind. Worse yet, Frederick would be called upon to approve and pay the man's fee and expenses, and the county rates were high enough already.

Reluctantly agreeing that the death was indeed suspicious, the coroner issued a warrant to impanel a jury and instructed Mr. Brixton, as local parish official, to carry it out. Brixton hurried to do so, asking Frederick's help in coming up with a list of substantial householders to serve as jurors.

A few hours later, men from all over the parish descended on the hotel, and if Frederick was not mistaken, he saw a gleam of satisfaction in Mr. Mayhew's eyes, the man no doubt thinking ahead to the meals and drinks he might sell, and perhaps a few rooms as well.

The twelve selected jurors were led into room three, and Frederick wished he could be privy to what was said.

Before he closed the door, Mr. Smith asked if there was anyone present in the hotel who could positively identify the victim as Ambrose Oliver. Someone who had been well-acquainted with the man even before he arrived at the abbey.

Frederick nodded. "Mr. Edgecombe, his publisher, is here."

Smith nodded. "Summon him directly."

Frederick felt stung by the man's officious manner but had to admit it was a wise precaution for a man of Oliver's celebrity.

Mr. Mayhew said, "He asked for a room last night. We've put him in number five. Just give me a moment." The hotel proprietor hurried away down the passage.

Less than a minute later, Mr. Edgecombe appeared and stepped into Mr. Oliver's room.

The door was left open, Smith perhaps assuming it would be a brief visit.

"State your name, if you please," the coroner began.

"Thaddeus Edgecombe."

"Your relationship to the deceased?"

"I am—was—his publisher."

"And can you testify to this man's identity?"

"Sadly, yes. That is Ambrose Oliver, the author."

"How long have you known the victim?"

"My brother was better acquainted with him, but I have known him these last two years at least."

"Very well, thank you, Mr. Edgecombe. If you will wait outside, we shall likely have more questions for you shortly." Smith closed the door behind him.

A few minutes later, the jury and Mr. Smith filed out again. *Awfully brief*, Frederick thought.

The men proceeded down to the coffee room to begin their deliberations.

That, Frederick could witness, because coroners' inquests, often held in public houses or inns, were open to the public. He hoped Ludlow Smith would prove him wrong and perform his duty well.

12

Reconvening in the coffee room, Mr. Smith requested refreshments for himself and the jury, which Mr. Mayhew happily supplied. More expenses for Frederick to pay.

Once settled, Mr. Smith began, "As a reminder, gentlemen, we are here to establish the identity of the victim, as well as the time, place, cause, and manner of death—whether natural, accident, suicide, unlawful killing, or willful murder. We have identified the victim and the place is obvious. Now to establish the time of death."

Mr. Edgecombe was officially sworn in, and the coroner continued his examination.

"When did you last see Mr. Oliver alive?"

"Yesterday. We were supposed to have dinner together, but when I went up to his room, he said he couldn't stop; he'd come up with a book idea at last. I was so foolishly, stupidly relieved. . . ."

"And the time?" Smith asked.

"Oh. Sorry. That was shortly after seven. He asked me to send up a tray. I agreed and went down to my dinner, sure I would learn more about this new idea soon, perhaps even read a chapter or two." He shook his head. "Now my hopes have been dashed and the future of the company too."

"Is your firm a large concern?"

"No. Just me and a clerk now my brother is gone. William was Mr. Oliver's first publisher. Sadly, he died more than a year ago."

Questions spun through Frederick's mind, and he wrote them in his notebook. How had his brother died? Natural causes? He must have been fairly young.

"I see. And was Mr. Oliver in good health?"

The publisher shrugged. "As far as I know. He ate and drank too much, as was plain to see, but he never mentioned consulting a physician."

"And what were you and he doing here at Swanford Abbey?"

"His idea. Said he needed dedicated time and solitude to focus. To devise a clever plot. Promised me he would finally overcome his stagnation and write the successful novel he's long promised me."

"Did Mr. Oliver have any family?"

Edgecombe shook his head. "He was an only child, and his parents are long gone. Perhaps a few distant cousins, but no close relatives as far as I know."

"And his heir?"

"No idea. And I don't see how it matters as all anyone will inherit are his debts."

"Had Mr. Oliver any enemies?"

Edgecombe huffed. "The man was adored by strangers and despised by those who knew him best."

"Why?"

"I suppose it's not the done thing to speak ill of the dead. But Oliver was not an easy man to get on with—vain and selfish, not to mention a philanderer. But I was only his publisher. I did not meddle in his private affairs."

"Was he meeting anyone here at the hotel?"

The man looked down, then peered up through smudged spectacles. "Besides me? Not that I was aware of."

Frederick noted the hesitation, even if Smith did not.

"And was that the last time you saw him?"

Edgecombe shook his head. "I briefly went back to his room after dinner. Just to . . . tell him something."

Tell him what? Frederick wondered.

Smith asked, "And what time was this?"

"I suppose between nine and half past. I was tempted to press for more details about the book but didn't want to interrupt him for long. I decided to wait till morning. I took a room here instead of making the trip back and retired early."

"Can anyone verify that?"

"Well, I imagine one of the staff saw me go upstairs. And Mr. George would have seen me had I returned again to room three."

"And I suppose you engaged this Mr. George?"

"It was Oliver's idea, but I . . . I was glad of his presence. He was there to keep out distractions and keep Oliver writing."

"How unusual."

Edgecombe's eyes glinted. "If you say that, you clearly don't know any writers, nor ever struggled to write a book yourself. Plenty of authors long for seclusion to create, away from distractions and interruptions."

"Ah. Well, any other questions, men?"

The jurors shook their heads.

Mr. Smith added, "Please do stay on here, Mr. Edgecombe. In case other questions arise before the inquest concludes."

"If I must." The publisher rose and took a seat midway back.

Mr. Smith next deposed Mr. George.

After he was sworn in, Smith said, "State your full name and place of residence, please."

"Jack George. Originally from London, but have resided in Birmingham for the last ten years."

"And how do you know the deceased?"

"I had a shooting gallery, where men could practice rifle shooting, fencing, boxing, and the like. Mr. Oliver came for a few months to train in self-defense."

"I had a shooting gallery" echoed in Frederick's mind. Past tense. He noted it.

"Did Mr. Edgecombe pay you to guard the author?"

George shook his head. "With respect, sir, he thought it a colossal waste of time and money."

"Yet he agreed to pay the bill, apparently."

"The hotel bill, yes. But Oliver engaged me himself. Made me promise not to let him out except for dinner, nor let anyone in."

"Why, exactly? I can understand keeping others out for privacy's sake, but why did you need to keep him in?"

George grimaced. "He had a gambling problem. Always drawn to whatever club he might find or game he might join. It's how he lost all the money he made from his writing. He also trifled with women.

"He had the best of intentions to stay in his room and work, but he knew himself well enough to know he'd be tempted to slip out and find a friendly game or a friendly female. I was there to dissuade him. He was that desperate."

"Why desperate? Was his publisher pressuring him unduly?"

George shrugged. "Mr. Edgecombe needled and wheedled, bribed and threatened. But no. That's not why he was desperate."

"Then why?"

"He owed money to the wrong people—that's why. Impatient, dangerous people. No new novel, no more money to pay off his debts."

"Are you suggesting some . . . moneylender or bookmaker might have killed him?"

"It's possible. Two nights ago, Mr. Oliver pointed out someone as we left the dining room. He thought it might be Isaac King, a man he'd once borrowed money from. He'd heard Mr. King had moved to Italy, so he hoped he was mistaken. Told me to alert him if I saw the man anywhere near his room."

"Did Mr. King approach his room?"

Mr. George shook his head. "The only man I saw come to the room was Mr. Edgecombe. No others—not while I was awake, anyway, though a fellow has to sleep sometime. I stayed at my post from eight in the morning until midnight. It's possible someone came after I went to bed, but if Oliver had called out, I think I would have heard him. My room is just down the passage."

"You saw no one else enter the room all week?"

"Only a pair of chambermaids."

"Together?"

"No. Just the one at a time. Mary came most often, and the other came up once in her stead. Don't know her name."

A second maid? This was news to Frederick.

"And when was the last time you saw a maid enter room three?"

"Last night. When Mr. Oliver didn't go down to the dining room, Mary brought his dinner to him."

"And before you were struck, did you hear nothing unusual from the room?"

"Nothing."

"Did you see or hear anything at all from Ambrose Oliver that morning?"

"No, sir."

"And was the door to his room locked or unlocked?"

George shrugged again. "I assumed it was locked as usual. I had no reason to try it."

"And did you have a key?"

"No, I did not."

"And you appeared at your post as usual this morning?"

"Yes, sir."

"And does the maid come at the same time every morning?"

He nodded. "At nine. Mr. Oliver was particular about when he had his breakfast."

"So Mr. Oliver was alive at nine last night and was dead by nine this morning." Smith made a note, then looked again at the witness. "And you saw nothing of your attacker?"

"No, sir. I was taken unawares." Jack George dipped his head. "To my shame."

"Very well, Mr. George. Thank you. You may go for now, but please remain in the hotel until the inquest concludes. May take another day or two."

"And who's to pay for my room?" he asked. "I've had no wages from Mr. Oliver."

Smith looked above the other heads and coolly met Frederick's gaze. "Sir Frederick handles the expenses related to inquests. Apply to him."

After reviewing his notes, Smith called up the next witness. The chambermaid timidly approached the front of the room and was sworn in.

"State your full name and place of residence, if you please."

"Mary Ann Hinton. And I live here, in the staff quarters."

"And how long have you been employed here?"

"Going on a year now."

"And you were the chambermaid assigned to Mr. Oliver's room?"

She nodded. "Room three, yes. And several other rooms besides."

"Please describe the last time you saw Mr. Oliver alive."

"I took him his dinner last night."

"How did he seem to you? Worried about anything? Agitated?"

"I couldn't say, your honor. He doesn't really speak to me. He unlocked the door for me and sat down again, going straightaway back to work."

"He said nothing to you?"

Mary winced in concentration. "When I came in with the tray, he said, 'Ah, it's you,' but nothing else that I recall."

"And earlier that day?"

"Every morning was about the same. I'd take up his breakfast at nine sharp. Then I would gather his laundry, and tidy up a bit. He didn't want me to stay long."

"And were you the only maid who attended that room?"

She blinked rapidly. "Yes. For the most part. Now and again, one of us fills in for the other, when we're busy or running behind."

At her vague answer, questions began ringing in Frederick's mind, but Smith went on.

"And this morning?"

"Started out as always. I took his breakfast upstairs just before nine. Then I rounded the corner and saw Mr. George on the floor with a bloody head. I thought he was dead! I screamed and dropped the tray. I must have fainted because next thing I remember, Miss Lane was bending over me, patting my cheek and calling my name."

"Miss Lane?"

"She's a guest here. I used to work for her family years ago, so we are some acquainted."

"And what was she doing outside room three?"

The girl shrugged. "Heard me scream and came running. Sir Frederick Wilford too."

"Anything else you can tell us?"

"No, your honor."

"Very well. Thank you, Miss Hinton. We'll let you know if we need to speak to you again."

She bobbed a curtsy and returned to stand at the back of the room.

When it was time for dinner, Rebecca found Lady Fitzhoward sitting on a padded settee outside the coffee room, apparently listening to the proceedings.

"You go on, Miss Lane," she said. "Tell them to put it on my bill as usual. I am finding this too interesting to miss."

"But are you not hungry?"

Lady Fitzhoward waved a dismissive hand. "I'll have something sent to my room later."

So Rebecca endured an awkward dinner on her own. As it turned out, Lady Fitzhoward had not missed much. The courses were late in arriving and not up to usual standards, the staff no doubt put behind schedule and distracted by the day's events. All around her, diners at their tables whispered among themselves, eyeing the other guests askance as though everyone was a possible killer.

Sir Frederick was not at dinner either, no doubt sitting in on the inquest, interested or even duty-bound as magistrate to attend.

Thomas was there, and Miss Newport dined with him, defying convention. The two smiled at one another and talked in low, intimate tones throughout the imperfect meal.

Rebecca ate a few bites of lukewarm soup and fallen soufflé, her stomach rebelling. Dread filled her until there was little room for food.

Had John . . . ? No. She could not imagine him striking anyone so violently. This was the lad who'd opposed his father's suggestion he enlist in the military because he hated the idea of bloodshed. Then again, John had been bitterly angry with the author and possessed a passionate temper.

Why had John come to the hotel . . . really? Especially when he rarely went anywhere. She saw him again in her mind's eye, stealing across Dodge's field early that morning. Had he done what he came for?

Please, God, let it not be true.

❧

After some additional discussion, Mr. Smith consulted his pocket watch. "The hour grows late." He turned to the hotel proprietor. "Mr. Mayhew?"

The owner snapped to attention, clearly ready to testify. "Yes, sir!"

"At your ease, Mr. Mayhew." Smith narrowed his eyes and worked his mouth as though sucking food from his teeth. "As you know, I questioned Mary Hinton, as she was directly involved, but I don't think it will be necessary to depose all of your sundry staff. However, I charge you with questioning them yourself, and if any of them has something useful to report, inform me tomorrow and we will hear from him or her then."

"Yes . . . sir," Mayhew repeated with far less enthusiasm. He added, "And might I summon the undertaker?"

"I don't see why not. I believe we are finished in there, unless any of the jurors wish to see the room or the body once again?"

Around the room, heads shook.

"You are free to do as you like with the room. We will plan to reconvene here at eleven a.m. tomorrow. That should give you sufficient time to question your staff." Smith turned a page in his leather-bound diary, then looked up. "One more thing, Mr. Mayhew, before you go. Most of the jurors are local men, but I trust you can find a room for me and any other outliers who have traveled some distance to be here?"

"Of course."

Mr. Smith gave a thin smile. "Sir Frederick will see to the charges."

Although the inquest had not yet officially adjourned, Frederick closed his notebook and followed Mr. Mayhew from the coffee room, surprised to see Lady Fitzhoward lingering nearby, apparently listening to the inquest from the corridor.

He nodded to acknowledge her and hurried on, catching up with the proprietor outside his nearby office door. He said, "I am surprised Mr. Smith asked you to question the staff yourself."

The man sighed. "As if I haven't enough to do with monthly invoices and orders due."

"I could question them for you, if you like," Frederick offered. "As magistrate, I have some experience and would like to be useful."

"Really? That is kind of you. Yes, if you would not mind."

Lady Fitzhoward walked in their direction. "Excuse me, please."

They moved to one side to allow her to pass. As she did, she looked up at him. "Careful, Frederick. Don't ask questions for which you don't really want to know the answers."

He flashed a look into her eyes, surprised at her breach of etiquette, as well as the strange warning. But she met his gaze without contrition and walked on.

Mayhew waited until she was out of earshot, then lowered his voice. "I take it you two are acquainted?"

"You would think so, would you not?"

Never one to criticize a guest, Mr. Mayhew said no more about the lady and returned to the former topic. "I accept your generous offer, if you are in earnest. When would you like to start?"

"Tonight, if possible."

"Well, most of my staff rise early, so I hate to keep them up too late. Perhaps you could start with the night clerk and the barman now and question the others first thing in the morning?"

"Very well. Where would you suggest we meet?"

Mayhew considered. "Perhaps the small office adjacent to mine. I used to employ an assistant manager but no longer."

"Whatever is most convenient."

"In that case, if you could question the night clerk and the barman at their posts, that would be most helpful. I will ask Mrs. Somerton to set up a schedule for the others to come to the office tomorrow morning."

"Excellent. Thank you, Mr. Mayhew."

"Thank *you*." The proprietor expelled a heavy sigh. "If it's not one thing, it's another. I hope a death in the hotel won't put people off coming here."

"Perhaps for a time, but people have short memories."

"I pray we can last that long."

Frederick tilted his head to survey the man. "I thought things were going well?"

"Oh, they are. Of course they are. Forgive me, I should not speak my every thought aloud. No need to trouble you with my petty concerns. I shall bid you good night and get back to the pile of paperwork on my desk."

Frederick nodded, then said, "Since the coroner is finished with room three, might I take another look?"

Mayhew hesitated. "I suppose that would be all right."

"You are welcome to supervise."

"I don't think that will be necessary, you being magistrate." The man added wryly, "And me being behind on everything." He quickly retrieved a key from his desk. "Here's the spare. I shall ask the undertaker to come in the morning. Just remember to lock the door when you leave."

Frederick thanked him and returned to the coffee room. Noah Brixton stood in the passage, leaning his head back against the wall, eyes heavy.

"Go home, Brixton. You'll need to rise in a few hours."

"Only if I want my bread to rise too." The young baker chuckled, even though weariness etched lines around his eyes.

Frederick clapped his shoulder. "I'll remain vigilant tonight. Get some sleep."

"Thank you, sir. The missus is more exhausted than I with the new babe to feed round the clock. But I'll be back in the morning, soon as I can."

"I know you will."

Inside, the inquest adjourned and the coffee room began to empty. Frederick caught Mary Hinton, Mr. George, and Mr. Edgecombe as they were leaving.

"May I ask you three to come upstairs for a few minutes? I would like your help in determining if anything is missing from Mr. Oliver's room. I thought, between you, you might be able to account for the man's belongings." Theft might have been motive for a break-in that resulted in Mr. Oliver's death, Frederick reasoned, though he kept that theory to himself.

Mary nodded her agreement. The men exchanged looks of surprise but raised no objection.

Frederick led the way with the key, while the others followed him upstairs.

He unlocked number three, saying, "Give me one moment."

Entering first, he saw the room appeared the same as it had that morning, except that the smoldering embers in the grate had gone cold. He spread a sheet over Mr. Oliver's body in deference to Mary. He noticed the man's key, watch, and purse lying on the side table and looked briefly inside, recording the contents in his notebook.

Then he stepped back out. "We'll do this one at a time, if you don't mind."

The chambermaid entered first, nervously plucking at her apron.

"You mentioned you were in here just last night, is that right?" Frederick asked.

"Yes, sir. When I brought up his dinner."

Frederick gestured around the room. "Notice anything missing? Anything not where it was?"

She looked around, studiously avoiding the shrouded figure, brow puckered in concentration.

"Take your time," he encouraged.

"Hard to tell, sir. I seem to remember more paper. Stacks of the stuff. Though I might be mistaken." She pivoted around once more. "Nothing else seems different."

"And was it customary for him to leave his key there on the table, and his watch and purse in plain view?"

"I don't know about his key, but the other two, yes, sir."

"Thank you." Frederick paused, then said, "I am also wondering about something Mr. George said during the inquest about a second maid. Did someone else attend this room yesterday?"

"Yesterday?" Mary frowned up at the ceiling as though thinking back . . . or was she avoiding his gaze?

"I . . . don't think so. Not that I recall."

"Are you sure?"

She shrugged. "Honestly, all the mornings run together. It's the same job day after day."

Not thoroughly convinced, yet doubting it could have any bearing on the author's death, Frederick decided to let it pass for the present.

"Very well. That is all for now."

Next, he invited in Mr. Edgecombe to look at the room.

"I doubt I can help," the publisher said. "I came to see him a few times but barely got past the threshold."

"The chambermaid seems to remember there being more paper in the room. Any idea why that might be?"

Edgecombe shook his head. "He'd finally come up with a new idea and was busy writing, yet I can't imagine he had time to write more than a few chapters. I had not yet seen them. He sent word that he needed a dictionary and more ink but nothing about paper."

Frederick said, "I looked in his purse and found only three pound coins and sixpence. Would he have had more money with him?"

"You suspect robbery?" The publisher snorted. "Unlikely. Oliver was broke."

"A stranger would not have known that."

Edgecombe shrugged. "Maybe."

Finally, Mr. George stepped reluctantly into the room.

He said, "I don't know that I would notice anything missing. I talked to him at the door now and again when he wanted something. Otherwise, I stayed out there. He didn't exactly invite me in to chat—not when he'd hired me to stand guard outside."

"I see. The chambermaid thought there had been more paper in the room. That mean anything to you?"

Mr. George looked thoroughly bewildered. "More paper? No, sir. No idea. He did ask me to send a message to Mr. Edgecombe about needing a dictionary and ink but nothing about paper."

"Very well. Thank you, Mr. George."

When the three had left, Frederick shut his notebook with a snap. The exercise had availed little, but he was not ready to give up. He still felt that the man's room, or the man himself, might hold more evidence than Mr. Smith had bothered to seek.

13

Notebook still in hand, Frederick walked down the corridor and knocked on Dr. Fox's door. Fox and his wife were playing a game of chess, but the physician said he would join him in a few minutes.

As Frederick walked back to room three, Miss Lane came up the main stairs.

"Good evening, Sir Frederick. We missed you at dinner."

"I attended the inquest."

"So I guessed."

She glanced from him to the door he was hovering near. "What are you up to, if I may ask?"

"I was just about to go in again and see if the coroner missed anything. Dr. Fox will be joining me shortly. Mr. Mayhew lent me a key."

She asked, "May I look too?"

He was taken aback by her request. There was still a body in the room, after all, although at least now it was covered.

"If . . . you would like."

"I would."

Why was she so interested in the man's death?

They entered, and he closed the door partway, glad Dr. Fox would soon be there for propriety's sake as well as for his medical opinion.

As they waited, Frederick thought again of the author approaching Miss Lane's room the previous night. Was he simply pursuing an attractive woman, or had he sought her out for some other reason?

He asked, "When Mr. Oliver came to your door, was he—forgive me—seeking an assignation, or . . . ?"

"Oh. I don't know. I hope not." She shuddered, a flush rising to her cheeks.

He added, "When I confronted him, he said something like, 'I want to speak to the guest inside—to see if she is who I think she is.' Seemed odd to me. When he knocked, did he call your name? Even know your name?"

She looked away in recollection. "Come to think of it, he never called me by name."

"Ah." Frederick concluded that Oliver had probably seen a young woman enter her room at some point and simply thought he'd try his luck.

She turned back to him. "Thank you again for sending him away."

He nodded, and the two of them began searching the author's room.

The desk held many quills in various stages of sharpening. Ink pots—some half-empty. And a few thick, leather-bound notebooks. He picked up the top one, flipping through several pages filled with scrawled lines. Might this be the beginning of the great book idea Oliver had promised his publisher? It seemed unlikely.

He moved to the chaise longue, unnerved anew to realize a dead man lay beneath that makeshift shroud.

Unbidden, a memory revisited him. Marina's body, lying broken and still, her head at an unnatural angle. Him staring in horror, then feeling for any signs of life and finding none. He'd whipped off the Holland cloth from a nearby settee and laid it over her, one shoeless foot sticking out, the missing kid slipper halfway down the stairs. . . .

With effort, he blinked away the horrid image.

On the octagonal writing table beside the chaise stood another quill propped in ink and two wadded pieces of paper. Might a clue lie within?

He unfolded the first wrinkled page and discovered not discarded words as he'd supposed, but a sketch. An amateurish drawing of a woman with dark eyebrows, wearing a mobcap and apron. Why draw the chambermaid? At least the drawing wasn't at all suggestive. Unflattering, actually. The man's drawing skill was even worse than his writing.

On the back were scrawled the initials *R. J.* followed by a list of names: *Rachel, Rosalind, Ruth, Rose, Rebekah* . . . Had the author been trying to remember someone's name? Or to name a character?

On the second discarded paper, Frederick found more words. Title ideas, he guessed. *The Last Temptress, Ancient Deeds, The Wronged Widow, Valley of Ashes,* and *The Doom of Druggers End.*

He tucked the pages into his own notebook. Then he looked over and saw Miss Lane digging through the desk and dressing table.

He asked, "Are you looking for something in particular?"

She glanced at him, then around the room, a line between her brows. When had she grown old enough to have such a line, even a charming one like that?

"I am surprised not to find more paper. His publisher told

us Mr. Oliver was writing away feverishly, so I assumed we would find a manuscript in here . . . or at least the pages he'd written so far."

He recalled Mary Hinton mentioning missing paper as well. "There is some writing in these notebooks, if you'd like to take a look."

She walked over to join him and flipped through the first notebook he'd indicated.

"No, this is not it," she murmured.

"How . . . would you know that?" he asked, his uncertainty now tinged with suspicion.

"I mean, these are not the first pages of a novel. These are just quick descriptions of several different ideas, and I'd wager *not* the one he'd missed dinner to write." She read aloud, "*The ghost of the abbess of a long-destroyed nunnery haunts a modern day 'Lady Abbess,' the mistress of a brothel.* Ugh." She shuddered. "I am glad he did not live long enough to write *that.*" Her gaze flew to his. "Forgive me. I suppose it is disrespectful to speak ill of the dead."

"I am the last person to judge you for that, I assure you."

Rebecca glimpsed a corner of paper sticking out from beneath the chaise and bent to retrieve it. She held up the page and saw written there, *Ashes From the Fire by Ambrose Oliver.*

She read the lines that followed, and her heart hitched.

In one of those beautiful valleys in which the Thames flows through lush green meadows and chalk hills stood an isolated villa in the bosom of an old wood, the home of a respectable but reclusive widow. . . .

Rebecca shook her head, not quite able to believe it. Here were her brother's words in another hand—not Rose's, but a man's handwriting—although the title had been changed slightly, and the author's name completely.

How could he? How dare he?

"Did you find something?" Sir Frederick asked.

"I did. I believe this is what he had been writing. Unless there are more pages somewhere, he did not get very far." She looked around the room again. Where was John's manuscript?

Sir Frederick squatted near the hearth. She walked over and lowered herself beside him. She saw the curled remnants of several pieces of paper among the ashes. An inferior draft used for kindling? Or destroyed evidence of plagiarism?

With careful fingers, he extracted a charred corner. It crumbled into dust.

He tried again, retrieving another fragment, and this time managed to lay the curled piece onto his palm. She peered over his shoulder. A few words were still discernible: *After the Fire by R. J. Stephens.*

The words were written in a hand she did recognize. Rose's.

"*After the Fire*," Sir Frederick read aloud. "Beyond the irony, the words mean nothing to me. Perhaps they would mean something to Mr. Edgecombe. And why would Mr. Oliver be using a pen name?"

"How many more pages are in there?" Rebecca asked, ignoring his question. "A whole book's worth?"

He frowned into the rubble. "I don't think so. Only a dozen or so, if I had to guess."

Sir Frederick carefully tucked the remnant between two pages of his notebook, and took the full page from her as well.

Had Ambrose Oliver been burning John's pages as he rewrote them? It certainly appeared that way.

Then where were the rest of them? Again she thought of John. Had he come to reclaim what was his?

Knuckles rapped and the door opened wider. Dr. Fox appeared in its threshold.

Sir Frederick said, "Thank you for coming."

"Glad to." The physician added wryly, "Jane won again, and I was not eager to start another match and suffer another defeat."

Sir Frederick said, "You remember Miss Lane, I trust?"

"Indeed. Good evening." The doctor bowed and Rebecca curtsied in reply.

Sir Frederick gestured to the shrouded figure. "Just wanted you to take one more look. Make sure we didn't miss anything. The undertaker will be here in the morning."

Dr. Fox nodded. He flipped back the sheet and studied the victim once more, starting with the back of his head. Rebecca was glad she would not be able to see the wound from where she stood.

"It's clear Mr. Oliver was struck with enough force to cause a serious contusion."

"Enough to kill him?"

"Apparently."

Sir Frederick frowned and looked from the victim to the door and back again. "What I don't understand is this. If Mr. Oliver was sitting there on the chaise, across the room from the door, how did his assailant sneak up on him to deliver the blow? Assuming whoever it was stole a key or picked the lock and let himself in, Oliver would have heard the door open and seen the person approach, likely with weapon in hand. Why sit there so complacently, so vulnerably? Why not rise to his full height and face his foe? Much harder to deliver a blow to the top of a man's head when he is well over six feet tall."

The older man nodded. "Good point. Perhaps he had fallen asleep and was a heavy sleeper."

"Or maybe he'd been drugged . . . or even poisoned."

Rebecca's pulse began to accelerate.

The doctor stared at him. "I say. What a thought."

"Why not?"

"Well, if true, who could have done it? The maid who brought his meals?"

Rebecca gasped. "Mary would never—!" She amended, "Not knowingly, that is."

Sir Frederick said, "Or the chef himself or anyone in the kitchen could have done it, and Mary unknowingly delivered drugged coffee or poisoned soup." He gestured to a tray holding a bowl, a cup, and a plate scraped clean. "There's what remains of the meal sent up last night."

Dr. Fox winced in thought. "If you are right, the culprit gave the drug time to work, then returned, struck the guard, and went inside to finish off the author."

Rebecca asked, "Why would the chef wish him any harm?"

"Perhaps he complained about the food."

Dr. Fox snorted. "Seems unlikely."

"I agree, though people have killed for lesser reasons."

Rebecca regarded the coffee cup and soup bowl, both mostly empty apart from murky dregs. Might Ambrose Oliver have been drugged? Probably only one of the hotel staff would have opportunity to adulterate food or drink sent up to the man, she reasoned, trying to reassure herself. But why would any of them do so?

Apparently having a similar thought, Sir Frederick lifted and sniffed both cup and bowl, then offered them to Dr. Fox. "I don't smell anything. But are not some poisons odorless?"

"I believe so."

"Is there any evidence he's been drugged or poisoned?" Rebecca asked, hoping her anxiety did not show.

"Nothing obvious. Not without an autopsy." Dr. Fox pointed

to Mr. Oliver's face and hands, and explained for her benefit, "We noticed these black smudges before, here on his lips and fingers, and assumed it was ink. Probably is. Arsenic poisoning can cause blackening of the tongue and lips, but with all the ink on his hands and shirt cuffs, I still think ink stains seem far more likely."

Sir Frederick nodded. "Any idea how long he has been dead?"

"I am no expert in postmortems, I'm afraid. I would estimate at least an hour or two before I first examined him this morning."

Sir Frederick said, "Logically speaking, he would have been killed soon after Mr. George was attacked. Someone struck George this morning between eight and nine. How long would you guess he remained senseless before Mary saw him and shouted the alarm? Would he have remained senseless a full hour?"

"He has a nasty head wound, true enough, so it's quite possible."

"So that probably means whoever did this struck Mr. George shortly after eight, and with him out of the way, somehow forced his way in and delivered the fatal blow to Mr. Oliver."

Rebecca thought of an alternate solution. She hesitated to suggest it but decided Mr. Oliver would probably not have invited her brother into his room. She said, "There is another option that requires neither drugs nor poison nor lock picking. Mr. Oliver might have known whoever it was and willingly let him or her in, and sat back down. Then this person could have taken him by surprise."

"And the weapon?" Frederick asked.

She thought, then said, "Perhaps concealed in a sleeve or under a cloak. Or it might have been something already here in the room."

"Good point."

They looked around for likely objects. The water jug, perhaps? No, the earthenware would have shattered. The fire iron? Frederick picked up the iron and wiped the end with his handkerchief. No trace of blood.

Dr. Fox asked, "Was the door unlocked this morning when you got there?"

Frederick shook his head. "It was locked. We used the maid's key to open it."

"To lock the room from the outside would require a key. Is Mr. Oliver's room key missing?"

"No, it's right there on the table," Frederick replied. He added, "The chambermaids have keys, as do Mr. Mayhew and Mrs. Somerton. Perhaps one of theirs has gone missing. I asked Mayhew to look into that, and have not yet heard back."

Frederick stepped to one window, then the next. "Latched. No one went out this way."

Dr. Fox picked up the cup and bowl. "There are a few tests for arsenic, although some dispute their validity. I could ask a colleague to examine the contents for us."

"Excellent," Sir Frederick replied. "Please do."

A current of urgency rippled through Rebecca. She was tempted to run off to the lodge to confront John right then but worried she'd be seen sneaking away and look suspicious. She was also reluctant to face her growing suspicions about who may have killed Ambrose Oliver. Perhaps someone with a close relationship to the chambermaid, who had a key to the man's room. . . .

After a few more minutes of discussion, the three departed. The doctor bid them good night and walked away. Rebecca, however, lingered in the passage. As Sir Frederick fished out the spare key to lock the door, she stepped closer and nervously licked dry lips.

"I know you asked us to remain in the hotel, but would it be all right if I made a brief visit to the lodge in the morning? I imagine word has spread quickly around the village, and I don't want Rose or John to worry. I only want to assure them I am all right. I would not be gone long."

He considered, then nodded. "Very well. But come back directly. It is unlikely the coroner will summon you, although he might take it into his head to do so, since you and I discovered the body."

"I will be quick," she said and turned to go.

He called after her. "I have been wondering. Early this morning, you said you thought you saw someone you knew outside the abbey?"

For a moment she stilled, heart pounding. Then she feigned an indifferent shrug. "In hindsight, I think it must have simply been Mr. Dodge. His field abuts the abbey grounds. It was foggy, you will remember."

"True."

But Sir Frederick did not look convinced.

After Dr. Fox and Miss Lane had returned to their rooms, Frederick walked downstairs to the hall. There he approached the desk and addressed the night clerk, explaining his reason for coming.

The young man nodded. "Mrs. Somerton mentioned you'd be stopping by."

The clerk gave his name and length of employment, and then Frederick asked, "Did you notice anything out of the ordinary late last night or in the small hours this morning? Anyone asking for Mr. Oliver's room number or loitering about?"

"No, sir."

"Do you stay on duty all night?"

"In a manner of speaking. I sit here at the desk until midnight, then I leave a sign near the bell and go into the back room to sleep. There's a cot there. Very kind of Mr. Mayhew to provide it. And the truth is, I rarely get summoned between midnight and seven. It's an easy job, really."

"But couldn't someone steal a key or get into the cash box while you sleep?"

"They could do. Which is why I lock them in that drawer there before I leave the desk unattended."

Frederick nodded. "So if someone were to enter or leave the hotel in the small hours, you wouldn't see them. Anyone could come and go as they pleased and commit a crime leaving no one any the wiser?"

The young man's Adam's apple rose and fell. "Not . . . exactly. I lock the front door there at midnight. And the barman locks the back door when he closes up for the night at one or two."

"And they remain locked until . . . ?"

"Seven. I unlock them before I go off duty."

"I see. Well, thank you. If you think of anything else, do let me know."

Next Frederick went belowstairs to the gentlemen's bar and billiards room. Dr. Fox and Thomas were there before him, preparing for a game, and an older gentleman sat alone near the door, cigar in hand and cognac glass at his elbow.

Frederick introduced himself to the barman, Mr. Heck, a small man with pointed features and merry eyes.

After a similar preamble, Frederick asked, "Did you meet Mr. Oliver during his stay?"

Mr. Heck looked one way, then the other, as though suspecting eavesdroppers. "I did, as a matter of fact. He asked me to keep it quiet-like. As he's gone now, I don't think it will do any harm. He came down a few times quite late. Had a drink and played a few hands of piquet with the fellows."

"I see. So much for sequestering himself in his room to write."

"Aw. A fellow has to take time off now and again. Keep the old cogs going."

"Did he meet any former acquaintances here, as far as you know? Anyone angry to see him? Threaten him?"

"Pah! Nothing like that. In Swanford? This may be an old convent, but it ain't London's Covent Garden!"

Frederick managed an awkward, closed-lip smile, then lowered his voice. "And that older gentleman, sitting alone. I saw him at dinner the other night." Mr. Oliver had clearly noticed him as well, Frederick recalled. "Do you happen to know his name?"

"I do. That's Mr. King. Ike King."

"*The* Ike King?"

"Yes, sir. But it ain't what you think. He lives abroad now with his new lady. He's only here in England to visit family."

"Did he ask you about Ambrose Oliver?"

The barman shook his head. "Not a word."

"And were the two men in here at the same time? Did they interact?"

"No. King has kept himself to himself, as far as I've seen."

"I see. Well, thank you, Mr. Heck."

Frederick crossed the room, planning to talk to his brother and Dr. Fox for a few minutes before turning in for the night.

Thaddeus Edgecombe entered just then, approached the bar, and ordered a whiskey.

Frederick walked over to him, pulling his notebook from his

pocket. "Mr. Edgecombe, good. I wanted to ask you about a few things we found in Mr. Oliver's room."

"A first-rate novel, I hope," the publisher said bitterly and downed his drink.

Frederick opened his notebook and spread out the page Miss Lane had spotted beneath the chaise.

"Is this Mr. Oliver's handwriting?"

The publisher studied it. "Yes." He murmured, "*Ashes From the Fire by Ambrose Oliver. . . .*" He read the opening lines silently, then said, "Tell me there is more."

"Not that we found."

Frederick also laid out the charred remnant, sketch, and list of titles.

"These mean anything to you?"

The man's gaze landed on the words *After the Fire by R. J. Stephens*. His eyes hardened. "I recognize neither the hand nor the name. Do you?"

"No." Frederick tucked away the pages.

Edgecombe ordered a second whiskey.

When the man's drink arrived, Frederick said, "You know, rather than trusting me and young Mr. Brixton to get to the bottom of this, you could engage a Bow Street runner. Since Mr. Oliver had no close family, it would likely fall to you to do so. Brixton and I will do what we can, of course, but in all honesty, we have little experience with murder."

"And the coroner?"

Frederick shook his head. "His role is to decide the cause and manner of death, not to track down and punish the perpetrator. That's a gap in our current system, unfortunately."

Edgecombe frowned. "It would be up to me to pay this runner, and what would be the benefit? There is no bringing back Oliver now."

"No," Frederick agreed. "Although justice would be served if the killer is apprehended." He watched Edgecombe with wary speculation. There had certainly been no love lost between publisher and author. Apparently Edgecombe had little interest in justice—he merely lamented the loss of his milch cow.

Frederick said, "You mentioned your brother's death. May I ask how he died?"

Edgecombe nodded. "Heart failure. He'd been under a great deal of pressure."

"Financial pressure?"

"Yes." Edgecombe threw back the second whiskey and slammed the glass to the table. "Ambrose Oliver drove him to an early grave."

14

The next morning, as arranged, Frederick began interviewing the rest of the staff. The effort required him to rise earlier than usual, but he didn't mind. He was eager to do his part and discover any useful information—and hopefully before the inquest reconvened, so he could attend the proceedings.

True to his word, Mr. Brixton returned to the abbey early as well. He now stood in the hall awaiting the arrival of the undertaker and would join Frederick later.

Mrs. Somerton sent staff members in, one after another with little pause in between, beginning with the kitchen maids, grooms, and porters. He received little information from any of the young, green lot.

Next came the chef, Monsieur Yves Marhic, a dark-haired man with bushy brows, whose black whisker points showed through his fair skin, although it was clear he had recently shaved.

Frederick regarded with interest the man dressed in white. French chefs were in high demand. He was curious why this one chose to remain at the Swanford Abbey Hotel, of all places. After greeting him, Frederick asked, "I wonder . . . do you like working here, Monsieur?" He added lightly, "In a place rumored to be haunted by nuns?"

The chef shrugged. "This does not trouble me. My own sister is such a one. Sadly, she lives far from here, and I do not see her often."

Frederick nodded, then launched into his official questions. "Mr. George mentioned that a chambermaid besides Mary Hinton delivered Ambrose Oliver's breakfast tray two days ago. Mary seems to have no recollection of this. Do you know who that might have been?"

The chef shook his head. "*Non. C'est* Mary. She delivers to room three *le petit-déjeuner* most excellent. Oh, and *le dîner* one night also. Alas, she could not deliver yesterday. Instead she drop the whole tray. Every morsel wasted." He spread his fingers wide. "All my work. Poof."

"I know Mary carried up the breakfast tray the morning Mr. Oliver died, but I am asking about the morning before that."

"Before?" The bushy brows lowered. "Mary, as I say. *Tous les jours*, Mary."

"Did you actually see her?"

"*Oui.* I am very particular *la cuisine* prepared to each guest's tastes be delivered to the correct room at the correct time."

"Would anyone else have seen her?"

Again he shrugged. "Perhaps Jacques, *mon* assistant. But with his head in the pots, eh, he is not the keen observer I am."

"And did Mr. Oliver enjoy your cuisine?"

"*Bien sûr! Mais*, the first morning, he sent back the marmalade. Detests the marmalade. And my coffee. My aromatic French *café*? Too strong, he says! Never before has my coffee been criticized. Alas, Monsieur Mayhew insists the patron must have his way. So. *Alors.* I make him the weak English coffee. *Beurk!*"

"You were angry with him."

The chef laughed. "You think I kill him for criticizing my coffee? Ho! A crime in France, perhaps. But not here, where an Englishman would not know a good cup of coffee if he bathed in it! *Héhéhé* . . ." The chef held his rounded stomach and laughed until tears leaked from his eyes.

"I did not intend to amuse you."

"*Merci, monsieur.* I have not laughed so well in many ages." He wiped his eyes with the hem of his apron.

"And had you any other reason to dislike Mr. Oliver?"

"Bah. *Non.* Why should I? I am not even sure I ever met him."

"Very well. Thank you, monsieur."

Next, Mr. Moseley came in, looking as smart as an officer in his regimentals. Frederick bit back a smile to see his father's former valet in his role as head porter or commissionaire of the Swanford Abbey Hotel. His fine livery, gold braid, and jaunty hat gave the mild-mannered man a proud bearing and seemed to lengthen his spine and broaden his once-thin shoulders.

"Good day, Mr. Moseley. I am glad to see you looking so hale. The livery suits you. I hope the position here does as well?"

"It does indeed, sir. I enjoy it. Out in the fresh air, welcoming guests and assisting them. Yes, I find it suits me very well. It seems the role I was born for."

"Good, good."

Mr. Moseley added, "And now and again, I see former acquaintances like you and your brother. And now Miss Lane too! Almost like old times."

As much as he was enjoying chatting with the older man, Frederick was aware of the ticking clock and pushed ahead with his questions.

Moseley listened, then shook his head. "No, sir. I did not see anyone enter the hotel who looked remotely suspicious. Not while I was on duty. And I am out there all day in all weather."

"And what are your hours?"

"Nine till eight."

"Goodness. That is a long shift. Don't you grow weary?"

"Not a bit of it. I move around, help with bags, open doors, and stop to have a bite to eat now and again. The time goes by quickly." Moseley sighed, then sent him a sad, sidelong glance. "I do miss your father, though. He was a good man."

"Thank you. So do I." Frederick paused, then asked, "Did you meet Mr. Oliver when he arrived?"

"I opened the door for him. That was all. I considered telling him I'd read his books, but I'd seen him rebuff someone else, so I thought the better of it."

"Whom did he rebuff?"

Moseley worried his lip before replying. "Robb Tarvin. I doubt there's anything in it, but I heard the two talking when Robb delivered the man here in his fly."

"What about?"

"I didn't hear all Robb said, but I could see the author didn't like it. He alighted rather abruptly, and what a scowl! I heard Robb ask Mr. Oliver to wait. He said something like, 'There's another error in chapter three.'

"But the big man held up his hand and said sharply, 'I have heard more than enough.'"

Moseley tsked and shook his head. "Poor Robb. Not a bad fellow, but always was something of a know-all. Doesn't realize folks don't like hearing their every mistake enumerated."

"Did Robb say anything else to Mr. Oliver?"

"Not to his face. But the author did not tip him, so Robb grumbled to me about it and called him a skinflint. I am sure he meant no real harm."

"I see. Well. Thank you, Mr. Moseley. I appreciate your time."

He excused the commissionaire and summoned the flyman. Robb Tarvin came in, removing his flat cap as he entered, and sat in the offered chair.

"I have just a few questions. I understand you delivered Mr. Oliver to the hotel?"

"That's right. He requested a ride when he wrote to secure a room. Mr. Mayhew sent me to Worcester to meet the Birmingham stage."

"And what did the two of you talk about on the way here?"

Robb shrugged. "This and that. Told him I'd read his books."

"That all?"

Robb hesitated, avoiding his gaze. "More or less."

"I have been told the two of you parted in an . . . unfriendly manner."

Robb jutted out his chin, nostrils flaring. "I suppose meddling Moseley told you that."

"Why did you not mention it?"

"Because Mr. Mayhew does not like us speaking ill of any guest, no matter if he *is* a miserly skinflint."

"So you argued with the author?"

"Not argued, exactly. But he didn't take it too kindly when I pointed out a few errors in his novels. Was only trying to be helpful."

"I see."

"I offered to read his next draft in advance, to review his facts."

"He declined?"

"That's right."

"And did you see him again after that?"

"No," Robb replied. Then he quickly modified, "Well, I

glimpsed him in the dining room one night, but I didn't talk to him."

Frederick regarded him with some surprise. "You were in the dining room?"

"No, I . . ." Robb lowered his head and shifted uneasily. "I simply looked inside . . . out of curiosity."

Frederick noticed the young man's neck redden and wondered what he was hiding.

"Where were you between, say, midnight and eight a.m. the day of Mr. Oliver's death?"

"Asleep in my bed." Robb's eyes widened. "Wait—you don't think . . . ? I was vexed with the man, I own, but I went nowhere near him. Didn't even know which room he was in. I rarely venture farther than the hall. Anyone can tell you that. And I've never once been upstairs."

"Then how did you know his room was up there?"

Robb blinked. "I . . . Most are, are they not?"

Frederick watched him squirm a moment, then replied. "Yes. Well . . ."

Mrs. Somerton knocked on the door to announce that the undertaker had arrived.

Frederick excused Robb and asked the head housekeeper if he could ask her a few questions while she was there.

Her eyes widened in surprise but she said, "Of course. Anything to help."

He smiled to assure her and began, "Did you have occasion to meet Mr. Oliver?"

"Unfortunately, no. I was overseeing the repair of the laundry mangle when he arrived. Raymond would have been at the desk, and Anton showed him to his room."

"You have keys to all the rooms, is that right?"

"I do, yes."

"None have gone missing?"

"No, sir. I take prodigious care of them."

"And no one else has mentioned any missing keys?"

"No, sir."

"And do you recall assigning anyone besides Mary Hinton to Mr. Oliver's room?"

"I do not. But that does not mean it might not have happened. The girls sometimes help each other out in a pinch. It is not forbidden."

Frederick nodded. "And who would Mary most likely ask for help, if the need arose?"

"Millie, I suppose. Although it could have been Lydia as well."

Frederick noted their names. "May I speak with them next?"

Mrs. Somerton obliged him, going to fetch the chambermaids. Mr. Brixton came in while he waited and sat down to join him.

When the maids arrived, Frederick asked them if they had delivered anything to Mr. Oliver's room. Both answered in the negative.

Strange. So perhaps Mr. George had been mistaken. But then, why had Mary Hinton seemed so nervous when he'd asked her about it?

Perhaps he should question her again.

But when he asked the helpful Mrs. Somerton, her mouth tightened and her chin gave an obstinate lift.

"Mary has already been questioned by the coroner. It's a busy time of morning. So if it's not absolutely necessary, I hate to call her away from her work just now."

Frederick consulted his pocket watch. The inquest would soon reconvene. He decided it was probably not important, since the murder did not occur until the next day. But for some reason, it troubled him.

"Very well. Who is left?"

The day clerk came in next, Mrs. Somerton taking his place at the desk for the time being.

Raymond said he had met Mr. Oliver briefly when he first arrived, but had not seen him afterward.

Frederick asked, "Did you notice anything out of the ordinary the morning he was found dead? Anyone asking for Mr. Oliver's room number or loitering about?"

"No, sir. Though I did see a man leave the hotel that morning."

"Oh? What time?"

"Just before you followed that young woman from thirteen into the blue parlour."

"Ah." Sweat prickled at the back of his neck. *So not Mr. Dodge* . . . Frederick felt Brixton's gaze on his profile but kept his on the clerk. "That would have been a little before nine."

"Who was the man?" Brixton asked.

"Don't know. Didn't see his face."

Frederick asked a few more questions, each as fruitless as the last.

He almost didn't bring in the youngest member of staff, the new page, but with a sigh, decided to finish what he'd started.

"Your name?"

"Billy Jackson."

"And how long have you worked here, Billy?"

"A whole month now, sir. Mrs. Somerton made mention of that fact just last night."

"Well done. Is this your first position?"

"No, sir. Not if you count mucking out the neighbor's pigsty and collecting his eggs. Did that since I were breeched. But I like this more. Pays better and I smell better too."

Brixton guffawed at that, and the boy grinned, showing a missing front tooth.

"And did you meet Mr. Oliver during his stay?"

"No, sir. Anton carried up his baggage and Mary his meals. I did clean his boots once, but that was as close as I got."

Disappointment balled in Frederick's chest. Nothing to learn from this lad either. About to dismiss him, he saw the boy sitting forward, eager to help. So he asked one more question, though he set aside his pen, expecting nothing useful.

"Did you notice anything out of the ordinary over the last few days? Anyone where they shouldn't be? Any unusual comings and goings?"

Billy's eyes lit. "Now you mention it, I did see one thing that surprised me, sir, but I ought not speak out of turn."

"Go on."

"Mrs. Somerton don't like us to gossip about the guests."

"In this instance, she will understand if you speak freely."

The lad considered, then smiled. "If she gets cross, I'll tell her you twisted my arm, shall I?"

"If you wish." Frederick grinned back, but his smile soon faded.

"I saw a man letting himself into one of the guest rooms. A lady's room."

The coy countenance of Selina Newport flitted through Frederick's mind. Had Thomas paid her a clandestine visit? He wouldn't put it past him.

"When was this?"

"The night before last. Around ten."

Brixton clarified, "The night before Mr. Oliver's body was discovered?"

The boy nodded.

"The man is a guest here, I'm assuming?"

"No, sir. At least, I had not seen him here before. I suppose he might have registered when I was busy elsewhere. But I've not seen him in the hall or dining room neither."

Probably not his brother, then. At least Frederick hoped not. "What did this man look like?"

The lad shrugged. "Ordinary. Dark hair, gentlemen's clothes, although wrinkled. In need of a shave."

Not terribly specific, though at least dark hair excluded Thomas. The flash of relief that it had not been his brother quickly transformed into something else. Dread.

"And which room did the man enter?" Brixton asked.

"Number thirteen." The lad lowered his voice. "Miss Lane's room."

The words struck hard. The thought of Miss Lane alone with a man in her hotel room sent bile coursing into his stomach.

"Are you sure?" Frederick asked. "Was it not perhaps the room of another woman, say, Miss Newport?"

"No, sir. She's in twelve."

Lady Fitzhoward's words from the day before revolved through his brain. *"Don't ask questions for which you don't really want to know the answers."*

He wished now he had not suggested Brixton join him for the remaining interviews.

Frederick swallowed and thought quickly. "I see. Well. Thank you for telling us, Billy. Now, I want you to promise not to tell anyone else, understand? As you said, it is not right to gossip about a lady. Mrs. Somerton wouldn't approve, and nor would I. There is very likely some . . . respectable explanation for what you saw, and I intend to find out. In the meantime, let's keep this between ourselves, all right? Have I your word?"

The boy's brow furrowed. "Yes, sir." Although he'd agreed, he looked puzzled and perhaps a little disappointed.

Frederick hoped he could count on his silence. Brixton's too. He also hoped the boy was mistaken.

The young page left, and Brixton departed to look in on

things at the bakery. Frederick, however, remained sitting in the small office, alone and motionless.

His emotions and resolve, however, swung back and forth like a pendulum.

There is a reasonable explanation, he told himself, much like he had told Billy. *Do not jump to conclusions or sully her reputation based on one lad's tale.* He reminded himself that he trusted Miss Lane and knew her to be virtuous.

The next moment, doubts chased each other through his brain. Yes, he'd known her as a girl, but really, how much time had they spent together in recent years? Very little since he married and none at all in the last two years. She may have changed.

His all-too-capable imagination conjured a vivid picture: a young man entering her room at night wearing a familiar smile. At the thought, jealousy wrenched his gut. He clutched his hands tight, striving to subdue the emotion. Had he been foolish to believe her the same sweet innocent he'd once known—to trust her? *Mr. Dodge, my eye.*

In the back of his mind, he realized his own past fueled the potency of his reaction. Suspecting a woman of meeting a man in clandestine fashion—a man not her husband—brought back all the old sickening feelings of betrayal.

His wife had played the innocent too. Lied straight to his face. Took other lovers and laughed behind his back.

Miss Lane is not Marina, he scolded himself.

And yet . . . she was definitely hiding something.

With great effort Frederick mastered his composure. *Stop it. Calm down. Talk to her before you do anything you might regret.*

Rebecca put on her outdoor garments, preparing to walk to the lodge to talk to John and reassure Rose. Would her brother tell her the truth?

Did she really want to know?

Someone knocked on her door, and Rebecca jumped. "Wh-who is it?"

"It's Mr. Brixton, the constable."

Alarms rang in her brain. She pressed a hand to her lurching heart and opened the door, endeavoring to look as composed as possible.

"Yes?"

"Good morning, Miss Lane. I'm on my way home, but first wanted to ask you a question."

She hesitated. "I am in a bit of a hurry myself."

"Will just take a moment. It's rather important."

"Very well."

He looked around to make sure they were not being over-heard, then began, "Thing is, we have a witness who says he saw an unknown man enter your room the night before Mr. Oliver's death."

Her stomach churned. "A strange man . . . in my room?"

"Yes, miss. I understand it's . . . delicate. But I wonder if you could tell me who it was. In case it might have some bearing on Mr. Oliver's death."

She shook her head. "I invited no strange man into my room, Mr. Brixton."

He looked over her shoulder as if trying to see inside. She swung the door wide. "You are welcome to search if you like."

"You deny it?"

"Adamantly." *Wait . . . John.* Realization dawned. *Of course. Though he is no stranger.* She swallowed. "Who says he saw this?"

"A young page. He is pretty positive. I realize it is awkward, but you see why we felt we must ask."

"We?"

"Sir Frederick and me. We've been interviewing people. To identify anyone whose testimony might be helpful to the coroner's inquest underway now."

Sir Frederick had heard of this? What must he think of her! But she couldn't name John without placing him under suspicion.

Rebecca's nerves jangled. How she dreaded being summoned to the inquest. It was bad enough to lie in an informal setting, but in a legal proceeding? *Please, God, no.*

"And what time was this . . . supposedly?" she asked.

"Around ten."

John had arrived earlier, before dinner, though he had also gone out and returned again later. She shook her head once more. "The lad was mistaken."

A way out flashed through her mind.

"Oh! I know what must have happened. A man did come to my door later that night. He knocked but I did not let him in."

"Who was it?"

"Ambrose Oliver."

"What?"

"That must be where the misunderstanding originated. The page must have assumed I let him in. But I never even opened the door to him."

The constable scratched his head.

"I know it sounds . . . odd," she said in a rush. "I thought it odd and rather disturbing at the time, which is why I did not answer his knock. Oh! Sir Frederick can confirm this. He heard Mr. Oliver knocking and calling through my door and told him to go back to his own room."

"Did he indeed?"

"Yes. You can ask him."

"I shall."

She looked up at him, hoping her face did not reveal her unease. "Anything else?"

"Not at present." He frowned at her bonnet and cloak as though just noticing them. "You were not thinking of leaving the hotel, were you?"

She raised her chin. "Only to reassure my family. I imagine they have heard about the death and may fear for my safety. I did ask permission, and Sir Frederick said it would be all right if I came back directly."

The normally friendly man's eyes darkened. "I shall verify that with him as well."

Rebecca walked to the lodge, full of self-reproach. When had she become such a liar? Yes, she had been trying to protect John, but that did not justify her actions. If she were called to testify at the inquest, would she have to lie again to protect herself? To save John? The commandment ran through her mind, *Thou shalt not bear false witness. . . .*

God, please help me make this right!

The cook-housekeeper came to the door, wiping stained hands on her apron. "Ah, Miss Rebecca. I am very glad to see you." Rose looked down ruefully at her red-smeared apron. "I apologize for my appearance. Caught me chopping the last of the beetroot. The first time you came home, the house was as untidy as you've ever seen it, and this time you find me covered in red stains. Probably thought I'd murdered someone or at least a chicken." Rose grimaced. "Sorry, that was an idiotic thing to say, considering what happened up at the abbey."

"You heard the news, then?"

"Yes. Robb Tarvin brought it. A regular town crier he is. I had just resolved to walk up to the abbey this afternoon to make sure you were all right. Come in, come in." Rose led the way back to the kitchen. "Just let me wash my hands and I'll put the kettle on."

"Thank you. Is John . . . ?"

Rose shrugged. "In his room as far as I know. Haven't heard a peep out of him all morning."

John would wait. Tea first. For courage.

The older woman bustled around the warm kitchen, wiping one end of the table, bringing out cups and saucers, and filling a plate with honey biscuits.

The two sat down, and while the tea steeped, Rebecca said carefully, "Rose, what would you do if you suspected your sibling had done something wrong? Would you try to protect them, or let them face the consequences?"

Rose slowly nodded, gazing off into her own thoughts. "As a younger woman, I was devilish angry over something mine did. I determined to banish her from my life and my heart. Easier said than done. Had I to do it over again, I would have forgiven Daisy. Not lost my only sibling over one wrongdoing. Family . . . once gone, there's no replacing them."

Rebecca considered this. She helped herself to a buttery sweet biscuit, then said, "Two nights ago, when John came to the hotel, did he—"

"He did come to see you, then?" Rose asked. "He said he was, but I admit I wondered if he had some other purpose in mind. He so rarely leaves the lodge."

"What other purpose?"

Rose added milk to their cups and poured the tea. "Oh, going to meet that Stoker fellow in the wood or to see a girl."

"Is John seeing someone? Or do you mean Mary?"

Rose shook her head. "Mary isn't the girl for him. She's got a good head on her shoulders, I can't deny. But John, well, don't be offended, but he's in no fit state to be courting anyone."

"I agree. Though I sometimes wonder if becoming interested in a woman might be good for him."

"That's crossed my mind too—that having someone depend on him might spur him to break some of his . . . habits . . . and settle down. But he's already got you and me depending on him—or at least me, if you're continuing on as a companion. And if that has not roused him to any sense of duty, I doubt another female would. Though I grant you, a pretty sweetheart might be more inspiring than either of us."

Rebecca nodded thoughtfully, then said, "I know John asked you to write a clean copy for him. Did he ask you for anything else? Or do anything . . . unusual?"

Rose dipped her chin and raised a brow. "This *is* John we're talking about."

"I know, but—"

"There was one thing that surprised me. A few days before you arrived, he asked me for a paintbrush. Like an artist would use. Said I hadn't one and if he tried to borrow my pastry brush I'd feed him gizzards and leeks for a week! I remembered your things in the attic and thought you might have a box of painting supplies up there. You used to draw and paint a little."

"A very little and very ill. Why did he want a paintbrush?"

"He didn't say. I heard him rattling around up there, so I assumed he found one. I was too busy trying to finish my house-work to pay much attention. Don't know if he put it back or not. I hope you don't mind."

"Not at all," Rebecca murmured, but her mind was spinning. "Did he ask for anything else?"

The older woman nodded. "Steak and kidney pie. But I told

him we had neither in the larder and an unpaid bill at the butcher's."

"Anything else?"

Rose screwed up her face. "Come to think of it, he also went down to the cellar for something. When he came up, he had cobwebs in his hair and said he'd seen signs of rodents down there." She shuddered. "Nasty place."

"Shall I summon the rat catcher?" Rebecca offered.

"No. We don't need another expense. John said we had some white arsenic down there that should do the trick."

Rebecca stared, stomach cramping. White arsenic? *Please, God, no . . .*

Rose's eyes shot open like a whipped-wide curtain. "You don't think John . . . ?" The housekeeper shook her head, expelling a long breath and answering her own question. "No. Of course not. Good thing Robb already told me the author was struck dead. If he'd been poisoned, one might be tempted to think . . . But no, John would never do that."

Rebecca prayed she was right.

⁓

Less than an hour later, Noah Brixton returned to the small office Frederick was using, with two cups of coffee in hand.

"Here you are, sir. I took the liberty of adding sugar and cream."

Frederick usually took neither, but he simply thanked the constable, his mind on other things.

Recalling the younger man's errand, he roused himself to ask, "How were things at the bakery?"

"Good, good." Brixton sat, legs sprawled in front of him. "So. About Miss Lane."

Frederick looked up sharply. "What about her?"

"Well, it seems to me we have a reliable witness who saw a gentleman enter her room, apparently with her permission, the night before Mr. Oliver's death. Yet the young lady denies it."

"Miss Lane denies it?" Frederick echoed, voice tight.

"Yes, sir. I took the liberty of stopping by her room before I went out. I asked her in confidence, and—don't worry—with due respect."

You take a lot of liberties, Frederick thought acidly but held his tongue. The man was only trying to do his job.

The constable went on, "With the inquest going on, and us with a lad who is pretty certain of what he saw . . . well, it's dashed awkward. One doesn't like to doubt the word of a respectable young lady—not without strong proof to the contrary."

"And she denied having a man in her room?" Frederick mulishly repeated.

"Yes, sir, as distinct as could be. I wonder if we ought to report it to the coroner. He might want to question her to see if she or this man knows something about Mr. Oliver's death. But I thought I should ask your advice first, both as magistrate and as the gentleman who got me elected in the first place."

Frederick attempted a light tone. "Perhaps you are regretting that now?"

The constable shrugged and looked down. "A bit."

Suddenly Brixton eyed him again. "She said you gave her permission to leave the hotel?"

Warily, Frederick replied, "Yes. . . ."

"She also said something about Ambrose Oliver knocking on her door that night, but that sounds farfetched to me."

"That's right!" Frederick affirmed, the tightness in his chest easing. "He did. I saw him myself. Though I believe it was

227

later than Billy reported. And he certainly did not go inside. I heard him at her door, asked him to return to his own room, and waited until he left."

"What did he want?"

"He'd been drinking, and Miss Lane is a young woman on her own. What do you think he wanted?"

"Ah."

"That must have been who Billy saw, and he confused the time. The man did make a spectacle of himself. And since Billy never met Mr. Oliver, he would not have recognized him."

"But the lad distinctly said he saw a man go *into* Miss Lane's room."

"I know what he said, but people make mistakes."

In his heart, Frederick knew Miss Lane was lying or at least hiding something. *Had* she entertained a man in her room at night? What would happen to her good name if she was questioned about it during the inquest? It would likely provide no evidence about Mr. Oliver but would damage her reputation beyond repair.

No. She would not be summoned to the inquest if he could prevent it. And if he was wrong, he would take the blame.

The girl he had long held affection for, as well as her honored father, should be protected from scandal and shame; and shame it would be either way—to confess the truth or to pledge herself to a lie.

He squared his shoulders. "At all events, you were right to speak to me first. Don't go to the coroner with this."

Brixton hesitated, expression somber. "If you think it best, sir."

"I do. We have no evidence that this is related to the Oliver case, and it is outside the coroner's mandate of determining cause of death. Take no further steps and tell no one to avoid injuring the lady's reputation unjustly. I shall speak to her in confidence about the matter. And if it turns out to be somehow related, I will report it to the justices myself. But for now, leave it and any recriminations with me."

Mr. Brixton nodded and blew out a puff of air. "Well, that spares me from an awkward job. Especially as our young witness is less likely to take an oath once he hears Miss Lane roundly denies it."

Frederick nodded, but was not at all certain he had done the right thing.

◈

Rebecca knocked on her brother's door and was not surprised when he didn't respond.

She knocked again. "John? It's Rebecca." Trying the latch and finding it unlocked, she announced, "I'm coming in," and gingerly opened the door.

She made out a rumpled mound on the bed and heard John's telltale snore.

As her eyes adjusted to the dim light, she saw a jar on his desk she had not noticed before, the handle of a paintbrush propped inside.

She sniffed the contents of the jar but smelled nothing. Beside the jar lay a small brown bottle on its side, empty.

She went and sat on the edge of the bed, sitting on something hard beneath the twisted blanket. She rose and fished out the offending object—another small bottle with a glass stopper, all but empty.

Carrying it to a thin shaft of light between the shutters, she pulled the stopper and took a whiff, instantly recoiling at the strong, sweet smell. A reddish-brown residue clung to the bottom like spoiled molasses. Tincture of opium, if she had to guess. Heavy on the opium.

Her heart sank.

She returned to the bed and, with her free hand, shook her brother by the shoulder. "John?" She patted his cheek to no avail. His breathing was shallow, and holding his wrist, she felt a sluggish pulse. Her brother would not be answering her questions anytime soon.

She heard a heavy sigh and glanced up. Rose stood there, shoulder against the doorframe. She looked from John's prone form to the bottle in Rebecca's hand. "It's as I feared. Apparently he did meet Leo Stoker."

The local man with an unsavory reputation was rumored to deal in smuggled liquor and other substances.

Rebecca winced. "Oh, John."

On his bedside table, she noticed a copy of a book their father had read to them as children, *The Arabian Nights Entertainments*. She picked it up, and for a moment, childhood memories warmed her.

Then she remembered John's favorite story from the collection, and the fleeting warmth froze in her veins.

15

The inquest reconvened, and Dr. Fox was the first to be sworn in and deposed.

Mr. Smith began, "As you were here in the hotel when the incident occurred, we will allow you to give your professional opinion on the cause of death."

"How gracious," Dr. Fox wryly replied.

Frederick heard the barb in his friend's tone, while the coroner's expression remained placid.

"Full name and residence?"

"Charles Fox, MD. I live at Woodlane, near Cheltenham."

"And what brought you here?"

"Sir Frederick Wilford is a friend of mine. I came to support the canal project he plans to undertake in the area. Meeting was a few days ago. I've stayed on for a bit of a holiday with my wife."

"I see. And you were called in when the victim was discovered?"

"Yes, after I treated Mr. George's head wound, I was asked to confirm Mr. Oliver's death and complete a cursory examination. I disturbed nothing, I assure you."

"How gracious of *you*," Smith countered. "Now, before

your deposition, I feel I should inform the jury that you are not a surgeon, nor a physician in general practice. You have little experience with bodily injury as you deal mostly with diseases of the mind. Is that not so? You are, in fact, a mad doctor."

Fox's face tensed. "I object to that term. My patients are not . . . mad dogs. They are human beings with personalities and emotions. Fears and hopes, like any of us. Yes, they may suffer from various manias or hysterias, but they are still humans created in God's image and deserving of dignity."

"Are you suggesting God is mad?"

"Heavens, no. But this fallen world has taken a harsh toll on many. My life's purpose is to rehabilitate those I can, and to protect and nurture those I can't."

"How noble," Smith replied with asperity.

"And I am, in fact, a duly licensed medical doctor."

"Very well. And your findings?"

"Mr. Oliver was struck on the back of his head with sufficient force to cause a contusion."

"The cause of death."

"I believe so. I also noticed the dark appearance of his lips and fingers. That gave me pause, wondering if the man might have been poisoned, but at the time, I concluded that the black marks were simply ink stains."

Smith nodded. "We concluded the same. Anything to add?"

Fox considered. "Only something Sir Frederick observed. That if Mr. Oliver were sitting on the chaise alive and well, reading or writing, he would have heard his door open. Why did he sit there instead of rising to challenge his assailant? To defend himself?"

"And your point?"

"Either he knew and trusted whoever entered, or perhaps he *was* drugged or poisoned and could not rise."

"You already said you discounted the black stains. Did you see any other evidence of poison or drugs?"

"No, but an autopsy might reveal telltale inflammation of the internal organs. I have sent the contents of the cup and bowl found in his room to be tested for traces of poisonous substances. The results may take some time."

Smith frowned. "That was quite presumptuous. The man was bludgeoned. You said it yourself. Struck with enough force to kill a man."

Dr. Fox sighed. "Yes."

"I see little reason to delay this process further by requesting an autopsy when the body has already been removed. But the jury will deliberate that option later. You are excused, Dr. Fox. Next, I would like to hear from the constable."

The young man was sworn in, then began, "Noah Brixton, born and raised right here in Swanford."

"And you are the current constable?"

"Yes. As well as local baker now my father's gone."

"Well, Mr. Brixton, anything useful to report?"

Brixton looked uneasily at Sir Frederick, then said, "No, sir. I thought I might, but turns out I was mistaken."

"Oh?"

"That's right."

"Very well. And as constable, what is your opinion of the manner and cause of death?"

"If I had to wager a guess, I'd say maybe a robbery gone wrong. Famous author staying in the hotel and all. Times are hard for some, and now and again, a man gets desperate, especially if he has a family to feed."

Smith said archly, "And do you have many robberies here in the metropolis of Swanford?"

Apparently aware he was being mocked, Brixton lifted his

chin. "A few, yes. A theft of hens and another from the church poor box."

"Large-scale crime indeed."

"The way I see it," Brixton went on, undeterred and warming to his theory, "is someone desperate-like heard Ambrose Oliver was staying here and decided to rob him."

"Even though we've heard testimony from others that Mr. Ambrose Oliver was in financial difficulty?"

"Well, a local man wouldn't know that, would he? He'd assume a famous author had money. Wouldn't you? He's written a few books that were quite popular, especially his last—*The Faded Rose of Wickwood*. Have you read it? Very affecting. The missus cried for hours. At all events, driven by worry for his starving children, this would-be thief sneaked up the stairs, struck Mr. George and Mr. Oliver, took what he could find, and left again."

Listening to Brixton weave his tale, Frederick thought the man had missed his calling. Perhaps he ought to have been a writer of affecting novels himself.

At least he had not mentioned Miss Lane.

Mr. Smith said, "As far as we know, nothing was stolen from the room. Mr. Oliver's purse containing three and six-pence was on the side table as well as a silver pocket watch."

Brixton nodded. "Maybe the intruder got scared, realized he'd killed a man when he never meant to, and hied it out of there, taking nothing."

"Diverting supposition, Mr. Brixton."

The constable beamed. "Thank you, sir."

Next, the coroner called on Mr. Mayhew again.

"Have you anything to report after questioning your staff?"

"No, sir, I—"

"You questioned everyone?"

The hotel proprietor sent Frederick an uncertain look.

Frederick had shared his findings with Mr. Mayhew just before entering the coffee room, though there had been little to report, since he'd decided not to mention the page's claim.

Mayhew shifted uncomfortably. "Actually, as there were so many to question in such a brief amount of time, Sir Frederick Wilford kindly offered to help conduct the interviews."

The coroner looked over at him, brows lifted in surprise, but not, Frederick thought, disapproval. "How kind."

"I am staying here and was happy to help." Frederick shrugged off the praise. "Mr. Mayhew is a busy man."

"Then perhaps we had better depose you next. I had planned to summon you at some point, as you were the one who discovered the body, were you not?"

Miss Lane had been with him—but would saying so cause the coroner to summon her as well?

Persons present when the crime was committed, along with the finders of the body, were all attached to appear at the trial before the itinerant justices. He did not want to put Miss Lane into a situation where she would feel compelled to lie in a public court.

"That's right," Frederick replied. He *had* gone in ahead of her, after all, and been first to see the body.

"Your name and residence?"

"Sir Frederick Wilford, baronet. I live locally, at Wickworth."

"And were you acquainted with the deceased?"

"I have seen him—here in the hotel dining room, for example. But we never formally met."

Frederick thought of seeing the man knocking incessantly at Miss Lane's door. He did not think it relevant to mention, nor worth the risk to her reputation.

"Tell us how you came to find the body."

"I was in the parlour when I heard a scream and a crash,

and ran upstairs to see what the matter was. After ascertaining that Mr. George and Miss Hinton were alive, I then went into room three."

"Was the door unlocked?"

"No, we borrowed the maid's key."

"We?"

Dash it. "Yes. Miss Lane heard the scream as well and followed me upstairs."

Smith made a note in his diary.

"But you were first on the scene?"

"Yes. I went in before anyone else and saw Ambrose Oliver lying on the chaise, eyes and mouth open. I felt for breath and a pulse, and finding none, realized he was dead."

"What did you assume was the cause of death?"

"I did not study the body nor the wound until Dr. Fox came in."

"But now, do you concur that the head wound was what killed him?"

Frederick hesitated. "He definitely had what appears to be a fatal head wound. But as Dr. Fox mentioned, I wonder if there might have been a secondary cause. He might have been drugged or poisoned first to allow the culprit entry and to prevent Mr. Oliver from defending himself. I do hope you will consider requesting an autopsy before it is too late."

The coroner's brow rose. "Even considering the fees involved?"

"Yes. I also wonder if it would not be prudent to question all the guests as well. It is likely that in a hotel like this with many people on the same floor, someone may have seen or heard something that might shed light on the crime."

"And are you offering to interview them yourself? Or are you suggesting we imposition every wealthy, respectable guest by demanding they appear at our inquest? Mr. Mayhew would not like that and neither would they. Gritty business, these depositions.

Nor do I see that I would be justified in doing so. Unless you have reason to believe one of the guests was involved?"

"No, sir. Not yet. But yes, I would like to ask them all a few questions. And you are right—my doing so would be less objectionable, I believe, to everyone. I would endeavor to be discreet."

"And you will inform me of any relevant information?"

"I shall indeed, without delay." Frederick's conscience smote him, for he could not be sure the visits to Miss Lane's room by Ambrose Oliver and an unknown man were not relevant.

Smith nodded. "Very well. I shall request the autopsy, and we shall adjourn until the results are reported. In the meantime, you may begin interviewing the guests. Mr. Brixton will help you, of course."

Frederick forced a smile. "Oh. Of . . . course."

That afternoon, Frederick knocked on his brother's door. Thomas opened it, well and fully dressed, complete with gloves and beaver hat in hand.

"May I speak with you a moment?" Frederick asked.

"Now? But I am meeting Miss Newport for another game of bowls."

"This won't take long."

Thomas huffed. "Are you asking as my brother or as magistrate?"

"Both. I plan to interview all the guests. Someone must have seen or heard something."

His brother's fair brows rose. "And what has Mr. Smith to say to this plan of yours?"

"He no doubt thinks it a waste of time but seems content to leave it to me and Brixton, assuming we continue to pay his expenses. I don't want to show partiality, so thought I ought to start with my own brother."

"Ah. And will you question Miss Lane as well?"

Frederick blinked before meeting Thomas's gaze. "Why do you ask?"

"Just making sure no one shows any partiality." Thomas gave a sly grin, then asked, "And who shall question you?"

"I have already been deposed by Mr. Smith."

"And I don't imagine you told him that Ambrose Oliver maligned you and your wife in his novel," Thomas replied. "That gives you a motive, ol' boy."

"You said I imagined the similarity in names." Frederick narrowed his eyes. "Do you actually think I had anything to do with the man's death?"

"No. But I could ask you the same question."

Frederick sighed. "I know. But we both saw the way Mr. Oliver looked at Miss Newport, and you do seem to know something about *her*."

Thomas raised his hands. "Truthfully, I know very little, beyond how irresistible she is. I met her last season, when she played Josephine in *An Actress of All Work*."

Frederick rolled his eyes.

Thomas sent him a scathing glance. "Look. I realize actresses have a certain reputation, but it is not deserved in this case. Selina is not a light-skirt. Some men, however, don't want to believe there can be exceptions to the general rule. I take it Oliver was one of those."

"She told you that?"

"Not in so many words. But I saw how she reacted to seeing him. I asked her about it later, and she shuddered and said, 'The man is a snake.'"

"Was she aware he would be here?"

"I don't think so. . . ." Thomas looked away, searching his memory. "No, I doubt she would have come in that case. At least, based on the vehemence of her reaction."

"Then why is she here?"

Thomas shrugged. "She was in the area. Sent me a note, letting me know."

"And you told me you did not arrange to meet her here."

"I didn't. Not directly. I may have mentioned this lovely hotel, and our ongoing refurbishments that might necessitate we stay here, but—"

"Don't insult my intelligence."

"Look, I understand this has the appearance of an . . . illicit liaison, but it isn't. Grant you, it might have been if I had my way, but Miss Newport is more of a lady than I realized, and I admire her for it."

"You lied to me."

"I did not. I told you I had a hint she might be here. But I did not invite her, nor did I know for certain she would come. Why are you so cross?"

"I don't know."

Thomas's lips quirked. "I could tell you, if you'd like."

"No, thank you. Are you saying you are in love with this Miss Newport? Hope to marry her?"

"Oh, now . . . let's not place the cart before the horse. I have spent but a few hours in her company. For the present, suffice it to say I admire her."

"Careful, Thomas. If you have genuine feelings for the woman, and Mr. Oliver wronged her, that might seem like motive enough to kill the man."

His brother's mouth fell open. "Me, kill a man I never met for trying to seduce a woman I barely know? Do you really think I would? Have you ever known me to be violent?"

"No, but if this comes out, Mr. Smith or another JP may take a different view."

"Well, then, don't tell them."

"I cannot promise that. I will need to speak to Miss Newport as well."

Thomas sighed. "You are determined to ruin this for me, are you not?"

"No. Only to get at the truth."

His brother looked at him soberly. "Tread gently, will you, ol' boy?"

Frederick hesitated, then promised, "I will try."

Thomas reluctantly agreed to ask Miss Newport to speak to Frederick before starting their match.

Finding the library and writing room unoccupied, Frederick sat down, idly fiddling with one of the chess pieces on the table. Mr. Brixton had yet to join him.

A few minutes later, Miss Newport appeared in the doorway.

Frederick rose. "Thank you for coming. Please sit down, if you would." He indicated the chair facing his.

Her tight lips expressed displeasure. "Very well." She gracefully sat, spreading her skirts around her.

He smiled in hopes of reassuring her. "As magistrate, I am conducting preliminary interviews with the guests, and will report anything relevant to the coroner."

Her eyes glittered with . . . what? Irritation? Fear? It was difficult to tell.

"Will I be called to give testimony at the inquest?"

"Not unless you have information that bears on this matter."

She clasped slim fingers together but said nothing.

Frederick asked, "So, what can you tell me about Ambrose Oliver?"

240

"Why should I be able to tell you anything?"

"I gather the two of you were some acquainted."

"Oh?" One arched eyebrow rose high. "And who told you that? Your sweetheart, I suppose?"

Frederick reared his head back. Sweetheart? He had no sweetheart. The only woman he was fond of was Rebecca Lane, but why would Miss Newport assume *she* had said something?

"Who do you mean by that?"

She lifted one shapely shoulder. "Miss Lane. Her chamber-maid received a message from Mr. Oliver requesting I come to his room. Miss Lane passed along the message to me. Of course, I did not go."

He absorbed that. Then noticing he was bouncing an agitated knee, he crossed one leg over the other.

Attempting a casual smile, he asked, "And why do you call her my 'sweetheart'?"

She studied him with interest. Was he red about the collar again? *Drat.*

"I observed the two of you during our game of lawn bowls," she replied. "And the night before last, I heard Mr. Oliver pounding on Miss Lane's door, trying to wheedle his way inside. My room is the next one down, past the night stair. At first, I thought perhaps he mistook the rooms and was looking for me. Thankfully not. Then I heard you coming to her aid."

"Ah. I see." Frederick relaxed a little. He said, "When Oliver saw you in the dining room, I thought his expression revealed recognition, or at least . . . interest."

A coy grin lifted her rouged lips. "You think it notable that a man should look at me with interest? You injure me, truly."

"It was more than that. My brother—only when I asked in my official capacity—confided that you had been . . . acquainted with the man, and unhappily so."

"Did he?" Her coy grin faded. "How . . . indiscreet of him."

"Again, he did not offer the information until I pulled it from him. I will add that he speaks of you highly, with both respect and regard."

"Now, that is more like it," she quipped, but her smug words did not hide her unease.

"He did not go into any detail, if that helps."

She smoothed her glove. "Because he does not know any details."

"Could you tell me, in confidence?"

"I don't like remembering it, let alone speaking of it. Nor do I see how it has any bearing on this matter. It is all a long time ago now."

"How long?"

"Oh, about three years. I thought him charming for about two seconds. Soon I realized his true character, and we . . . had a falling out."

"And you have not seen him since?"

"No."

"Until you came here."

"Obviously."

"Did you know he would be here?"

She huffed. "I would hardly have come had I known."

"Not even to see Thomas?"

She shook her head. "I could have easily seen your brother at another time. There was no urgency to see him this particular week."

"But you did not leave once you knew Oliver was here."

"No." Her fair eyes glinted. "I am not frightened off so easily. Nor am I the malleable fool I once was." She lifted her chin. "I have done nothing to be ashamed of. If anyone should have left, it ought to have been him."

"You got your wish. He did leave. Permanently."

She frowned. "See here, if I killed every man who tried to take advantage of me, I would get little else done. I did not kill Ambrose Oliver."

"But you are not sorry he's dead?"

She looked down at her clasped hands, and then up again. "In a way, I am. Sorry for whoever that lecher wronged so badly that they were driven to such a desperate act—to risk his or her own life to take another's." A shudder passed over her frame.

Frederick studied her ashen countenance and realized he believed her, even as he doubted whether he should. She was, after all, an actress.

16

Stepping out of the library and writing room a short while later, Frederick saw Rebecca Lane coming through the garden door in cloak and bonnet, a book under her arm.

"Miss Lane, could you join me for a few minutes?"

Her gaze flew to his, showing alarm rather than pleasure. Even so, she entered without protest and sat in the chair he indicated.

Sliding the book onto her lap, she folded her hands, entwining gloved fingers tightly.

He resumed his seat. "How was everything at the lodge? Did you reassure Rose and your brother?"

"As . . . best I could."

He nodded. "I noticed you brought back some reading material."

"Just . . . one of my father's books."

"Well. I have undertaken to question all of the guests with the intention of notifying the coroner of anyone with information to share. Pray, do not be offended. I even interviewed my own brother."

He gave a small smile at that, but she remained somber. "I understand."

Noah Brixton appeared in the threshold, hat in hand, out of breath.

"Sorry. Had to refire the ovens. Ah, Miss Lane." He made to tip his hat, only to realize it was in his hand.

Sir Frederick silently cursed the man's timing but made do with pointing to a nearby chair.

Then he returned his attention to Miss Lane. "To begin with, when did you last see Mr. Oliver? Alive, that is?" He winced at his lack of tact.

She looked upward, eyes shifting to the right. "Let me think. We all expected him at dinner two nights ago, but he did not make an appearance at his usual time. Nor at all, that I saw. Mr. George either. Mr. Edgecombe, however, came to the dining room, in quite a happy mood."

"And you didn't see Mr. Oliver after that? Not until you and I discovered his body?"

"Right." She scratched an eyebrow. "As you know, he knocked on my door late that night. So I heard his voice, though I did not see him."

Here she sent Mr. Brixton a significant look.

Brixton leaned forward. "Excuse me, sir, but Miss Lane didn't really answer the question. She said when she *didn't* see him, but not when she did."

"Oh." She blinked rapidly.

Seeing her discomfort, the desire to help rose in Frederick like Brixton's half-peck loaves of bread dough.

He suggested, "Did you see him at dinner the night before that—the last night he appeared in the refectory?"

"Yes! That's it . . . I did see him then." She added awkwardly, "Alive."

Frederick nodded and continued, "And had you met him or seen him before his stay here?"

Miss Lane hesitated. "Saw him, yes. Although only from a distance."

"Where?"

"Birmingham. I went there with John a few times, when he went to call on Mr. Edgecombe. Not the Mr. Edgecombe here now, but his brother. On one occasion, I saw Mr. Oliver leaving the office."

"And why did John meet with Mr. Edgecombe?"

"He hoped the publisher would help him with . . . his novel, but sadly, no."

"Your brother worked for Mr. Oliver at one point, did he not?"

She swallowed. "Just for a few months, about three years ago. William Edgecombe arranged it. John assisted Mr. Oliver with clerical tasks to free up his time to write."

"A good experience?"

"No. Though John learned some valuable lessons. And he still aspires to be published." She smiled but the expression did not reach her eyes.

He was about to probe further into the Lanes' dealings with the author, but before he could, Mr. Brixton took over.

"With your brother living nearby, may I ask why you are staying here at the abbey?"

"I came to Swanford to visit him, but when I got to the lodge, I found him . . ." She paused, and Frederick saw a flurry of emotions pass behind her eyes. Worry? Fear? Shame?

"Preoccupied with . . . his writing." She shrugged. "At all events, Lady Fitzhoward was staying here, so I took a room as well."

Not the clearest answer, Frederick realized, though he did not interrupt.

"And who is that lady to you?" Brixton asked. "A friend?"

"In a manner of speaking. I am her companion."

Frederick said, "Speaking of John, has he been to see you here at the hotel?"

Again, she blinked those wide hazel eyes. "John, here? When he sent me away for peace and quiet?" She chuckled but it sounded false.

Frederick's heart sank. Rebecca, the innocent girl he'd known, the darling vicar's daughter, was lying to him again.

He sat there feeling deflated. He felt more than saw Brixton's concerned gaze on his profile.

The younger man cleared his throat and asked another question. "Don't mean to embarrass you, miss, but any idea how and why Ambrose Oliver came to your room? Had he seen you, say, in the dining room, and somehow managed to learn your room number?"

"I don't know. I suppose he might have asked the clerk or one of the maids for my room number. Or perhaps he saw me go inside at some point when I did not see him."

Frederick roused himself to say—for Brixton's benefit as well as Rebecca's—"Miss Newport heard him knocking that night too. Apparently her room is nearest yours. She wondered if Oliver thought he was knocking on *her* door. She also indicated that you were aware of her previous acquaintance with the author."

"Did she?" Miss Lane's white throat convulsed. "Did she say how I knew?"

"Something about your chambermaid receiving a message from Mr. Oliver and you passing it along for her?"

"Oh yes. That's right. I did."

Frederick frowned. "Speaking of chambermaids. We still don't know which one entered Mr. Oliver's room the day before he died."

She nibbled her lip. "Is that . . . important?"

He grimaced. "Probably not. Bothering me though. Like something stuck in one's teeth. Or a missing chess piece." He nodded toward the nearby game board. "Only a pawn, but still . . . troublesome. I think I will question Mary Hinton again." He added on a chuckle, "Or line up all the maids and ask Mr. George to identify one!"

Brixton laughed, but Miss Lane did not seem to find it at all amusing.

Frederick glanced at the questions outlined in his notebook and asked, "And have you seen or heard anything else that might help us? Anything suspicious while you have been here?"

"Actually, yes." She took a deep breath and upon its exhale said, "I saw the abbess."

Not this again. A flicker of disapproval tightened his mouth. "Miss Lane . . ."

"I did! In the corridor yesterday morning, as well as my first night here. And of course I thought I saw her going belowstairs that night I . . . happened into you and your brother. At least, I know I saw a figure in a black-hooded gown that *looked* like a nun's habit, from what I've seen in paintings."

Brixton laughed again, but this time Frederick silenced him with a glare.

"Are you seriously telling us you saw an apparition . . . thrice?"

"Or a real person who looked like one, yes." She pursed her lips in frustration and Frederick saw her at six years old, pouting when she'd been denied something.

"I thought *you* would believe me, if no one else did. Apparently, I was wrong." She stood, tucking the book under her arm. "Are we through?"

Her eyes glinted and her nostrils flared. Yes, he feared they were through before they had even begun.

———

Brixton excused himself to use the water closet. During his absence, Frederick took a few notes and was about to summon the next person when Lady Fitzhoward threw open the door with a bang.

"Miss Lane says you are interviewing guests. As I don't wish to be disturbed during my nap later, I am here to be questioned now."

"Th-thank you, my lady."

Lady Fitzhoward entered, hair piled high in ornate style, its thickness in contrast to her sparse eyebrows. A wig perhaps? Her gown was equally ornate, a rich brocade in plum and grey. Her fashionable dress and coiffure fostered the illusion of a forty-year-old, while her lined face and drooping eyelids belied the appearance. He guessed her to be sixty at least.

And she still seemed familiar to him.

The woman sat without waiting to be asked, as befitted her station or at least her assurance.

Raising her chin, she asked, "You are questioning everyone, I understand?"

"Yes, even my brother. Showing no partiality, you see."

"Very thorough."

He decided an indirect approach might be more fruitful. "I gather you are a keen observer of human nature, my lady. What can you tell me about Mr. Oliver and your fellow guests?"

"Flattering my mind, ey? At my age, I'll take what I can get. A rum bunch the lot of them, Mr. Oliver included. I had not planned to stay on so long, but I found the company diverting."

"How so?"

She chuckled. "Where do I begin? First, having the esteemed, some might say eccentric, author staying here ensconced in his room with a henchman at his door, who even stood guard while he dined, added a certain excitement. Then there was the titillating appearance of the beautiful Miss Newport and the romantic tension with your brother, and the hints of some unhappy history with Mr. Oliver. Add to that spicy stew the rumors about an abbess's ghost? Why, it was all deliciously Gothic, don't you think? And now a murderer among the guests? I was right to stay on."

Her conclusion intrigued him. "I know you listened to the inquest. You didn't believe the constable's theory of a desperate would-be thief?"

She shook her head. "You wouldn't be questioning the guests if you thought Oliver was killed by some hapless stranger. I am sure you have better things to do with your time, like admire my pretty young companion. Or meet with more wealthy investors in hopes of seeing your canal plans come to fruition."

"True." *Thunder and turf.* He had called her a keen observer, but perhaps a bit too keen for comfort. He was glad Mr. Brixton had stepped out.

He shifted and asked, "Were you acquainted with Mr. Oliver—before coming here, I mean?"

"No. Never met him, except through his books." She watched him closely. "Have you read them? If you read the latest, I imagine you did not much enjoy it."

He decided to let that pass without comment and said instead, "Tell me about yourself, my lady."

Her grey-blue eyes glimmered. "What would you like to know?"

"To begin with, where are you from, if I may ask? You mentioned your husband being from Manchester, but nothing about yourself." In reality, simple curiosity drove him more than any conviction that her history might be relevant.

"Oh, I have lived in several places, and I travel a great deal."

"And your given name is Marguerite?"

"That's right."

"And your husband's name?"

"Donald. He died over a year ago. I miss him, yet I am grateful we had so many happy years together. Since his death, I have lived primarily in hotels and inns. I love them. No clutter. Everything fresh and clean. No reminders of the past . . ."

"I can understand that. Have you any children?"

"Impertinent question! Sadly, we remained childless, despite our best efforts. Donald did have a son with his first wife, who died young trying to bear him a second. His son and I don't get on."

"And how did you and your husband meet?"

"Goodness! Has my romantic history some bearing on the author's death?"

"Doubtful. It is just . . . you seem familiar to me, my lady. I am trying to work out why."

"As I said, I have traveled extensively and lived in many places."

"Yet, I have only ever lived here."

"Come. Surely you went away to university and spent seasons in London as most young bucks do."

"True. I have spent several weeks in Town. And my brother spends most of his time there now."

"There, you see? Perhaps our paths crossed then."

"If you say so."

"It is all I am prepared to say. Can we not leave it at that?"

"Very well. For now. Can you think of anything else that might have a bearing on Mr. Oliver's death?"

She slowly shook her head. "I think you have extracted quite enough information from me for one day, young man." She rose. "If you will excuse me, I am tired. Feel free to arrest me or let me go and have my nap."

Frederick stood. "By all means, my lady. Rest. I did not intend to wear you out."

She dipped her head as majestically as any royal and turned to go. And in truth, she did seem a little unsteady on her feet.

After asking Brixton to meet him back there in an hour, Frederick took a respite to stretch and have an early dinner in the coffee room. He'd been up since dawn and had eaten nothing all day.

First, he walked out through the garden to clear his mind. Evening was approaching, but the air was still mild and the breeze refreshing.

Seeing Miss Lane sitting on a bench near the fountain, eyes downcast, he hesitated. So many questions and emotions had run through him in recent hours, and he was uncertain how to proceed, especially where she was concerned.

Walking closer, he asked, "Daydreaming, Miss Lane?"

She looked up with a start. "Just thinking."

He sat beside her, heedless of keeping a proper distance, dispirited when she averted her gaze.

"Look at me," he said, his tone more commanding than he'd intended.

She obeyed, blinking up at him, her expression fearful.

He gentled his voice. "I believe that, at heart, you are a good and honest person, and you must have an important reason for withholding the truth."

Miss Lane lowered her head but not before he saw her face mottle red and white in mortification.

252

Regret stabbed him. "I have no wish to shame you. I want to help. To do that, I need to know the truth. I will wait a little longer for you to confide in me, but I can't wait forever."

"Thank you," she whispered.

He leaned closer and said, "And I hope you know you can trust me, with whatever it is." He pressed her hand and rose to take his leave. "Good evening, Miss Lane."

After a simple meal, Frederick asked Mr. Brixton to join him in questioning Isaac King. If he were truthful with himself, Frederick felt a bit uneasy about interviewing this particular guest. His reputation had preceded him.

"Mr. King. Thank you for agreeing to speak with us."

The impeccably dressed older man raised his palms in a magnanimous gesture. The jeweled ring on his little finger sparkled. "I don't mind. I would say I have nothing to hide, but at my age that is not entirely true." He gave a self-deprecating smile. "However, I can honestly say I have nothing to hide in this particular matter."

"Good. Now, during the inquest, Mr. George—who was employed by Ambrose Oliver in a . . . protective role—testified that his employer owed money to . . ." Frederick consulted his notes and quoted, "'impatient, dangerous people.' The coroner asked if he was suggesting a moneylender or bookmaker might have killed him, and George replied, 'It's possible.'"

Mr. King shook his head, expression as placid as his tone. "Are you accusing me? Nonsense. If a man does not repay what he owes, I take the collateral he pledged when I made the loan—not his life. Why do you think I demand security? I am no fool."

"Clearly not. And Ambrose Oliver? What security did he offer?"

The dark eyes glinted. "What could he offer? The man owned almost nothing. The profits of his next book, of course."

Frederick said, "Not exactly as guaranteed as, say, an indebted lord's property or family jewels."

"True. Perhaps I took an unwise risk in Mr. Oliver."

"So you came here to . . . remind him . . . of his debts?"

"Not at all." Isaac King spread his hands. "My lady and I reside in Naples these days, but I returned to visit my daughter, who has recently given me another grandson."

"And you originally left England to avoid prosecution, I gather."

"What an ugly rumor! Tsk tsk. You must never have been to Napoli or you would know a man needs no other persuasion to sojourn there than the pleasure of his lady love."

The man was charming and well-spoken, Frederick would give him that. He certainly did not fit the image of a dangerous moneylender.

Brixton spoke up, "Can you account for your whereabouts between midnight and nine the morning of Mr. Oliver's death?"

King nodded. "I was down in the bar until midnight or so, then returned to my room for the remainder of the night. My manservant can vouch for me."

Brixton nodded. "Thank you. I shall confirm with him."

Frederick made a note, thought, then added, "You can understand that it stretches credulity that you just happened to be staying in this out-of-the-way hotel when a man in your debt was killed here. I saw him react when he noticed you in the dining room. He was not happy to see you."

Again, the expressive hands lifted. "Is any man happy to see someone to whom he owes money?" Mr. King shook his head, then sighed. "Very well, perhaps I came here to remind him that I had not forgotten his debt, even though a sea separated us."

"How did you know he would be staying here?"

"Ah!" The man's eyes glimmered. "Now that *is* interesting.

I received an anonymous letter notifying me of his plans. No idea who sent it. Perhaps someone who wanted me here as scapegoat. In any case, I did not harm Mr. Oliver, and now I am without recourse. I suppose I could appeal to his publisher, but I gather no new book will be forthcoming. So I have lost by the man's death." He pressed a hand to his breast. "I tell you upon my honor, which I realize you may doubt, that I had nothing to do with his death. Nothing."

"Very well. Thank you for your candor, Mr. King."

"Am I free to go?"

"Please wait until the inquest concludes," Frederick requested, although he knew that if the man decided to flee to Naples, there was little he or Brixton could do to stop him.

Isaac King rose. "As you wish. The barman here serves an excellent brandy from the Cognac region. Eighteen eleven was an outstanding year."

After Mr. King left, Brixton went to find his manservant while Frederick sat there for several minutes, pondering. Did he believe the moneylender innocent? Not in everything, but in the case of Ambrose Oliver's death? Despite himself, Frederick had liked the man and was tempted to believe his version of events. And beyond the circumstance of his presence, they had no real evidence against him. Not that men had not been hung for less.

Should he suggest that Mr. Smith question King during the inquest? Frederick felt oddly reticent to do so. It seemed too easy, too convenient to lay the blame at the feet of a notorious moneylender. There were those who would happily convict a man for that fact alone. Thankfully, this jury was only to decide the cause and manner of death. Convicting any suspects would wait till trial at the county assizes.

Would there be any justice for Ambrose Oliver? Despite the author's contemptible character, he felt compelled to seek it.

While Brixton was talking with Mr. King's manservant, Frederick questioned the other guests—a middle-aged couple named Mr. and Mrs. Curtis, followed by Mrs. Sizemore and her daughter. All expressed disappointment that they'd not seen more of the famous author during their stay but could shed no light on his death.

Then Frederick questioned Lady Fitzhoward's maid, Nicole Joly.

"Have a seat, please, mademoiselle."

The thin, dark-haired woman sat and folded her hands primly in her lap.

"You are employed by Lady Fitzhoward—is that right?"

"Yes."

"And how much do you know about her . . . her history, family, et cetera?"

Miss Joly reared her head back in surprise. "What has this to do with that man's death? Is that not why you question us?"

"Yes." Not wishing to cast suspicion on the woman's employer, Frederick retreated. "I am simply trying to gauge if you have been with her long."

"Oh. Three years."

"And what do you do when you are not attending Lady Fitzhoward? I see her often in the library or garden alone, so . . ."

She frowned. "You suggest I am idle?"

"No. Merely wondering where you spend your time."

"In my room. I sew for my lady. Take care of her clothes. Remove the small stains or dirt from the hems."

"And do you dine with the staff, or . . . ?"

She shook her head. "The chef sends up the special food to my room. He cooks for me his favorite dishes he says the English would not appreciate. Oh. I should not tell you that part."

"I shan't repeat it, never fear. And what did you do before you started with Lady Fitzhoward? Had you been lady's maid for someone else first?"

"*Non.* I worked in a dress shop, so I knew how to sew. And she taught me to arrange the hair. She is quite particular and likes it just so. And I learn to apply the cosmetics. My lady is most patient, though she says I make her look like . . . what is the English saying, the mutton as lamb?"

He nodded. "And have you been to Swanford before?"

"Me? *Non.* But I think my lady was here long ago. At least, she has some acquaintance in the area."

"Do you know who?"

"Not the name. After she delivered Miss Lane here to visit her brother, she planned to send a note to this acquaintance and see if the invitation arrived."

"No invitation was forthcoming?"

Miss Joly raised her hands. "She did not send her note. She changed her mind and decided to stay in the hotel."

"Did she say why?"

Miss Joly winced in memory. "Something like, 'It is best to leave the past in the past'?"

"I see."

Her dark eyes studied him. "How inquisitive you are! I thought you would ask about the night the author died."

"I am getting to that. *Did* you see or hear anything the night of Mr. Oliver's death? Anything that might help us?"

"*Non.*" She scrunched her face in thought. "Wait. The night before last?"

"Right. The body was discovered yesterday morning."

She considered. "Most often my lady goes to bed early. But that night, she wanted to sit on her veranda and think.

"She said she would call for me when she was ready to retire.

But Monsieur Marhic made for me the *coq au vin* and sent up the French bread and wine." She kissed her fingertips. "Ah! Delicious. I confess I ate too much and fell asleep.

"In the morning I awake with a start and realize if my lady had called during the night, I did not hear. I hurried into her room, afraid she would be vexed. But no. She had removed her over robe herself and went to bed that way. She said she had stayed up late and did not wish to disturb me."

"Is she always so understanding?" he asked.

Miss Joly shook her head. "Sometimes she is peevish, but more often she is . . . understanding, as you say."

"And did you venture out of your room that night?"

"No. I wanted to go down and thank Monsieur Marhic, but I fell asleep as I said."

He made a note. "And lastly, have you seen or heard anything unusual since you have been here?"

She tilted her head to one side, her long, narrow face puckering. "Unusual . . . how?"

"Well, I don't mean to lead you, but one person staying here reported seeing a ghost. Or at least, someone dressed as a nun or abbess."

He expected the French woman to scoff, but instead her expression brightened. "*C'est vrai?* Ah! I like to hear that. For I did see such a one. That night, I look out the window and I see a figure dressed in black with the white, em, how do you say . . ." She circled her face with a finger.

"Wimple."

"*C'est ça.* Wimple. I thought I drank too much wine. I turn to look, *mais non*, the carafe is still quite full. I look out again, but she has disappeared. Who else saw it?"

"Perhaps I should not say, as the young lady in question has experienced some ridicule over it."

"Not from me. Not when I saw it too!"

"Very well, it was Miss Lane."

"Miss Lane?" Her dark eyebrows rose. "This surprises me. So practical and serious." She wrinkled her nose.

"You two don't get on?"

"Oh yes, now. I admit I was jealous at first. Before she came, I was companion to my lady as well as maid. I even dined with her when she felt lonely. Then Miss Lane came, so young, so pretty, so well-spoken. Ah well. She is kind to me, so I overcome my bad feelings."

"I am glad to hear it."

"And now we have this in common!" Miss Joly leaned back in her chair, shaking her head with apparent wonder.

When she said nothing further, he thanked the woman for her time.

After seeing her out, Fredrick sat heavily back down, exhausted. Talking to people did that to him on the best of days, and this had not been the best of days.

17

The next morning, as Frederick went downstairs to breakfast, he steeled himself to report to the coroner, wishing he had more to tell him.

Mr. Smith, standing in the hall at the reception desk, looked up at his approach. "Ah, Sir Frederick. I was just leaving you a note. We shall have the autopsy results tomorrow, according to Mr. Brown. So we shall reconvene then."

The coroner asked nothing about Frederick's interviews with the guests, and Frederick was relieved for the reprieve.

"Thank you for telling me."

"Well, I'm off." Smith pulled on his gloves. "There's been a death in Rushwick. Sounds like an accident, so I expect to be back before the day is out. Tomorrow morning at the latest."

Frederick nodded. "Godspeed."

Walking through the passage, he saw Jack George leaving the coffee room and raised a hand. "Mr. George, just the man I was hoping to talk to. May I ask you a few more questions?"

"Very well. Though I've already told the coroner what I know." The man gestured to a table just inside the coffee room door and the two sat down.

Frederick said, "First of all, just a point of curiosity. I have heard you referred to as both Mr. George and Sergeant George. Which is it?"

The man lifted his chin in acknowledgment. "Mr. George will do. I was a trooper in the army but didn't advance to officer. Still, some call me Sergeant as a term of respect, and I don't correct them."

Frederick nodded his understanding and asked, "You told the coroner that you '*had* a shooting gallery.' Do you no longer?"

The lines around the man's eyes and mouth tightened. "That's right. Numbers were down. Could no longer justify the rent on the place."

"I am sorry to hear it."

"Not as sorry as I was."

"You mentioned Mr. Oliver came to your training gallery for only a few months."

He nodded. "Right. Not long enough to gain much strength or skill. Never saw a fellow sweat so much—had to stop and catch his breath every other minute."

"Was he still coming when you decided to close?"

"No, but he remembered me when this situation came up and asked me to accompany him. With the gallery closed, I was in need of a job, so I agreed."

"When Mr. Edgecombe was questioned, he said he was glad you were here to keep Mr. Oliver writing. But something you said seemed to call that into question."

George shook his head. "Edgecombe didn't want me here. As I said, he thought the whole situation a waste of time and money. He agreed to pay the author's hotel bill, but Mr. Oliver was supposed to pay me. Which, true to form, he did not."

"I will cover the cost of your stay, but I am afraid I cannot reimburse your lost wages as well."

Mr. George held up a palm. "Would not ask it of you. Not your responsibility."

Frederick said, "You also mentioned seeing another maid enter Mr. Oliver's room in Mary's stead."

"Yes, though I don't know which one it was or her name."

"What did she look like?"

"Barely saw her, truth be told, with that floppy cap over her face."

"So you may have been mistaken about it being someone else?"

"It's possible. Look, I don't want to get Mary into any trouble. She seems a good girl, quiet and respectful."

"Could you at least tell if she was young or old? Fair or dark? Pretty?"

He looked down in concentration. "Young, I think. Dark. Beyond that I couldn't say. Only got a glimpse. She ducked her head, I recall, shy-like or scared. I worried Oliver might have tried something with her, but she scurried off before I could find out."

Frederick watched him with interest. "And what would you have done if he had tried something?"

Mr. George looked up. "And her unwilling?"

Frederick nodded.

The trooper's eyes glinted, and Frederick was put in mind of a fierce dog they'd once had. He didn't bark, but he did bite.

Then Mr. George leaned back in his chair and crossed his arms. "Advised her to take care in the man's presence."

"That all?"

He gave a casual shrug. "What else?"

Frederick wondered but changed tack. "And what will you do now?"

"Now?"

"After this is over, I mean."

George shrugged again. "Don't know. I had not thought that far. Wasn't sure how long this job would last."

Frederick nodded. "Not long at all, as it turns out."

~

Rebecca considered attending divine services at All Saints that Sunday but instead sat alone in the dim abbey chapel, the wrought iron chandelier with its white tapers unlit above her, the ornately carved wooden pew hard beneath her, and the air sharp with the acrid smells of snuffed candles and turpentine polish.

She gazed up to the colored panes of stained glass depicting the Messiah's suffering, crucifixion, and resurrection. Sunlight brightened the scene and burned her heart.

What have I done? she inwardly lamented, but she knew very well. She had lied to Sir Frederick and sinned against God and her own conscience.

She thought back to her conversation with Frederick in the garden the previous evening, when he'd confronted her about withholding the truth. She had anticipated anger, but the eyes that met hers were gentle and disappointed, which was almost worse. She had felt ashamed but also grateful to the kind, patient man, who somehow still believed her to be good and honest.

Sadly, she was neither.

I am sorry. Please forgive me. The silent plea seemed to echo inside her troubled soul.

She whispered aloud, "What should I do?"

But the words again echoed across the empty chapel and back to her from the stone walls, apparently unheard and unanswered.

Rebecca pressed a hand to her eyes as tears threatened. She had to make a decision, and make it soon.

Later that morning, Rebecca came upon Lady Fitzhoward in the library and writing room, studying a series of framed prints on the wall.

As Rebecca stepped into the room, her employer glanced over her shoulder. "Ah, Miss Lane. Have you seen these?"

She must have walked past them, but there had been little of beauty or color to attract her attention. Now she joined the woman in her perusal of the trio of architectural floor plans in gilded frames.

"You just missed Mr. Mayhew," Lady Fitzhoward said. "He told me about these. The first is the original abbey as it was in the Middle Ages."

Rebecca surveyed the black lines on yellowed parchment: the square cloisters at the heart of the monastic building, the long nave of the former church, as well as the chaplains' room and chapter house in the very space where they were now standing.

The woman gestured to the second frame. "This is a plan for the manor house built over and around the original abbey after the dissolution."

Rebecca nodded, recognizing the hall, long gallery, and bed-chambers, the gaping wound of the destroyed church like a missing appendage. She also noted the addition of a Tudor courtyard with its stables and coach house.

Finally, Lady Fitzhoward pointed to the third frame, the more recent plans to convert the manor into a hotel. The hall, cloisters, and stable yard were still there, but much had been added and changed.

Rebecca leaned closer and pointed from plan to plan to plan. "Look. The night stair is there in all three."

Lady Fitzhoward nodded. "And there are other constants as well."

Rebecca studied the drawings again and identified the constants as she found them. "The cloisters. The remaining chapel, although the wall has been rebuilt and the entrance moved. The cellars . . ." She slowly scanned the plans, following each drawn wall, wishing she had her reading spectacles. "Mr. Mayhew said the abbess's room is now room three. . . ."

"Mm-hm."

"And what is this below it? This little . . . curl or hook in the otherwise solid wall?"

Lady Fitzhoward screwed up her eyes, the crepey skin around them webbing into deep lines. "You tell me. My old peepers are not what they used to be."

"I have spectacles upstairs if you'd like to borrow them," Rebecca offered lightly, knowing she would refuse.

"Ha. You know I am too proud to acknowledge any imperfections." She gave a self-deprecating smirk. "Well, when you work it out, let me know. I think I shall retire to the veranda and pretend to read."

Lady Fitzhoward turned and walked from the room, her echoing footfalls growing softer and fading away.

Rebecca continued to stare at the plans, but they blurred before her as a memory filled her mind—one of Rose telling her and John a story. While Rose talked, she'd sipped from a glass of homemade plum wine, which tended to make her wistful about the past.

"When I was young, the abbey was home to the Sharington family," Rose explained. "I was quite close to their lady's maid. She slept in a small room adjoining the lady's bedchamber, so she would always be at her mistress's beck and call.

"Oh, but we were cheeky girls." Rose shook her head, smiling fondly. "I would walk over there and let myself in through the chapel, which was open to visitors in those days. From there, I would sneak up the servants' stairs to her room. She was supposed to be mending for her mistress, but instead we would sit shoulder-to-shoulder on her little bed and drink wine and whisper and giggle like a pair of giddy fools." The housekeeper's eyes twinkled. But a moment later, those same eyes filled with tears. "I still miss her, after all these years."

"Did she move away, or . . . ?" Rebecca let her question dangle, not wanting to say the words *pass away*.

Thankfully, Rose nodded. "She moved away many years ago now. Before you were born. You must think me a right nattering goose to still remember her, let alone miss her, but I do."

The memory faded. Rebecca went upstairs to room thirteen and retrieved her spectacles. Wearing them, she returned and again studied the prints. She helped herself to pen, ink, and a sheet of hotel stationery and sketched a plan of her own.

She then wandered out into the cloisters. Following her sketch, she walked past the night stair toward the chapel, then turned and walked along the passage that ran parallel to the church ruins outside. Nearing the next corner, she again consulted her drawing. From where she stood, the blue parlour would be on the other side of the wall in front of her and the hall to her right. Above her would be room three, formerly the abbess's private chamber. She looked at her rough rendering of the old plans. Was anything still here? Some trace of the "servants' stairs" Rose had mentioned? Or were they long gone, demolished during the hotel renovations?

Peering into that dim corner, Rebecca saw a small alcove she'd walked past without noticing before. On the left was an arched stone bay that had once, perhaps, been a low doorway leading into the long-ruined nave. If it had once been a passageway, it had been bricked up long ago. On the right was a crude wooden door—low and a foot or more above the ground. The planks were painted a dull grey, with iron hinges and a sliding bolt. Rebecca assumed it was now some sort of storage cabinet, if it was used at all.

Or was it?

After attending church with his mother, Frederick returned to the abbey. He came in through the garden door and walked through the cloisters, determined to have another look in room three. He wanted to work out how a perpetrator managed to not only enter the room but also to lock the door behind himself when he left.

As he turned the corner, he saw a woman lurking in the shadows.

A pert female figure backed from a dim alcove. The trim waist, hair, and profile were painfully familiar. His heart sank to see her sneaking around. What was she up to?

"Miss Lane?"

She jerked and whirled, clearly startled and perhaps guilty. Her eyes, wide behind spectacles, met his and skittered away again into the dark corner, which made him suspect she had been meeting someone.

Rebecca placed a hand to her chest. "You gave me a start."

Looking past her, he saw that she was alone. Even so, he told himself to remain aloof and objective in her company, more the magistrate and less the lovelorn fool. "What are you doing skulking about down here?"

"Just exploring. Fascinating old place."

"Yes . . ." he absently replied. Gaze lingering on her face, he said, "I have never seen you wear spectacles before."

"Oh." She quickly removed them, tucking them into the reticule dangling from her wrist. "Mostly for reading."

"And what were you reading down here?"

"I . . . was, em, trying to follow the floor plans from the library." She held up a sketch as proof. "And where are you headed?"

"Back up to number three. I still have Mayhew's key."

"May I come along?"

He vacillated, mind and heart wrestling. "Well . . . I suppose that would be all right. Though I am surprised you would want to see it again."

"Actually, I am very keen to do so."

He looked at her in consternation, her expression strangely eager. Why?

As they crossed the hall to the main stairs, Miss Lane said, "May I ask what you are hoping to find?"

In a low voice, Frederick replied, "I am still wondering how the perpetrator managed to enter undetected, and then lock the door behind himself when he left."

"You assume whoever it was stole a key?"

"Or possessed one legitimately."

"Do you suspect one of the staff?"

He shook his head. "I don't, and yet, besides the maids, only Mrs. Somerton and Mr. Mayhew had keys to the room. And there is no other way in."

"That may not be true."

Surprise flashed through him. "What do you mean?"

"I believe there may be another way into that room. At least, there used to be."

Frederick shook his head. "The windows were latched from the inside, remember?"

She nodded. "Even so. There may be another way."

He looked at her doubtfully. "Show me."

When they reached the top of the stairs, Miss Lane paused to pick up a lamp from a table in the passage. She said, "In the days when this was an abbey, room three was part of the abbess's private chamber."

"Yes, I heard." He unlocked the door and opened it, gesturing for her to precede him and hesitating a moment before closing it after them.

She continued, "Lady Fitzhoward and I studied the floor plans in the library. There is what appears to be a small spiral staircase leading to and from this room—one the abbess probably used to go to and from the cloisters below and into the church beyond. After the abbey closed and Mr. Sharington renovated the building into a family home, this room became his wife's bedchamber. Her lady's maid slept in a small room adjoining it, with a second door leading to a servants' stairway, so the maid could come and go without disturbing her mistress or being seen by guests."

"How do you know all this?"

"Rose told John and me about it a few years back. She and the lady's maid were friends."

He looked around the room. "Where would it be?"

"I am not sure." Rebecca went to the closet and opened it. A coat and discarded cravat hung from hooks on the wall, and a two-tier wooden shelf for shoes or hat boxes sat on the floor. It had been pushed to the right side, Mr. Oliver's hat atop it, looking abandoned and forlorn.

"That is only a closet," Frederick observed.

Miss Lane nodded. "I assume the former maid's room was done away with during hotel renovations, leaving only this."

She eyed the set of low shelves. "In my room, the shelves are set against the back of the closet."

"In mine as well."

She felt along the seam for some sort of hidden latch, searching all the way to the floor. Nothing. She straightened and in mild frustration pushed the rear panel. The panel popped open, and cool, musty air wafted out at them.

He gaped. "Why did Mr. Mayhew not tell us about this?"

"I doubt he knows. Remember, he bought this place after the first investors went bankrupt. Most of the work had already been done. In the floor plans, the stairs appear as a tiny curl within the wall. Easy to miss. Or he may have assumed the stairs had been removed, since they are now completely hidden from view."

"Surely someone else must know of this. The workmen? The maids?"

She shook her head. "You can ask Mr. Mayhew, but I believe most of the present staff were hired after the renovations were completed."

"And what about servants from the Sharington days—are any of them still alive and in the area?"

"Not that I am aware of."

"And Rose told you about this?" he asked again.

"Yes, apparently she used to sneak over here to visit her friend, no one any the wiser."

Some fleeting glimmer of an idea teased the edges of Frederick's mind and faded away as quickly. What was it? He tried to call it back to no avail.

He peered into the shadowy space, the light from the lamp descending into the shaft, revealing the uppermost stairs—chalky grey stone, almost white—curving sharply away into the darkness below.

Miss Lane extended the lamp farther into the space, into this hidden capsule of medieval architecture.

"I will go first," Frederick offered. The tightly wound stairs would be best navigated one at a time. His shoulder brushed the wall as he slowly descended.

"Right behind you," she whispered.

Partway down, a narrow shaft of light pierced the darkness. Studying it, he saw that a little section of masonry had been removed from the vaulting to form a squint. He had to bend to position his eye to it. People in earlier generations had been shorter, and he was above average height for the present age. Through the slit, he could see a small slice of the cloisters.

There, he glimpsed Miss Newport standing in the walkway, talking to someone he could not see. The woman reached out her hand, a look of consolation or resolve on her pretty face. "It will be all right," she said, and walked away, out of view.

He wondered whom she'd been talking to. Thomas? Not like him to need consoling.

Frederick then descended a few stairs to allow Miss Lane to look through the squint after him.

She mused, "Do you suppose the abbess used this hole to spy on the nuns in the cloisters?"

"Maybe."

Frederick continued down the stairs until they abruptly ended at a wall. He felt around its surface. Not a wall but a wooden door, the faintest lines of light showing through its vertical boards.

He tried pushing it open. It did not give. "I think it's locked from the outside. Or perhaps this is permanently sealed and not a door at all."

She said, "I will go around and unbolt it."

Frederick would have offered to go himself but knew there was no decent way to move past her in the confined space. He asked, "Do you know where it is?"

"Yes. I know."

Rebecca made her way back up the spiral stairs and let herself from room three, shutting the door quietly behind her.

Hoping to avoid a lengthy encounter with Lady Fitzhoward or anyone else, she decided not to use the closer, more public main stairway and instead hurried through the gallery passage and down the night stair, returning to the cloisters that way. Reaching the southwest corner, she paused. Seeing only a waiter in the courtyard, clearing a table, she stepped into the shadowy alcove.

Leaning near the plank door, she whispered, "Sir Frederick? Can you hear me?"

No answer. Disappointment flared. Perhaps this was not the same door after all.

She tugged the sliding bolt, but it did not give. Using both hands, she took a broader stance and pulled again. It stuttered to the side.

"Miss Lane?" Frederick asked, his voice close by.

"I'm here," she whispered back.

She pulled, and he apparently pushed, and the plank door creaked open toward her, revealing cobwebbed corners, dust, and the handsome, intent face of Sir Frederick Wilford.

He lifted his chin and looked out in amazement. "So there *was* another way into the room."

She nodded. "By the way," she said. "I called your name a moment ago. Did you not hear me?"

"Sorry. I had retraced my steps to the squint. I found something interesting on the wall near it. Come and see."

He extended his hand.

She put her hand in his, lifted one foot to the door's bottom lip, and ducked her head. He pulled her into the entombed spiral staircase.

"Up here," he said in a hushed voice. "It is another wall painting, like the ones Mr. Mayhew showed us."

She shut the plank door behind herself and followed him up and around the sharp curve of the stairs.

"See it?" he whispered.

The glow from the squint, aided by the lamp, revealed a drawing on the wall nearby. Compared to the preserved paintings of St. Andrew and the abbess in the library, this was far simpler. The figure of a rabbit had been scratched into the limestone. Amateurish, almost childish. Below it were the words *JOHAN fecit hoe*. Perhaps, Rebecca mused, the name of the abbess or chaplain who had drawn it.

"What does it mean?" she asked.

He lowered the lamp to study the words.

"John did this."

The simple translation chilled her.

She shivered and attempted to keep her voice light. "Why a rabbit?"

"In Christian art, I believe they are a symbol of the resurrection."

"Really? I did not know that."

"And in secular art, a symbol of fertility."

She felt her neck grow foolishly warm at the word. *Silly creature! You are a grown woman, not a schoolgirl.*

"Or so they taught us at university," he said dryly. "Come. Let's go up."

When they returned to room three, Sir Frederick lingered in the closet, eyeing the repositioned shelves. Rebecca looked as well. Had someone let themselves into Mr. Oliver's room and pushed the thing aside to get in?

Or had someone moved it for them?

Mary flashed through her mind. Mary going daily into Mr. Oliver's room. Mary with her head near John's, the two whispering together. But Rebecca kept those thoughts to herself.

Frederick said, "This opens possibilities, does it not? No key needed to sneak into or back out of this room."

Rebecca nodded, wondering dully if she had just made things worse for her brother, if indeed *John did this*.

"I think I will talk to Mr. Mayhew again," Sir Frederick said. "Ask if he knows of any builders still in the area. But . . . let's keep this discovery to ourselves for now, all right? I am not sure why, but I think it might be a wise precaution."

"I agree." In the meantime, Rebecca longed to ask some questions of her own.

She noticed a chalky-white smear on Frederick's shoulder, and automatically reached up to wipe at it, saying, "You must have brushed against something."

Her fingers lingered. Rubbing again, she felt the firm, rounded muscle beneath his sleeve.

Frederick had turned his head to try to see the offending mark, but now his focus returned to her.

He placed his hand over hers, and for a moment they stood that way in utter stillness. Rebecca felt the warmth of his gaze on her face and the warmth of his hand on hers. Pulse racing, she looked up at him, tall and darkly handsome, his deep brown eyes fixed on her so intently that she struggled to breathe.

Suddenly recalling her brother's possible crime, icy reality cascaded over her and she snatched her hand away.

"There. Good as new."

"Thank you," he said, his voice a low rumble.

She nodded and thought, *If only the rest of this calamity could be remedied as easily as a chalk smear.*

18

So much for my resolve to remain aloof and objective in Miss Lane's company, Frederick thought as he walked away from her. He could still feel her hand on his shoulder, touching him, almost . . . caressing him. He squeezed his eyes shut as though to blot out the memory. *Imbecile*. She had merely wiped dirt from his sleeve like any friend would.

And yet he could not forget the look on her face when she'd gazed up at him, eyes wide, lips softly parted. He'd been tempted to kiss her then and there, despite her lies or at least her evasion. What a fool he was. When she'd pulled her hand away, he immediately wanted it back.

"Good as new?" Hardly.

With a concerted effort, Frederick returned his focus to the present task. He went to speak to Mr. Mayhew again and found him in his office.

"What can you tell me about the workmen who renovated this building into a hotel?"

"Precious little!" Mayhew sat back and pursed his lips. "By the time I bought the place, the builders and stonemasons had moved on to other jobs. I had to hire new men for the finishing work—joiners mostly, and a few plumbers—to complete what the others had started."

"And what about servants from the building's days as a private house—any of them employed here now?"

"I don't think so. Goodness, the only person old enough might be Abe Plaskitt, our gardener."

"I see."

Mayhew tilted his head. "Why do you ask?"

"Oh, merely following up a theory."

Frederick was still reluctant to tell the man about the secret stairway, not ready to make that news public. Perhaps because he thought he might yet use it to his advantage. Or perhaps because he feared revealing it might somehow endanger Miss Lane.

As Rebecca descended the stairs and looked down upon the hall below, she saw Dr. Fox in his blue frock coat sitting with a companion near the fireplace.

Noticing her, the doctor stood. "Ah, Miss Lane. May I present my wife, Mrs. Jane Fox."

Rebecca walked over, footsteps echoing until she reached the plush carpet. She curtsied. "How do you do."

Mrs. Fox inclined her head in return, her expression friendly and interested. "A pleasure to meet you, Miss Lane. My husband tells me you are an old friend to the Wilford family."

"Yes, we have that in common."

Dr. Fox smiled in acknowledgment. "We have just returned from a stroll and were about to order chocolate to warm our bones. Will you join us?"

"Thank you, yes. That is very kind."

Rebecca sat down and began chatting with the woman while her husband ordered their drinks.

Mrs. Fox was a pretty, petite woman with a pleasant demeanor, dressed simply in olive green.

When Dr. Fox sat back down, Rebecca said, "Sir Frederick mentioned something about your medical specialty. Could you tell me about your practice?"

"Yes, if you'd like. I have an asylum for people suffering from various mental and emotional disturbances. You may have heard me called a 'mad doctor.'"

Rebecca had heard Thomas Wilford refer to him as such, but didn't acknowledge it. Instead she said, "Sir Frederick describes you as a highly reputable physician with new and humane methods."

The man nodded, eyes warm. "Frederick understands me. I detest the terms *idiot*, *madmen*, and the like. For centuries, ignorant people, many with little or no medical training, have mistreated or imprisoned those with mild hysterias, restless agitation, and even common melancholia. Some make no distinction between the truly insane and a merely nervous patient, for whom confinement should continue no longer than necessary. Often such dear souls are harmless, yet have been forced to endure barbaric practices like purging, shackles, ice baths, narcotics, and worse."

"My dear," his wife protested gently. "Miss Lane may not wish to hear all the gruesome particulars."

"Ah. Forgive me."

"Nothing to forgive," Rebecca said, swallowing back the queasiness his words had caused. "I asked and find it most fascinating."

Their cups of chocolate arrived along with a plate of crisp almond biscuits. For a few minutes the conversation turned to other topics: the history of the hotel, the enjoyment of their holiday, the many games of chess they had played, and the strange disruption of Ambrose Oliver's death.

When Mrs. Fox finished her chocolate, she set down her cup and said, "Will the two of you excuse me? I have ordered a bath."

Her husband rose and helped her to her feet. "Of course, my love."

Mrs. Fox turned to Rebecca and said earnestly, "Please do continue your discussion without me. My dear husband is always glad to find someone who is genuinely interested in his work."

Rebecca smiled at the woman, happy to oblige them both.

Dr. Fox sat back down, and Rebecca said, "You had begun to tell me about your asylum."

He crossed one leg over the other. "Yes. Woodlane is a hospital for the curable and a comfortable retreat for the incurable. We offer compassionate, therapeutic, moral treatment."

"Forgive me, but what does that mean?"

He entwined his hands over one knee. "As opposed to places like Bethlehem Hospital, or 'Bedlam,' which primarily restrain the severely deranged, my specialty is providing professional guidance in a safe environment to help the anxious or depressed, and those suffering from manias or hysterias. We employ gentle, long-term treatments to restore mental, emotional, and spiritual health."

Rebecca thought the doctor sounded rather like a pamphlet but also sincere. "And may I ask what inspired this calling of yours?"

He nodded. "My father and brothers manage a large asylum near Bristol. They do good work overall and have been quite successful. I agree with the majority of my father's practices, though not all. He has on occasion resorted to cold shower-baths, strait-waistcoats, and manacles for the most refractory patients. He also believes removing a patient from his home influence is of the utmost importance.

"At Woodlane, I have changed what I disagreed with while preserving the best of my father's methods in a smaller, more homelike setting. For example, we have abolished all use of restraints and encourage visits and correspondence with loved ones to stave off feelings of abandonment. We promote physical and mental activity. Patients have access to my personal collection of books, and I encourage participation in regular divine services, which I find has a positive, peaceful effect. And I invite patients, in turns, to spend evenings with my family so I might observe any improper behaviors and help to check them. I want my patients to lead as active and normal a life as possible while with me, with the aim of returning them to a *fully* normal life as soon as reasonable."

"Impressive. Where is Woodlane?"

"Just north of Cheltenham."

He leaned forward and looked at her closely, speculation glimmering in his eyes. "As my good wife said, I always appreciate an attentive audience, but may I ask to what your questions tend? Is there a particular sufferer you have in mind?"

Rebecca hesitated. The newspapers often reported accounts of wrongfully issued lunacy certificates and people held against their will for minor oddities, differences in religion, or simply so a family member could gain control of someone's finances. Would she endanger John by mentioning her concerns?

Perhaps something in her expression betrayed her whirling thoughts, for he said in fatherly tones, "You may speak to me in confidence, my dear. If it is a loved one you are concerned about, I can promise I have no intention of intruding into your private affairs or forcing a certificate of lunacy into your hands. But I would like to help, if I can."

Rebecca pressed dry lips together. "You are very kind. May I ask, are any of the people who come to your asylum . . . cured? Is such a thing even possible?"

"I have seen many return to soundness of mind and to liberty. Of course, not everyone can be 'cured,' as you say. Some will never recover, despite our best efforts. For many who suffer from severe mental derangement, release is not the right answer, especially those who may pose a threat to themselves or others.

"And even those with more minor complaints may continue to struggle with depressions of spirit, but they can learn to ignore the vile voices in their minds that torment them with doubts, lies, and thoughts of self-harm. We encourage them to battle paralyzing fears with prayer and right thinking and a reliance on God's strength. A wise prescription for all of us in this troubled age, I'd say."

"Yes," she murmured. "True."

"I wish I could say I had a magic potion, a regimen of healthful diet, exercise, and therapeutic practices that would return all to soundness. Sadly, I cannot. But I don't give up hope. And neither, Miss Lane, should you."

She forced herself to meet his inquisitive gaze, then quickly looked away again.

He added, "Sir Frederick has visited Woodlane."

"Has he?"

"Yes, as magistrate, one of his duties is to inspect asylums."

"I did not realize."

"So if you are not comfortable asking me more . . . specific questions, you might wish to talk with him."

"Thank you. I—"

At that moment, Sir Frederick entered the hall from the rear passage and, seeing them, walked over.

He smiled at her and said to the doctor, "Good day, Charles."

"Ah, Frederick. I was just telling Miss Lane that you are familiar with my methods."

His face stilled. "Because of Marina, do you mean?"

Dr. Fox's lips parted and lines of remorse scored his brow. "No, no. I said nothing of your late wife. I only said that you have visited Woodlane several times in your role as magistrate."

"Ah yes, the quarterly inspections." Frederick glanced at her, then away again. "A commendable establishment." He shifted from foot to foot. "Well. Only wanted to greet you. I will leave you to your talk."

He bowed and walked away before either could protest.

Dr. Fox sent her a telling look.

Rebecca nodded and replied, "I will consider your advice."

Frederick walked away, feeling like a blundering oaf. Of course Charles had not mentioned Marina's disturbing behavior. He was too discreet for that. It was he who'd blurted out her name, embarrassed himself and the others too. *Dashed fool.*

He guessed Miss Lane had heard the rumors about his wife's death. He wondered if she believed them. Would she exonerate him if she knew all? Why should she, when he owned a share of the blame?

When he'd met Miss Marina Seward, he'd been instantly taken by her beauty and charm and astonished that she seemed to find him charming in return. Everyone said Frederick was lucky to marry her. At the time, he'd agreed. But later he had cause to repent of his choice.

The first few years of their marriage had been difficult. Strained. Marina had remained distant from him, despite his best efforts. He'd concluded his efforts were lacking and had no idea how to bridge the ever-widening gap.

Then one night she announced she had something to tell him. Frederick had steeled himself for the worst—a deadly diagnosis, perhaps, since she had recently consulted a physician. But what she told him was good news, at least to him. Marina was expecting a child.

A child to love? An heir to the estate? He was elated. It felt like the sun finally rising after a long, dark night.

Marina, however, was clearly unhappy. Said she was not ready to be a broodmare and lose her figure. Insisted she was not meant to be a mother and possessed no maternal instincts.

Frederick had tried to reassure her, saying her doubts were only natural and that she would learn. *They* would learn together. She scoffed.

His wife started leaving Wickworth more often without saying where she was going or why. When she was home, she insisted on taking long walks alone. She drank too much and ate too little. Frederick began to fear she would injure her health or that of the babe. Or even that she would take measures to destroy the child.

He wrote to his friend Dr. Fox, whom he knew to be a capable, discreet physician who treated people with disturbances of the mind, including female hysteria and unnatural feelings.

Knowing Marina would resist going to the man's establishment, he asked his friend to come to Wickworth at his earliest convenience.

Dr. Fox came as a personal favor and met with his wife. Of course, Frederick hoped Charles would suggest some cure, some simple treatment that could be completed before the child's birth. But in the end, Dr. Fox was not convinced she was hysteric so much as flighty, devilishly vain, and selfish. Even so, he gently counseled Marina and prescribed rest and a healthful diet.

When she lost the child—whether by God's design or her own—Frederick had been devastated. His wife might not love him, but his child would have.

One evening Marina came into his bedchamber and found him weeping. Even now, Frederick's face burned in shame at the memory.

She stood, hands on slim hips, and rolled her eyes. "What are you crying about?" she said, voice dripping with disdain. "The child was not even yours."

At that, she'd turned and swept from the room. Fury and incredulity burned away his tears and drove him to his feet. He strode after her and caught up with her at the top of the stairs.

"Then whose?" he demanded.

"Does it matter?"

She started to turn away again, but Frederick grabbed her arm to stop her. She jerked away so forcefully that she lost her balance and fell backward down the stairs.

Even thinking about it now, his heart lurched, that startling, breath-stealing terror seizing him anew.

He'd lunged, reaching for her, but only caught the ribbon tie around her waist, which tore as she fell, and fell, and fell . . .

In a blind panic, Frederick hurried down the stairs after her, shouting for the footman to summon a doctor.

But it was too late. She had broken her neck and died instantly.

Despite everything, sorrow had swamped him. He'd never meant her any harm, never wished her ill.

How often he'd rehearsed that moment, wishing he had acted more quickly to stop her fall. He knew some people suspected he'd pushed his unfaithful wife to her death, but he had not. Even so, he knew he was not blameless.

The constable, physician, and coroner had unanimously declared it an accident and exonerated him. But the guilt still hung heavy on his soul.

———

Rebecca watched Sir Frederick leave, but her thoughts soon returned to John. Her dear, disturbed brother who could spew hateful disparagement one minute and sweet consolation the next. He needed help—more than she or Rose could give him. Could Dr. Fox help John? Maybe. But her brother would never willingly agree to enter an asylum.

She thanked Dr. Fox again and walked through the cloisters, lingering in that reverent place to add a prayer to all the thousands that had been offered there over the centuries.

Oh, God, please help us. I don't know what to do. Please give me wisdom.

One minute her heart broke for John, her little brother who'd lost his mother young and whose father could never relate to his more artistic ways. Who, being small for his age as well as sensitive, had suffered taunts from bullies and betrayals by childhood friends. And later had suffered a hope-crushing blow when the manuscript he had worked on so long and arduously had been published as another's.

The next minute, her anger kindled against him. Yes, John had suffered setbacks and disappointments, but many people had suffered far worse—incurable illnesses, unjust imprisonment, the loss of children, limbs, or sight. And not all of those people felt sorry for themselves, lay in bed all day bemoaning life's unfairness, numbed pain with drink, and spent the household money on opium. And most certainly, they did not take revenge, kill anyone, and ruin their family's lives!

Rebecca sighed heavily. It was easy to blame John for her current misery. But she knew she had wrongs of her own to confess. Sins of omission. Outright lies. They gnawed at her. When she prayed, God seemed silent and forgiveness not forthcoming. Was that perhaps because she had yet to confess to the man she had deceived—a man she deeply admired, yet whose trust she had taken advantage of and broken?

Her chest tightened with a growing realization. Every minute she delayed would only worsen her wrongdoing and widen the breach.

Frederick returned to his room and lay on the bed, planning to rest awhile. He was surprised when someone knocked on his door a short while later. Thomas, he supposed, or perhaps Dr. Fox inviting him to play a game of chess in the library.

He opened the door, but instead of either man, Rebecca Lane stood there, face pale and stricken, a book in her arms.

"Rebecca . . . em. Miss Lane. What is it? What's wrong?"

"I am so sorry."

"About what?" He glanced down the quiet corridor. "I would invite you in, but that would not be the done thing. Perhaps we might talk downstair—"

"No. I must confess all now. In private. And after I tell you what I must, concerns about my reputation will not be uppermost in your mind."

Frederick stared at her, wanting to hear her out, yet filled with misgiving.

He made a decision. "Very well, come in. But keep your voice down." He let her into his room and closed the door, though he worried they might be heard through the wall.

"I hate that I have lied to you," she said. "The guilt has been clawing at my insides."

"Go on." Frederick leaned against a bedpost and braced himself, thinking about the man seen entering her room and fearing what she would tell him.

She implored, "Please don't line up all the chambermaids and ask Mr. George to identify one. And don't question Mary again. At least, not about the second maid who went into Mr. Oliver's room."

"Why not?"

"It was me."

"You?" Disbelief washed over him, followed by disapproval. "Why on earth would you go into that man's room, especially alone?"

She winced at his vehement reaction. So much for keeping their voices down.

"For John. He asked me to give his manuscript to Mr. Oliver in hopes he would recommend it to his publisher. But Mr. Oliver almost never left his room alone, that I saw. And Mr. George shooed me away when I tried to approach the author's room as myself. It was all I could think of."

Frederick pressed a hand to his forehead. "Rebecca . . ."

"Nothing happened! I asked him and he said he would consider it."

"Nothing else?"

"No. Well . . ."

"Well what? No more lying, if you please."

"He asked me if I knew Selina Newport. When I said I knew who she was, he told me to ask her to come and see him. Seemed confident she would."

"For what purpose, if that is not indiscreet to ask?"

"I don't know."

"And you relayed Oliver's request, saying it had come from your chambermaid?"

Miss Lane nodded, looking abashed. "I did. But I have no idea if she went or not."

"Miss Newport claims she did not go."

A new thought struck him. "Has this anything to do with why Mr. Oliver came to your room?"

"No. Mr. Edgecombe had told him John Lane's sister was staying at the hotel. That's why he came—to see if I was the 'maid' who'd given him the manuscript."

"I see." He expelled a rueful sigh. "Anything else to tell me?"

Rebecca lowered her head, then raised it again. "John did come here. To ask if I had delivered his novel into Mr. Oliver's hands. He spent part of the night sleeping in my armchair. I believe it was him the page saw entering my room, and him I saw leaving that morning when you came upon me in the parlour."

"The morning we found Mr. Oliver dead?"

She nodded, tears streaming down her cheeks.

His heart squeezed. "Why are you crying? You don't think John struck Mr. Oliver?"

"I don't think he would, but . . . "

"But what? Had he some reason to resent the man?"

She nodded and swiped at her wet cheek. He longed to wipe away her tears himself, to draw her into his arms and tell her everything would be all right. Even as he doubted it would be.

Shoving his hands behind his back to keep from reaching for her, he guessed, "Because Oliver was a successful author and John is not yet published?"

She shook her head. "It's more than that. When John worked briefly as his secretary, he asked Mr. Oliver to read his first novel, hoping he would recommend it to his publisher or at least offer some advice. Mr. Oliver read it and told John it was not good enough, not publishable—that he should start on something new or give up writing altogether."

"Difficult to hear, I can imagine, but surely not enough to kill a man over, years later."

"You're right. Though at first John believed the man's harsh criticism. He was bitterly disappointed, ranted and raged, and burned all his notes and old copies. Eventually he seemed to calm down and began working for the newspaper.

"But then, the following year, when Mr. Oliver's new novel was published, John discovered it was *his* book. His story, his characters, his plot. Mr. Oliver had stolen it. He had changed the title and some names and places, but the story, the words, whole paragraphs and pages of description and dialogue—all John's."

Stunned, Frederick said, "You should have come to me. Perhaps I might have helped, talked to our solicitor, something."

"We did try to assert John's claim. We first met alone with William Edgecombe. He asked for proof, and sadly, we had very little. Mr. Oliver had never returned the pages John had given him, and John had destroyed his early drafts after Mr. Oliver's rejection—on *his* advice, we then realized, no doubt hoping to protect himself from just such charges. John hired a lawyer for a short while, but he had little money for his fees. And at any rate, the lawyer told John he had no real case, not without proof. John did find an early outline, but the man said he could have written that anytime, even after Oliver's novel was printed. He offered little hope.

"Later, John and this lawyer met again with Mr. Edgecombe along with Mr. Oliver, who of course denied everything and said that ideas are two a penny and can't be owned. That even if they'd started with the same idea, it would become a completely different novel in a skilled author's hands. In the end, Mr. Edgecombe, eager to avoid scandal, offered John a small settlement on the understanding that he would drop the matter.

In turn, Edgecombe's own lawyer threatened John with an action for libel should he breathe a word of his 'baseless charges' to anyone.

"John accepted the settlement. I told him he should not, for the amount was not worth giving up his right to reclaim what was his. But John rashly agreed, saying it was his word against Ambrose Oliver's and why would anyone believe him?"

Frederick said, "Could you not testify to John's authorship yourself?"

She again looked down, clearly embarrassed. "No, to my shame. John had asked me to read his manuscript at one point, and I'd meant to, but at the time, I was reading a novel I loved, *Pride and Prejudice*, so I kept putting it off. It was terribly selfish of me, I admit.

"The truth is, I had learned from a young age that John is highly sensitive to any criticism. Especially from me. He didn't really want my opinion, he wanted my unmitigated praise, which I doubted I could give him. When this happened, John felt betrayed that I had never read the manuscript. I have felt guilty ever since."

Frederick slowly nodded. "I believe I understand. Thank you for telling me."

Sudden realization twisted Frederick's gut. "Wait . . . are you saying John wrote *The Faded Rose of Wickwood?*"

Miss Lane reddened all the more. "Yes, although under a different title. I am sorry. Apparently in John's version, any correlation to real people and places was more subtle, but after Oliver changed the names and made a few vague references less vague . . . well. John never meant to hurt you, I know."

"And here I vilified Ambrose Oliver. . . ."

"You were justified, though perhaps not for the precise reason you thought."

He ran an agitated hand through his hair as though to calm his whirling thoughts. "Why would John want you to give Mr. Oliver his new manuscript when the man had stolen the last one?"

Rebecca's eyes turned down at the corners. "I asked the same thing. He told me he had tried every other way he knew to get a publisher to read it. Mr. Edgecombe won't look at any submissions unless they come to him through one of his authors. John said he was desperate enough to try one more time."

"But wouldn't Oliver think it a trap—receiving another manuscript from John?"

She nodded. "That is why he asked Rose to make a second copy, and used a pen name this time—R. J. Stephens."

"Ahh," Frederick murmured, recalling the burnt fragment.

She added, "*If* Mr. Oliver gave it to his publisher, John planned to reveal his true identity then."

"And if Oliver stole it again?"

"John had kept copies this time, to protect his interests. He'd learned from his mistakes. Rose read it through, and I read a few chapters as well—all I had time for. I recognized John's words on the page we found under Mr. Oliver's chair."

"So you think John *was* trying to trap Oliver . . . and succeeded?"

Miss Lane hesitated. In lieu of answering, she asked a question of her own. "Have you ever read *The Arabian Nights*?"

He felt his brow furrow in confusion. "I . . . think so. I certainly recall your father describing some of the tales in it."

She nodded. "He read them to us when we were younger—at least those he deemed fit for children. John's favorite was 'The Vizier and the Sage.' Do you remember that one?"

Frederick thought back. "Not the details. Though it sounds familiar."

Expression grave, Rebecca handed him the book she'd brought. "Then perhaps you should refresh your memory."

When Miss Lane had gone, Frederick sat in one of the room's chairs and opened the volume of *The Arabian Nights Entertainments*. He searched the contents until he came to "The Vizier and the Sage Duban."

He flipped to the page indicated, slid a candle lamp closer, then settled back. As he began reading, the old story returned to him.

Duban was a wise healer who cured a king of leprosy. A jealous advisor or "vizier" told the king that Duban was planning to poison him, so the king sentenced the sage to death. Duban seemingly accepted his fate, and offered the king one of his prized books full of wisdom so that the ruler might heal himself should he grow ill again.

Later, after Duban's death, the king opened the book and turned through the pages, surprised to find them blank. He continued to flip through the book, separating the sticky pages by licking his fingers, thereby absorbing the poison Duban had spread there. He quickly began to die, realizing in his final moments that this was his punishment for killing the man who had cured him.

Cheery tale, Frederick thought, then stilled as apprehension prickled over him. His heart pounded dully, and bile as sour as vinegar rose in his throat.

Miss Lane had asked him to read this story for a reason. An awful, chilling reason.

Merciful God, please, no.

19

When Rebecca left Sir Frederick's room after her confession, she'd felt only partially relieved. She had not been able to force out the last words. To admit she feared John may have poisoned Ambrose Oliver.

She had returned to her room with no intention of leaving the hotel, but the relentless inner turmoil that had driven her to confess now drove her to put on her things and walk back to the lodge to confront her brother finally and fully.

As she entered Fowler's Wood, the last of the waning daylight filtered through the tree branches, dappling the dirt road with shadows. Rebecca had forgotten how early the sky darkened at this time of year—especially in the wood.

Ahead, the road curved around a sprawling yew. Anything or anyone might lie beyond. She shivered. Perhaps she should have started out earlier or hired Robb Tarvin to drive her.

Too late. She kept walking. The farther she went, the thicker the wood became and the darker.

A branch snapped behind her, and she halted, looking over her shoulder. She could see no one, nor did she hear any footsteps, so she continued on.

To encourage herself, she whispered, "Not long now, brave Becky."

The road curved again, and another branch snapped—closer this time. She drew in a sharp breath and turned.

Footsteps shuffled to a stop somewhere out of sight. Was someone following her?

"Who's there?" she called, endeavoring to remain calm, although her voice sounded young and high-pitched.

"Halloo . . . ?" Rebecca hailed and waited, but there was no answer. Her hands felt damp within her gloves. Should she start running?

She made herself walk on, the back of her neck bristling all the while.

Sudden pounding footfalls shook the ground from the opposite direction. A large animal came tearing through the trees. A scream rose in her throat as the creature burst onto the road, charging straight at her.

She recognized the Fenchurches' Irish wolfhound, though the beast looked terrifying with his teeth bared.

"Ranger, no," she commanded with all the authority she could muster. "Ranger, stop!" She braced herself as the dog leapt into the air.

He landed at her feet, panting eagerly up at her.

Rebecca sagged in relief. "You remember me. Good boy." She petted his wiry head, which reached higher than her waist.

A moment later, Ranger tensed, low growl at the back of his throat. He sprang into motion, kicking dirt onto her skirt as he loped away down the road. In pursuit of what? Or whom?

Rebecca strode briskly on her way, now and again glancing nervously over her shoulder.

She passed through the tall hedge and saw the welcome glow

of candlelight twinkling from the windows of the underkeeper's lodge. Her spirits lifted at the sight.

She knocked and let herself in.

Rose looked up from her mending with pleasure. "Ah, Miss Rebecca. You're out late."

"Yes, I . . ." She turned to the window and stared out. "I heard someone in the wood. I think he may have been following me."

"Who?"

"I did not see. Are you expecting anyone?"

"No."

Rebecca knew it wasn't someone simply passing through, as the road led only to the lodge and to the Wilfords' parkland and hunting ground beyond. There was not a farm or cottage for miles.

Rebecca tried to shrug it off. "Probably someone from the estate, then."

"At this time of day?" Rose said. "I doubt it. More likely that vile Leo Stoker. He's taken to meeting John in the wood since I made it clear he wasn't welcome here. He supplies your brother with smuggled liquor and those little brown bottles. I don't mean to speak out of turn, but you have a right to know where all the money goes."

Rebecca frowned. "The newspapers describe how terribly addictive opium is. Does he not realize?"

"He says, 'It's only laudanum. Doctors prescribe it all the time, so don't act so scandalized.'"

"What does he think laudanum is?" Rebecca protested. "A mixture of opium and alcohol!"

"I know." Rose sighed heavily and shook her head. "I wish John would tell Leo Stoker to take his foul stuff and never come back. Indeed I do." The older woman looked at her in concern. "You don't think Leo or whoever followed you wished you harm, surely?"

"Probably not," Rebecca admitted. "Though whoever it was certainly frightened me. Thankfully Ranger came along—the Fenchurches' dog? He ran down the road and probably scared off whoever was there."

"Good."

Rebecca studied Rose's careworn face, noticing how much she had aged in the last few years.

Rebecca sat down near her and said, "I know it has not been easy for you, caring for this place and for John. A thankless task, I imagine."

"Only when you're not here." Rose raised a palm. "No criticism intended. Your allowance and having one less to feed here have helped, I can't deny."

Even so, regret weighed down Rebecca's soul. "Is John at least . . . civil . . . toward you?"

Rose hesitated, then said, "I am not the first housekeeper to feel uneasy around her master, to never know if I'm to receive a word of praise or rebuke. But it is hard sometimes, especially as he was once such a sweet lad and so fond of me."

Tears pricked Rebecca's eyes. Over a sudden lump in her throat, she managed, "I am sorry." She swallowed and said, "I hope you realize we would be lost without you. Especially John, although he might not admit it. However, I would understand completely if you wanted to find another place, somewhere more . . . pleasant."

"And where would I go? Who would give me another place, at my age?" Rose shook her head. "I don't know what will become of me if John has to give up this lodge."

"Don't worry about that. If all else fails, I am sure Sir Frederick will find another place for you. But . . . did not a certain yeoman farmer express interest in you? I remember him calling here. You might yet have a home and kitchen of your own."

"Oh," Rose said with a dismissive wave. "That was years ago. Mr. Fletcher brought me eggs and invited me to walk around his farm. He was very amiable—he just wasn't for me. I know it's foolish, especially after all this time, but I was in love once when I was young. And even now, I can't help but compare every other man to him, and they all come up wanting. Not that there have been many, mind, but a few. I was not as pretty as Daisy, but he admired me, or so I thought. He moved away and married, yet I still think about him from time to time."

"Where is he? Any idea?"

"No. I've not heard a word from or about him in thirty years. I try to tell myself he'd be fat and bald by now, though I know better. He'd still be trim, and have that full head of hair. It might be silver, but he'd still have it. And laughing eyes and a devilish smile." She shook her head. "I'd be embarrassed to see him, old hag that I am, round and wrinkled, my figure long gone."

"You are not a hag at all," Rebecca assured her. "And a few pounds and wrinkles would not matter. Not to a man who cared for you."

Rose smirked. "You've read too many romance novels. A man may admire a woman's mind or virtue, but the attraction starts by what he *sees*. Unless, maybe, he's blind." Rose added with a saucy wink, "Know any blind men with a snug home and sunny kitchen?"

Rebecca grinned. "I am afraid not."

"Nor I—more's the pity."

Rebecca set her gloves and bonnet on the side table and stood. "Well, I had better talk to John." To herself she added, *Before I lose my nerve.*

Rebecca knocked and gingerly opened the door, expecting to find John asleep under the bedclothes, perhaps suffering the ill effects of drink . . . or worse.

Instead she found him sitting in his desk chair, turned to face the window, the fading evening light illuminating his profile.

"What are you doing sitting here in the dark?" she gently asked.

"Hating myself."

"Oh, John."

"You would think I would be happy he's dead, would you not?"

She bit her lip, then said softly, "Are you?"

He shook his head. "Maybe for a few minutes, but after? No. It's all vanity. Futility. Over."

She took a deep breath and said, "Your manuscript was not in Mr. Oliver's room. I looked. We did find a few burnt pages in the grate—your title page and a few others, but not your whole manuscript. Do you know what happened to it?"

He gestured vaguely to a stack of paper half-hidden by a discarded pair of trousers.

She swallowed, her heart beating hard. "So you went to his room to retrieve it?"

He nodded.

"When?"

"You know when. The night I came to the hotel. I started having doubts after you gave it to him."

"Why? Did you have reason to believe Mr. Oliver might be killed?"

He winced.

She looked again at the jar on his desk, the paintbrush still propped inside. She also recalled the pages hanging on a line in the spare room, left to dry.

"I have to ask. Did you spread arsenic on the pages I gave to Ambrose Oliver? Is that why you were looking for a paintbrush and rat poison? To kill him?"

She waited for him to deny it, to burst out in shocked anger. Yet he simply sat there, eerily calm.

Gaze still on the window, he asked softly, "Like that story in *The Arabian Nights*?"

She nodded, and he nodded back, which confused and frightened her.

He said, "If Oliver would have simply passed the manuscript on to his publisher, he would not have been harmed, or so I thought. Only if he lingered over it, licking his fingers page after page, as is his habit, would he ingest enough to hurt him, to suffer as I have suffered. It would be his fault, not mine. He would poison himself by his own perfidy."

"Oh, John." Rebecca moaned, feeling as though her chest had collapsed, stealing her breath, her hope.

"Then I changed my mind," he said. "I decided I could not do it. I didn't believe he'd give it to Edgecombe, but even so, I realized it was a risk. And Edgecombe had seen you there and might suspect our involvement.

"That night I came to the hotel, I waited until morning. When I worked for Oliver those few months, I learned his habits. I knew he stayed up half the night, burning the midnight oil. I learned from Mary when that guard fellow came on duty and went in earlier. I knew he would not see me enter, but I did not want him to hear me either."

"You went up the abbess's staircase?"

He glanced over. "Ah, so you remember Rose's stories too." She nodded.

John went on, "At the top of those stairs, I listened and heard nothing, so I carefully inched open the door. Still I heard nothing, so I opened the panel all the way—slow going because of something in front of it—and stepped into the closet. I tripped over those low shelves and froze, sure Oliver would wake up and come to investigate. I held my breath, ready to retreat, but still . . . nothing.

"So I opened the closet door and entered the room. I was surprised to find his bed empty. Then I saw him sprawled on the chaise near the hearth. The fire had burned low, but a lamp gave off some light.

"At first I assumed he must have fallen asleep and hadn't heard me because he'd been drinking. Liked to drink, I recalled. Yet as I tiptoed closer, I saw his eyes were open though he lay unnaturally still. I watched his chest but saw no sign of its rising and falling. I put a hand in front of his mouth, but felt no breath. He was dead.

"I was stunned. Truly. His lap desk had fallen to the floor, and looking at the pages spread about"—John gestured again to the stack of paper—"I deduced that he had begun copying mine.

"I gathered up the manuscript. The title page and first few chapters were missing. I searched and searched but could not find them. I concluded he must have burned them.

"On the pages in his handwriting, I saw many words I recognized and others I did not. I was too nervous to stand there reading, so I picked up all I could find."

She asked, "Did you notice if the outer door was locked or unlocked?"

He nodded. "Unlocked. I locked it and set the key on the table, not wanting that guard dog of his nor anyone else to come into the room and discover me there. When I had what I came for, I slipped out the way I had come."

"I saw you leaving that morning, crossing Dodge's field. I wondered what you were doing."

"You haven't told anyone, have you? The coroner hasn't asked to question you?"

She shook her head. "I have told only Sir Frederick."

"Sir Frederick?" John repeated in alarm. "Why would you tell him?"

"Someone saw you enter my room that night and reported it. I had to tell him it was you. If you had seen how he looked at me. The shocked disappointment . . ."

"What is that to my life?"

"I was not certain about the poison then, though I did wonder."

He grimaced. "But the poison didn't kill him. Robb came by and told us he was bludgeoned."

"They are awaiting results of the postmortem. Sir Frederick thought he might have been poisoned or drugged as well. Otherwise, why would he just sit there and let someone strike him?"

"Oh . . ." John sat back hard, expression troubled.

Rebecca asked tentatively, "Are you sure he was already dead when you got there? You did not . . . strike him out of anger? In revenge?"

His eyes grew large. "I did not lay a hand on him! You must believe me, Becky."

"I want to, John. But you have lied before, so it is difficult to believe you now, as much as I long to. Especially when you freely admit to poisoning the paper."

He sighed deeply. "Oh well. What's the noose to me now? I've lost everything. That man stole from me in life and will now steal from me by his death."

John jerked a hand toward the pile of pages. "There's nothing to live for anyway. I am a terrible writer. I've finally accepted the truth of it."

"That is not true."

He nodded. "It is. I read the paragraphs Oliver rewrote. Based on mine, yes, but better. He left my opening lines, then omitted the next few pages and revised the first scene. So much more vivid and compelling than my rubbish."

"No, John. Beyond some changes, it was still your writing—writing he thought good enough to steal. Perhaps all you need is a skilled editor."

"Ha. Even if you're right, it's too late."

"But you have your early drafts. And most of Rose's clean copy. You can prove Oliver intended to steal it. This time you have proof."

He threw up his hands. "How do we explain how Oliver got the manuscript in the first place, not to mention how I retrieved it? If I go to Edgecombe now, with Oliver's few pages and mine, he'll realize I was in his room, that I took them and maybe did worse."

"I don't mind admitting I gave them to him. But you're right, I don't know how to explain the rest without implicating you."

John shook his head. "It's not worth the risk. He'd probably take the pages Oliver wrote and hire a hack to finish the book. Tout it as Ambrose Oliver's last work. He'd never admit to any similarities nor publish my version."

"He might—when you show him you have already written the rest of the novel."

"It's too late," John repeated, expression desolate. "I've lost my right to publish this book as much as if Oliver had stolen it whole."

"There must be something we can do. Let's talk to Sir Frederick. If you confess and convince him of your change of heart, perhaps he will understand. Be lenient."

"It's not solely up to him, though. He'd feel honor-bound to report it to the coroner or take it up with the other JPs."

He probably would, Rebecca realized. "I don't know what to say," she lamely replied, adding to herself, *Nor what to do.*

Oh, John. How could you even think of poisoning someone—and you a vicar's son? She swallowed the reproof, pressed her brother's arm, and said, "I will think of something. In the meantime, don't lose heart, all right?"

Worried John might harm himself, she took the white arsenic from his room and carried it outside to dispose of it, pouring it over a patch of weeds.

Rebecca then donned her mantle and prepared to leave the lodge.

Rose called sternly into John's room, "You walk your sister back now. It's late."

He grumbled something under his breath.

Rebecca began, "That's all right, Rose. I—"

Then John stumbled to the door, pulling on his coat as he did so. "I'll walk her as far as the village. She'll be safe enough from there."

Rose sniffed. "Very well."

Her brother walked through the wood beside her, hands in his pockets, head down. She thought of raising the subject of the laudanum but decided he looked beaten down enough already. Besides, his problems went far beyond those bottles.

They encountered no one in the wood, but John still jumped at every scurry of nocturnal animal or call of an owl.

He walked her as far as the church, as promised.

"Thank you," she said, pressing his arm once more. "Remember—don't give up. While there is life, there is hope."

"Yeah," he murmured, though he did not sound convinced.

When he left her, Rebecca pulled the hood of her mantle

over her hair, preferring not to be recognized while walking alone after dark.

As she neared the public house, she veered to the opposite side of the cobbled street to avoid being seen from its windows. Voices and laughter from within told her the place was crowded.

The door opened and a man exited.

She ducked her head and walked on, but it was too late. He'd spotted her.

"Becky?" Robb Tarvin asked, then jogged over to join her.

Her stomach sank. "Good evening. I am just on my way back to the abbey."

"I'll walk with you."

She noticed the smell of ale on his breath and smoke on his clothes. "No need. I shall be all right."

He fell into step beside her anyway, one hand tucked into his pocket. "You ought not walk alone at night. Some men might take that as an invitation. Or think you are not concerned about your reputation."

"That is not the case, as you well know. I was simply visiting John and Rose and the hour grew late."

"Either way, I'm heading to the abbey myself."

She made do with a nod and quickened her pace as they turned into Elderberry Lane, wanting to keep the uncomfortable interlude as brief as possible.

"What's the hurry?" he said, lengthening his stride.

A few possible replies played through her mind, but she discounted them, afraid they might be misconstrued. *I am eager for my bed.* Or *I am cold.* She settled for "I am tired."

"Then slow down. You're making *me* tired."

She moderated her pace . . . a little.

They passed a few shuttered shops and cottages, many with

dark windows, but not all. Which was worse, she wondered, to be seen at night walking alone or with a man?

Robb extracted his hand from his pocket, swinging both arms to keep up with her. She noticed a pristine bandage wrapped around his hand. "What happened to you?"

He glanced at it, as if surprised it was there. "Oh, em, nothing much. Blasted horse bit me."

Realization flaring, she whirled on him. "Horse, my eye! I would wager anything that's a dog bite. *You* followed me into the wood, did you not? Trying to scare me?"

Lantern light from the village hall illuminated his roguish grin. "I was only hoping it would make you come running into my arms. But that dashed Ranger ran at me instead."

"Serves you right." She turned and strode on.

"Did you think the ghost of the abbess was following you? I heard from Brixton you saw it again."

She knew he was teasing her but raised her chin. "That's right. I did see someone in a black gown. But tonight I see only a mean-spirited scoundrel."

"Aw, don't take on so, Becky. I am sorry, all right? Only meant a bit of fun."

"I did not appreciate the joke."

They walked the rest of the way in grudging silence.

Frederick fastened a few buttons of his greatcoat against the evening's chill and pulled his hat low on his head. He'd been walking the hotel grounds, gathering his thoughts. Now he paused and looked up at the building. Light twinkled from a window near the far end—Thomas's room. The other upper-story windows remained dark. He identified Rebecca Lane's room at the opposite end, with its small balcony overlooking the garden.

Was she safe in bed? Sleeping peacefully? Or perhaps she was tossing and turning, wrestling with doubts and questions, as he would no doubt do if he tried to fall asleep. Questions plagued him even now, walking alone in the brisk night lit by a quarter moon.

Was he doing the right thing by protecting her? Or was he opening himself up to betrayal and humiliation all over again?

Growing cold, he walked on to warm himself, striding around the corner of the building, past the chapel with its stained-glass windows, and past the fallen ruins of the former abbey church. As he neared the front of the hotel, footsteps crunched up the gravel drive.

He glanced over and saw a tall man and a slight woman approaching the hotel together on foot.

Near one of the cone-shaped topiaries lining the drive, the young man pulled the woman abruptly into his arms and bent his head.

Frederick looked away, not keen to witness young passion, but then the woman's gasp of protest caught his ear.

Passion was one thing. But not when it was unwelcome.

He started across the spongy grass of the manicured lawn toward the couple. The female figure turned her face away, and moonlight shone on her profile. Rebecca.

Illogical jealousy curdled his stomach, though he had no romantic claim on her nor any right to expect fidelity.

"Robb, stop it."

The sound of her voice quickened his stride.

"Come on, Becky. Don't be like that. We're old friends."

Concern washed away Frederick's jealousy, and anger quickly swept in to take its place.

"Your father said I could do anything I set my mind to," Robb said evenly. "And I set my mind on having you."

"That is not going to happen."

Nearing them, Frederick said, "Miss Lane. Mr. Tarvin. Am I intruding?"

Both heads turned in his direction.

"Yes," Robb snapped.

"No," Rebecca said, rather breathlessly, and pulled away from the young man.

Robb said, "I was just escorting Miss Becky back to the hotel." He reached for her arm, but she stepped farther away.

"And for that I thank you, but for nothing else," she coldly replied. "You . . . mistook the matter. Good night, Mr. Tarvin."

"Mr. Tarvin now, is it? Weren't so formal-like before the high-and-mighty baronet showed up."

"That's enough," Frederick said sternly. "I believe Miss Lane wishes you to leave, if you would be good enough to oblige her."

"So you can walk her to her room instead? Oh, sure." Robb frowned at Rebecca. "And you'll no doubt thank him more sweetly than you did me."

Robb turned and stalked away.

Frederick looked at her questioningly. "Shall I throttle him?"

"No, thank you. Although I am glad you appeared when you did."

"Are you?"

"Definitely. As you may remember, my father championed him as a boy, and he believes that allows him a certain . . . familiarity. He also assumes I admire him as my father did, but I don't."

"He said you are friends."

"As children we were, yes. He often came to the vicarage to borrow a new book or discuss some scholarly tome with Father. I sometimes joined them. As we grew older, his . . . interest . . . changed. Mine did not. He thinks my parents were encouraging him where I was concerned, and I have not had the heart to tell him the exact opposite was true. They sought to encourage his education, but that was all."

"I trust he understands that now."

She sighed. "I hope so."

"May I escort you inside? I promise to behave in a more gentlemanlike manner than our wayward Mr. Tarvin."

"Yes, you may."

They strolled toward the hotel entrance. She stumbled over a clump of grass, and he quickly took her hand and tucked it under his arm.

"You went to the lodge again?" he asked.

"Yes, I hope you don't mind. I wanted to discuss a few things with John."

He looked down at her, close to his side, and all those feelings of protectiveness washed over him once more. "Can you tell me what you learned? I will help if I can."

"I know you would try." She sighed again.

He said, "I read the *Arabian Nights* story you suggested."

"Oh."

"You don't think—"

"May we talk about it tomorrow?" she said abruptly. "I am tired and need to think. I shall be more myself after a night's rest."

He hesitated. "Very well."

At the bottom of the stairs, he paused, fearing tongues would wag when the two of them showed up together in the hall. Hopefully it would be quiet at this time of the night.

Instead, when they entered, they found the hall alive with candlelight and music.

Miss Newport sat at the pianoforte, playing and singing, while a few others stood or sat nearby, listening. Thomas turned the pages of music for her, watching in adoration.

Thankfully, with all eyes on the beautiful singer, no one paid them much heed.

Then Thomas looked up, just noticing them. "Is she not divine? Join us!"

Miss Lane smiled wanly back, then leaned closer to Frederick. "You stay. I am going upstairs."

"Are you certain?"

"Yes. I think it would be best."

Probably wise, he realized. Tongues would definitely wag if they went upstairs together.

As tempting as that thought was, he pushed it from his mind.

Rebecca continued across the hall, through the passage, and out into the cold, dark cloisters, leaving the cheerful warmth and music behind. The cloisters were lit only by a few torches, flickering in the breeze and casting ethereal shadows on the medieval stone walls.

She hurried along, her slippers all but silent on the paving stones, when a figure darted into view between the pillars on the other side.

Rebecca stifled a gasp and stopped dead, leaning into the wall as though it might hide her. Robed in black from head to foot, even the figure's face was concealed by a dark veil. It passed through the archway, then turned sharply, disappearing up the night stair.

Rebecca's pulse pounded. *There are no such things as ghosts*, she told herself, *except for the Holy Ghost*. And religious habit or not, Rebecca sensed nothing holy about the being now hurrying up the stairs.

Over the sound of her thumping heart, she heard the padding of feet, followed by a scuffle-slap. The figure had . . . tripped?

Ghosts didn't stumble, and this evidence of humanity gave her the courage to creep forward.

Reaching the bottom of the stairs, Rebecca craned her neck to look up and caught a glimpse of the fluttering black gown and booted feet. Boots? The hand on the railing seemed surprising large and . . . masculine. Then the figure rounded the railing and slipped from view.

Rebecca started slowly up the stairs, listening for any returning footfalls and trying not to stumble herself.

At the top, she vacillated between retreating into the relative safety of her room and turning right to follow whoever it was to see what she—or he—was doing.

Curiosity spurred her on—as well the desire to prove that she had not imagined the sightings.

She tipped her head around the corner just enough to see along the corridor. There, the robed figure slipped into the room beyond the stairway. Miss Newport's room.

Miss Newport?

Apprehension washed over Rebecca. It made sense. An actress had access to costumes. But no. She had just seen Miss Newport downstairs, singing. And the hand and boots had appeared more like those of a man.

Who, then, had just entered the woman's room—disguised as the ghost of the abbess, or at least a nun? And why?

A shiver ran over her.

Hearing the door click shut behind whoever it was, Rebecca paused a moment, considering. What should she do? Knock and see who answered? Confront whoever it was face-to-face? She quailed at the thought. Someone rounded the corner, and Rebecca gasped and pressed a hand to her chest.

Miss Newport stopped, appearing both startled and amused. "Miss Lane? What is it?"

"Oh! You frightened me."

"You look as if you have seen a ghost."

"I have."

"The ghost of the abbess?" Miss Newport asked, humor fading.

Rebecca nodded. "It, em, he went into your room." She pointed with a shaky finger.

The woman's eyebrows rose. "He?"

"I believe so. I only caught a glimpse."

"I thought it was an abbess."

"The person wore a habit, yes. But I think the boots and hand I saw belonged to a man."

Miss Newport narrowed her eyes. Rebecca saw doubt there . . . and something else. Fear? Maybe. Or was it irritation?

"Shall I call for someone?" Rebecca asked. "Mr. Mayhew or Sir Frederick?"

"No. I can take care of myself. I have experience with strange males trying to sneak into my room. But dressed as a nun? That is a new low."

"How did he get inside?"

Miss Newport lifted a casual shoulder. "I often neglect to lock my door until I retire for the evening. Don't like carrying a reticule to hold my key. Spoils the silhouette."

Selina reached for the handle and put her rouged mouth close to the wood. "Ghost? Beware, I am coming in! And Miss Lane is here with me, so don't try anything!" She slanted Rebecca a wry grin.

The woman was mocking her. She apparently didn't believe her.

Miss Newport opened the door and looked inside.

Rebecca held her breath, then crept closer. Ready, though terrified, to lend assistance if needed.

A tense moment's pause hung in the air. Then Selina swung the door wide and announced, "Vanished, apparently. Ghosts walk through walls, after all. See? Empty."

Rebecca peered inside. The room was dim and did appear empty. "Perhaps the balcony?" she suggested.

"Ah." Miss Newport opened the balcony door and looked out, then closed it again. "All clear."

"But—I was so sure I saw . . . someone enter."

"There, there, Miss Lane. No harm done."

Miss Newport lay a comforting arm around her shoulders. "This place has a strange effect on people. Enough to give anyone nightmares. It's no wonder you thought you saw something frightening. After all, a man recently died here."

She shepherded her out the door. "You know, Miss Lane, you remind me of my sister." Selina's eyes abruptly filled with tears. "She had an imagination too. And so sweet and innocent." Selina sniffed and swiped at the tears with her free hand. "Come, I'll walk you to your room."

There Rebecca bid her good night and closed the door, turning the key to lock it. But she was still not convinced she had imagined the figure.

Her gaze landed on her balcony door across the room. She hurried over and opened it, wincing at its creak. She stuck her head outside and looked at the balcony to the left of hers. It was empty, as Selina had said, although Rebecca thought she heard a metallic click of the door closing.

Or was she imagining things again?

A short while later, Mary came in to help her prepare for bed.

"I have news." Mary's eyes gleamed impishly, and she waggled her brows. "I saw your ghost. The abbess in black."

"Just now?" Rebecca asked.

"No. This morning. After I left your room. I didn't say any-thing, afraid Mr. Mayhew would think me mad and send me packing. But since you saw her too . . ."

Relief and confusion tangled within Rebecca. "I am glad I am not the only one who saw . . . whoever it was, but—"

"Oh, I know who it was." Mary's tone was matter-of-fact. "I didn't guess straightaway. At first I thought it really was a ghost. But her veil slipped for just a moment before she replaced it. Guess who?"

Rebecca opened her mouth to wager a guess, but before she could, Mary blurted, "Miss Newport!"

Incredulity struck. She had just seen the "abbess" and Miss Newport within seconds of each other. It couldn't be.

Likely noticing her silent frown, Mary went on, "She is an actress, I hear, so it's not so surprising. Probably playing a trick on someone."

"Did she see you?" Rebecca asked. "Know that you saw her?"

Mary shook her head. "I don't think so. I was coming down the night stair when she came out of the chapel. Gave me a turn, I can tell you, seeing that shrouded figure comin' out of there of all places. But then I glimpsed her face and felt a world better."

"I can imagine."

Rebecca wasn't sure what she felt besides bewildered. Were there two "ghosts"? What on earth was going on?

20

On Monday morning, Mr. Smith reconvened the coroner's inquest in the Swanford Abbey coffee room. Frederick attended, eager to hear the autopsy report.

"As you know," Smith said, "the body of Ambrose Oliver was taken to an operating theatre in Worcester, where a post-mortem was performed. I received the results." He lifted a signed document and then summarized, "Using the Rose and Metzger methods, no evidence of poisoning was detected, nor was there any sign of inflammation or damage to the internal organs beyond what is normal for a man of his age and cor-pulence. The surgeon, Mr. Brown, concludes that Ambrose Oliver was killed by a blow to his cranium and the subsequent trauma to his brain."

He sent Frederick a smug look. "As we originally thought."

Relief and uncertainty wrestled within. Frederick knew he should be relieved for Rebecca's sake, especially, but something was still nagging him.

The coroner faced the jurors and asked, "Do you need to retire?"

The foreman replied, "I don't think that necessary, your honor."

The jury talked among themselves for a few minutes, quickly agreeing on a verdict, which was duly noted and relayed to the coroner.

Smith nodded and pronounced, "The jury has reached a verdict of unlawful killing by person or persons unknown."

Mr. Smith looked from juror to juror. "Thank you for your service, gentlemen. You are now dismissed. Be sure to give an account of any expenses to Sir Frederick Wilford before you go."

Afterward, Dr. Fox followed Frederick out of the coffee room. "Are you satisfied?"

"Not quite."

"If it helps put your mind at ease," Charles said, "I received a message from my colleague who tested the contents of Mr. Oliver's cup and bowl. The available tests are not foolproof, but he detected no obvious narcotic, nor, employing the reduction method, did he find any traces of arsenic."

Frederick nodded, not really surprised. Thinking of the sage's poisoned pages, he considered asking Dr. Fox to test the burnt remnant as well. But since the autopsy had revealed no evidence that Ambrose Oliver had been poisoned, it seemed a waste of time.

"So we are back where we started. If Mr. Oliver was not drugged nor poisoned, why did he sit there while his assailant approached?"

"Perhaps the killer entered with gun drawn and told him not to move."

"Maybe. But then why go behind him to deliver the blow?"

"Shooting him would be too noisy."

"True. However, to me only one explanation makes sense—the one Miss Lane suggested. Mr. Oliver must have been acquainted with whoever it was, willingly let him or her in, then sat back down, not suspecting he was in any danger."

"Who, then? His publisher?"

"I don't know. Yet."

Rebecca walked beside Lady Fitzhoward on the way to the refectory for luncheon, listening halfheartedly while the woman talked about departure plans and possible destinations.

As they passed the quiet coffee room, Lady Fitzhoward said, "The inquest is over, by the way. I happened to . . . overhear . . . the verdict."

"Oh?" Rebecca felt sweat prickling her brow.

"Unlawful killing by person or persons unknown."

"And the cause?" Rebecca asked, thinking, *Please not poison, please not poison . . .*

"As expected. The blow to the head. No evidence of poison."

"Oh, good!" Relief overwhelmed her.

Lady Fitzhoward looked at her askance. "Is it?"

"Well, yes. Poisoning would show such . . . premeditation, while a blow might have been struck in a moment of anger."

"I am glad you approve," the older woman dryly replied, then returned to her one-sided debate about where to travel next.

Could Rebecca go off again with Lady Fitzhoward, knowing what she knew? Leave John as he was—his already troubled self and now his attempt to poison Ambrose Oliver, aborted though it was?

Having heard the results of the autopsy, a part of her wished she had never mentioned the *Arabian Nights* to Sir Frederick, never hinted at her own suspicions. Should she say nothing more about it and leave her brother to Rose's care as she had the last few years, or should she share John's confession with Sir Frederick and let justice take its course?

She knew how Frederick's logical mind worked, knew he must wonder about, if not outright suspect, her brother. After all, if John was willing to poison Ambrose Oliver, then was he not the most likely to have struck him as well—resorting to a surer method? But Rebecca didn't want to believe that. It had to be someone else. She thought again of Mary seeing Miss Newport dressed as the abbess. Had Miss Newport killed the man? Mr. Oliver would certainly have let her into his room. If only Rebecca could prove it.

Entering the dining room, she saw Frederick sitting with an elegant older woman dressed in a fur-trimmed redingote and matching hat.

Noticing them, Sir Frederick stood. "Ah, Lady Fitzhoward, Miss Lane. Allow me to introduce my mother."

His mother turned toward them. When Lady Fitzhoward remained still and silent, Rebecca dipped a curtsy. "A pleasure to see you again, my lady."

The dowager's light brown hair held a touch of silver, fine wrinkles framed intelligent brown eyes, and her jawline had softened, yet she was still a handsome woman.

"Miss Lane. How are you keeping?"

"I am well, thank you. And you are in good health, I trust?"

"Tolerably well, yes."

Her gaze fixed on Lady Fitzhoward, eyes narrowing, sunlight from the arched refectory windows giving them a steely tint.

"Lady . . . Fitzhoward . . . did you say?"

"That's right," Rebecca's employer replied in equally cool tones.

"You seem familiar to me, yet your name does not."

Lady Fitzhoward met the woman's challenging stare and said mildly, "Yet it is my name."

The dowager Lady Wilford said, "I do not know any Fitzhowards."

"And yet I have heard a great deal about the Wilfords."

One of the dowager's dark eyebrows rose expectantly, but Lady Fitzhoward did not expand on her reply.

Rebecca began to grow uncomfortable. Sir Frederick, clearly also noticing the tension, shifted and said soothingly, "Do you know, Mamma, I thought Lady Fitzhoward seemed familiar too when I first met her here in the hotel."

He smiled from one woman to the other but neither returned the gesture.

His mother's gaze remained on Lady Fitzhoward. "And your husband was . . . ?"

"Sir Donald Fitzhoward."

"Would I have met him?"

"Doubtful. He was from the north. Manchester."

"And his title?"

"Mamma!" Frederick protested in dismay.

Lady Fitzhoward's eyes glinted. "I shall save you the trouble of consulting *Debrett's Peerage*. My husband was knighted for service to the crown. He was not a baronet, as was your late husband."

"Ah."

Lady Fitzhoward inhaled and said, "I do hope that satisfies

your curiosity. Now, if you will excuse me, I find I am not hungry after all." She turned and walked away, head held high.

Even so, Rebecca noticed the slight tremor of her hand.

Voice low, Sir Frederick said to his mother, "It was unlike you to pry like that. I must say you were rather rude."

"I don't know what came over me. I am sorry to embarrass you."

Rebecca turned to go. "I shall take my leave as well."

"No, do stay, Miss Lane," the dowager urged. "I apologize to you too. And please join us." She gestured to a waiter, and Rebecca was soon seated with a bill of fare.

The older woman glanced briefly at the day's selections, then set down the card, her brows knit. "It is just . . . I know I have seen that woman before in some other context. And she was not the wealthy widow of a knight then."

Rebecca said, "She is the widow of Sir Donald Fitzhoward. That I can attest to. He was a successful manufacturer. He developed some improved piece of machinery—I forget what— that helped many others in his trade."

"Trade." The dowager shuddered. "I do wish monarchs would cease granting knighthoods to ignoble persons."

"Mamma, you sound terribly haughty."

"I suppose I do. In my day, knighthoods were awarded for bravery, as a military honor, that sort of thing. Not to every tradesman who devised a new mousetrap."

"Well, whatever it was made him a rich man," Rebecca defended. "He left his wife with an impressive house and fortune."

"No children?"

"He had one son with a first wife, who died young. Sir Donald left everything to his second wife. He has long been estranged from his son."

"Perhaps because the son disapproved of his second wife."

"Mamma!" Frederick protested again.

Rebecca felt a spar of loyalty straighten her spine. She did not like admitting she'd needed her position, but neither did she like hearing her employer unfairly maligned.

"Before you say more, my lady, I think it fair to tell you that I am companion to Lady Fitzhoward and have been for a twelve-month now. And while she may possess her share of asperity, she has also been generous and kind to me."

"Lady's companion?" Frederick's mother repeated, taken aback.

Rebecca forced herself to hold the woman's gaze, overcoming the urge to duck her head in embarrassment. "Yes."

Lady Wilford sucked in a breath. "Oh! That's it!"

"What is, Mamma?" Frederick asked. "Are you suggesting Lady Fitzhoward was once—" he chuckled uneasily—"a lady's companion?"

Staring off into her memory, the dowager said, "Not . . . exactly."

After luncheon, Sir Frederick rose to walk his mother out to the Wilford carriage. Rebecca bid them good-bye and started toward Lady Fitzhoward's room to make sure she was all right.

As Rebecca stepped into the cloisters, she saw it again—the black habit billowing out behind a retreating figure.

Her heart lurched. Someone was masquerading as the abbess once more. Miss Newport? Or the unknown man?

What should she do? Go back into the hall and remain out of sight? Or confront whoever it was, although the prospect terrified her?

Sir Frederick appeared behind her, as if hearing her silent cry for help.

"Miss Lane." He studied her expression and his eyes narrowed. "What is it? What's wrong?"

Rebecca pointed to the swathed figure striding quietly through the opposite side of the cloisters.

She whispered, "I know you did not believe me when I said I saw a ghost. But there. Look. Tell me I am imaging *that*."

His jaw tightened. "I see it too. And it is no ghost."

In a flash, Frederick sprinted around the corner and shouted, "Stop!"

With the swiftest glance over his or her shoulder, the figure began running. Rebecca glimpsed a pale face framed by a white wimple. Not a veiled specter this time.

Frederick chased the fleeing figure around the cloisters and through the door that led back into the hall. The figure's gait struck Rebecca as feminine this time. What was Miss Newport up to now?

Rebecca turned and hurried after them.

She had just reached the hall when Sir Frederick caught up with the dark figure, grabbed her shoulder, and whirled her around to face him.

Rebecca slowed, then stopped altogether, mouth slack in dawning dismay.

The woman staring back at them was plain, middle-aged, and not familiar in the least.

Frederick had rarely been so embarrassed—for Miss Lane and for himself.

"I am sorry," Miss Lane said, yet again. "It was my fault."

They had all gathered with Mr. Mayhew in his office—Rebecca, Frederick, and Sister Celeste Marhic.

"I am the reason Sir Frederick chased after you," Rebecca explained. "I thought you were . . . someone else."

The woman raised a skeptical black brow. "Who? You have other nuns in this place? Chase them as well?" The sister's accent was wry and decidedly French.

Miss Lane's face reddened. "No. Not exactly."

Mr. Mayhew spoke up, saying in diplomatic tones, "May we ask what brings you to our hotel?"

"My brother is chef here," the woman replied. "Monsieur Yves Marhic?"

"Ah yes. Of course."

"Our order lives now in Winchester, but I am here to visit my brother for his birthday."

Siblings are siblings, wherever and whatever else they may be, Frederick mused, thinking of Thomas's birthday visit.

"Why did you run?" he asked.

The woman looked at him, eyes dark and sincere. "If you experienced what I have, young man, you might run too." Despite her accent, she spoke excellent English.

"During the revolution, many *religieux* were persecuted, pressured to deny their vows, and if they refused . . . executed. Some of us fled to save our lives. Perhaps we were wrong to do so. Weak. But we are human too—fearful and faithful at once. Now many of us live as exiles. Even here, we are discouraged from wearing our habits. I traveled here in secular clothing, coward that I am.

"But in this place built by a woman of faith, I receive courage to don my habit once more. *Béni soit Dieu!* Today, I walk through the cloisters where many sisters have poured out their prayers. I feel close to them. Close to God.

"But then?" She gestured toward Frederick. "This man chases me. Shouts at me, and all the terror comes rushing back. I ran, instinct taking over, to my shame."

321

"You have no reason to feel ashamed," Frederick assured her. "It is I who am deeply ashamed of my actions."

"Again, it is my fault alone," Miss Lane insisted. "You see, there are legends about this place being haunted by the ghost of an abbess who is buried here. Over the last few days, I have seen someone dressed much like you, and I thought . . . Well, again, please forgive me."

The woman watched her with interest. "If you saw someone dressed like this before today, it was not me. Either a ghost, as you say, or another nun, which I doubt, or someone with reason to disguise themselves."

"Yes," Miss Lane agreed.

But what exactly was that reason?

After the awkward interview was over and all had dispersed, Rebecca happened to pass Mr. Mayhew in the corridor.

"Again, I am sorry, Mr. Mayhew," she said. "I hope I have not caused Sister Celeste too much hardship, nor you."

"Not at all, Miss Lane. Sister Celeste is all gracious forgiveness, as one might expect. I have put her in a better room at no extra cost and have sent up a hot bath and tea tray with my compliments. I have also given her brother time off to spend with her. He is cooking for the pair of them now. Both seem well satisfied."

"I am relieved to hear it. And . . ." she added sheepishly, "somewhat surprised you have not tossed me out for the trouble I have caused."

He regarded her, his expression thoughtful. Then he said, "You and I are not well acquainted, Miss Lane, but Sir Frederick clearly thinks highly of you, and that is good enough for me.

Not to mention, I believe Lady Fitzhoward would see me put out of business if I dared speak one word against you." He ended his little speech with a grin, and she returned the gesture, chagrined and grateful in turns.

Rebecca continued through the hotel, looking for Sir Frederick. Eventually, she saw him in the courtyard. She pushed through the door and approached him, still not sure what or how much to say.

He turned at her approach, his expression difficult to decipher.

She clasped damp fingers together and said, "Again, I am sorry about Sister Celeste."

He waved a gracious hand. "It is over. And I am sorry about my mother's rude behavior toward your employer."

"That *was* rather surprising."

"Yes, and out of character for her. She said nothing else about the matter after her outburst. Even so, it made me all the more curious about Lady Fitzhoward's past."

Rebecca said, "I believe she was here years ago and has friends in the area. That is all I know."

"And where does she go from here?"

"She has not yet decided. Brighton, most likely."

"And will you go with her?"

"That, em, depends."

"On what?"

"John. You. What happens next. . . ."

He stepped closer. "You had better explain."

She took a deep breath, resisting the urge to back away. "I heard the inquest verdict and the autopsy results."

"Yes. No evidence of poison found in Mr. Oliver's body." He watched her carefully. Waited.

Her stomach seemed to twist one way, then the other as

her inner struggle continued. *Tell the truth. Tell him. No, say nothing. Walk away. Save John.*

But would sparing John from repercussions really save him?

No. She admitted the truth to herself. She could not save her brother. Never could. Never would. She was not God. Sobering words from the book of Hebrews rumbled through her mind. *"It is a fearful thing to fall into the hands of the living God."* But was it not also the only place to find forgiveness and restoration?

When she said nothing, Frederick said gently, "Are you wishing now you had never mentioned the sage and his poisoned pages?"

She ducked her head in shame, then forced herself to lift her eyes. "Yes. A part of me is."

"And the other part?"

"Is so tired of secrets and lying to protect him. Rose and I have tried to help. We keep . . . holding out branches as to a drowning man, but he *won't* take them."

He nodded, slowly and solemnly. "Did John poison the manuscript pages he asked you to deliver to Ambrose Oliver?"

She stared unseeing, blood roaring in her ears. Should she? Dare she? *God forgive me, for John never will!*

She licked dry lips and replied, "Yes. He confessed as much to me."

Again he nodded. Something flashed in his dark eyes, but otherwise she saw no change in his expression. He must be an excellent magistrate with that calm, inscrutable countenance.

He asked, "And did John return to Mr. Oliver's room to take back his manuscript and to finish what he'd started, this time by striking the man?"

"No!" Rebecca exclaimed, then quickly amended, "He

changed his mind and sneaked into Mr. Oliver's room to retrieve the pages before he could consume a harmful amount of
arsenic. Yes, he took back his manuscript—except the pages
Mr. Oliver had already copied and burned. And he took the
plagiarized pages as well, except the one we found under the
chaise. But John did *not* strike him. The author was already
dead when John climbed the abbess's stair."

"Any proof of that?"

"No, though I believe him."

"I want to believe him too, but I also need proof. Did John
see or hear anything that might point to another suspect?"

Rebecca's mind whirled. "Not that he said . . . though he
mentioned finding the door unlocked. He locked it himself
and laid the key on the table. And . . . there's something
else. Not from John, but Mary told me she saw Miss Newport dressed in a nun's habit. Why would she disguise herself
unless she was up to no good? Might she have killed Mr.
Oliver?"

Sir Frederick grimaced. "I know you are desperate to spare
John, but we can't lodge accusations without proof."

"And Mary seeing her is not proof?"

He shook his head. "Unless Mary saw her coming out
of room three with weapon in hand, no, it is not sufficient
proof."

"I saw the figure fleeing down the corridor that very morning!"

"But you did not see her face or a weapon?"

"No." Again, Rebecca lowered her head, feeling defeated.

He cupped her chin and gently lifted her face to his. "Do not
despair. We are not beaten yet."

His dark brown eyes held hers. She wanted to sink into their
depths and stay there forever.

Then Frederick leaned close, bringing his cheek near hers. His breath tickled her ear as he whispered, "Don't lose heart, brave Miss Rebecca."

Too late, she thought. She had already lost her heart to him all over again.

21

Later that afternoon, the Wickworth steward came to the abbey with a letter delivered by special messenger. Frederick read the contents with grim interest. The report was relevant but inconclusive, sending questions and theories volleying through his mind. How to best marshal his thoughts?

Frederick summoned two people to join him in the library and writing room. While he waited for them, he sat, knee bouncing, considering how to proceed. He found himself staring at the chess pieces on the game table before him. An idea formed.

When his guests arrived, Frederick rose and gestured to chairs on either side of his. "Please, be seated."

Miss Lane sat first, and his brother took the other chair.

Thomas regarded the chessmen, then looked awkwardly from Rebecca to Frederick. "This is a two-person game, Freddy. I feel like a fifth wheel, or is it a third? I don't enjoy being gooseberry."

"I have not asked you here to play chess," Frederick said. "The game has already been played. We are here to determine the role of each player." He gave them a sheepish glance. "Please humor me. I think better aloud."

Thomas winked at Rebecca. "And with an audience, apparently."

Frederick remained serious. "You two are here because I trust you and value your insight."

"You must be joking." Thomas sat up straighter. "I had better pay attention, then."

Frederick gestured to the pieces carved of light and dark wood. "Don't read too much into the colors. I am aware that no one is perfectly pure nor completely evil. Most of us are somewhere in between. However, for illustration purposes . . ." Frederick picked up the darker of the two kings. "Ambrose Oliver. A man whom many despised for different reasons and is now dead." He laid the piece flat on its back.

"Let us consider those reasons." He picked up the pair of dark rooks resembling castles. "The publishing house of the two Edgecombe brothers. William Edgecombe was driven to near bankruptcy, not to mention ill health due to the strain of working with Ambrose Oliver: his endless requests for advances, his empty promises of a forthcoming manuscript, and publishing another man's work as his own. That cost Edgecombe more money in legal fees and to pay off the young writer in question."

"Abominable!" Thomas interjected. "How did you learn that?"

"I'll explain in a moment." Frederick continued, "William Edgecombe died, leaving his brother, Thaddeus, holding the bag, with debts and a justifiable hatred of Ambrose Oliver."

He lifted a rook high. "He was the one man Mr. George would allow into Ambrose Oliver's room, no questions asked. Thaddeus Edgecombe had the opportunity and the hatred. However, even though he detested Oliver, he needed him too. He was the firm's best chance of recovering financially. Because of that, I don't believe he did it. Either of you have reason to think he did?"

"I have no idea." Thomas raised his palms. "I never even met the man."

Miss Lane said, "I briefly met both brothers, and while not well acquainted, I believe them reputable and respectable. I don't think Mr. Edgecombe would stoop to murder."

With a solemn nod, Frederick removed the dark rooks from the chess board.

Then he lifted one of the dark knights. "I briefly considered the moneylender, Isaac King. Yes, Mr. Oliver owed him money. Yes, he came to the abbey to warn him that debt had not been forgotten. Yet, like Mr. Edgecombe, I believed him when he said he wanted Oliver alive for financial reasons. Moreover, it struck me as too easy that he should be guilty—like the emblematic villain in a melodrama. An obvious, hackneyed solution."

Frederick set the knight aside.

"I asked Mr. King how he knew Ambrose Oliver would be staying here. He said he received a letter notifying him of that fact, as though someone wanted him here to take the blame. I wonder who it was."

Then his fingers hovered over a dark bishop before picking up a pawn. "Rebecca Lane."

She sucked in a breath.

"Only a pawn?" Thomas teased. "I think she ranks higher than that!"

Frederick sent him a quelling look. "In this 'game,' one does not wish to rank high in terms of suspicion."

"Oh."

"I did suspect Miss Lane initially. Not of killing Ambrose Oliver, but I knew she had lied to me. And I knew she was hiding something—or several things."

Rebecca dipped her head, clearly mortified.

He looked at her with compassion and gentled his voice.

"I also know you had compelling reasons. Reasons of family loyalty and the desire to protect those you love."

"Yes," she breathed.

Frederick went on, "Miss Lane went into room three disguised as a maid and gave Oliver her brother's manuscript, asking him to recommend it to his publisher. Instead, desperate for a new novel to pay his debts, Oliver began to rewrite that manuscript as his own, as he had done once before."

"The devil!" Thomas said. Then his eyes widened. "Ah! John Lane was the young writer you mentioned?"

"Yes." Frederick picked up the dark bishop. "John set a trap for Ambrose Oliver. This time armed with copies and witnesses that the novel was actually his."

With a look at his well-meaning but indiscreet brother, Frederick chose his next words carefully, "We know he was tempted to . . . take revenge. We know he changed his mind and sneaked back to retrieve his manuscript. For a time, I wondered if he had struck the author while he was in the room. As much as I hated to think it, John Lane was the most likely suspect. He had the motive and the opportunity."

Thomas blinked, then sent Miss Lane a pained, sidelong glance.

Countenance pale, she said, "You use the past tense. Does that mean John is no longer your primary suspect?"

Frederick heard the plea in her voice and wished he could assure her all was well. But the most he could say was, "He is not my only suspect."

He picked up the second dark bishop. "Mary Hinton. She helped Miss Lane enter Mr. Oliver's room in secret. Beyond that, however, I don't believe she was involved in any wrongdoing." He removed her piece from the board.

He next picked up a white bishop. "We shall let this represent Dr. Fox. He has been exceedingly helpful throughout this process and will hopefully continue to offer his services." He set the piece beside John's on the edge of the board without further explanation.

Then he selected another pawn. "Robb Tarvin met Mr. Oliver in Worcester and delivered him here in his fly. Robb offered to review the author's next book for errors and was soundly rebuffed. He was not pleased to be rejected, nor to receive no gratuity."

"Sounds like Robb," Miss Lane murmured. "But I can't see him taking revenge for something so minor. He might resent the man's success and strike out with words, but not with a weapon."

"I agree with you."

Frederick began clearing away the remaining pawns and several other pieces. "After questioning everyone, I don't believe any of the other hotel staff were directly involved, including Mayhew and Mrs. Somerton." He lifted the white rooks and set them aside.

"Who is the white knight?" Thomas asked eagerly. "I do hope it's me."

"It is," Frederick agreed. "Although your role has been more dupe than gallant knight."

"Dupe?" Thomas protested, lower lip protruding. "You must be joking. I am chivalry personified."

"Yes, yes. Very well."

"And when you questioned me earlier, you said you believed I was not involved."

"Not knowingly. But you certainly played your part in instigating our stay here and meeting with Miss Newport."

"Miss Newport? What has she to do with this? Nothing, surely."

"I will get to that. But first . . ." He lifted the remaining king. "Before you chide me for making myself the other king, I would be happy to make myself a pawn, if you prefer. Either way, I don't think it right to exclude myself from examination."

"You did have a motive, after all," Thomas reminded him.

Frederick conceded the point. "Yes, I resented Ambrose Oliver because of his unflattering allusions to me and my wife in his previous novel. There were also rumors that Marina might have had an affair with the man, though I doubt it. Either way, I give you my word, as a gentleman, a Wilford, and a justice of the peace, that I had nothing to do with Mr. Oliver's death. If that is not sufficient and either of you wish to question me further, now is your chance."

"I believe you," Miss Lane said softly.

"So do I." Thomas winced and shifted in his chair. "While we are clearing the air, I want to make sure you don't . . . That is, I gather there was another rumor that *I* might have been involved with Marina. She did, em, flirt with me, which is one of the reasons I began staying in London. But I give you my word, as a gentleman, a Wilford, and a white knight, that nothing happened. I hope you believe me."

Frederick sighed. "I do, but thank you for saying so."

He removed his and Thomas's pieces. Left remaining on the chess board were the dark king, lying flat, one white knight, and both queens.

Frederick slid forward the remaining knight. "The brave knight, Mr. George. Sworn to protect a man he clearly did not like or respect. In the end, he failed to do so. Beyond that, I have no proof he was involved." He looked to his companions. "Have you?"

Thomas shook his head. "I never met him either."

Miss Lane said thoughtfully, "From my brief interactions

with him, I agree he did not esteem Mr. Oliver, but he seems honorable. Though, come to think of it, he is another man Mr. Oliver would probably have let into his room."

"Good point. Had he a motive?"

"Not that I am aware of." Rebecca considered, then added, "He did warn me to take care around Mr. Oliver. Implying he was something of a rake, as we have heard. Mr. George, however, was polite and respectful to me, and to Miss Newport, the one time I saw them together."

Interest flared. "You saw them talking?"

"Only very briefly. He helped her unlock her door when it stuck."

"Do they know one another?"

"I don't think so. They seemed to me polite strangers."

Frederick remembered seeing Miss Newport talking to someone in the cloisters. Might it have been Mr. George? He tucked that possibility away in his mind.

Frederick next moved forward the white queen. "Selina Newport. She came here, supposedly to see Thomas again. But we soon learned she had an unhappy past with Ambrose Oliver. I wrote to my solicitor and received his reply today. He asked around the theatre for me and found someone willing to talk for a few shillings."

"You spied on her?" Thomas exclaimed. "Went behind my back to ferret out information against her?" Anger sparked in his usually mild eyes.

"Yes, I confess I did. The man my solicitor spoke to said he remembered Ambrose Oliver making unwelcome advances to Selina Newport, without success. So the author turned his attention to her younger sister, who was visiting."

Rebecca said, "Selina mentioned she failed to protect her little sister somehow. Oh . . ." Her eyes grew round.

Frederick glanced at his brother. "If Oliver took advantage of the girl, that would give Miss Newport a motive."

Thomas sullenly crossed his arms. "Even if true, it does not mean . . . Not Miss Newport. It must not . . ." He nodded toward the chess pieces. "You have made her the white queen, after all."

Frederick slid the dark queen beside it.

"Lady Fitzhoward?" Thomas blurted.

Both of them looked at him in surprise.

"Well," he defended, "you said she seemed familiar and secretive."

"True," Frederick allowed. "And she says some rather strange things. She was also oddly interested in the inquest. Miss Lane, you know her best. Do you have any reason to suspect her? Had she any grudge against Mr. Oliver?"

Rebecca shook her head. "No. She has read his books but only came to Swanford now because I wanted to see John. We had no idea Mr. Oliver would be at the hotel. Lady Fitzhoward has said nothing against the man, except, perhaps, to criticize his self-importance."

Frederick nodded. "There is something mysterious about the woman, to be sure, but I don't see her striking anyone a fatal blow. She barely made it up the stairs unsupported."

"If not her, then who is that?" Thomas gestured toward the dark queen.

"The abbess."

"Abbess?" Thomas repeated, incredulous. "Surely you don't mean a ghost."

"I do. Not a real ghost, of course, but someone masquerading as one."

"A prank, no doubt."

Frederick shook his head. "Why would someone disguise

themselves this last week of all weeks, when murder was afoot? I shall never believe it a coincidence or harmless prank. No. Someone wished to move around the hotel without being identified. And what a . . . dramatic way to sneak around a place rumored to be haunted! At first it seemed only Miss Lane saw this 'ghost.' But later Lady Fitzhoward's maid admitted to seeing it as well, as did Mary Hinton."

Thomas frowned. "But you saw how the author looked at Miss Newport. If she *had* gone to his room, which I doubt, he would have let her in, no disguise needed."

"But if she wished to leave it again, without being recognized?"

Frederick set the queens back to back. "I believe the two queens are one and the same person. In fact, Mary Hinton clearly saw Miss Newport's face while the woman was dressed in the costume."

His brother's mouth fell open. He asked in alarm, "Are you saying Miss Newport killed Ambrose Oliver, while in disguise?"

The clock ticked once while the two waited—twice more while they stared at him.

Frederick huffed a sigh. "I don't know. I feel as though I am missing something. And even if I fully suspected her, I don't have evidence to prove she struck anyone. Masquerading as a nun or ghost may be strange, but it's not illegal."

He ran a hand through his hair. "Well, I have kept you two long enough. I daresay it is time to dress for dinner. Thank you for obliging me. If you think of anything else, let me know. In the meantime, please keep this between us." He sent his brother a pointed look.

Thomas scowled. "Of course I won't repeat it. It's all supposition—a bag of moonshine! Do you suppose I want to tell Miss Newport my pompous brother has been poking about for skeletons in her closet? And even suspects her of murder?" He stood abruptly, his chair scraping the floor, and stalked from the room.

Frederick felt his neck heat and glanced ruefully at Rebecca. "Sorry about that."

She rose, and Frederick followed suit.

"I did not realize his feelings for her ran so deep," Rebecca said. "He is more like you than I thought, longing to protect those he cares about." She flushed. "Not that you . . . I did not mean to imply . . ."

"It is all right if you did." He held her gaze. "I do care, Miss Lane. Very much."

He slowly leaned down and pressed a feather-soft kiss to her cheek. He heard her sharp inhale of surprise, but not, he hoped, displeasure.

❧

After dinner that evening, Rebecca returned to her room and began packing. She would leave the next day, she decided. She had already stayed at the Swanford Abbey Hotel too long and spent too much of her meager savings. And in return? She had thought she was helping John. Instead, he was now under suspicion for murder.

The conviction grew that she could not go off again with Lady Fitzhoward with things as they were. She would move back into the lodge and try to help her brother—and Rose— through whatever came next.

With a heavy heart, Rebecca pulled her valise and bandbox from her closet. As she did so, the low rumble of voices caught her ear. She realized her closet must abut that of room twelve behind the night stair. Rebecca usually kept her closet door closed, and she supposed Miss Newport had little cause to talk to herself, but now, stepping farther into the dim space, Rebecca heard the rise and fall of conversation. A higher voice. A lower one. She could not identify the voices, although she assumed the higher one belonged to Selina Newport.

Was Miss Newport meeting with a lover? Or the man Rebecca had once seen disguised in nun's attire?

Even though Sir Frederick did not seem convinced Selina was guilty, Rebecca's suspicions mounted. Had the actress disguised herself to go to and from the author's room without being identified, much as Rebecca had done, although with a far more malevolent intent? Had she struck him and Mr. George as well?

Rebecca strained to hear but could make out only rare words amid the muffled flow of conversation. She quietly shut the closet door and tried to think. Frederick said they had no proof. What if she could get evidence for him?

An idea came to her. She wanted to know what was going on next door, and here was an opportunity to do so.

More than curiosity drove her now. She felt or at least hoped that discovering who had killed Mr. Oliver might help to exonerate John.

Dare she?

Rebecca pulled on her deep blue pelisse and kid gloves and slipped out onto the dark balcony.

Clouds covered the moon, and the balconies to the left of hers were empty. No one would see her.

Rebecca eyed the space separating her balcony from the next. Eight feet? More? She wished she had a board or something to lay over the gap, but she had nothing. Her gaze fell to a narrow wall ledge between the two railings. Was it wide enough to cross? Was she brave enough to attempt it? For John?

She took a deep breath. Would it be that much more difficult than climbing the garden wall or a tree? She looked to the stone veranda far below. It would certainly be more dangerous.

She dragged the wrought-iron chair to the rail, grimacing as it rattled and whined, and then stood atop it. From there, she stepped carefully onto the ledge, hands outstretched for balance. One foot on the rail, one on the ledge, Rebecca sought a handhold on the wall. A row of decorative bricks protruded at regular intervals. Grasping one of these, she breathed a prayer and stepped out, placing both feet on the ledge. Pressing close to the wall, she inched her right foot over, grasped the next brick, then slid her left foot over. Her heel slipped from her flat leather shoe, and she teetered, then gripped the wall tight. She wished she'd taken the time to lace on her half boots.

Pausing to catch her breath and regain her courage, Rebecca sidestepped again, and again. Soon the other balcony was in reach, and she carefully stepped onto its rail. Taking another breath, she leapt down as gracefully as she could, dropping low and wincing when her shoes thudded onto the balcony floor. She held her breath and looked toward the door. One second, two, three. When the door remained closed, she exhaled in relief.

Rebecca straightened and crept across the balcony toward the door. A few inches of candlelight shone through a narrow opening between the curtains. She tiptoed closer until she could see inside.

She hoped she would not find herself spying on a romantic encounter. How mortifying for all.

At first she saw only a slice of the room. Dressing chest, table, and, thankfully, an empty bed.

Then she saw a man standing with his back to the balcony. Selina, in the black habit, stood nearby, her face revealed within the frame of the white wimple.

The man held a weapon in his hand.

Rebecca stifled a gasp, fear for Selina thrumming through her. It appeared to be a short, blunt, lethal-looking mace. The mere sight of it sent horror sluicing through her.

Selina reached for it, but he raised it over his head—to elude her or to strike her? Rebecca held her breath. What should she do? Knock? Flee?

But Selina did not look frightened. She looked sad yet resolute. She shook her head and said, "No."

The man lowered his arm, and she took the weapon easily from his hand, the fight gone out of him.

Miss Newport's face appeared over the man's shoulder and one of his arms wrapped around her waist. The embrace struck Rebecca as protective rather than romantic, the image marred only by the mace still clutched in her hand.

Suddenly Selina stilled, staring straight at the balcony door. Rebecca pulled back.

"I think someone's out there," Selina said.

"What? I'll go and see." The man's voice seemed familiar. "You hide that. And get rid of that garb."

Pulse drumming, Rebecca quickly climbed back up onto the rail and stepped to the ledge—just as the balcony door opened behind her. She found herself praying words from the Psalms, *"Hide me under the shadow of thy wings. From the wicked that oppress me, from my deadly enemies."*

Glad for her dark pelisse, Rebecca clung to the wall, her face turned away, scared to move lest she be seen or heard, yet also scared to remain where she was, within reach of the man . . . and the mace.

Rain began to peck against her exposed cheek. *Oh no.* Rain would make the ledge slick and her escape even more dangerous.

For a moment longer the door remained open. She waited, tense, barely breathing, anticipating a shout or feet rushing toward her, but they did not come. The door closed.

Rebecca squeezed her eyes tight and breathed a prayer of thanksgiving.

Keeping her face averted, just in case, she moved as quickly as she could across the ledge. She jumped back onto her own balcony, striking her ankle on the wrought-iron chair, and slipped into her room. Pain flaring, she closed the door, bolting it for good measure.

Rebecca stood catching her breath, limbs trembling and ankle throbbing. She lifted her hem and saw the gash on her ankle bone and the blood flowing down her slipper and onto the floor. *Fiddle!* She grabbed a handkerchief and tied it around her ankle to staunch the blood, deciding she would clean up the rest later.

Putting her ear to the outer door and hearing nothing over her own ragged breaths, she cracked it open and looked down the corridor. No one in sight.

Suddenly a door opened down the passage and the black-clad "abbess" stepped out, veiled once again, and walked in her direction. Rebecca gingerly shut her door and waited for the footsteps to pass.

Then she opened the door again and listened, hearing the faint sound of footsteps descending the night stair.

Had Miss Newport hidden the weapon in her room, or was she, or perhaps the man, going somewhere now to dispose of it? Rebecca longed to ask Sir Frederick to accompany her but worried she would lose sight of the furtive figure if she delayed.

Slipping her room key into her reticule, Rebecca left number thirteen and tiptoed down the night stair. Following slowly and cautiously, she reached the lower passage in time to hear the chapel door close.

Rebecca stood there, heart pounding, afraid to enter the dark chapel alone. If she could be sure it *was* Miss Newport, she would brave it, believing she could best the slender woman in a skirmish if need be . . . unless she had that mace with her. But having seen masculine boots and hands protruding from the same gown once before, Rebecca hesitated. She could not fight a man, mace or no. It would be foolhardy to follow him into the dark, remote chapel and put herself in harm's way.

Lord, what should I do?

No answer was forthcoming.

She slowly tiptoed toward the chapel door, thinking she would peek in and see what was happening. If he or she was about to hide the weapon, maybe Rebecca could spy out the hiding place and return later with Sir Frederick.

Drawing near, she reached for the door, only to have it flung open in her face. Selina Newport emerged from the chapel in ordinary dress, nothing in her hands.

Miss Newport's eyes widened. "Miss Lane! I almost ran you down. Forgive me. I didn't see you there."

"Is . . . is anyone else in the chapel?"

"Only God, I hope. I was praying. Oh, but I did see a nun enter and leave again by the outside door. Apparently we have one staying here now."

Rebecca blinked. She doubted Selina had told the truth. *Now what?*

Miss Newport took her arm. "Shall we go into the hall together? Perhaps I might play while you sing."

Rebecca ignored the woman's tug and remained where she was. "I . . . don't really sing."

"Were you going in to pray as well?"

"I was, yes. If you will excuse me?"

Miss Newport gave no sign of leaving. Her eyes held Rebecca's, alight with challenge and suspicion. Then her expression changed, like the drawing of a curtain, or the donning of a mask.

She smiled. "Of course. I won't keep you." She gave a little wave and sauntered away, hips swaying.

When Miss Newport had disappeared down the passage and, presumably, into the hall, Rebecca looked around to make sure no one was watching and then entered the chapel. Moonlight shimmered through the stained-glass windows. And someone had left tallow candles burning on the brass candelabra, flames casting flickering light and shadow on the ancient stone walls. Rebecca walked slowly up the aisle, then paused to survey the dim interior.

If Miss Newport had concealed the weapon and habit in here, where would be a likely hiding place?

The small adjoining sacristy? The altar ambry or communion cabinet?

Her gaze landed on the stone baptismal font with its heavy wooden cover, crowned by a cross. Her senses stilled, centered on the font, moonlight from the tall, narrow lancet windows shining on it.

She had never lifted the cover off a font before. Finding it exceedingly heavy, she widened her stance, pushed it to the side, and reached in, trying to feel whether anything was inside. She felt something hard lying in a nest of coarse fabric—a smooth handle followed by a bulbous knob. The mace.

She slid the cover farther, afraid it would topple with a clang and a shuddering wobble to the floor.

Rebecca carefully pulled the wooden handle until the mace's brass head was free. Just touching it made her shiver. She set it down momentarily, tugged out the long swath of material, and replaced the cover.

Then she wrapped the mace in the material and wadded it up as compactly as she could.

She turned and started back down the aisle just as the outer door into the chapel opened. She ducked behind a column.

Footsteps slapped the stones, echoing across the vaulted space. Boot steps.

Pulse as rapid as a swift's wings, Rebecca peered around the column and saw the shadowy silhouette of a man approaching the baptismal font.

A shaft of moonlight from the sword-shaped window sliced across his face.

Mr. George?

Rebecca tiptoed as quietly as she could to the door leading back into the hotel. She waited until the man was as far away as possible before taking a deep breath, pushing open the door, and sliding out.

"Hey!" the man shouted. "What are you doing there? Stop!"

For a fraction of an instant Rebecca considering running upstairs to her room and locking the door. In the next, she thought of the flimsy lock on the least important guest room, occupied only occasionally by a valet or lady's maid without valuables to safeguard. She dismissed the idea. A strong man could likely break it down in a matter of seconds, and she had no idea how to use a mace.

Terror shook her. She had to act quickly.

On impulse, she tossed her reticule toward the stairway, hoping it might convince anyone pursuing her that she had gone up the night stair. Then she ran in the other direction through the cloisters. Out in the courtyard, rain was falling in earnest now, obscuring her view of the other side.

She hoped she could make it across the cloisters and into the safety of the more public reception hall, but from behind, she heard the chapel door screech open.

Rebecca ducked into the shadowy corner alcove, opened the low door, and climbed onto the spiral staircase, shutting herself inside just as running boot steps clattered across the cloister's flagstone floor.

She had plunged herself into darkness, except for the thinnest crack of torchlight leaking around the door panels. She prayed the man had not somehow heard about the hidden entrance. How ironically awful to be caught in the abbess's stairway by one of the abbess's "ghosts."

Heart beating hard, she pressed her free hand into her aching side, and told herself to calm down. If he came to the lower door, she would hurry up into room three and escape from there down the main stairway, in view of the clerk on duty.

The footsteps in the cloisters stopped. Hearing nothing for a time, Rebecca rose and carefully climbed halfway up the spiral stairs until she reached the squint. She positioned her eye to the slit . . . and saw Mr. George. Her mouth fell open. She had been so sure he was a chivalrous, honorable man.

He stood in the cloisters, head cocked to the side, hands extended, fingers splayed, as though alert to any sound. Dust tickled her nose, and Rebecca put a finger beneath her nostrils, hoping not to sneeze.

He began walking slowly, calmly, in her direction and stopped abruptly below the squint.

She held her breath.

Then he continued around the corner toward the hall or perhaps beyond.

Unsure what to do next, Rebecca thought again about slipping upstairs into room three. But what if someone was staying there now? She had not heard that the room had been put back into circulation, but she couldn't be sure. She seemed safe where she was for now, so she decided to remain. However, if Mr. George opened the bottom door she would scramble up like a rabbit from its burrow and face whatever consequences or person she might find above.

At the thought, and aided by the faint light coming through the squint, she found and traced the childish rabbit scratched into the wall and the artist's signature: *John did this*. Thank heavens those words had not turned out to be as prophetic as she'd feared.

Rebecca sat down on the stone steps to think. Setting the wrapped mace on the step beside her, she tried to breathe normally, swallowing often to dampen her throat, which had begun to feel scratchy from the stirred dust. She was afraid to cough.

How long should she wait? She couldn't remain in that dark, cramped cocoon all night. Her bladder would revolt, not to mention the rest of her. She was growing chilled already. And even if she hid for hours, might not Mr. George simply wait outside her room until she returned?

Lord, give me wisdom. Please protect me.

22

Frederick was descending the main stairs when Mr. George strode into the hall, looking harried.

"Sir Frederick, have you seen Miss Lane?"

"Not recently. Why?"

"I came in through the chapel a few minutes ago. I'm afraid I may have startled her. She ran out in a fluster. Must have thought I was another ghost." He gave a small chuckle, but the humor didn't reach his eyes.

Frederick surveyed the hall. "I don't see her. Which way did she go?"

"I thought this way." George looked past him into the blue parlour, empty except for Thaddeus Edgecombe.

"Perhaps she returned to her room?" Frederick guessed. "I did not see her on my way down but may have missed her. Shall we go and see?" Mild concern simmered in his veins. Had Rebecca seen the abbess again? Might Miss Newport have threatened her?

"I am sorry to trouble you," Mr. George said. "I am probably worrying for nothing."

Together the two men went upstairs and through the gallery passage to number thirteen.

Frederick knocked and the door creaked open. Discovering the door unlatched increased his uneasiness.

"Miss Lane? It's Sir Frederick and Mr. George. Are you all right? Are you in there?"

He tentatively opened the door wide, and by the light of a lamp on the dressing table saw the room was empty.

Something on the floor caught his eye. Frederick picked up the lamp and trained its flickering light on the wet, red smear. "What in heaven's name? There's blood here."

Clearly stunned, George muttered, "Thunder and turf."

Frederick rose, now in full alarm mode. If anything had happened to Rebecca, he'd never recover. Never forgive himself. *Please, God, let her be all right.* Aloud, he said, "Let's make sure she has not gone to Lady Fitzhoward's room."

They hurried down to the Grand Suite on the ground floor, but Lady Fitzhoward had not seen her.

"Is something wrong?" the woman asked.

"Probably nothing," Frederick said, striving to reassure her as well as himself. "But we shall keep looking."

The two men continued across the cloisters and returned to the hall, but there was still no sign of her. "Let's split up," Frederick suggested.

"If you think it best," George replied. "Though you are more likely to know where she might have gone."

Frederick did have an idea where Rebecca might hide if she was frightened. But he didn't want anyone to follow him there.

Mr. Edgecombe saw them and waved Mr. George into the parlour. "Are you sure Oliver said nothing to you about his plans for his next book?"

While Edgecombe occupied Mr. George, Frederick hurried back upstairs alone.

⚜

After what seemed an eternity, Rebecca began to believe Mr. George had given up the search. *Maybe I should—*

Click.

Panic gripped. Focusing her hearing, she realized the sound had come not from below but from above.

Then came the wooden pop of the panel door opening.

Rebecca rose to a crouch, prepared to scurry down the stairs, willing to risk a sprained ankle and anything else to escape.

"Rebecca?" a man whispered. "It's me."

Frederick.

Rebecca released a pent-up breath. *Thank you, God.*

Then she managed a weak "I'm . . . here."

She wanted to walk up to meet him, but her legs seemed suddenly made of jelly, and she sank to the steps once more. Why now did she tremble? Was the shock only now hitting her?

"Are you all right?" he asked.

She heard the scrape of footsteps on the stairs, and light shone around the curve of the central pillar.

"What is it? What's wrong? Here, let me help you up." He set down the candle lamp and reached for her, running his hands along her arms until he found her limp fingers. He grasped them and pulled her to her feet.

"Are you injured?"

She shook her head. A grazed ankle didn't merit mentioning.

"You are shaking." He pressed his back as far as he could to the outer wall and gently pulled her onto the same stair, bringing her nearer to eye level, although she still had to look up to see into his face.

Their hands, trapped between them, were all that separated them in the narrow space.

He studied her, concern tightening his familiar features. "Were you hiding?"

She nodded, lips trembling.

"From Mr. George?"

She blinked. "H-how did you know?"

"He came into the hall looking winded and asked if I had seen you."

"Oh. Yes." In utter relief at Frederick's presence, Rebecca closed her eyes and leaned forward, resting her cheek against his chest.

She heard the strong, rapid beating of his heart and took comfort in the sound.

He tugged his hand free, and for one awful second she thought she'd offended him, but then both of his hands bracketed her shoulders, drawing her nearer, holding her close.

He smelled of spices and safety, childhood memories and unrequited love.

Rebecca breathed him in deeply, wanting to slow down this moment, press it between the pages of her favorite book. . . .

She sneezed.

"Here, let's get you out of this dusty place." He picked up the lamp and carefully helped her up the stairs, his strong, steady hand enveloping hers.

He led her through the closet, set aside the lamp, and closed the panel behind them.

Then he turned to her and rubbed her arms. "Are you cold?"

Without waiting for a reply, he picked up a folded blanket

from the foot of the bed and draped it around her shoulders. "Here. This should help."

He rubbed her arms again through the thick wool and tucked his chin to look into her face. "What happened? Mr. George said he saw you running from the chapel in a panic."

She swallowed but found it difficult to speak through a tight throat, her body still trembling.

He tucked a wayward strand of hair behind her ear. "We tried your room first, but it was empty. You had not locked it, you know."

Had she not?

"We also saw blood on the floor. Are you certain you are not hurt?"

"Only c-cut my ankle."

"That's a relief. I did not want anyone to follow me, so I waited until Mr. Edgecombe cornered George with some question, then let myself in here."

"You s-still have the k-key?"

Frederick nodded. "Mayhew has not asked for it back, and guessing I might want to look again, I held on to it. Now I am glad I did."

"S-so am I." Her shivering slowly subsiding, she added, "Though you frightened me half to death when you opened that panel."

He bit his lip. "Can you tell me what happened?"

She nodded. "You will probably think I am seeing things again, but . . ." She went on to tell him what she'd seen in Miss Newport's room and in the chapel.

When she'd finished, she looked up into his face, wincing in anticipation. "You don't believe me, do you."

Uncertainty lined his forehead. "It is just so strange. Are you saying Miss Newport and Mr. George are in league together?

That they both may have disguised themselves as the abbess at different times?"

She nodded. "I saw a man wearing the habit once—saw masculine boots and hands—though not his face, so I can't be positive it was him."

"Why would Mr. George walk around the hotel dressed that way?"

"To not be seen somewhere he shouldn't be, like entering Miss Newport's room? Or maybe to deflect suspicion away from her?"

He frowned. "And you saw them arguing over a . . . mace?"

"Yes, he tried to keep it from her."

"Are you sure? Those haven't been used in battle for hundreds of years."

"I can prove it. Wait one moment—I forgot it on the stairs."

She started back toward the closet, but he forestalled her with a hand to her arm. "I'll go. What am I looking for?"

"The habit and mace I found hidden in the baptismal font."

Picking up the lamp, he again descended the stairs, returning less than a minute later with the bundle in his hand.

He slowly unwound the black fabric, stillness settling over him as he regarded the mace, its brass knob gleaming by lamplight.

"It's rather short—ceremonial, perhaps."

"Does it not seem a likely weapon?"

"A likely weapon indeed." He tested its weight in his hands. "I will ask Dr. Fox his opinion, but I think even slight Miss Newport could have killed a man with this."

His brows knit. "What is the connection between Jack George and Selina Newport? I can't imagine the two of them being romantically involved. He is far too old for her."

"Age is not important to everyone."

His gaze shot to hers, then away again.

"Actually," she said, "the way the man embraced her did not strike me as romantic, but more . . . paternal. Might he be her father?"

He shook his head. "No. Remember at dinner? She mentioned her parents were gone. Her father died in the war."

"That's right." An idea came to Rebecca. "Her father was a military man, and Mr. George is a former trooper. . . ."

"As were many thousands of other men."

"I realize the chance of a connection is slim. Just a thought."

"It is a possibility, though this is all supposition, not solid evidence."

"I would say that mace is quite solid."

"Having a mace does not necessarily prove she used it on Ambrose Oliver. But if you are right, does that mean she struck Jack George with it too?"

"Perhaps. Though if she did, Mr. George must not know it."

"You did not actually see one of them hide it in the font?"

"No, but they had it in her room."

He cocked his head to one side. "How exactly did you see that, by the way?"

"Oh." She glanced down, face heating. "I . . . I am afraid I peeked in from her balcony. I climbed over from mine. That's how I cut my ankle."

He slowly shook his head, surprise and mild censure in his expression. "Rebecca, Rebecca." He drew himself up. "Well, we shall leave that for later. Now, to decide what to do next." He stared off into the distance, then swiftly back at her. "Do you have reason to fear Mr. George? Did he threaten you?"

"Well . . . when he saw me leaving the chapel, he shouted for me to stop, and when I didn't, he followed me."

"He told me you seemed frightened and he was concerned about you."

"I *was* frightened—of him!" Another thought struck her. "Did you find my reticule near the night stair? I tossed it there, hoping to misdirect him."

"I did not see it. Maybe it's still there."

Looking first to make sure the corridor was quiet, he held the door for her and locked it behind them. After returning the lamp to its place on the passage table, they walked through the long gallery to the night stair.

"There it is." He jogged to the bottom of the stairs, bent to retrieve the small stringed bag, and brought it up to her.

Accepting it from him, she noticed it felt suspiciously light. She looked inside. Her few coins and hairpins were still there. But that was all.

"My room key is missing."

Another shaft of terror pierced her. Had Mr. George taken it . . . for later?

"Perhaps someone returned it to the front desk," he suggested. "Or to your room. Shall we look there first?"

Turning toward the door of number thirteen, which was still unlocked, she opened it and glanced inside, glad Frederick was with her.

"Has anything been disturbed?" he asked.

"No, but I don't see the key either." She looked up at him. "You will think me foolish, but I don't want to stay here tonight. I think I will walk back to the lodge."

"All that way at this time of night? And in the pouring rain? I would offer you a ride, but all I have here is a horse, and Tarvin's fly is not covered. I believe the other rooms are occupied except for number three. I hesitate to suggest it with its unsecured second entrance, but if you want, we could ask to have it readied for you."

She shook her head. "I don't want to trouble anyone. I just want to be safe."

He considered a moment, then said, "Gather your things and come with me."

She blinked up at him in mute surprise, then collected the rest of her belongings into her partially packed valise. "Where are we going?"

"I know it is not the done thing, but you can have my room. I will share with Thomas next door."

"That is kind of you, but—"

"It will likely cause tongues to wag, I can't deny. If you prefer not to . . . " He looked at his pocket watch. "Perhaps I could take you to the dower house. It isn't as far as the lodge, and Mamma has a guest room."

"Heavens, no. Your mother retired long ago, I imagine. I would hate to disturb her."

"True." He paused, then said, "But I agree with your decision to sleep elsewhere. I don't like the thought of you being alone in this room off by itself. So what's it to be? Wake my mother or take my room?"

"Are you sure you don't mind?"

"Not in the least. I wouldn't sleep otherwise, worrying about you."

He led her down the corridor. As they passed the door to number twelve, her skin prickled as though she were being watched.

When they reached his room, Sir Frederick unlocked the door and quietly ushered her inside. He closed the door behind them, though he stood with his back against it. "You will be safe here. Thomas or I will be right next door. The sheets are fresh. I did lie on that pillow for a short rest, but otherwise, all should be clean for you."

"Don't you need to gather your . . . night things?"

"Yes. Pray pardon me as I do. It will take just a minute."

"You needn't clear out everything. I will likely go to the lodge tomorrow, now the inquest is over."

"Very well. That would be quicker." He gathered what looked like a nightshirt and his toiletries.

"That should tide me over." He returned to the door. There, he pressed his lips tight as he considered. "Before I go to bed, I am going to find Mr. George, let him know you are safe, and make sure he means you no harm. I will not mention your change of rooms but will make it clear you are under my protection, just in case. I won't be gone long, and in the meantime, I shall ask Thomas to remain vigilant. After that, I shall be next door the rest of the night. All right?"

She nodded.

"I hope you will be able to sleep." He handed her his key. "Secure the door when I leave, and don't hesitate to knock on the wall or to call out if you need anything."

"Thank you. I shall feel better knowing you are nearby."

When he closed the door behind himself, she locked it.

Then Rebecca set her valise on the dressing chest, opened it, and extracted teeth-cleaning things and a hairbrush.

Someone knocked on the door.

Her nerves jangled.

Thinking Frederick may have forgotten something, she went to the door and asked softly, "Yes?"

"It's Tommy."

Relief. She unlocked and opened the door a crack, glad she had not yet undressed.

His eyebrows rose. "You really are in there. Had to see it for myself. Thought Freddy had a bad dream or spied a mouse in his room. Hasn't crawled into bed with me since I was four."

Frederick appeared behind his brother.

"Hush, man, and get back to your own room."

"I wish it were still only my room. I won't sleep a wink with him driving his pigs to market all night."

Frederick grasped him by the shoulder, turning him toward the adjacent door. "That's only when I have a cold, and I feel perfectly well."

"Thank heaven for that."

Rebecca closed the door with a small smile on her lips. Perhaps this was a good idea after all—assuming Lady Fitzhoward didn't find out. And she should have thought to tell Mary where she was. It was too late now. She was *not* going to wander the abbey late at night trying to find her. She shivered. Either way, she would work it out in the morning, which would arrive all too soon.

Now, how to get out of her dress and stays? She wished she had worn a frock that fastened in the front that day and her more comfortable wraparound stays.

Another light tap sounded on the door. "Miss?"

Mary's voice. At this rate, everyone in the hotel would know she had switched rooms, which to her ear sounded less shocking than saying she'd moved into Sir Frederick's! She opened the door.

Mary said, "Sir Frederick found me knocking on your door. I'd come earlier, but you weren't there so I came back. He said you didn't feel safe in your room. Something about a rat?" The girl shuddered. "And here I thought those were only in the cellars."

Instead of lying, Rebecca said, "He offered me his room for the night. He is sharing with his brother. It was kind of him to let you know where to find me. I hope you did not think the worst."

The girl grinned. "I've seen stranger things here—that I can tell you."

"Oh, like what?"

"Well, let's just say you're not the first lady I've found in the wrong room. Nor gentleman!" Mary's gaze swept over her. "Now, let's get you out of that frock and into your night-dress."

After Mary left, Rebecca pulled back the counterpane and fresh sheet and climbed into the bed, which was higher and wider than hers had been. Giddy excitement tickled her stomach as she settled into Frederick Wilford's bed—at least the one he'd slept in the last several nights. She laid her head on the one indented pillow, the same pillow he'd rested on earlier. A whiff of his spicy cologne enveloped her. Citrus and cloves. She turned her face into the pillow and breathed deeply, instantly feeling her nerves calmed and her senses . . . stirred.

She remembered her younger days when she used to dream of kissing Frederick and becoming his bride. Her girlish imagination had never ventured beyond that, and certainly not as far as the bedroom. Oh, but she had longed to kiss him.

There, in the warm embrace of his bed, she admitted to herself that she still did.

After asking Thomas to remain alert for any sound or call from Miss Lane, Frederick went out, bent on finding Mr. George and satisfying himself that he posed no threat to Rebecca.

He found him belowstairs in the bar.

Upon his entrance, Mr. Heck said, "Sorry, sir. I've already taken last orders."

"That's all right. Just want to speak with Mr. George there." Frederick walked over to his table.

"Find her?" the man asked.

"I did. May I join you for a few minutes?"

"Suit yourself."

Frederick sat down and explained the situation.

"She said what?" Mr. George stared at him. "Can you imagine a man like me dressing up as a woman, let alone a nun? The fellows would never let me hear the end of it! Why on earth would I do such a thing?"

"That is what I am trying to find out."

Mr. George shook his head, lips pressed into a regretful smile. "Look, I don't like to say anything against a lady. But let's remember this is the same young woman who reported seeing a ghost—a ghost who turned out to be a living, breathing nun. I'd put it down to a vivid imagination and too many Gothic novels—that's my guess."

"Then why did you chase her into the cloisters?"

"Chase her? What would you do if you saw a young lady bolt from a room? Would you not think she was in danger? Maybe needed help? Would you stand there and do nothing?"

"No," Frederick allowed, then studied the man's face. "Has Miss Lane any reason to fear you?"

Mr. George's nostrils flared. He looked genuinely offended. "I am a man of honor where women are concerned. Ask anyone. I do my best to protect them, though I have not always succeeded. Miss Lane has nothing to fear from me."

Frederick relaxed a bit, finding he believed him. On this point, at least.

"May I ask your connection to Miss Newport?" Frederick didn't mention he'd been seen in Miss Newport's room—first, because Rebecca had seen only his back there, and second, because then he'd have to explain how Rebecca had managed it. The role of Peeping Tom was not a flattering one.

George made a face. "Connection?" He chuckled. "I hope

you are not suggesting a romantic one. You could not be more wrong. I have known her since girlhood."

Frederick wanted to ask more, about the mace and the chapel, but Mr. George abruptly stood. "Look. It's late. In my current temper, and after two whiskeys, I might say something terribly rude. Can this not keep till morning?"

"Are you staying on here?"

"I had planned to go tomorrow, but I'll not leave until we talk again."

Frederick held his gaze. "Very well. I will take you at your word, as a man of honor."

George's eyes glinted, then he turned on his heel and strode away.

Frederick would have liked to detain Mr. George and demand more answers. He had reason to suspect Miss Newport, but had insufficient grounds to demand anything of this man.

Frederick returned to Thomas's room. His brother was in bed but had left one lamp burning low. Frederick sat in a chair near him and asked, "Did Miss Newport ever mention Mr. George to you? Hint at any connection?"

"Mr. George? The guard?"

Frederick nodded. "He and Miss Newport pretended not to know one another. But they were seen talking again tonight."

Thomas sat up in bed with a frown. "I don't understand. Are you suggesting Selina is involved with this George fellow?"

"In some way, yes. Although not romantically. He admitted he has known her since her girlhood."

Thomas blinked, his complexion sallow by lamplight. "You think they were in on it together? That Selina . . . ? I can't believe it. Wait! You said you had no proof she struck anyone."

Frederick narrowed his eyes. "Forget I said that."

"What!"

"For now. Forget I said that."

Miss Lane had described the former trooper as protective, and Jack George was certainly not one to stand by and do nothing when a young woman was in danger. Especially a woman he cared about.

Frederick said, "I think this will be exceedingly difficult to prove. But I have an idea."

Thomas glared at him. "Are you still determined to try to pin this on her? I know Marina gave you cause to distrust women, but now you are prejudiced against them, and suspect them all of foul play! I pity Miss Lane." He abruptly rolled over, turning his back on him.

Frederick had rarely seen his brother so angry. Was there a trace of truth in his accusation?

He sighed and undressed for bed, already dreading the morrow and hoping his plan did not go awry.

23

The following morning, Frederick knocked softly on Miss Lane's door. A few moments later, she opened it. She had already dressed, though her hair was still down around her shoulders like a curtain of rich honey-brown silk.

He dragged his gaze from it and went on to describe his plan, such as it was, in a low voice. He hoped and prayed it would work, and the true killer would be revealed.

A flash of nervous excitement lit her eyes as she gathered her hair. "I shall be out in two minutes."

Thomas had angrily refused to take any part in the scheme, trumped-up or not, so Frederick alone assembled the other players, assigned them their roles, then waited with them for the opening act to begin.

On cue, Noah Brixton pounded on the door of number twelve. "Open up! It's the constable!" Another barrage of knocking. "Mr. Mayhew is here with a key and we'll not hesitate to use it."

Roused by the noise, curious guests opened their doors and peered out.

"What's going on?" someone called.

Miss Newport slowly opened her door, fully dressed and appearing supremely beautiful, and supremely poised. "What is it?" she asked with cool indifference.

She really was a skilled actress.

Mr. Brixton proclaimed, "Selina Newport, I am taking you into custody for the murder of Ambrose Oliver."

Deadly calm, she replied, "I did not kill him."

"That's for the court to decide."

She stilled, then said evenly, "Very well. Allow me to gather my things." She retrieved her reticule and valise, and a few moments later, they paraded through the corridor toward the main stairs.

Mr. Brixton held her arm, and Frederick walked on her other side. Mr. Mayhew and Miss Lane trailed behind them, watching. Witnessing.

Mr. George came out of number four, drawn by the hubbub.

"Hey! What has happened? What are you doing? Where are you taking her?"

Brixton said, "Miss Newport is being arrested on suspicion of murder."

"Murder?" Mr. George thundered. "What? No!"

Frederick nodded. "She was seen hiding a wicked-looking mace in the chapel's baptismal font. A probable murder weapon, according to Dr. Fox. She was also seen dressed as a nun, running away from room three the morning Ambrose Oliver was killed. We are holding her over for trial."

Selina Newport's face, stoic till now, showed a ripple of fear. Even so, she lifted her chin and said resolutely, "Don't worry about me. It's all right."

"Thunder and turf," George muttered. "It's not all right."

"It was my fault," she said.

"No, it dashed well wasn't. It was his."

Mr. George turned to Frederick. "Let her go, and I will tell you what really happened."

"Don't!" Selina called. "There is no use in both of us being destroyed by this."

George winced. "Bit late for that, lass."

"Uncle Jack, no. I don't want anything to happen to you. You're all I have left."

"And you're all I have left. Please. It's my responsibility. My right."

Tears glimmered in Selina's eyes. She opened her mouth to speak but hesitated, lips trembling.

Jack George stepped near and laid a hand on her shoulder. "Do you trust me?"

A short while later, Frederick led Mr. George into the small office where he'd conducted his earlier interviews.

"I will tell you all," he said. "But you must let Selina go."

"I can make no promises until I hear the truth."

"You strike me as a fair man, Wilford. So I will trust you. Just you, though, if you please." He shot the constable a look.

When Brixton opened his mouth to object, Frederick said, "It's all right. I shall apprise you later. Please keep Miss Newport in custody here in the hotel for now."

"Yes, sir."

When the two of them were sitting alone together behind closed doors, Mr. George drew a deep breath and said, "None of this is Selina's fault, though she blames herself for Edie's death."

"Edie was her younger sister?"

"Yes. My best mate's girls. I was their guardian and raised them after their parents' deaths."

"She called you uncle."

Mr. George waved a dismissive hand. "Term of affection—that's all."

Frederick nodded. "Go on."

"The whole thing started a few years ago. Selina was performing in a theatre in Cheltenham, living in a pair of rooms in a lodging house. Edie begged to go and stay with her sister for a time. Have an adventure. I didn't like it, but they cajoled and I've always been too soft when it comes to those girls. I figured they could look out for each other. But the reality was, Selina worked long hours. The novelty of loitering behind stage soon wore thin, and Edie began spending more time on her own.

"I knew something was wrong as soon as she came home. She was quiet. Tense. Teary. Though I didn't guess the worst of it for several months when she could no longer hide the fact that she was with child. She was barely more than a child herself. Only sixteen.

"She wouldn't tell me who the man was. Said she knew I'd kill the lecher and end up hung for it.

"As far as I knew, she didn't tell her sister either. Yet I could see Selina felt guilty, so I figured Edie must have met the man through her or the theatre.

"For a time, I agreed to let it lie. For Edie's health and peace of mind. Then she died. . . ."

Jack George shook his head, a bitter twist to his lips. "The midwife couldn't turn the babe. I ran for a doctor, but by the time I located him and basically dragged him back, it was too late. She'd lost too much blood. Lost the babe as well."

His voice thickened. "Selina and I were mad with grief. I had promised their father to protect his girls, and I failed. I would have gladly given my life for hers if I could."

Another regretful shake of the head. "After Edie died, I swore to myself I would find out who was responsible and make him pay. Took time, asking around the theatre and the lodging house. Finally, I found a girl who had cleaned for Selina.

"She told me who she thought it was, who used my Edie ill. He talked Edie into letting him into Selina's place. Said he'd left something, his gloves or some such, although the maid assured him she'd not seen them. He told the maid to leave, and the timid thing obeyed, but not before she heard Edie call the man by name—Mr. Oliver.

"Edie had mentioned in one of her letters home that she'd met the author at the theatre. I'm sure she never imagined he'd show up at her door and refuse to take no for an answer.

"I didn't tell Selina what I'd learned, didn't want her involved. I asked around until I learned where Oliver lived. Not far from me, actually. I didn't strike directly, hoping to keep my neck out of the noose. Instead I slipped a printed notice under his door, advertising my gallery and tailor-made to appeal to his vanity. 'Men of letters, important, learned gentlemen, deserve to keep their bodies in as fit condition as their minds.' I also offered a very good price.

"It worked. He came, notice in hand, and asked for a trial. He blustered about how he had some fencing experience, written about it anyway, which must count for something. All the while I agreed and clucked, pretending to be impressed. I trained him, and got to know him, and garnered his trust.

"Then I began playing on his fears. I'd learned he was a habitual gambler. Always sure he would win, and always losing. Under the hatches in debt. I told him a man had come to the gallery, sniffing around, asking about him. I dropped the name of the moneylender, Isaac King, and could see it frightened him.

"I bided my time. Not eager to get myself arrested while one of my beloved wards might still need me. But Selina has grown up and grown hard since Edie's death—almost too hard, I sometimes think. She has the determination and strength to survive in this world, strength Edie did not have.

"At all events, I sent Oliver a letter. I write a better hand than you would suppose. In it, I wrote: 'Pay up or pay the consequences.'

"He came to the gallery and said he was done with fencing. He wanted to learn to fight hand to hand. To defend himself.

"Eventually, he grew desperate. No new book, no more money. He convinced his publisher he needed to get away, to some quiet place out of town where he could work without distractions.

"He came to my lodgings and asked me to accompany him. I said it was propitious timing, as I had recently closed the gallery. Oliver told the publisher I would be here to keep him accountable, to keep him writing. But I saw the panic in his eyes and knew it was bravado. He mostly wanted me here for protection, should an angry moneylender learn where he'd gone and come to collect—or dole out punishment."

"So he trusted you," Frederick said.

The man's eyes glinted. "More fool him. I even wrote to Mr. King in Naples. Paid a pretty penny for his direction too. A gamble, I knew. One that didn't pay in the end."

Frederick asked, "Why did Miss Newport come here to the abbey . . . really?"

George grimaced. "When she wrote of her plans to come to Swanford, I was wary. I guessed she had set her sights on a man. Knowing Mr. Oliver was staying here, I worried she might be meeting him."

"To take revenge herself?"

"Didn't say that. I would ask you not to put words in my mouth, sir."

"Very well."

"No. Turns out she was here to see your brother. I was relieved, though I could see she'd have little chance there. She'd reached too high."

"Tell me what happened the day Mr. Oliver died."

Mr. George nodded. "I went to his room rather early that morning, just after sunrise. I knocked and identified myself. He let me in, cross as a badger—didn't like being woken early. He must not have been asleep long, for his fire had not yet gone out.

"I said, 'Sorry, sir. But with Mr. King staying in the hotel, I thought it would be wise to make certain all the windows are locked and there's no other way in.'

"He bid me get on with it, lit a lamp, and sat down. Said he might as well get some work done since he was up.

"I made a pretense of making sure the windows were secure, working my way around the room until I was positioned behind him. Then I pulled out the mace, which I'd hidden beneath my coat."

Here Mr. George gave a humorless chuckle. "Do you know where I got that old relic? Oliver himself gave it to me instead of paying his bill for the training. Some admirer of his books had given it to him, and he passed it on to me and considered his debt settled. And now it truly is settled."

George sent him a piercing look. "You no doubt think me a heartless villain for what I did. I don't ask for mercy, only for understanding. Ambrose Oliver ended forever the happiness of the only two creatures I loved in all the world." His voice grew hoarse. "He ruined our sweet Edie, left her with child, and denied all responsibility. Left her to die. And he left Selina feeling responsible and miserable. That man was more my enemy than any foreign soldier I faced in battle. So yes, I struck hard—one decisive blow."

"And after?"

His shoulders drooped. "Selina came along sometime later, wearing her idiotic disguise. I was just sitting there outside the room, mace in hand. I'd expected to feel victorious. Relieved. Satisfied that justice had been done. But I felt none of those things. Only numb."

"Why did she wear the habit?" Frederick asked.

Again George shrugged. "I had written back to warn her Oliver would be here, hoping she wouldn't come. She came anyway, and brought along that costume, having just played a nun in *Measure for Measure*. She thought she might frighten him, deliver a message from beyond the grave that his vile deeds would not go unpunished, like *Richard III* visited by the ghosts of those he killed. And if scaring Oliver failed, she could at least come to my room without being seen or thought to be doing anything improper."

"Did she go into Mr. Oliver's room? We know he sent a message through . . . one of the maids, asking her to come."

George hesitated. "She came to the door, but I turned her away." He shifted. "At all events, that morning I told her I'd done it—Ambrose Oliver was dead."

"How did she react?"

"She said, 'Well, don't just sit there. Go. Run. Hide.'"

Jack George smiled wryly. "I declined. I said running would make my guilt obvious. The authorities would quickly track me down."

"Selina retorted, 'And sitting there with a weapon in your hand won't shout your guilt? You are not thinking clearly.'

"She told me to give her the mace so she could hide it. Then she thought a moment and told me to lie down on the floor, to not move or open my eyes until someone came and raised the alarm. I knew Mary would be coming at nine with Oliver's breakfast, but I still didn't understand. So I remained sitting in the chair, confused, and asked Selina how lying on the floor would help.

"She said it would appear as though I'd been struck by the assailant before he went into Mr. Oliver's room.

"I told her no one would believe that. Not without a head wound. I am not the actor she is.

"Selina said I would not have to act. She also said she knew better than to try and surprise me, because my reactions are too fast. She said I would have to let her.

"'Let you what?' I asked.

"She said, 'I am sorry to have to hurt you. But it's all I can think of.' Then she looked me in the eye and asked, 'Do you trust me?'

"And I bowed my head."

Mr. George exhaled a deep breath and rubbed the back of his skull, apparently without realizing he did so.

"For a while after that, I hoped I might go free, that the verdict of death 'by person or persons unknown' would stand. But I was and still am willing to face the consequences. Truth is, I have experienced enough of this weary world. Selina, however, has so much life ahead of her. She might yet fall in love, marry, and raise a family of her own. Given the chance."

He held Frederick's gaze. "I failed to protect Edie, but let me protect Selina now. Leave her out of it. She may have guessed what I planned to do, but she did nothing herself."

"Nothing except strike you to provide an alibi?"

"I will deny it till my dying day, which will be here soon, I imagine. Besides, who would believe it? That slight, feminine Selina, my own loving ward, knocked down a man like me—a former trooper and expert fighter? Everyone knows the infamous moneylender, Mr. King, was here, rings on his fingers and vengeance in his eyes. You accuse her and I'll say *he* struck me, to get to Oliver. Which version do you think a jury will believe?"

The man had a point. "Are you saying you will confess under oath to Ambrose Oliver's murder if Selina is left out of it?"

"Completely out of it, yes."

When Frederick did not respond, Mr. George added, "Please, young man. Have you never wanted to protect someone you love . . . a woman you love? She has done nothing wrong. Has punished herself for years because of her sibling's suffering . . ."

Frederick thought of Rebecca and her guilt over not being able to protect John from Mr. Oliver's cruelty.

Mr. George continued, ". . . while Ambrose Oliver has gone on with his eat, drink, and gamble life without a backward glance or a glimmer of remorse for what he did to our beloved Edie. Our hearts."

The man's voice cracked and Frederick felt his resolve crack with it.

"You will confess in court?"

"I will. Once I have your word as a gentleman that no harm shall come to Selina."

Frederick considered. He still suspected Miss Newport might have been more involved than Mr. George let on—or at least had been tempted to harm the author herself. Yet knowing he could not prove it, he concluded this was likely their only chance for a conviction. He felt no satisfaction at the triumph . . . if triumph it was.

He said, "I reserve the right to tell Miss Lane and Thomas in confidence about your relationship with Selina, and that she was aware of what you did and did not report it. I promise it will go no further."

The man's mouth twisted. "To warn your brother off?"

Frederick held his gaze. "You are not the only one who feels duty-bound to protect his family."

Mr. George hesitated, then nodded. "I understand."

"Then yes," Frederick promised. "You have my word."

A short while later, Frederick followed as Mr. Brixton led Jack George across the hall toward the hotel's front door. He glimpsed Miss Lane and Lady Fitzhoward sitting near the fire. Both turned solemn faces toward the grim procession.

Miss Newport appeared at the top of the stairs and gripped the railing tightly. She called down, her usually eloquent voice as plaintive as a little girl's, "I am sorry, Uncle Jack. So sorry!"

He looked up, neck craned, and called back, "It's all right, Selina."

She vehemently shook her head. "I still feel like it's all my fault. I can't forgive myself."

Expression adamant, he said, "Then *I* forgive you, and I love you. Never forget."

She raised a hand in farewell, and the tears streaming down her face were no act.

When the men had left and the hall was quiet once more, Rebecca leaned closer to Lady Fitzhoward and explained the morning's events as best she knew them.

"Ah. I heard a commotion upstairs and wondered what was going on." The older woman gazed thoughtfully into the distance. "So it was the guard dog after all."

"It seems so, yes." Rebecca felt strangely sad for Miss Newport and even for Mr. George, whom Selina apparently looked on as an uncle. She was relieved John had been exonerated in the bludgeoning, but her relief was tempered by what her brother *had* done, and by what she must tell her employer.

Lady Fitzhoward inhaled deeply, then thumped the floor with her stick. "Well, now that's over, we can get on with our plans. What do you say to Easter in Canterbury, and then on to Calais?"

She saw the hope in the woman's eyes and hated to disappoint her. "I am sorry, my lady, but I cannot go with you. I can't leave John when he . . ." Her words trailed off as she struggled with how much to say. The truth was she did not want John to face whatever was coming alone. Nor did she feel it right to leave the whole burden on dear Rose. After all, Rebecca was John's only remaining family. His sister.

For some reason, the word *sister* echoed through her mind. *Sister, sister, sister . . .*

She blinked and looked up to find Lady Fitzhoward watching her, waiting for her to finish her sentence, eyes narrowing when she did not.

Rebecca swallowed and finished lamely, "I can't leave him. Not now."

Lady Fitzhoward sighed. "I was afraid of that. Ah well. I admire you for putting family first, even if it is devilish inconvenient for me. Never mind. I will go and see those friends I put off visiting before. Joly will miss her French chef serving up savory reminders of home. But life, I find, often serves us disappointments instead."

Rebecca managed a wan smile and pressed her hand. "Goodbye, my lady. You have been very kind to me, and I hope our paths cross again."

"So do I, Rebecca."

It was the first time the older woman had called her by her Christian name. Rebecca wondered if it would be the last.

When she crossed the cloisters, Sir Frederick was waiting for her at the bottom of the night stair, hat in hand.

"Miss Lane, I wanted to speak with you before I go to the lodge." He gestured her into the library and closed the door most of the way behind him.

He explained, "Mr. Brixton is taking Jack George to the county gaol to await trial."

"He confessed to striking Mr. Oliver?" she asked.

"Yes."

"Then your plan succeeded. Well done."

He flinched. "No need for congratulations. It is a sad business all around."

"I agree."

He looked at her, expression somber. "As your friend, I am relieved to prove John was not ultimately responsible for Mr. Oliver's death. As magistrate, however, I cannot ignore what John did. I could authorize a warrant to search the lodge, seize John's manuscript, and have Dr. Fox's colleague test the pages for arsenic."

She ducked her head, dread weighing down her soul anew.

"But as John has already confessed to attempting it and changed his mind before harm could be done, I don't think that will be necessary—assuming he cooperates and accepts the consequence I intend to require."

"Which is?" Rebecca asked, a tremor sweeping over her. What would it be? Imprisonment? Transportation?

"At least one year at Woodlane Hospital under Dr. Fox's care." He held up a preemptive hand. "Before coming to this decision, I considered *all* of John's actions. He may have planned to trap Mr. Oliver into stealing his manuscript and ingesting poison if he did so, but he repented and retrieved the pages. Because of that, I feel a stay in a private asylum a more fitting consequence than prison. I hope it will reform his weaknesses of character and mind. And at the end of a twelvemonth, it will be up to Dr. Fox's professional recommendation whether John remains there or is released."

"Thank you."

Rebecca's relief was quickly followed by worry. "But the fees!"

"Will be covered. Never fear."

Never fear . . . Oh what a heavenly ideal. What joy and freedom it must be not to live with constant guilt and fear. "And if he does not cooperate?"

"Then I will have no choice but to pursue charges of attempted murder. The judges on the Oxford circuit are stern and unyielding, so I would anticipate a severe penalty, especially considering Mr. Oliver's fame."

"Please be sure you make that clear to John. Otherwise, I doubt he would go willingly."

"I shall." He started to leave, then turned back, eyes downturned with regret. "I am sorry, Miss Lane."

"It is not your fault."

"Nor yours."

"I wish I could believe that."

"And I wish this didn't have to come between—" Sir Frederick broke off, then finished stolidly, "I hope it won't spoil our . . . long friendship."

"I hope so too. But how can it not change things?"

"You are probably right." He shifted and tightened his grip on his hat. "If you would like to bid your brother farewell, we can wait a bit."

"Yes, thank you. I must gather my bags, but I shall be there shortly."

He nodded. "Very well."

Sir Frederick managed a sad smile, bowed, and then walked away, looking as dejected as she felt.

24

Stepping out of the hotel a few minutes later, Rebecca saw Robb Tarvin and paused at the bottom of the steps.

Before she could decide whether to speak to him or not, he raised a hand and jogged over to her.

"Hoped to catch you," he panted. "Wanted to apologize." He dipped his head, then earnestly met her gaze. "Sorry I acted like a brute before." Robb grimaced and then added, "I have a jealous nature, Mum says, and she's right. That's no excuse, though. Pray forgive me."

Seeing his sincere contrition, Rebecca took pity on him. "All is forgiven," she said, then added, "and please forgive me for any . . . misunderstanding. I wish you every happiness."

"And I you, Miss Lane."

He expelled a relieved breath and, with a glance at her valise, said, "Finally leaving this old place for good?"

"I believe so." She decided to offer her old friend an olive branch. "By the way, I saw Kitty Fenchurch the other day. We talked for some time."

"Oh? And what did you and Kitty talk about?"

"You, among other things."

"Me?"

"She speaks very highly of you, you know."

He shook his head. "Kitty Fenchurch is a silly creature. A fine figure, I own. But not an ounce of sense between her ears."

"Maybe. But within that fine figure lies a kind and loving heart. And she admires you, Robb."

He slanted her a wry look. "Trying to fob me off on Kitty?"

Rebecca huffed. "Fob you off? Kitty is a pretty young woman from a good family."

He said wistfully, "She isn't you."

Rebecca shook her head. "But you will always have my friendship, Robb." She smiled. "If you want it."

"I do."

Before leaving, Rebecca asked him to deliver her trunk to the lodge when he had time. He was heading out on another job but promised to see to it when he returned.

When Rebecca reached the lodge a short while later, she found Sir Frederick and Dr. Fox there before her. Upon her entrance, the two men stepped out to give her time to say good-bye to her brother in private.

She set down her things and took a deep breath, bracing herself for John's anger and remonstrances. Then she entered the sitting room.

He stood before the hearth staring up at the mantelpiece. Was he thinking of their family portrait, which had hung there until he sold it? Anger again nipped at her. Remembering Rose say, *"Your living, breathing family is more important than any portrait,"* Rebecca bit her tongue. Now was not the time.

She noticed with relief that his hair had been recently washed and he had shaved as well. A half-filled valise lay open on the sofa.

He looked at her over his shoulder, his face taut. "Tell them, Becky. Tell them it's not my fault. Ambrose Oliver ruined my life. It's his fault. He did this to me."

His voice pitched higher with desperation. "Don't let them take me away, Becky. Talk to Sir Frederick. He likes you. Always has. Tell him to let me go."

She resolutely blinked back tears, and spoke over a tight, burning throat. "No, John. What Mr. Oliver did was wrong, but that does not justify what you did. Life is precious. And only God has the right to end it."

When he didn't respond, she added, "Do you not realize that if Mr. Oliver *had* died from the arsenic, I would share the blame, as I delivered the poisoned pages myself?"

"But I had to do something!" he blurted, with little apparent remorse.

"You are wrong, John. And you need to accept responsibility for your actions. It could be worse—you should be grateful for Sir Frederick's mercy, and for God's."

He frowned and opened his mouth to argue, but she went on, "This is a good thing. Or can be, if you let it. A chance to put the past behind you. To heal."

"I can do that here. I don't want to leave."

Rebecca shook her head and walked closer. "You need more help than Rose or I or those little brown bottles can give you. I believe Dr. Fox can help you."

"I don't want—"

"John." She pressed his hand, tightly. "Better this than prison." For several weighty moments, she held his gaze, then with forced brightness said, "Now, have you got everything you need?" She looked at the valise, stuffed haphazardly with clothes. "You forgot paper and ink and your favorite books." Rebecca began moving around, gathering things.

The fight seemed to go out of him, and he pushed the hair from his face, shoulders slumped. "I am sorry, you know. Never meant to put you in danger. I never should have involved you or Rose or Mary. . . ."

Rebecca paused in her packing. Yes, poor besotted Mary. And what would happen to Rose once John was no longer here to pay rent on the lodge? They would worry about that later. If John was willing to admit he was wrong, there might be hope for him yet.

"I forgive you, John," she said earnestly. "And God will too. Ask Him."

He hung his head.

Rebecca sniffed and said, "Now, listen to Dr. Fox and do as he advises. You have nothing to lose and everything to gain."

"I hope you're right."

Rose came in from wherever she had been hovering, and no doubt listening, and embraced John, cheeks streaked and handkerchief in hand. "I shall be praying for you, my lad."

While her brother's back was turned, Rebecca slipped into the valise their father's small *New Testament & Psalms* and their mother's three sketches to remind him of family and home.

When John walked out the door, only then did Rebecca let the tears come. She and Rose stood at the window side by side, watching his departure in a duet of soft weeping.

After the men disappeared from view, Rose wiped her eyes with the wadded handkerchief and blew her nose. She said, "Reminds me of the day Daisy left. Although there were more harsh words than tears that day. The tears came later. . . ."

Rose looked up at the clock. "Good heavens. The day's half gone and I haven't given a thought to dinner. Are you hungry?

I'm afraid there's little in the larder. Perhaps some cheese . . ." The woman trudged into the kitchen and Rebecca followed.

There, the cook-housekeeper lifted the domed lid off the cheese keeper. Empty. "Sorry, Miss Becky."

"That is all right," Rebecca assured her. "It's been quite a day already, has it not? And it's only midafternoon."

Rose lifted her market basket to the table and reached for the punched tin box, which held her household funds. "I shall go into the village and find something." She shook the box, and a few small coins clacked together. "Not much in our coffers, sadly."

"I'll go," Rebecca offered. "I have some money left. Lady Fitzhoward paid more of my bill than I expected."

"But you just got here."

"I don't mind. I feel too restless to sit now anyway. My pulse is still racing after that scene."

"Mine too. Very well. Get some ham and cheese. Fruit, if you want it. And I'll make some savory scones. I'm sure I have enough flour and such for that."

"Sounds an excellent plan."

Donning her outdoor things, Rebecca picked up the market basket and left the lodge. She strode through Fowler's Wood— glad it was daytime—and into Swanford. Her steps were light and her spirits surprisingly buoyant with relief.

She walked past the church and vicarage without flinching and waved to Mr. Fenchurch coming out of the public house.

Rebecca was halfway to the High Street when the word *sister* echoed through her mind once again.

She stopped then and there on Elderberry Lane and walked back to Henwick Cottage on the corner. Rose's childhood home. She recalled Lady Fitzhoward staring up at it with a sad, faraway look in her eyes.

Little scraps of remembered conversation began falling over Rebecca's mind like reviving rain.

"I haven't spoken to mine in years. . . ."

"Have you been to Swanford before, my lady?"

"A lifetime ago. . . ."

Understanding flickered, then flamed to life.

Rebecca hurried down the lane and turned up the High Street, passing by the butcher's shop and cheesemonger's without stopping. Heart rate accelerating, she walked as fast as she could all the way back to the Swanford Abbey Hotel.

She let herself in through the garden door and started to turn right toward her employer's room, hoping the woman had not already left.

At some faint sound, or internal urging, Rebecca turned left instead, toward the library and writing room. If nothing else, she told herself, she would take a final look at the painting of the abbess.

Pausing in the threshold, she glanced inside.

There sat Lady Fitzhoward, shoulders slumped, head bowed, all alone.

Rebecca stood still and silent, transported back to the day almost a fortnight ago when she'd stepped into the parlour of the inn they'd stayed in prior to coming here.

Rebecca had been surprised to come upon Lady Fitzhoward sitting in a high-backed armchair, her posture sagging. She appeared to sink into herself. To shrink. She looked almost like a child in that massive chair.

In her veined hands, she'd held a letter. Lady Fitzhoward stared down at it, face grey but eyes wide.

"What is it?" Rebecca had asked. "Not bad news, I hope."

Lady Fitzhoward started as though awakening. "What? How

should I know?" She struggled up with effort. "I have not yet stooped to reading your letters. Our forwarded post arrived this morning." She thrust the unopened letter toward Rebecca, adding, "From home."

Rebecca looked at the postal markings and recognized Rose's handwriting. "It's from my brother's housekeeper."

"Rose, I believe you call her?"

Rebecca nodded.

"What is her surname, by the way?"

"Watts."

"Rose Watts?"

"Yes."

"She never married?"

"No. Why do you ask?"

The woman shrugged. "Merely curious. You speak of her often."

"We are fond of her," Rebecca replied, thinking of the housekeeper's generous nature and tart, forthright tongue.

Then she studied Lady Fitzhoward's face once more, wondering why she looked so disconsolate.

"My lady, is something the matter? Are you not feeling well?"

"I am perfectly well. Quit fussing and read your letter."

"All right." Rebecca opened the seal and unfolded the page. As she read about Rose's growing concerns over John's behavior, and her plea that Rebecca return to Swanford as soon as possible, all other thoughts faded away.

Now Rebecca felt a quiver of unease to find Lady Fitzhoward looking similarly dejected, although this time she held no letter.

"What are you doing here, my lady?" she asked gently. "I thought you were visiting friends for Easter?"

The woman shook her head. "The truth is, I haven't any

friends. I told you that so you wouldn't feel sorry for me. And my sister and I have been estranged for thirty years."

Rebecca held out her hand. "Then come home with me."

⁂

Engaging Robb to drive them, they made a brief stop for provisions at the High Street shops, then rattled through Fowler's Wood. The late afternoon sunshine slipped through the tree branches like bars of yellow gold. Birdsong and the smell of wildflowers filled the air with promises of springtime.

Arriving at the lodge, Rebecca opened the door for Lady Fitzhoward and gestured her inside.

Rose met them in the entryway and drew up short, clearly startled.

Rebecca said, "Rose, this is Lady Fitzhoward."

The housekeeper stared at her for three full ticks of the clock, then her mouth tightened. "No, it isn't."

"It is."

Lady Fitzhoward, looking tense and pensive, rested gloved hands rather heavily on her walking stick. "Rosie," she said simply.

"Daisy," Rose replied.

How strange to hear her exacting employer referred to as a sweet, humble flower!

Lady Fitzhoward glanced at her and explained, "Never liked the name, so I changed it when I left here."

Eyes narrowed, Rose blurted, "You didn't marry him, then?"

"Elias Westergreen? No." Lady Fitzhoward looked down, then said somewhat sheepishly, "I might have done. But we'd got no farther than Manchester when he left me for an innkeeper's daughter named Modesty, which was an irony, I can tell you."

Rose shook her head, lip curled accusingly. "I've imagined you married to him all these years and hated you for it."

"I know," Lady Fitzhoward softly replied.

"Why didn't you tell me?"

"And share my disgrace and shame? You would have enjoyed that, I wager."

"I would have, indeed!" Rose snapped, then amended, "For a few minutes. Or a year."

"As I thought."

Rose huffed. "Why not? You stole him from me."

"Or rather I borrowed him for a few days. Honestly, I spared you a great deal of heartache and betrayal."

"Just because he left you does not mean he would have left me."

Rebecca winced at the harsh words, but Lady Fitzhoward merely inhaled a long breath.

"Perhaps. Although, I went back through that part of Manchester not long ago and stopped at that same inn. And guess what? Modesty was working there again. As buxom as ever, but otherwise aged and weary. Elias had left her too. Left her to raise a child alone. Left a whole string of women by now, I imagine."

"Well." Rose lifted her double chin, her sharp gaze sweeping over Lady Fitzhoward's fine gown. "You don't seem to be suffering too badly. You have done pretty well for yourself, even so."

"Yes," Lady Fitzhoward allowed. "I fell in love with an older widower and broke my heart when he died."

"At least you had a husband. And money, by the looks of it. Probably a grand house too."

Lady Fitzhoward nodded. "I have decided to sign over the house to his son. I cannot stand to be there without Donald. I have a small annuity and a settlement I am going through somewhat rapidly with all my traveling and investments."

Rose gestured toward Rebecca. "Well, when the Lanes are through with me, I'll end in the poorhouse, no doubt. Perhaps we can go together." She froze, seemingly realizing what she'd said. Her sister stilled as well.

Lady Fitzhoward said, "You think I would live with you in a poorhouse?"

Rose's eyes flashed. "Heaven forbid! You're too good for me now, my *lady*, is that it? Pardon me."

"That is *not* it," her ladyship retorted. "I may not have as much money as I once did, but we can do better than the poorhouse. A small cottage like this one might suit us rather well."

Rose tilted her head, expression vulnerable. "Oh?"

"With your industry and my . . . charm"—Lady Fitzhoward gave a self-deprecating grin—"we might deal very well together."

The two sisters held each other's gazes, hope and uncertainty wavering there.

Rebecca took advantage of the break in conversation to excuse herself. Lifting the basket, she said, "You two must have a great deal to discuss. I will just, em, take this food into the kitchen."

After a brief trip to the larder to stow the food they'd stopped to purchase, Rebecca grabbed her shawl and slipped outside to let the sisters talk in peace.

As she strolled across the front garden, a man rode up on horseback.

Curious, Rebecca walked to the gate. Sir Frederick Wilford dismounted and looped a rein over the gate post.

"Sir Frederick, I . . . I did not expect to see you again so soon."

He glanced beyond her into the empty garden. "May I ask what you are doing out here alone?"

"Just giving Rose a little privacy to talk with her sister."

He reared his head back in surprise. "Her sister?"

"Yes. Lady Fitzhoward, the former Daisy Watts."

His brow furrowed. "Daisy? I thought her name was Marguerite?"

Rebecca nodded. "She told us she never liked the name Daisy and changed it when she left here."

"Ah . . . and Marguerite is the French word for daisy, after all."

"Is it?"

"Yes. No wonder she looked familiar."

"I am surprised I did not guess the connection earlier," Rebecca said, "but their situations and demeanors were so different, especially after thirty years apart. And with the different names . . ."

He nodded. "I would never have guessed either. And how is it going in there?"

"After a tense beginning, things are looking more promising."

"Good, good." He shifted from foot to foot. "Well, John and Dr. Fox have set off all right."

Rebecca swallowed. "I am . . . relieved to hear it."

He grimaced. "Again, I am sorry, Miss Lane. I could not in good conscience ignore his actions."

She ducked her head, mortified anew. "I know." Keeping a tight grip on her composure, she said, "Thank you for showing mercy to my brother."

In her heart of hearts, Rebecca wondered if John had truly repented. Had he really worried she might be implicated, or had he simply wanted his prized pages back? Perhaps realizing almost too late that if his manuscript killed Oliver, he would never be able to claim it as his own.

Or maybe it had been a combination of those factors.

In the end, the poison had not been what had killed Ambrose Oliver. And they could all take some comfort in that.

Frederick looked up and squinted into the slanting afternoon sunshine. "Well. I just wanted to let you know. And to make sure you were all right. I . . . hope you do not despise me for it."

"Of course not."

"Thomas does. He is still angry with me for arresting Miss Newport as a ploy to force Mr. George to confess."

"He will forgive you in time."

"I pray you are right." He picked at a loose paint sliver on the gate. "So . . . do you and Lady Fitzhoward depart soon, or will you delay, now that she has been reunited with her sister?"

"I am not certain of her plans. But I believe we will be here for some time."

He looked up and something sparked in his eyes. "Good. I . . ." His Adam's apple rose and fell. "I hope we shall see you again, while you are here."

She managed a wobbly smile. "I would like that."

The lodge door opened, and Lady Fitzhoward stepped outside, her cane noticeably absent. Indeed, she seemed more spry than usual as she crossed the garden toward them.

"Frederick." She raised a hand. When she reached them, she said, "Yes, I know I should call you Sir, but after all, we played ball together on the village green."

His dark brows rose. "Did we really?"

She nodded. "Rose and I met there almost weekly. She and I talked while you ran about. And then you would beg me to play with you and I always obliged. The last time must have been when you were about five years old. Such a polite, handsome boy you were"—she grinned—"and still are."

387

"Thank you. I wonder if that is why you seemed familiar to me, or if I simply noticed a resemblance to your sister."

"If the former, I am surprised you would remember. If the latter, I am flattered. Either way, thank you for not pressing me for details earlier. I was not yet ready to reveal my connection here, which I feared irreparably severed. Not so, thank God. Well, I shan't keep you. Do forgive the interruption."

"Not at all."

Lady Fitzhoward returned to the lodge. Rose held the door open for her and waved to them, and the sisters walked inside arm in arm.

Sir Frederick returned his gaze to Rebecca, seemed about to say something, then hesitated. "Well. I will leave you." He untied the rein and mounted his horse. "Good-bye, Miss Lane. Please give Rose my regards."

"I shall."

Rebecca watched him ride away, feeling deflated. Had his words been merely polite platitudes? She doubted he would call again or invite her to Wickworth after the awful business with John as well as her own lies and misdeeds. After all, she was no wealthy, renowned beauty like Marina Seward had been, and never would be.

"Good-bye, Sir Frederick," she whispered, after he was too far away to hear. She was afraid it truly was good-bye, and wished that little word did not sound so final.

25

One morning a few days later, as Rebecca and the pair of reunited sisters were talking together in the sitting room, the sound of an approaching carriage drew Rebecca to the window. A barouche-landau came up the wooded lane, pulled by matched bays. The equipage was familiar, as was the coachman.

"Who is it, Miss Rebecca?" Rose asked.

"The Wilford carriage."

"It is rather early for visitors, is it not?" Lady Fitzhoward patted her coiffure, making sure every hair was in place.

As Rebecca watched, the dowager Lady Wilford alighted with the help of a liveried footman. Then she strode up the path, looking like a woman on a mission.

"It's the dowager," Rebecca announced, beginning to perspire.

Rose pressed a hand to her fichu-covered bosom. "Heavens above."

"Heaven help us," Lady Fitzhoward grumbled under her breath.

A knock sounded. Rebecca moved to answer it, but Rose

forestalled her, adjusted her lace-trimmed cap, and opened it herself.

With the utmost politeness, Rose said, "Your ladyship, what an unexpected pleasure."

The dowager Lady Wilford inclined her regal head. "Rose. You are well, I trust?"

"Yes, thank you. Do come in and be seated."

The dowager entered with a solemn air and sat down. She looked across the room at Marguerite "Daisy" Fitzhoward and said, "That lady, I understand, is your sister?"

"Yes, my lady," said Rose, with evident delight. "We have lately been reconciled after some thirty years."

"How nice for you," the dowager said, glancing around the small sitting room. "I trust our steward is keeping everything in good order?"

Rose hesitated, and Lady Fitzhoward opened her mouth, perhaps prepared to launch into a litany of needed repairs, but Rebecca spoke before either could do so.

"We, em, have no complaints."

"I am glad to hear it."

Rebecca wondered at the reason for the woman's call. Had she heard about John and wished to express her disapproval? For even though Rebecca had come and gone freely at Wickworth as a girl, she had never been close to Lady Wilford, and she'd certainly never entertained her in the humble lodge. As the woman's silence lengthened, Rebecca grew increasingly puzzled.

Rose, with great civility, offered refreshment, but the dowager declined.

"I shan't stay long," she said, then turned to face Lady Fitzhoward. "I came to apologize for my rude behavior when last we met. It was only that I could not place you and, at my age, lapses in memory are so vexing. Now that we are to be neighbors, I hope you will pardon me."

Lady Fitzhoward narrowed her eyes. "You apologize even though you must now know I was once a lady's maid?"

"Yes. As I recall, Lady Sybil spoke very highly of you and your unmatched skill in dressing hair. Even now, I quite envy your coiffure."

"Well, in that case, we shall let bygones be bygones." Lady Fitzhoward's mouth quirked. "As it happens, I may have to return to arranging my own hair. My lady's maid fancies herself in love with the hotel's French chef."

"Ah. That is a pity." The dowager rose. "Well, thank you for receiving me. And now I shall bid you good-day." Turning, she said, "Miss Lane, perhaps you would walk me to the carriage?"

"Oh. Of course."

Both sisters raised their sparse brows high in surprise. The twin looks might have been comical were Rebecca not so uneasy.

Pausing to don her mantle, Rebecca attended her august guest outside.

In the garden, the dowager stopped and lowered her voice. "Is it true that your brother was sent to an asylum?"

Rebecca's face heated. Before she could fashion a reply, the woman went on, "Frederick will tell me next to nothing. And Thomas left for London in a pet after giving me only the scantest account. In his anger, some of what he said was unintelligible and certainly not repeatable."

She looked at Rebecca earnestly. "I cannot believe the son of our former vicar could be involved in any wrongdoing. His being sent to Dr. Fox's asylum seems a patched-up business."

Rebecca forced her chin up. "I am afraid I cannot contradict the report about my brother. He is . . . not well. We believe a year or more under Dr. Fox's care will help him."

"I see. I am grieved indeed to hear it." The dowager studied her. "Tell me . . . is my son courting you?"

Taken aback, Rebecca faltered, "H-he is not."

Rebecca expected the woman to be relieved. For while Rebecca might be a gentleman's daughter, she was without connections or fortune. And her brother's mental state called into question the family's soundness as well.

But instead of showing pleasure, the dowager's countenance fell. She said, "Frederick's wife was a diamond of the first water, descended from a respectable and ancient family. Their fortune was splendid. You, Miss Lane, are nothing at all like her."

The dowager glanced over and, perhaps seeing Rebecca's injured expression, raised her hand. "That, my dear, is a compliment."

She went on, "For years I blamed myself. I had encouraged him, extolling Miss Seward's impressive connections and dowry. How I have repented of that. He has, however, exonerated me. Says he was bound and determined to marry her at any price. Dazzled by her beauty and what appeared to be her charming nature, which was, in the end, a ruse. 'Favour is deceitful, and beauty is vain' has never been more true."

"Why are you telling me this?" Rebecca asked.

"Because I know you once admired and cared for my son."

"That was years ago."

"And now?"

Rebecca swallowed, but pride kept her from replying.

"Never mind," the dowager said. "I would say it is none of my affair. But once a mother, always a mother. We never stop caring for our children, even when they become adults. When their hearts break, ours break with them. Of course, we are no longer the ones they turn to for advice and comfort. Relegated to the background we may be, yet our children forever remain in the forefront of our thoughts and prayers."

With a tremulous smile, Rebecca confessed, "You make me miss my own mamma."

The dowager patted her shoulder. "I may have once nurtured selfish hopes that my sons would marry wealthy, lovely young ladies to give me pretty grandchildren and to add to the prosperity of the estate. But life has doled out some hard lessons. Now all I want is for my sons to marry kind and virtuous women who share our faith and will honor their marriage vows. I will not ask for pedigree or dowry or even that she likes me." She gave Rebecca a wry grin. "The latter of which, I suppose, is impossible."

"Not at all, my lady."

The dowager Lady Wilford signaled the footman to open the door, then turned back to her. "I will take my leave before I meddle further. Good day, Miss Lane."

Rebecca curtsied. "Thank you for coming, and for . . . thinking of me."

When Rebecca returned to the house, Rose asked, "Well? What did she want to talk with you about?"

Rebecca summarized their conversation.

Lady Fitzhoward nodded with satisfaction. "That bodes well."

"Don't read too much into it," Rebecca cautioned her, and herself. "I don't think Sir Frederick will be eager to spend time with me after my behavior at the hotel, not to mention John's." Rebecca sighed and dropped into a chair.

The sisters exchanged knowing glances.

Rose said, "I believe it is time."

"Time for what?" Rebecca asked moodily.

"To pull your old riding habit out of storage. Is it still in that trunk in the attic?"

"I believe so, though no one has suggested riding."

Rose turned to her, a shrewd glint in her eye. "Then *you* suggest it, my girl."

"Would that not be terribly forward? Besides, I don't exactly want to remind him of myself as a little girl, forever pestering him to ride."

"I saw how he looked at you at the hotel," Lady Fitzhoward said. "He looked at you as a man looks at a woman—an attractive woman."

Rose nodded. "It's obvious you care for him and he for you. Don't you doubt it."

"Do you think so?" Hope flared and then faded as quickly. "I don't know. . . ."

Lady Fitzhoward shook her head, lips compressed. "Don't be a fool, Rebecca. Rose and I don't agree on much, but we agree on this. Sir Frederick admires you. All he needs is a little encouragement."

"But I—"

"Listen to me." Lady Fitzhoward sat forward. "I have had one great love in my life with Donald. If there was even a chance I could have more time with him, I would not waste it shilly-shallying."

Rebecca considered, biting her lip. Was it possible?

When she protested no further, Rose said eagerly, "I'll go and fetch the habit."

A short while later, Rose returned with the deep green riding habit, brushed, smoothed out, and sprinkled with rose water. Rebecca donned the long skirt and close-fitting jacket—closer-fitting than she recalled, but she managed to fasten the jacket buttons while Rose laced the back of the skirt.

"Is it too tight, do you think?" Rebecca fretted.

Lady Fitzhoward stepped back to survey her. "Yes, it is tight. In all the right places."

The sisters shared wry grins, and Rebecca blushed.

"What a pity," Rose added. "Sir Frederick might notice your figure."

Lady Fitzhoward advised, "Take shallow breaths."

Frederick had spent a few days at home, feeling exhausted and defeated. He hoped he had not ruined forever his relationship with Thomas, nor lost any chance he might have had with Miss Lane. Whenever she saw him, would she always think of the consequence he'd doled out to her brother?

The canal project also seemed doomed to fail before it had begun, much like his relationship with Rebecca.

The footman brought in a silver salver with two letters upon it. The first was from his solicitor, bearing the unexpected news that Lady Fitzhoward had bought a significant number of shares in the canal project. Surprise and relief flooded him. That was something, at least.

The second was from Thomas.

> *Sorry, old boy. May have overreacted. I know you meant well and were just trying to do your duty and fill Papa's shoes as magistrate. Better you than me!*
>
> *In the meantime, I hope you have not let that sweet-faced Miss Lane slip through your fingers.*
>
> *On the subject of romance, I have renewed my acquaintance with a most charming redhead. An opera singer.*
>
> *(Ha ha. Knew that would get a rise out of you!)*

*Only joking, but she is a peach and I shall look forward
to introducing her to you and Mamma soon.*

> *Yours, etc.*
> *Tommy*

Frederick slowly shook his head, a tolerant grin lifting his mouth. He was pleased to receive this conciliatory gesture from his brother, although it didn't fill the hole in his heart.

He walked upstairs. In the corridor outside his bedchamber, he stood before a framed family portrait. Husband, wife, daughter, son. The family had not been perfect, but they had loved one another. Would he never have a family of his own? A loving wife? Children? A part of him thought he should just let Rebecca go. Let her find someone younger who had never married. But he was not ready to give her up. He liked her too much. Loved her, actually.

With a sigh of resignation, he reached up, took the frame down from the wall, and wrapped it in brown paper.

Feeling restless, he walked downstairs and through the house, his footsteps echoing through the lofty Wickworth gallery. He stopped abruptly beneath another oil painting. It was one he'd never really taken the time to appreciate. By Titian, he believed, painted in dark, drab colors, the only spot of light the one shining behind Christ's head as He hung there on the cross. Beside Him was the "good thief" in the shadows, one arm still strapped to his cross, the other raised in praise, gazing up to heaven in reverent expectation.

Frederick recognized it for what it was—a portrait of Christ's mercy, His unmerited forgiveness and grace.

As Frederick stood there, he heard a still, small voice whisper deep in his soul, "I forgive you, and I love you."

Heart burning within him, Frederick strode resolutely across the hall to stand below one more portrait.

His wife's.

How beautiful Marina looked. How lifeless. How cruel. Frederick took a deep breath, asked God for strength, and whispered, "I forgive you, and I love . . ."

The sound of soft slipper treads caught his ear, and he turned in surprise.

"Rebe . . . Miss Lane." His pulse accelerated as he took in her flushed, lovely face and form-fitting riding habit. Concern and cautious hope tangled within him. "I am glad to see you, but has something happened? Something else, that is?"

Rebecca breathed a prayer and gathered her courage. "No. I hope you don't mind me showing up like this unannounced."

"Not at all."

"I passed your mother outside. She said there was no need to stand on formality between old friends. In fact, she insisted on letting me in through the garden door herself."

"Ah." He glanced behind her. "Did she not stay?"

"No. Busy helping your gardener ready the flower beds, apparently." *Or trying to give us privacy*, Rebecca thought.

She turned toward the wall. "May I ask what has so captured your attention?"

Looking up at the portrait, she realized he'd been staring at his wife's beautiful face, beautiful . . . everything. Rebecca felt daunted, her confidence draining away, like water from a punctured pot. *"You, Miss Lane, are nothing at all like her."* Then she reminded herself what else his mother had said. *"That, my dear, is a compliment."*

Rebecca took a steadying breath and said, "She truly was lovely."

"Yes. Though I am not pining for her, if that is what you think. I was . . . forgiving her." He glanced at Rebecca. "Marina may have been unfaithful, but contrary to rumors, her fall was an accident. I did not push her. I hope you believe me."

"I do. Completely."

He exhaled in relief. "Good. Shall I show you what inspired me to forgive?"

Rebecca wordlessly nodded.

He led her to another oil painting, this one in the gallery. It was a portrait of Christ on the cross, with one of the criminals crucified beside him, the man's eyes raised to heaven. The old words whispered through her mind, *"Thou shalt be with me in paradise."*

"I've walked past this a thousand times," he said. "But today was the first time I stopped and really looked. Really *saw*."

She watched his dear profile as he spoke, relishing the sweet intimacy of his confession and this moment, and hoping not to do anything to break the tantalizing spell.

"You may think me daft," he added, "but as I stood here, I thought I heard a voice whisper, 'I forgive you, and I love you.'"

"Like Mr. George said to Selina as he was taken away," Rebecca observed.

He nodded, and for a moment, they both stared up at the portrait of the Savior.

Then Rebecca said, "I have accepted God's forgiveness for my deception. But I still need yours."

"You have it." Holding her gaze, he took her hand, raised it to his lips, and kissed her fingers. Her skin warmed and tingles of pleasure swept through her.

As if suddenly remembering something, he said, "Oh. I have something for you. I had planned to bring it to the lodge, but now you're here. . . ."

"What is it?"

"Come with me."

She eagerly followed him across the hall, up the stairs, and along the corridor. Near the door she knew led to his bedchamber, she noticed an empty place on the wall in a long row of regularly spaced portraits. On the floor, propped against the wall, was a rectangle wrapped in brown paper. He lifted it and held it toward her.

Afraid to hope, she tentatively tore away one corner, then ripped away more. *Yes.*

"I am returning it to you," he said. "I never should have agreed to purchase it. John said he needed the money, and I am a dupe, apparently."

"You are kind and generous and always have been." She stared down at the family portrait. Her father, mother, herself as a girl, and John as a toddler. Seeing it again, her heart swelled with love and the sting of loss.

"Thank you," she whispered, aware of the tears filling her eyes but powerless to stop them.

"The truth is," he added, "I was afraid if I did not buy it, John would sell it to someone else, and you might never see it again."

"Had it been hanging there, before now?" She pointed to the empty spot on the wall.

He nodded. "For nearly a twelvemonth. I wanted to hang it somewhere I would see it often, which I did, whenever I went to my . . . bedchamber."

At the word, said in that tone, her chest gave an odd palpitation and her mouth went dry. She looked up at him, her gaze drawn to his mouth. His lips.

Then reality intruded.

"You keep it," she said in a shaky little voice and pushed the painting toward him. "I don't know where I shall be living. I have no proper home to give it."

He bent to set the painting down, then rose. Framing her shoulders with warm hands, Frederick gently guided her to face him. He reached up and stroked her jaw, then cupped the side of her face, looking deeply into her eyes. "Nothing would give me greater pleasure or honor than to share my home with you, Rebecca Lane." He slid his thumb over her bottom lip, then slowly leaned close, touching her mouth with his in an achingly slow, sweet kiss. Raising his head, he said in a husky voice, "Say you will marry me and bring this dusty place to life. I love you, and will do everything in my power to be a good husband to you."

Her heart lodged in her throat, she found it difficult to speak.

When she didn't immediately reply, his eyes dimmed. "Please don't tell me I am too old or have waited too long."

Her eyes filled with a new wave of tears, and happiness beat a rhythm in her veins.

With a trembling grin, she said, "It has been a rather long wait. But I love you too. I always have and always will."

Pleasure brightened his dear face. "And here I feared I had lost my chance with you."

"Thankfully, God offers second chances." Rebecca gazed into his adoring eyes, raised herself on tiptoes, and pressed her lips to his as she had long dreamed of doing.

He wrapped his arms around her and gently kissed her back. Then he pulled her against him, arms tight around her waist, as if he couldn't get close enough. He angled his head and passion deepened their kiss.

It had definitely been worth the wait.

Eventually they broke apart, foreheads resting together.

Then, hand in hand, they walked back downstairs. In the

hall, he smiled down at her. "I notice you are dressed for riding. May I hope that means you will ride with me?"

"Yes, happily." She glanced around. "But first, let's do one other thing."

Together, they ran laughing through the house, lifting the Holland cloths off the furniture, and with them, the dark cloud that had hovered over Wickworth for too long.

Afterward, they set out together on horseback, with occasional stops to talk about their future or steal a kiss. The long, glorious ride was worth the minor discomfort of her restricting jacket. By the time they returned, Rebecca was quite breathless—and her tight habit was only partly to blame for it.

The following week, Easter arrived in Swanford bright and beautiful, bringing with it the promise of new life.

As if in response, the bluebells in the woods raised their heads in praise, and the wild daffodils danced in the soft breeze.

The whole village seemed to turn out for church. Rarely had Rebecca seen All Saints so crowded, its pews filled with old and young pressed together in a crush of souls eager for worship—or perhaps for the hot cross buns, simnel cake, and delicious Easter dinner to come.

Near her, Daisy and Rose sat shoulder to shoulder, sharing a prayer book once again after many years apart. It warmed Rebecca's heart to see it.

Across the aisle, in the Wilford family pew, Sir Frederick turned to find her amid the throng and their gazes met and held, love and longing communicated in that single glance. In two months' time, they would be husband and wife, and Rebecca would move into Wickworth and make a home with him there for the rest of their lives.

She was aware of John's absence but not unduly pained by it.

The day before, Rebecca had visited him at Woodlane. John appeared to be settling well into his new home, had been pleased to see her, and seemed to hold no grudge against Sir Frederick for sending him there. He'd even begun writing a new book, extolling Woodlane's calm, quiet setting as ideal for creativity.

For all his faults, perhaps Ambrose Oliver had been right about the benefits of solitude for writing.

Rebecca had left the visit with her brother feeling free and without crippling guilt for the first time in years.

Presently, as the divine service drew to its close, the congregation sang in joyous celebration of Christ's resurrection and the unparalleled hope it secured.

Afterward, the two sisters stopped to talk to friends, including Abe Plaskitt, the elderly gardener who'd recognized Daisy at the abbey. Now Rebecca understood why he'd called her a flower.

Then they headed back to the lodge together, Daisy and Rose followed by Rebecca and Sir Frederick, arm in arm. The sisters looked back at them and shared smug looks.

Thomas and his new ladylove were expected at Wickworth for Easter dinner with Frederick and their mother. Rebecca had been invited to join them, but she'd politely declined. She would become the new Lady Wilford soon enough, but for now, she chose to spend the holy day at the lodge, enjoying the dear sisters' company while she could. The two were soon to depart on a fortnight's holiday. Rose was not ready to travel anyplace as far-off and disconcertingly foreign as Calais or Paris, but she was quite eager to accompany her sister to the seaside resort of

Brighton and there see the Royal Pavilion of King George IV, which was well on its way to completion.

Rebecca chuckled at the thought of the well-traveled Daisy showing her more sheltered sister parts of their country she would never otherwise have seen. Rebecca could well imagine the two of them sight-seeing, laughing together, and occasionally squabbling, all the while having a much-deserved good time.

Reaching the lodge, the sisters continued inside while Rebecca and Sir Frederick lingered in the garden, warm and fragrant now that April had arrived.

Rebecca smiled brightly at her cherished intended. Frederick met her gaze, held her face in both hands, and gave her a tender, lingering kiss.

The church bells rang out over the sun-showered village, and the shadows of Swanford Abbey were dispelled at last.

Author's Note

Thank you for reading! I hope you enjoyed *Shadows of Swanford Abbey*. Now, just a few notes to share with you: Swanford Abbey is a fictional place, inspired by visits to the historic Lacock Abbey in Wiltshire, England, as well as photos and floor plans of the Stanbrook Abbey Hotel in Worcestershire, where I long to stay one day. My fictional abbey's history closely parallels that of Lacock, which was founded by Lady Ela, Countess of Salisbury, who is indeed buried in the abbey.

The abbess's hidden spiral stairway really does exist in Lacock Abbey (complete with squint), now walled up except for a small opening. I didn't see it during my visits, but later, when studying floor plans (much like Rebecca does), I noticed the small curl in the wall, and came across a mention of the staircase in one of my research books, and later found an online photo of the stairway opening. I love discovering that kind of historical detail and weaving it into a novel.

When travel plans for 2020 were curtailed, I looked for someplace in the US to visit to help me capture the sights and smells of a nunnery-turned-hotel. That led to a weekend stay in the lovely Celeste Hotel not far from my home in St. Paul, Minnesota. I was thankful for the personal tour and background information the hotel staff kindly provided. While the Celeste is far more modern than my fictional abbey, it was still wonderfully atmospheric and conducive for writing. My stay there inspired some of the descriptions in the book.

Woodlane is a fictional asylum based on the real institution of Edward Long Fox (and his sons) in Bristol called Brislington House (with some improvements). If you are interested in reading more about how mental health issues were dealt with in previous centuries, you might want to read *Inconvenient People* by Sarah Wise or *A Gentleman's mad-doctor in Georgian England: Edward Long Fox and Brislington House* by Leonard Smith.

The characters in the novel are also fictional, but you are correct if you guessed that my Mr. (or Sergeant) George was loosely inspired by a similar character in Charles Dickens's *Bleak House*.

Other nods to favorite novels include Agatha Christie's *At Bertram's Hotel* (the flavor of chapter 2's description of the reception hall), Elizabeth Gaskell's *North and South* (a phrase or two of Sir Frederick's discussion with the constable about a man seen entering Rebecca's room, and his decision to protect her), and Jane Austen's *Pride and Prejudice* (the dowager Lady Wilford's visit to the lodge borrows a few lines from Austen's Lady Catherine). And Lady Fitzhoward's aversion to doctors was inspired by Austen's Lady Denham, who said, "Let us have none of that tribe at Sanditon."

The moneylender in the novel is also fictional, but was inspired by a "fashionable and patronized moneylender" of the era known as Jacob "John" King.

Rest assured, the despicable Ambrose Oliver is *not* based on any authors I know. We can all be glad of that.

Thank you to Nancy Mayer for her class, *Constables, Coroners, and Courts*, and for answering my legal questions. Also thank you to Yves Marhic for helping me with French.

I am grateful for the helpful input I received from Cari Weber, Anna Paulson, talented author Michelle Griep, and my agent, Wendy Lawton. Warm gratitude also goes to my editors, Karen Schurrer, Hannah Ahlfield, and Raela Schoenherr, and my entire team at Bethany House Publishers.

Finally, thank you again for reading my books. I appreciate you! For more information about me and my other novels, please follow me on Facebook or Instagram, and sign up for my email list via my website, www.julieklassen.com.

Discussion Questions

1. What did you think of the book's ancient abbey setting? Does the idea of staying in an abbey-turned-hotel appeal to you? Why or why not?

2. Did you have a favorite character? Were you surprised by the relationships revealed between any characters, or did you guess at the connections early on?

3. This novel takes place before the establishment of a police force as we know it today. Were you familiar with the practice of "coroner's inquests" ahead of an actual trial? Learn anything new?

4. Rebecca feels guilty about her brother's condition and feels duty-bound to try to help him. How might you have responded differently?

5. Did any of the descriptions of mental asylums and their practices surprise you?

6. Several characters choose to forgive in the closing chapters. How easy is it for you to forgive someone who has done wrong or caused you pain? Any experiences to share?

7. How early did you figure out the identity of the killer? What convinced you? Did you enjoy the mystery element of this novel?

8. Do you feel the various characters involved in Mr. Oliver's death received the consequences they deserved? Was justice served?

About the Author

Julie Klassen loves all things Jane—*Jane Eyre* and Jane Austen. Her books have sold over a million copies, and she is a three-time recipient of the Christy Award for Historical Romance. *The Secret of Pembrooke Park* was honored with the Minnesota Book Award for Genre Fiction. Julie has also won the Midwest Book Award and Christian Retailing's BEST Award, and has been a finalist in the RITA and Carol Awards. A graduate of the University of Illinois, Julie worked in publishing for sixteen years and now writes full-time. Julie and her husband have two sons and live in a suburb of St. Paul, Minnesota. For more information, you can follow her on Facebook or visit www.julieklassen.com.

Sign Up for Julie's Newsletter

Keep up to date with Julie's news on book releases and events by signing up for her email list at julieklassen.com.

More from Julie Klassen

Laura Callaway daily walks the windswept Cornwall coast, known for many shipwrecks but few survivors. And when a man with curious wounds and an odd accent is washed ashore, she cares for him while the mystery surrounding him grows. Can their budding attraction survive, and can he be returned to his rightful home when danger pursues them from every side?

A Castaway in Cornwall

◊ BETHANYHOUSE

You May Also Like . . .

While Benjamin investigates a mysterious death, evidence takes him to a remote island on the Thames. There, Isabelle is trapped by fear and has a recurring dream about a man's death. Or is it a memory? When a murder brings everyone under suspicion, and the search for truth brings secrets to light, she realizes her island sanctuary will never be the same.

The Bridge to Belle Island by Julie Klassen
julieklassen.com

Visit the idyllic English village of Ivy Hill, where friendships thrive, romance blossoms, and mysteries await. As the villagers of Ivy Hill search for answers about the past and hope for the future, might they find love along the way?

TALES FROM IVY HILL: *The Innkeeper of Ivy Hill, The Ladies of Ivy Cottage, The Bride of Ivy Green* by Julie Klassen
julieklassen.com

Haunted by an old secret and the shadows of his past, gentleman Richard Brockwell prefers to stay away from Ivy Hill—until his mother threatens to stop funding his carefree life unless he returns for Christmas. Will Christmastime in Ivy Hill, with all of its divine hope, unforeseen surprises, and unexpected romantic encounters, work its magic in his heart?

An Ivy Hill Christmas by Julie Klassen
A TALES FROM IVY HILL NOVELLA
julieklassen.com

BETHANYHOUSE

More from Bethany House

When his reputation is threatened, Aaron Whitworth makes the desperate decision to hire a circus horse trainer as a jockey for his racehorses. Most men don't take Sophia Fitzroy seriously because she's a woman, but as she fights for the right to do the work she was hired for, she finds the fight for Aaron's guarded heart might be a more worthwhile challenge.

Winning the Gentleman by Kristi Ann Hunter
HEARTS ON THE HEATH
kristiannhunter.com

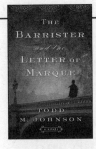

As a barrister in 1818 London, William Snopes defends the poor against the powerful—but that changes when a struggling heiress arrives at his door with a mystery surrounding a missing letter from the king's regent and a merchant's brig. As he digs deeper, he learns that the forces arrayed against them are even more perilous than he'd imagined.

The Barrister and the Letter of Marque by Todd M. Johnson
authortoddmjohnson.com

When a renowned profiler is found dead in his hotel room and it becomes clear the killer is targeting agents in Alex Donovan's unit, she is called to work on the strangest case she's ever faced. Things get personal when the brilliant killer strikes close to home, and Alex will do anything to find the killer—even at the risk of her own life.

Dead Fall by Nancy Mehl
THE QUANTICO FILES #2
nancymehl.com

⧫ BETHANYHOUSE

You Are Invited!

Join like-minded fans in the **Inspirational Regency Readers** group on Facebook.

From book news from popular Regency authors like Kristi Ann Hunter, Michelle Griep, Erica Vetsch, Julie Klassen, and many others, to games and giveaways, to discussions of favorite Regency reads and adaptations new and old, to places we long to travel, you will find plenty of fun and friendship within this growing community.

Free and easy to join, simply search for "Inspirational Regency Readers" on Facebook.

We look forward to seeing you there!